broken

Karin Slaughter grew up in a small south Georgia town and has been writing since she was a child. She is the author of the international bestsellers *Blindsighted*, *Kisscut*, *A Faint Cold Fear*, *Indelible*, *Faithless*, *Skin Privilege*, *Triptych*, *Fractured*, *Genesis* and *Broken*. She is also the author of the darkly comic novella *Martin Misunderstood*, and editor of and contributor to *Like a Charm*, a collaboration of British and American crime fiction writers. She lives in Atlanta.

Praise for Karin Slaughter

'This is without doubt an accomplished, compelling and complex tale, with page-turning power aplenty'
Sunday Express

'No one does American small-town evil more chillingly . . . Slaughter tells a dark story that grips and doesn't let go'
The Times

'Another brilliantly chilling tale from Slaughter'
heat

'Slaughter knows exactly when to ratchet up the menace, and when to loiter on the more personal and emotional aspects of the victims. Thoroughly gripping, yet thoroughly gruesome stuff'
Daily Mirror

'Beautifully paced, appropriately grisly, and terrifyingly plausible'
Time Out

KARIN SLAUGHTER

broken

arrow books

Published by Arrow Books 2011

4 6 8 10 9 7 5 3

First published in Great Britain in 2010 by
Century
Random House, 20 Vauxhall Bridge Road,
London SW1V 2SA

www.randomhouse.co.uk

Addresses for companies within The Random House Group Limited can
be found at: www.randomhouse.co.uk/offices.htm

The Random House Group Limited Reg. No. 954009

A CIP catalogue record for this book
is available from the British Library

Penguin Random House is committed to a sustainable future for
our business, our readers and our planet. This book is made from
Forest Stewardship Council® certified paper.

Printed and bound in Great Britain by Clays Ltd, Elcograf S.p.A.

Typeset by SX Composing DTP, Rayleigh, Essex

For Victoria

'Karin Slaughter has never been better'
Evening Standard

'Taut, mean, nasty and bloody well written. She conveys a sense of time and place with clarity and definite menace – the finely tuned juxtaposition of sleepy Southern town and urgent, gut-wrenching terror'
STELLA DUFFY

'Taut and tight and tinged with terror'
Houston Chronicle

'A story that roars its way through the final pages, Slaughter's thriller is scary, shocking and perfectly suspenseful'
BookPage.com

'Slaughter's gift for building multi-layered tension while deconstructing damaged personalities gives this thriller a nerve-wracking finish'
USA Today

'A page turner . . . has more twists than a Slinky Factory'
People

'A debut novel that blows your socks off. Karin Slaughter has immediately jumped to the front of the line of first-rate thriller writers . . .'
Rocky Mountain News

'Superb . . . Slaughter keeps the emotional tension high throughout'
Publishers Weekly

Also by Karin Slaughter

Blindsighted
Kisscut
A Faint Cold Fear
Indelible
Faithless
Triptych
Skin Privilege
Fractured
Martin Misunderstood
Genesis

Like a Charm (Ed.)

broken

PROLOGUE

Allison Spooner wanted to leave town for the holiday, but there was nowhere to go. There was no reason to stay here, either, but at least it was cheaper. At least she had a roof over her head. At least the heat in her crappy apartment occasionally worked. At least she could eat a hot meal at work. At least, at least, at least . . . Why was her life always about the least of things? When was there going to come a time when it started being about the most?

The wind picked up and she clenched her fists in the pockets of her light jacket. It wasn't so much raining as misting down a cold wetness, like walking around inside a dog's nose. The icy chill coming off Lake Grant made it worse. Every time the breeze picked up, she felt as if tiny, dull razors were slicing through her skin. This was supposed to be south Georgia, not the freaking South Pole.

As she struggled for her footing along the tree-lined shores, it seemed like every wave that lapped the mud brought the temperature down another degree. She wondered if her flimsy shoes would be enough to keep her toes from getting frostbite. She had seen a guy on TV who'd lost all his fingers and toes to the cold. He'd said he was grateful to be alive, but people will say anything to get on TV. The way Allison's life was going right now, the only program she'd end up on was the nightly news.

There'd be a picture – probably that awful one from her high school yearbook – beside the words 'Tragic Death.'

The irony was not lost on Allison that she would be more important to the world if she were dead. No one gave a crap about her now – the meager living she was scraping out, the constant struggle of keeping up with her classes while juggling all the other responsibilities in her life. None of it would matter to anybody unless she turned up frozen on the lakeshore.

The wind picked up again. Allison turned her back to the cold, feeling its freezing fingers probe her rib cage, squeeze her lungs. A shiver racked her body. Her breath was a cloud in front of her. She closed her eyes. She chanted her problems through chattering teeth.

Jason. School. Money. Car. Jason. School. Money. Car.

The mantra continued well past the penetrating gust. Allison opened her eyes. She turned around. The sun was going down faster than she'd thought. She turned around, facing the college. Should she go back? Or should she go forward?

She chose to go forward, tucking her head down against the howling wind.

Jason. School. Money. Car.

Jason: Her boyfriend had turned into an asshole, seemingly overnight.

School: She was going to flunk out of college if she didn't find more time to study.

Money: She wasn't going to be able to live, let alone go to school, if she cut back any more hours at work.

Car: Her car had started smoking this morning when she cranked it up, which was no big deal since it had been smoking for months, but this time the smoke was on the inside, coming through the heating vents. She'd nearly suffocated driving to school.

Allison trudged along, adding 'frostbite' to her list as she rounded the bend in the lake. Every time she blinked, it felt like her eyelids were cutting through thin sheets of ice.

Jason. School. Money. Car. Frostbite.

The frostbite fear seemed more immediate, though she was reluctant to admit that the more she worried about it, the warmer she felt. Maybe her heart was beating faster or her walking pace was picking up as the sun began to set and she realized that all of her whining about dying in the cold might come true if she didn't hurry the hell up.

Allison reached out, bracing herself against a tree so that she could pick her way past a tangle of roots that dipped into the water. The bark was wet and spongy under her fingertips. A customer had sent back a hamburger at lunch today because he said the bun was too spongy. He was a big, gruff man in full hunting gear, not the sort of guy you'd expect to use a delicate word like 'spongy.' He had flirted with her and she had flirted back, and then when he left there was a fifty-cent tip on his ten-dollar meal. He'd actually winked at her as he walked out the door, like he was doing her a favor.

She wasn't sure how much more of this she could take. Maybe her grandmother had been right. Girls like Allison didn't go to college. They found work at the tire factory, met a guy, got pregnant, got married, had a couple of more kids, then got divorced, sometimes in that order, sometimes not. If she was lucky, the guy didn't beat her much.

Was that the kind of life Allison wanted for herself? It was the kind of life that was written in her blood. Her mother had lived it. Her grandmother had lived it. Her aunt Sheila had lived it until she pulled a shotgun on her uncle Boyd and nearly took his head off. All three of the Spooner women had at some point or another thrown away everything for a worthless man.

Allison had watched it happen to her mother so often that by the time Judy Spooner was in the hospital for the last time, every bit of her insides eaten away from the cancer, all Allison could reflect on was the waste of her mother's life. She'd even *looked* wasted. At thirty-eight years old, her hair was thinning and nearly all gray. Her skin was faded. Her hands were clawed from working at the tire factory – picking tires off the belt, pressure-testing them, putting them back on the belt, then picking up the next tire, then again and again, over two hundred times a day, so that every joint in her body ached by the time she crawled into bed at night. Thirty-eight years old and she welcomed the cancer. Welcomed the relief.

One of the last things Judy had told Allison was that she was glad to be dying, glad that she didn't have to be alone anymore. Judy Spooner believed in heaven and redemption. She believed that one day streets of gold and many mansions would replace her gravel drive and trailer-park existence. All Allison believed was that she had never been enough for her mother. Judy's glass was perpetually half empty, and all the love Allison poured into her over the years would never fill her mother up.

Judy was too far drawn into the muck. The muck of her dead-end job. The muck of one worthless man after another. The muck of a baby holding her down.

College was going to be Allison's salvation. She was good at science. Looking at her family, it made no sense,

4

but somehow she understood how chemicals worked. She understood at a basic level the synthesis of macro-molecules. Her grasp of synthetic polymers came hand in glove. Most important, she knew how to study. She knew that somewhere on earth, there was always a book with an answer in it, and the best way to find that answer was to read every book you could get your hands on.

By her senior year in high school, she had managed to stay away from the boys and the drinking and the meth that had ruined just about every girl her age in her small hometown of Elba, Alabama. She wasn't going to end up being one of those soulless, washed-out girls who worked the night shift and smoked Kools because they were elegant. She wasn't going to end up with three kids by three different men before she hit thirty. She wasn't going to ever wake up one morning unable to open her eyes because some man's fist had beaten them shut the night before. She wasn't going to end up dead and alone in a hospital bed like her mother.

At least that's what she'd been thinking when she left Elba three years ago. Mr. Mayweather, her science teacher, had pulled every string he could grab to get her enrolled in a good college. He wanted her to get as far away from Elba as possible. He wanted her to have a future.

Grant Tech was in Georgia, and it wasn't far away in miles so much as far away in feeling. The college was enormous compared to her high school, which had a graduating class of twenty-nine people. Allison had spent her first week on campus wondering how it was possible to be in love with a place. Her classes were filled with kids who had grown up with opportunities, who'd never considered *not* going to college straight out of high school.

None of her fellow students snickered when she raised her hand to answer a question. They didn't think you were selling out if you actually listened to the teacher, tried to learn something other than how to give yourself French tips or weave extensions into your hair.

And the area around the college was so pretty. Elba was a blight, even for south Alabama. Heartsdale, the city where Grant Tech was located, felt like a town you'd see on television. Everyone tended their yards. Flowers lined Main Street in the spring. Total strangers waved at you with a smile on their face. At the diner where she worked, the locals were so kind, even if they were bad tippers. The town wasn't so big that she got lost. Unfortunately, it wasn't so big that she didn't meet Jason.

Jason.

She'd met him her sophomore year. He was two years older, more experienced, more sophisticated. His idea of a romantic date wasn't sneaking into a movie and doing it quick in the back row before the manager kicked you out. He took her to real restaurants with cloth napkins on the tables. He held her hand. He listened to her. When they had sex, she finally understood why people called it making love. Jason didn't just want better things for himself. He wanted better things for Allison. She'd thought what they had was a serious thing – the last two years of her life had been spent building something with him. And then suddenly, he had turned into a different person. Suddenly, everything that had been so great about their relationship was the reason it was falling apart.

And, as with her mother, Jason had somehow managed to make it all Allison's fault. She was cold. She was distant. She was too demanding. She never had time for him. As if

Jason was an affectionate saint who spent his days wondering what would make Allison happy. She wasn't the one who went on all-night benders with her friends. She wasn't the one getting mixed up with weird people at school. She sure as hell wasn't the one who got them involved with that jerk from town. How could that be Allison's fault if she had never even seen the guy's face?

Allison shivered again. Every step she took around this damn lake, it seemed like the shoreline squeezed out another hundred yards just to spite her. She looked down at the wet ground beneath her feet. It had been storming for weeks. Flash floods had taken out roads, cut down trees. Allison had never been good with bad weather. The darkness got to her, tried to pull her down. It made her moody and tearful. All she wanted to do was sleep away the time until the sun came back out.

'Shit!' Allison hissed, catching herself before she slipped. The cuffs of her pants were caked in mud, her shoes nearly soaked through. She looked out into the churning lake. The rain was sticking to her eyelashes. She brushed back her hair with her fingers as she stared at the dark waters. Maybe she should let herself slip. Maybe she should let herself fall all the way into the lake. What would it be like to let herself go? What would it feel like to let the undertow take her farther to the center of the lake where her feet no longer touched the ground and her lungs could no longer find air?

This wasn't the first time she'd thought about it. It was probably the weather, the relentless rain and dreary sky. Everything seemed more depressing in the rain. And some things were more depressing than others. There had been a story in the paper last Thursday about a mother and child

7

who'd drowned in their Volkswagen Beetle two miles outside of town. They were within spitting distance of the Third Baptist Church when a flash flood cut through the street and whisked them away. There was something about the design of the old Beetles that made them able to float, and this newer model had floated, too. At least at first.

The church crowd who'd just left their usual potluck were helpless to do anything for fear of getting caught up in the flood. They watched in horror as the Beetle spun around on the surface of the water, then tipped over. Water flooded into the cab. Mother and child were tossed into the current. The woman they interviewed in the paper said she would go to sleep every night and wake up every morning for the rest of her life seeing that little three-year-old's hand reaching out from the water before the final time the poor thing was pulled down.

Allison could not stop thinking of the child, either. Even though she had been at the library when it happened. Even though she'd never met the woman or the child or even the lady who spoke to the paper, she could see that little hand reaching up every time she closed her eyes. Sometimes, the hand grew larger. Sometimes, it was her mother reaching out for her help. Sometimes, she woke up screaming because the hand was pulling her down.

If she was telling the truth, Allison's mind had turned toward dark thinking long before the newspaper story. She couldn't blame the weather completely, but certainly the constant rain, the unrelenting overcast, had churned up inside of her mind its own kind of despair. How much easier would it be if she just gave in? Why go back to Elba and turn into some toothless, haggard old woman with eighteen kids to feed when she could just walk into the lake and for once take control of her destiny?

She was turning into her mother so fast that she could almost feel her hair going gray. She was just as bad as Judy – thinking she was in love when all the guy was interested in was what was between her legs. Her aunt Sheila had said as much on the phone last week. Allison had been whining about Jason, wondering why he wouldn't return her calls.

A long drag on her cigarette, then, during the exhale, '*You sound just like your mother.*'

A knife in her chest would have been faster, cleaner. The worst part was that Sheila was right. Allison loved Jason. She loved him way too much. She loved him enough to call him ten times a day even though he never picked up. She loved him enough to hit reload on her stupid computer every two minutes to see if he had answered one of her nine billion emails.

She loved him enough to out here in the middle of the night doing the dirty work that he didn't have the balls to do.

Allison took another step closer to the lake. She could feel her heel start to slip, but her body's automatic need for self-preservation took over before she fell. Still, the water lapped against her shoes. Her socks were already soaked. Her toes were beyond numb, to that point where a sharp pain seemed to pierce through the bone. Was that what it would be like – a slow numbing falling into a painless passage?

She was terrified of suffocating. That was the problem. She'd loved the ocean for maybe ten minutes as a kid, but that had changed by the time she turned thirteen. Her idiot cousin Dillard had held her under the water once at the municipal pool, and now she didn't even like to take baths because she was afraid she'd get water up her nose and panic.

If Dillard were here, he'd probably push her into the lake without her even having to ask. That first time he'd held her head down under the water, he hadn't shown a bit of remorse. Allison had thrown up her lunch. She was racked with sobs. Her lungs were burning, and he'd just said, 'Heh-heh,' like an old man who pinches the fire out of the back of your arm just to hear you squeal.

Dillard was Sheila's boy, her only child, more disappointing to her than his father, if that was even possible. He huffed so much spray paint that his nose was a different color every time you saw him. He smoked crystal. He stole from his mama. The last Allison heard, he was in prison for trying to rob a liquor store with a water pistol. The clerk had cracked open his skull with a baseball bat by the time the cops got there. The result was that Dillard was even dumber than before, but that wouldn't have stopped him from passing up a good opportunity. He would've given Allison a good shove with both hands, sending her headfirst into the water as he let out his little cackle. 'Heh-heh.' All the while she'd be flailing, working her way up to drowning.

How long would it take before she passed out? How long would Allison have to live in terror before she died? She closed her eyes again, trying to think about the water surrounding her, swallowing her. It would be so cold that it would feel warm at first. You couldn't live long without air. You'd pass out. Maybe the panic would take hold, sending you into some kind of hysterical unconsciousness. Or maybe you would feel alive – shot through with adrenaline, fighting like a squirrel trapped in a paper bag.

She heard a branch snap behind her. Allison turned, surprised.

'Jesus!' She slipped again, this time for real. Her arms flailed out. Her knee collapsed. Pain took away her breath. She slammed face-first into the mud. A hand grabbed the back of her neck, forcing her to stay down. Allison inhaled the bitter coldness of the earth, the wet, oozing muck.

Instinctively, she struggled, fighting the water, fighting the panic that flooded into her brain. She felt a knee jam into the base of her spine, pinning her firmly to the ground. Burning pain seared into her neck. Allison tasted blood. She didn't want this. She wanted to live. She *had* to live. She opened her mouth to scream it at the top of her lungs.

But then – darkness.

MONDAY

ONE

Fortunately, the winter weather meant the body at the bottom of the lake would be well preserved, though the chill on the shore was bone-aching, the sort of thing that made you strain to remember what August had been like. The sun on your face. The sweat running down your back. The way the air conditioner in your car blew out a fog because it could not keep up with the heat. As much as Lena Adams strained to remember, all thoughts of warmth were lost on this rainy November morning.

'Found her,' the dive captain called. He was directing his men from the shore, his voice muffled by the constant shush of the pouring rain. Lena held up her hand in a wave, water sliding down the sleeve of the bulky parka she had thrown on when the call had come in at three this morning. The rain wasn't hard, but it was relentless, tapping her back insistently, slapping against the umbrella that rested on her shoulder. Visibility was about thirty feet. Everything beyond that was coated in a hazy fog. She closed her eyes, thinking back to her warm bed, the warmer body that had been wrapped around her.

The shrill ring of a phone at three in the morning was never a good sound, especially when you were a cop. Lena had woken out of a dead sleep, her heart pounding, her hand automatically snatching up the receiver, pressing it to her ear. She was the senior detective on call, so she in turn had to start other phones ringing across south Georgia. Her chief. The coroner. Fire and rescue. The Georgia Bureau of Investigation to let them know that a body had been found on state land. The Georgia Emergency Management Authority, who kept a list of eager civilian volunteers ready to look for dead bodies on a moment's notice.

They were all gathered here at the lake, but the smart people were waiting in their vehicles, heat blasting while a chill wind rocked the chassis like a baby in a cradle. Dan Brock, the proprietor of the local funeral home who did double duty as the town coroner, was asleep in his van, head back against the seat, mouth gaping open. Even the EMTs were safely tucked inside the ambulance. Lena could see their faces peering through the windows in the back doors. Occasionally, a hand would reach out, the ember of a cigarette glowing in the dawn light.

She held an evidence bag in her hand. It contained a letter found near the shore. The paper had been torn from a larger piece – college ruled, approximately eight and a half inches by six. The words were all caps. Ballpoint pen. One line. No signature. Not the usual spiteful or pitiful farewell, but clear enough: *I WANT IT OVER.*

In many ways, suicides were more difficult investigations than homicides. With a murdered person, there was always someone you could blame. There were clues you could follow to the bad guy, a clear pattern you could lay out to explain to the family of the victim exactly why their loved one had been stolen away from them. Or, if not why, then who the bastard was who'd ruined their lives.

With suicides, the victim is the murderer. The person upon whom the blame rests is also the person whose loss is felt most deeply. They are not around to take the recriminations for their death, the natural anger anyone feels when there is a loss. What the dead leave instead is a void that all the pain and sorrow in the world can never fill. Mother and father, sisters, brothers, friends and other relatives – all find themselves with no one to punish for their loss.

And people always want to punish someone when a life is unexpectedly taken.

This was why it was the investigator's job to make sure every single inch of the death scene was measured and recorded. Every cigarette butt, every discarded piece of trash or paper, had to be catalogued, checked for fingerprints, and sent to the lab for analysis. The weather was noted in the initial report. The various officers and emergency personnel on scene were recorded in a log. If a crowd was present, photographs were taken. License plates were checked. The suicide victim's life was investigated just as thoroughly as with a homicide: Who were her friends? Who were her lovers? Was there a husband? Boyfriend? Girlfriend? Were there angry neighbors or envious co-workers?

Lena knew only what they had found so far: a pair of women's sneakers, size eight, placed a few feet away from the suicide note. Inside the left shoe was a cheap ring – twelve-karat gold with a lifeless ruby at the center. The right shoe contained a white Swiss Army watch with fake diamonds for numbers. Underneath this was the folded note.

I want it over.

Not much of a comfort for those left behind.

Suddenly, there was a splash of water as one of the

divers surfaced from the lake. His partner came up beside him. They each struggled against the silt on the lake bottom as they dragged the body out of the cold water and into the cold rain. The dead girl was small, making the effort seem exaggerated, but quickly Lena saw the reason for their struggle. A thick, industrial-looking chain was wrapped around her waist with a bright yellow padlock that hung low, like a belt buckle. Attached to the chain were two cinder blocks.

Sometimes in policing, there were small miracles. The victim had obviously been trying to make sure she couldn't back out. If not for the cinder blocks weighing her down, the current would have probably taken the body into the middle of the lake, making it almost impossible to find her.

Lake Grant was a thirty-two-hundred-acre man-made body of water that was three hundred feet deep in places. Underneath the surface were abandoned houses, small cottages and shacks where people had once lived before the area was turned into a reservoir. There were stores and churches and a cotton mill that had survived the Civil War only to be shut down during the Depression. All of this had been wiped out by the rushing waters of the Ochawahee River so that Grant County could have a reliable source of electricity.

The National Forestry Service owned the best part of the lake, over a thousand acres that wrapped around the water like a cowl. One side touched the residential area where the more fortunate lived, and the other bordered the Grant Institute of Technology, a small but thriving state university with almost five thousand students enrolled.

Sixty percent of the lake's eighty-mile shoreline was

owned by the State Forestry Division. The most popular spot by far was this one, what the locals called Lover's Point. Campers were allowed to stake tents. Teenagers came here to party, often leaving behind empty beer bottles and used condoms. Occasionally, there would be a call about a fire someone had let get out of control, and once, a rabid bear had been reported, only to turn out to be an elderly chocolate Labrador who had wandered away from his owners' campsite.

And bodies were occasionally found here, too. Once, a girl had been buried alive. Several men, predictably teenagers, had drowned performing various acts of stupidity. Last summer, a child had broken her neck diving into the shallow waters of the cove.

The two divers paused, letting the water drip off the body before resuming their task. Finally, nods went around and they dragged the young woman onto the shore. The cinder blocks left a deep furrow in the sandy ground. It was six-thirty in the morning, and the moon seemed to wink at the sun as it began its slow climb over the horizon. The ambulance doors swung open. The EMTs cursed at the bitter cold as they rolled out the gurney. One of them had a pair of bolt cutters hefted over his shoulder. He slammed his hand on the hood of the coroner's van, and Dan Brock startled, comically flailing his arms in the air. He gave the EMT a stern look, but stayed where he was. Lena couldn't blame him for not wanting to rush into the rain. The victim wasn't going anywhere except the morgue. There was no need for lights and sirens.

Lena walked closer to the body, carefully folding the evidence bag containing the suicide note into her jacket

19

pocket and taking out a pen and her spiral-bound note-book. Crooking her umbrella between her neck and shoulder, she wrote the time, date, weather, number of EMTs, number of divers, number of cars and cops, what the terrain was like, noted the solemnity of the scene, the absence of spectators – all the details that would need to be typed exactly into the report.

The victim was around Lena's height, five-four, but she was built much smaller. Her wrists were delicate, like a bird's. The fingernails were uneven, bitten down to the quick. She had black hair and extremely white skin. She was probably in her early twenties. Her open eyes were clouded like cotton. Her mouth was closed. The lips looked ragged, as if she chewed them out of nervous habit. Or maybe a fish had gotten hungry.

Her body was lighter without the drag of the water, and it only took three of the divers to heft her onto the waiting gurney. Muck from the bottom of the lake covered her head to toe. Water dripped from her clothes – blue jeans, a black fleece shirt, white socks, no sneakers, an unzipped, dark blue warm-up jacket with a Nike logo on the front. The gurney shifted, and her head turned away from Lena.

Lena stopped writing. 'Wait a minute,' she called, knowing something was wrong. She put her notebook in her pocket as she took a step closer to the body. She had seen a flash of light at the back of the girl's neck – something silver, maybe a necklace. Pondweed draped across the victim's throat and shoulders like a shroud. Lena used the tip of her pen to push away the slippery green tendrils. Something was moving beneath the skin, rippling the flesh the same way the rain rippled the tide.

The divers noticed the undulations, too. They all bent

down for a better look. The skin fluttered like something out of a horror movie.

One of them asked, 'What the—'

'Jesus!' Lena jumped back quickly as a small minnow slithered out from a slit in the girl's neck.

The divers laughed the way men do when they don't want to admit they've just soiled themselves. For her part, Lena put her hand to her chest, hoping no one noticed that her heart had practically exploded. She took a gulp of air. The minnow was floundering in the mud. One of the men picked it up and tossed it back into the lake. The dive captain made the inevitable joke about something being fishy.

Lena shot him a hard look before leaning down toward the body. The slit where the fish had come out was at the back of the neck, just to the right of the spine. She guessed the wound was an inch wide, tops. The open flesh was puckered from the water, but at one point the injury had been clean, precise – the kind of incision that was made by a very sharp knife.

'Somebody go wake up Brock,' she said.

This wasn't a suicide investigation anymore.

TWO

Frank Wallace never smoked in his county-issued Lincoln Town Car, but the cloth seats had absorbed the fug of nicotine that seeped from every pore in his body. He reminded Lena of Pig Pen from the Peanuts comic strip. No matter how clean he was or how often he changed his clothes, the stench followed him like a dust cloud.

'What's wrong?' he demanded, not even giving her time to shut the car door.

Lena shucked her wet parka onto the floorboard. Earlier, she had thrown on a jacket with two shirts underneath to help fight the cold. Still, even with the heat blasting, her teeth were chattering. It was as if her body had stored up all the chill while she was standing outside in the rain and only let it out now that she was safely sheltered.

She held her hands up to the vent. 'God, it's freezing.'

'What's wrong?' Frank repeated. He made a show of pulling back his black leather glove so he could see his watch.

Lena shivered involuntarily. She couldn't keep the excitement out of her voice. No cop would ever admit it to a civilian, but murders were the most exciting cases to work. Lena was so pumped through with adrenaline that she was surprised the cold was getting to her. Through chattering teeth, she told him, 'It's not a suicide.'

Frank looked even more annoyed. 'Brock agree with you?'

Brock had gone back to sleep in his van while he waited for the chains to be cut, which they both knew because they could see his back molars from where they were sitting. 'Brock wouldn't know his ass from a hole in the ground,' Lena shot back. She rubbed her arms to coax some warmth back into her body.

Frank took out his flask and handed it to her. She took a quick sip, the whisky burning its way down her throat and into her stomach. Frank took a hefty drink of his own before returning the flask to his coat pocket.

She told him, 'There's a knife wound in the neck.'

'Brock's?'

Lena gave him a withering glance. 'The dead girl.' She leaned down and searched her parka for the wallet she had found in the pocket of the woman's jacket.

Frank said, 'Could be self-inflicted.'

'Not possible.' She put her hand to the back of her neck. 'Blade went in about here. The killer was standing behind her. Probably took her by surprise.'

Frank grumbled, 'You get that from one of your textbooks?'

Lena held her tongue, something she wasn't used to doing. Frank had been interim police chief for the last four years. Everything that happened in the three cities that comprised Grant County fell under his purview. Madison and Avondale carried the usual drug problems and domestic violence, but Heartsdale was supposed to be easy. The college was here, and the affluent residents were vocal about crime.

Even without that, complicated cases had the tendency

to turn Frank into an asshole. Actually, life in general could turn him into an asshole. His coffee going cold. The engine in his car not catching on the first try. The ink running dry in his pen. Frank hadn't always been like this. He'd certainly leaned toward grumpy for as long as Lena had known him, but his attitude lately was tinged with an underlying fury that seemed ready to boil to the surface. Anything could set him off. In the blink of an eye he'd turn from being manageably irritated to downright mean.

At least in this particular matter Frank's reluctance made sense. After thirty-five years of policing, a murder case was the last thing he wanted on his plate. Lena knew that he was sick of the job, sick of the people it brought him into contact with. He had lost two of his closest friends in the last six years. The only lake he wanted to be sitting in front of right now was in sunny Florida. He should've had a fishing pole and a beer in his hands, not a dead kid's wallet.

'Looks fake,' Frank said, opening the wallet. Lena agreed. The leather was too shiny. The Prada logo was plastic.

'Allison Judith Spooner,' Lena told him, watching Frank try to peel apart the soaked plastic picture sleeves. 'Twenty-one. Driver's license is from Elba, Alabama. Her student ID's in the back.'

'College.' Frank breathed out the word with something like despair. It was bad enough Allison Spooner had been found on or near state property. Add to that the fact that she was an out-of-state kid attending Grant Tech, and the case just got twenty times more political.

He asked, 'Where'd you find the wallet?'

'In her jacket pocket. I guess she didn't have a purse. Or maybe whoever killed her wanted us to know her identity.'

He was looking at the girl's driver's license photo.

'What is it?'

'Looks like that little waitress who works at the diner.'

The Grant Diner was on the opposite end of Main Street from the police station. Most of the force ate there for lunch. Lena stayed away from the place. She usually brown-bagged it, or, more often than not, didn't eat.

She asked, 'Did you know her?'

He shook his head and shrugged at the same time. 'She was good-looking.'

Frank was right. Not many people had a flattering driver's license photo, but Allison Spooner had been luckier than most. Her white teeth showed in a big smile. Her hair was pulled back off her face, revealing high cheekbones. There was merriment in her eyes, as if someone had just made a joke. This was all in sharp contrast to the body they had pulled out of the lake. Death had erased her vibrancy.

Frank said, 'I didn't know she was a student.'

'They usually don't work in town,' Lena allowed. Grant Tech's students tended to work on campus or not at all. They didn't mix with the town and the town did its best not to mix with them.

Frank pointed out, 'The school's closed this week for Thanksgiving break. Why isn't she home with her family?'

Lena didn't have the answer. 'There's forty bucks in the wallet, so this wasn't a robbery.'

Frank checked the money compartment anyway, his thick, gloved fingers finding the twenty and two tens glued together with lake water. 'She could've been lonely. Decided to take the knife and end it herself.'

'She'd have to be a contortionist,' Lena insisted. 'You'll see when Brock gets her on the table. She was stabbed from behind.'

He gave a bone-weary sigh. 'What about the chain and cinder blocks?'

'We can try Mann's Hardware in town. Maybe the killer bought them there.'

He tried again. 'You're sure about the knife wound?'

She nodded.

Frank kept staring at the license photo. 'Does she have a car?'

'If she does, it's not in the vicinity.' Lena pressed the point. 'Unless she carried forty pounds' worth of cinder blocks and some chains through the woods . . .'

Frank finally closed the wallet and handed it back to her. 'Why is it every Monday just gets shittier and shittier?'

Lena couldn't answer him. Last week wasn't that much better. A young mother and her daughter had been taken by a flash flood. The whole town was still reeling from the loss. There was no telling what they'd make of a pretty, young college girl being murdered.

She told Frank, 'Brad's trying to track down somebody from the college who can get into the registrar's office and give us Spooner's local address.' Brad Stephens had finally worked his way up from patrol to the rank of detective, but his new job didn't have him doing much more than his old one did. He was still running errands.

Lena offered, 'Once the scene is cleared, I'll work on the death notification.'

'Alabama's on central time.' Frank looked at his watch.

'It'll probably be better to call the parents direct instead of waking up the Elba P.D. this early in the morning.'

Lena checked her own watch. They were coming up on seven o'clock, which meant it was almost six in Alabama. If Elba was anything like Grant County, the detectives were on call during the night, but not expected to be at their desks until eight in the morning. Normally at this time of the day, Lena would be just getting out of bed and fumbling with the coffeemaker. 'I'll put in a courtesy call when we get back to the station.'

The car went quiet except for the brushing sound of rain against steel. A bolt of lightning, thin and mean, sparked in the sky. Lena instinctively flinched, but Frank just stared ahead at the lake. The divers weren't worried about the lightning. They were taking turns with the bolt cutters, trying to disentangle the dead girl from the two cinder blocks.

Frank's phone rang, a high-pitched warble that sounded like a bird sitting somewhere in the rain forest. He answered it with a gruff 'Yeah.' He listened for a few seconds, then asked, 'What about the parents?' Frank grumbled a string of curses under his breath. 'Then go back inside and find out.' He snapped his phone shut. 'Jackass.'

Lena gathered Brad had forgotten to get the parents' information. 'Where does Spooner live?'

'Taylor Drive. Number sixteen and a half. Brad's gonna meet us there if he manages to get his head out of his ass.' He put the engine in gear and slung his arm over the seat behind Lena as he backed up the car. The forest was dense and wet. Lena braced her palm against the dashboard as Frank slowly made his way back to the road.

'Sixteen and a half must mean she's in a garage apartment,' Lena noted. Many of the local residents had converted their garages or empty toolsheds into the semblance of a living space so that they could charge exorbitant rent to the college students. Most students were so desperate to live off campus that they didn't ask too many questions.

Frank said, 'Gordon Braham's the landlord.'

'Brad found that out?'

They hit a bump that made Frank's teeth clamp together. 'His mother told him.'

'Well.' Lena searched her mind for something positive to say about Brad. 'Shows initiative that he found out who owns the house and the garage.'

'Initiative,' Frank mocked. 'That kid's gonna get his head shot off one day.'

Lena had known Brad for over ten years. Frank had known him even longer. They both still saw him as a goofy young boy, a teenager who looked out of place with his gun belt tightened high on his waist. Brad had put in his years in uniform and passed the right tests to garner his gold detective shield, but Lena had done this job long enough to know that there was a difference between a paperwork promotion and a street promotion. She could only hope that in a small town like Heartsdale, Brad's lack of street smarts wouldn't matter. He was good at filling out reports and talking to witnesses, but even after ten years behind the wheel of a squad car, he still tended to see the good in people instead of the bad.

Lena had been on the job less than a week when she'd realized that there was no such thing as a truly good person.

Herself included.

She didn't want to waste time worrying about Brad right now. She flipped through the photographs in Allison Spooner's wallet as Frank made his way through the forest. There was a picture of an orange tabby cat lying in a ray of sunshine, and a candid snapshot that showed Allison with a woman Lena assumed was her mother. The third photo showed Allison sitting on a park bench. On her right was a man who looked a few years younger than she was. He was wearing a baseball cap pulled down low and had his hands tucked deep into the pockets of his baggy pants. On Allison's left was an older woman with stringy blond hair and heavy makeup. Her jeans were skintight. There was a hardness to her eyes. She could have been thirty or three hundred. All three of them sat close together. The boy had his arm around Allison Spooner's shoulders.

Lena showed Frank the picture. He asked, 'Family?'

She studied the photo, concentrating on the background. 'Looks like this was taken on campus.' She showed Frank. 'See the white building in the back? I think that's the student center.'

'That girl don't look like a college student to me.'

He meant the older blonde. 'She looks local.' She had the unmistakably trashy, bleach-blond air of a town-bred girl. Fake wallet aside, Allison Spooner appeared to be several rungs up on the social ladder. It didn't jibe that the two would be friends. 'Maybe Spooner had a drug problem?' Lena guessed. Nothing crossed class lines like methamphetamine.

They'd finally made it to the main road. The back wheels of the car gave one final spin in the mud as Frank pulled onto asphalt. 'Who called it in?'

Lena shook her head. 'The 911 call was made from a cell phone. The number was blocked. Female voice, but she wouldn't leave her name.'

'What'd she say?'

Lena carefully thumbed back through her notebook so the damp pages would not tear. She found the transcription and read aloud, '"Female voice: My friend has been missing since this afternoon. I think she killed herself. 911 Operator: What makes you think she killed herself? Female voice: She got into a fight last night with her boyfriend. She said she was going to drown herself up by Lover's Point." The operator tried to keep her on the line, but she hung up after that.'

Frank was quiet. She saw his throat work. His shoulders were slumped so low that he looked like a gangbanger holding on to the steering wheel. He'd been fighting the possibility that this was a murder since Lena got into the car.

She asked, 'What do you think?'

'Lover's Point,' Frank repeated. 'Only a townie would call it that.'

Lena held the notebook in front of the heating vents, trying to dry the pages. 'The boyfriend is probably the kid in the picture.'

Frank didn't pick up on her train of thought. 'So, the 911 call came in, and Brad drove out to the lake and found what?'

'The note was under one of the shoes. Allison's ring and watch were inside.' Lena bent down again to the plastic evidence bags buried in the deep pockets of her parka. She shifted through the victim's belongings and found the note, which she showed to Frank. '"I want it over."'

He stared at the writing so long she was worried he wasn't minding the road.

'Frank?'

One of the wheels grazed the edge of the asphalt. Frank jerked the steering wheel. Lena held on to the dash. She knew better than to say anything about his driving. Frank wasn't the type of man who liked to be corrected, especially by a woman. Especially by Lena.

She said, 'Strange note for a suicide. Even a fake suicide.'

'Short and to the point.' Frank kept one hand on the wheel as he searched his coat pocket. He slid on his reading glasses and stared at the smeared ink. 'She didn't sign it.'

Lena checked the road. He was riding the white line again. 'No.'

Frank glanced up and steered back toward the center line. 'Does this look like a woman's handwriting to you?'

Lena hadn't considered the possibility. She studied the single sentence, which was written in a wide, round print. 'It looks neat, but I couldn't say if a man or woman wrote it. We could get a handwriting expert. Allison's a student, so there are probably notes she took from classes or essays and tests. I'm sure we could find something to compare it with.'

Frank didn't address any of her suggestions. Instead, he said, 'I remember when my daughter was her age.' He cleared his throat a few times. 'She used to draw circles over her *i*'s instead of dots. I wonder if she still does that.'

Lena kept quiet. She had worked with Frank her entire career, but she didn't know much about his personal life beyond what most everyone else in town knew. He had two children by his first wife, but that was many wives ago. They'd moved out of town. He didn't seem to have contact with any of them. The subject of his family was one he never broached, and right now Lena was too cold and too wired to start sharing.

She put the focus back on the case. 'So, someone stabbed Allison in the neck, chained her to some cinder blocks, threw her in the lake, then decided to make it look like a suicide.' Lena shook her head at the stupidity. 'Another criminal mastermind.'

Frank gave a snort of agreement. She could tell his mind was on other things. He took off his glasses and stared at the road ahead.

She didn't want to, but she asked, 'What's going on?'

'Nothing.'

'How many years have I been riding with you, Frank?'

He made another grunting noise, but he relented easily enough. 'Mayor's been trying to track me down.'

Lena felt a lump rise in her throat. Clem Waters, the mayor of Heartsdale, had been trying for some time to make Frank's job as interim chief a more permanent position.

Frank said, 'I don't really want the job, but there's nobody else lining up to take it.'

'No,' she agreed. No one wanted the job, not least of all because they would never in a million years match the man who'd held it before.

'Benefits are good,' Frank said. 'Nice retirement package. Better health care, pension.'

She managed to swallow. 'That's good, Frank. Jeffrey would want you to take it.'

'He'd want me to retire before I have a heart attack chasing some junkie across the campus quad.' Frank took out his flask and offered it to Lena. She shook her head and watched him take a long pull, one eye on the road as he tilted back his head. Lena's focus stayed on his hand. There was a slight tremor to it. His hands had been shaking a lot lately, especially in the morning.

Without warning, the rain's steady beat turned into a harsh staccato. The noise echoed in the car, filling up the space. Lena pressed her tongue to the roof of her mouth. She should tell Frank now that she wanted to resign, that there was a job in Macon waiting for her if she could bring herself to make the leap. She had moved to Grant County to be near her sister, but her sister had died almost a decade ago. Her uncle, her only living relative, had retired to the Florida Panhandle. Her best friend had taken a job at a library up North. Her boyfriend lived two hours away. There was nothing keeping Lena here except inertia and loyalty to a man who had been dead for four years and probably hadn't thought she was a good cop anyway.

Frank used his knees to hold the steering wheel steady as he screwed the cap back on the flask. 'I won't take it unless you say it's okay.'

She turned her head in surprise. 'Frank—'

'I mean it,' he interrupted. 'If it's not okay with you, then I'll tell the mayor to shove it up his ass.' He gave a harsh chuckle that rattled the phlegm in his chest. 'Might let you come along to see the look on the little prick's face.'

She made herself say, 'You should take the job.'

'I don't know, Lee. I'm gettin' so damn old. Children are all grown up. Wives have moved on. Most days, I wonder why I even get out of bed.' He gave another raspy chuckle. 'Might find me in the lake one day with my watch in my shoes. But for real.'

She didn't want to hear the tiredness in his voice. Frank had been on the job twenty years longer than Lena, but she could feel the weariness in his tone like it was her own. This was why she had been spending every free minute of her time taking classes at the college, trying to get a bachelor's degree in forensic science so she could work on the crime scene investigation end instead of enforcement.

Lena could handle the early morning calls that yanked her from sleep. She could handle the carnage and the dead bodies and the misery that death brought to each and every moment of your life. What she could not take anymore was being on the front lines. There was too much responsibility. There was too much risk. You could make one mistake and it could cost a life – not your own, but another person's. You could end up getting someone's son killed. Someone's husband. Someone's friend. You found out fairly quickly that another person dying on your watch was far worse than the specter of your own death.

Frank said, 'Listen, I need to tell you something.'

Lena glanced at him, wondering at his sudden openness. His shoulders had slumped even more and his knuckles were white from gripping the steering wheel. She ran through the catalogue of things she might be in trouble for at work, but what came out of his mouth took her breath away. 'Sara Linton's back in town.'

Lena tasted whisky and bile in the back of her throat. For a brief, panicked moment, she thought she was going to throw up. Lena could not face Sara. The accusations. The guilt. Even the thought of driving down her street was too much. Lena always took the long way to work, bypassing Sara's house, bypassing the misery that churned up every time she thought of the place.

Frank kept his voice low. 'I heard it in town, so I gave her dad a call. He said she was driving down for Thanksgiving today.' He cleared his throat. 'I wouldn't'a told you, but I've stepped up patrols outside their house. You'd see it on the call sheet and wonder – so, now you know.'

Lena tried to swallow the sour taste in her mouth. It felt like glass going down her throat. 'Okay,' she managed. 'Thanks.'

Frank took a sharp turn onto Taylor Road, blowing through a stop sign. Lena grabbed the side of the door to brace herself, but the movement was automatic. Her mind was caught up in how to ask Frank for time off during the middle of a case. She would take the week and drive over to Macon, maybe scope out some apartments until the holiday was past and Sara was back in Atlanta where she belonged.

'Look at this dumbass,' Frank mumbled as he slowed the car.

Brad Stephens was standing outside his parked patrol car. He was wearing a tan suit pressed to within an inch of its life. His white shirt almost glowed against the blue striped tie that his mama had probably laid out for him with the rest of his clothes this morning. What was obviously bothering Frank was the umbrella in Brad's hand. It was bright pink except for the Mary Kay logo stitched in yellow.

'Go easy on him,' Lena tried, but Frank was already getting out of the car. He wrestled with his own umbrella – a large black canopy that he'd gotten from Brock at the funeral home – and stomped over to Brad. Lena waited in the car, watching Frank berate the young detective. She knew what it felt like to be on the other end of Frank's tirades. He had been her trainer when she first entered patrol, then her partner when she made detective. If not for Frank, Lena would've washed out of the job the first week. The fact that he didn't think women belonged on the force made her damned determined to prove him otherwise.

And Jeffrey had been her buffer. Lena had come to the realization some time ago that she had a tendency to be mirror to whoever was in front of her. When Jeffrey was in charge, they did everything the right way – or at least as right as they could. He was a solid cop, the kind of man who had the trust of the community because his character came through in everything he did. That was why the mayor had hired him in the first place. Clem wanted to break the old ways, to pull Grant County into the twenty-first century. Ben Carver, the outgoing chief of police, was as crooked as a stick in water. Frank had been his right-hand man and just as jagged. Under Jeffrey, Frank had changed his ways. They all had. Or at least they had as long as Jeffrey was alive.

Within the first week of Frank being put in charge, things had started to slip. It was slow at first, and hard to spot. A Breathalyzer result had gone missing, freeing one of Frank's hunting buddies from a DUI. An unusually careful pot dealer at the college was suddenly caught with a huge stash in the trunk of his car. Tickets disappeared. Cash was missing from the evidence locker. Requisitions turned iffy. The service contract for the county cars went to a garage Frank had part ownership in.

Like a dam breaking, these small cracks had led to larger issues until the whole thing burst open and every cop on the force was doing something they shouldn't do. Which was one of the biggest reasons Lena had to get out. Macon didn't do things the easy way. The city was bigger than the three cities of Grant County combined, topping out at a population of around a hundred thousand. People sued if they were wronged by the police, and they tended to win. Macon's murder rate was one of the highest in the state. Burglaries, sex crimes, violent crimes – there was plenty of opportunity for a detective, but even more work for a crime scene tech. Lena was two courses away from getting her criminal science degree. There were no shortcuts in evidence collection. You dusted for prints. You vacuumed the carpets for fibers. You photographed the blood and other fluids. You catalogued the evidence. Then you handed it all off to someone else. The lab techs were responsible for doing the science. The detectives were responsible for catching the bad guys. All Lena would be was a glorified cleaner with a badge and state benefits. She could spend the rest of her life processing crime scenes, then retire young enough to supplement her pension with private investigation work.

She would end up being one of those asshole private detectives who were always putting their noses where they didn't belong.

'Adams!' Frank slammed his hand on the hood of the car. Water splashed up like a dog shaking itself. He was finished yelling at Brad and was spoiling for someone else to rip into.

Lena took the dripping wet parka off the floor and put it on, tightening the strings on the hood so her hair wouldn't get soaked. She caught a look at herself in the rearview mirror. Her hair had started to twist into curls. The rain had brought out her Irish Catholic father's roots and managed to suppress her Mexican grandmother's.

'Adams!' Frank yelled again.

By the time she got out of the car, he was concentrating another tirade on Brad, yelling at him about how he was wearing his gun holster too low on his belt.

Lena forced her lips into a tight smile, trying to give Brad some silent support. She had been a dumb cop herself many years ago. Maybe Jeffrey had thought she was worthless, too. The fact that he had tried to turn her into something worthwhile was a testament to his determination. One of the few reasons Lena could give herself for not taking the job in Macon was thinking that she could do something to help Brad be a better cop. She could keep him away from the corruption, train him to do things the right way.

Do as I say, not as I do.

'Are you sure this is it?' Frank demanded. He meant the house.

Brad's throat worked. 'Yes, sir. That's what the college had on file. Sixteen and a half Taylor Drive.'

'Did you knock on the door?'

Brad seemed unsure of which answer was the right one. 'No, sir. You said to wait for you.'

'You got a phone number for the owner?'

'No, sir. His name is Mr. Braham, but—'

'Christ,' Frank muttered, stalking up the driveway.

Lena couldn't help but feel sorry for Brad. She thought about reaching up and patting him on the shoulder, but he tilted his bright pink umbrella the wrong way and ended up sending a sheet of rain down on her head.

'Oh,' Brad breathed. 'Gosh, I'm sorry, Lena.'

She pressed down some expletives that wanted to come and walked ahead of him, joining Frank.

Sixteen and a half Taylor Drive was a one-story garage that was slightly deeper than a minivan and twice as wide. 'Converted' was a loose term, because the structure had not been altered well on the outside. The roll-up metal door was still in place, black construction paper covering the windows. Because of the overcast day, the lights inside the apartment showed through the cracks in the aluminum siding. Tufts of pink fiberglass insulation were matted down by rain. The tin roof was rusted red, a blue tarp covering the back corner.

Lena stared at the structure, wondering why any woman in her right mind would live here.

'Scooter,' Frank noted. There was a purple Vespa parked by the garage. A bike chain attached the back wheel to an eyebolt screwed into the concrete drive. He asked, 'Same chain as what was on the girl?'

She saw a flash of bright yellow under the wheel. 'Looks like the same padlock.'

Lena glanced toward the main house, a split ranch with a sloping gable on the front. The windows were dark. There was no car by the house or on the street. They would have to find the landlord for permission to go into the garage. She flipped open her cell phone to call Marla Simms, the station's elderly secretary. Between Marla and her best friend, Myrna, they represented a combined Rolodex of every person in town.

Brad pressed his face up to one of the windows in the garage door. He squinted, trying to see past a rip in the construction paper. 'Jeesh,' he whispered, backing up so quickly that he almost tripped over his feet. He drew his gun and went into a crouch.

Lena's Glock was in her hand before she thought about putting it there. Her heart had jumped into her throat. Adrenaline made her senses sharpen. A quick look over her shoulder showed Frank had drawn his weapon, too. They all stood there, guns pointed toward the closed garage door.

Lena motioned for Brad to move back. She kept a low crouch as she walked up to the garage window. The tear in the construction paper seemed larger now, more like a target she was about to put her face in front of. Quickly, she glanced inside. There was a man standing at a folding table. He was wearing a black mask. He looked up as if he heard a noise, and Lena ducked down again, her heart racing. She stood still, counting off the seconds as her ears strained to hear footsteps, a gun loading. There was nothing, and she slowly let out the breath she'd been holding.

She held up one finger to Frank: one person. She mouthed the word 'mask,' and saw his eyes widen in surprise. Frank indicated his gun and she shrugged as she shook her head. She hadn't been able to see whether or not the man was holding a weapon.

Without being told, Brad walked toward the side of the building. He went around the back, obviously checking for exits. Lena counted the seconds, reaching twenty-six by the time he showed up on the other side of the building. Brad shook his head. No back door. No windows. Lena indicated that he should go down the driveway and serve as backup. Let her and Frank handle this. Brad started to protest, but she cut him with a look. Finally, he hung his head in surrender. She waited until he was at least fifteen feet away before nodding to Frank that she was ready to go.

Frank walked toward the garage and leaned down, wrapping his hand around the steel handle at the base of the roll-up door. He checked with Lena, then yanked up on the handle hard and fast.

The man inside was startled, his eyes going wide behind the black ski mask covering his face. He had a knife in his gloved hand, raised as if to charge. The blade was long and thin, at least eight inches. What looked very much like dried blood was caked around the handle. The concrete beneath his feet was stained a dark brown. More blood.

'Drop it,' Frank said.

The intruder didn't comply. Lena took a few steps to her right, closing any escape routes. He was standing behind a large cafeteria table with paperwork strewn across it. A twin bed was angled out from the wall so that between the bed frame and the table, the entire room was cut down the middle.

'Put down the knife,' Lena told him. She had to turn sideways to get past the bed. There was another dark stain on the concrete under the bed. A bucket with brown water and a filthy-looking sponge was beside it. She kept her gun trained at the man's chest, stepping carefully around boxes and scattered pieces of paper. He glanced nervously between Lena and Frank, the knife still raised in his fist.

'Drop it,' Frank repeated.

The man's hands started to lower. Lena let herself exhale, thinking this was going to go easy. She was wrong. Without warning, the man shoved the table violently to the side, slamming it into Lena's legs, sending her back onto the bed. Her head grazed the frame as she rolled onto the concrete floor. A shot rang out. Lena didn't think it was from her gun, but her left hand felt hot, almost on fire. Someone shouted. There was a muffled groan. She scrambled to stand. Her vision blurred.

Frank was lying on his side in the middle of the garage. His gun lay on the ground beside him. His fist was clamped around his arm. She thought at first that he was having a heart attack. The blood seeping between his fingers showed that he had been cut.

'Go!' he yelled. 'Now!'

'Shit,' Lena hissed, pushing away the table. She felt nauseated. Her vision was still blurred, but it sharpened on the black-clad suspect bolting down the driveway. Brad was standing stock-still, mouth open in surprise. The intruder ran right past him.

'Stop him!' she screamed. 'He stabbed Frank!'

Brad jerked around, giving chase. Lena ran after them, sneakers slapping against the wet ground, water flying up into her face. She rounded the end of the driveway and flew down the street. Ahead, she saw Brad gaining on the suspect. He was taller, fitter, every stride closing the gap between him and the intruder.

Brad yelled, 'Police! Stop!'

Everything slowed. The rain seemed to freeze in midair, tiny droplets trapped in time and space.

The suspect stopped. He reared around, slicing the knife through the air. Lena reached for her gun, felt the empty holster. There was a popping sound of metal breaking through flesh, then a loud groan. Brad crumpled to the ground.

'No,' Lena gasped, running to Brad, falling to her knees.

The knife was still in his belly. Blood seeped into his shirt, turning the white to crimson. 'Brad—'

'It hurts,' he told her. 'It hurts so bad.'

Lena dialed her cell phone, praying the ambulance team was still at the lake and not making the half-hour trip back to the station. Behind her, she heard loud footsteps, shoes pounding pavement. With startling speed, Frank sprinted past her, yelling with uncontrolled rage. The suspect turned around to see what hell was about to be unleashed upon him just as Frank tackled him to the asphalt. Teeth shattered. Bones snapped. Frank's fists were flying, a windmill of pain raining down on the suspect.

Lena pressed the phone to her ear. She listened to the rings that were going unanswered at the station.

'Lena . . .' Brad whispered. 'Don't tell my mom I messed up.'

'You didn't mess up.' She used her hand to shield the rain from his face. His eyelids fluttered, trying to close. 'No,' she begged. 'Please don't do this to me.'

'I'm sorry, Lena.'

'No!' she yelled.

Not again.

THREE

Sara Linton no longer thought of Grant County as her home. It was of another place, another time, as tangible to her as Rebecca's Manderley or Heathcliff's moors. As she drove through the outskirts of town, she couldn't help but notice that everything looked the same, yet nothing was quite real. The closed military base that was slowly reverting to nature. The trailer parks on the bad side of the railroad tracks. The abandoned box store that had been converted into a storage center.

Three and a half years had passed since Sara had been home, and she wanted to think that her life was okay now, getting closer to a new normal. Actually, her current life in Atlanta looked a lot like it would have if she had stayed there after medical school instead of moving back to Grant County. She was the chief pediatric attending in Grady Hospital's emergency room, where students followed her around like puppy dogs and the security guards carried multiple clips on their belts in case the gangbangers tried to finish the job they started on the streets. An epidemiologist who worked for the Centers for Disease Control on Emory's campus had started asking her out. She went to dinner parties and grabbed coffee with friends. Occasionally, on the weekends, she would take the dogs to Stone Mountain Park to give the greyhounds space to run. She read a lot. She watched more television than she should. She was living a perfectly normal, perfectly boring life.

And yet, the minute she saw the sign announcing that she had officially entered Grant County, her carefully constructed façade started to crack. She pulled over to the side of the road, feeling a constriction in her chest. The dogs stirred in the back seat. Sara forced herself not to give in. She was stronger than this. She had fought tooth and nail to climb out of the depression she'd spiraled into after her husband's death, and she was not going to allow herself to fall back in just because of a stupid road sign.

'Hydrogen,' she said. 'Helium, lithium, beryllium.' It was an old trick from her childhood, listing out the elements from the periodic table to take her mind off the monsters that might be lurking under her bed. 'Neon, sodium, magnesium . . .' She recited from memory until her heart stopped racing and her breathing returned to normal.

Finally, the moment passed, and she found herself laughing at the thought of Jeffrey finding out she was chanting the periodic table on the side of the road. He'd been a jock in high school – handsome, charming, and effortlessly cool. It had tickled him no end to see Sara's geeky side.

She reached around and gave the dogs some attention so they would settle back down. Instead of starting the car again, she sat for a while, staring out the window at the empty road leading into town. Her fingers went to the collar of her shirt, then lower to the ring she wore on a necklace. Jeffrey's Auburn class ring. He'd been on the football team until he got tired of warming the bench. The ring was bulky, too big for her finger, but touching it was the closest she could come to touching him. It was a talisman. Sometimes, she found herself touching it without remembering putting her hand there.

Her only consolation was that there was nothing left unsaid between them. Jeffrey knew that Sara loved him. He knew there was no part of her that did not belong wholly and completely to him, just as she knew that he felt the same. When he died, his last words were to her. His last thoughts, his last memories, all were of Sara. Just as she knew that her last thoughts would always be of him.

She kissed the ring before tucking it back into her shirt. Carefully, Sara pulled the car off the shoulder and back onto the road. The overwhelming feeling threatened to come back as she drove farther into town. It was so much easier to push away the things that she had lost when they weren't staring her right in the face. The high school football stadium where she had first met Jeffrey. The park where they had walked the dogs together. The restaurants where they ate. The church that Sara's mother had occasionally guilted them into attending.

There had to be one place, one memory, that was untouched by this man. Long before Jeffrey Tolliver even knew there was such a thing as Grant County, she'd had a life here. Sara had grown up in Heartsdale, gone to the high school, joined the science club, helped out at the women's shelter where her mother volunteered, done the occasional odd job with her father. Sara had lived in a house Jeffrey had never stepped foot in. She'd driven a car he'd never seen. She had shared her first kiss with a local boy whose father owned the hardware store. She had gone to dances at the church and attended potlucks and football games.

All without Jeffrey.

Three years before he entered her life, Sara had taken the part-time job of county medical examiner in order to buy out her partner at the children's clinic. She had kept the job long after her loan had been paid off. She was surprised to find out that helping the dead was sometimes more rewarding than saving the living. Every case was a puzzle, every body riddled with clues to a mystery that only Sara could solve. A different part of her brain that she hadn't even known existed was engaged by the coroner's job. She had loved both her jobs with equal passion. She had worked countless cases, given testimony in court on countless suspects and circumstances.

Now, Sara could not remember one detail from any of them.

What she could vividly recall was the day that Jeffrey Tolliver had strolled into town. The mayor had wooed him away from the Birmingham police force to take over for the retiring chief of police. Every woman Sara knew practically tittered with joy whenever Jeffrey's name was mentioned. He was witty and charming. He was tall, dark, and handsome. He'd played college football. He drove a cherry red Mustang, and when he walked, he had the athletic grace of a panther.

That Jeffrey set his sights on Sara had shocked the entire town, Sara included. She wasn't the type of girl who got the good-looking guy. She was the type of girl who watched her sister or her best friend get the good-looking guy. And yet, their casual dates turned into something deeper, so that a few years later, no one was surprised when Jeffrey asked her to marry him. Their relationship had been hard work, and God knew there had been ups and downs, but in the end, she had known with every fiber of her being that she belonged to Jeffrey and, more important, that he belonged completely to her.

Sara wiped her tears with the back of her hand as she drove. The longing was the hardest part, the physical ache her body felt at the memory of him. There was no part of town that didn't slap her in the face with what she had lost. These roads had been kept safe by him. These people had called him friend. And Jeffrey had died here. The town he'd loved so much had become his crime scene. There was the church where they mourned his death. There was the street where a long line of cars had pulled over as his casket was driven out of town.

She would only be here for four days. She could do anything for four days.

Almost anything.

Sara took the long way to her parents' house, bypassing Main Street and the children's clinic. The bad storms that had followed her all the way from Atlanta had finally subsided, but she could tell from the dark clouds in the sky that this was only a temporary reprieve. The weather seemed to fit her mood lately – sudden, violent storms with fleeting rays of sunshine.

Because of the coming Thanksgiving holiday, lunchtime traffic was nonexistent. No cars were snaking a long line toward the college. No noontime shoppers were heading into downtown. Still, she took a left instead of a right at Lakeshore Drive, going two miles out of her way around Lake Grant so that she would not drive past her old house. Her old life.

The Linton family home, at least, was welcoming in its familiarity. The house had been tinkered with over the years – additions tacked on, bathrooms added and updated. Sara's father had built out the apartment space over the garage when she went away to college so that she would have a place to stay during summer break. Tessa, Sara's younger sister, had lived there for almost ten years while she waited for her life to start. Eddie Linton was a plumber by trade. He had taught both his girls the business, but only Tessa had stuck around long enough to do anything with it. That Sara had chosen medical school instead of a life navigating dank crawl spaces with her sister and father was a disappointment Eddie still tried his best to cover. He was the kind of father who was most happy when his daughters were close by.

Sara didn't know how Eddie felt about Tessa leaving the family business. Around the time Sara had lost Jeffrey, Tessa had gotten married and moved her life eight thousand miles away to work with children in South Africa. She was as impulsive as Sara was steady, though no one would have guessed when the girls were teenagers that either of them would be where they were today. The idea of Tessa as a missionary was still hard for Sara to believe.

'Sissy!' Tessa bounded out of the house, her pregnant belly swaying as she angled herself down the front stairs. 'What took you so long? I'm starving!'

Sara was barely out of the car when her sister threw her arms around her. The hug turned from a greeting into something deeper, and Sara felt the darkness coming back. She was no longer certain that she could do this for four minutes, let alone four days.

Tessa mumbled, 'Oh, Sissy, everything's changed.'

Sara blinked back tears. 'I know.'

Tessa pulled away. 'They got a pool.'

Sara laughed in surprise. 'A what?'

'Mama and Daddy put in a pool. With a hot tub.'

Sara wiped her eyes, still laughing, loving her sister more than words could ever convey. 'You're kidding me?' Sara and Tessa had spent most of their childhood begging their parents to put in a pool.

'And Mama took the plastic off the couch.'

Sara gave her sister a stern look, as if to ask when the punch line was coming.

'They redecorated the den, changed all the light fixtures, redid the kitchen, painted over the pencil marks Daddy made on the door . . . It's like we never even lived there.'

Sara couldn't say she mourned the loss of the pencil marks, which had recorded their height until the eighth grade, when she had officially become the tallest person in her family. She grabbed the dog leashes from the passenger seat. 'What about the den?'

'All the paneling's down. They even put up crown molding.' Tessa tucked her hands into her expansive hips. 'They got new lawn furniture. The nice wicker – not the kind that pinches your ass every time you sit down.' Thunder made a distant clapping sound. Tessa waited for it to pass. 'It looks like something out of *Southern Living*.'

Sara blocked the back door of the SUV as she wrangled with her two greyhounds, trying to snap on their leashes before they bolted off into the street. 'Did you ask Mama what made her change everything?'

Tessa clicked her tongue as she took the leashes from Sara. Billy and Bob jumped down, heeling beside her. 'She said that she could finally have nice things now that we were gone.'

Sara pursed her lips. 'I'm not going to pretend that

50

doesn't sting.' She walked around the car and opened the trunk. 'When's Lemuel coming?'

'He's trying to get a flight out, but those bush pilots won't take off unless every chicken and goat in the village buys a ticket.' Tessa had come home a few weeks ago to have the baby in the States. Her last pregnancy had ended badly, the child lost. Understandably, Lemuel didn't want Tessa to take any chances, but Sara found it odd that he hadn't yet joined his wife. Her due date was less than a month away.

Sara said, 'I hope I get to see him before I leave.'

'Oh, Sissy, that's so sweet. Thank you for lying.'

Sara was about to respond with what she hoped was a more artful lie when she noticed a patrol car driving down the street at a slow crawl. The man behind the wheel tipped his hat at Sara. Their eyes met, and she felt herself tearing up again.

Tessa stroked the dogs. 'They've been driving by like that all morning.'

'How did they know I was coming?'

'I might've let it slip at the Shop 'n Save the other day.'

'Tess,' Sara groaned. 'You know Jill June got on the phone as soon as you left. I wanted to keep this quiet. Now everybody and their dog'll be dropping by.'

Tessa kissed Bob with a loud smack. 'Then you'll get to see your friends, too, won't you, boy?' She gave Bill a kiss to even things out. 'You've gotten two calls already.'

Sara pulled out her suitcase and closed the lift gate. 'Let me guess. Marla at the station and Myrna from down the street, both trying to milk every ounce of gossip.'

'No, actually.' Tessa walked alongside Sara back to the house. 'A girl named Julie something. She sounded young.'

Sara's patients had often called her at home, but she didn't remember anyone named Julie. 'Did she leave a number?'

'Mama took it down.'

Sara lugged her suitcase up the porch stairs, wondering where her father was. Probably rolling around on the plastic-free couch. 'Who else called?'

'It was the same girl both times. She said she needed your help.'

'Julie,' Sara repeated, the name still not ringing any bells.

Tessa stopped her on the porch. 'I need to tell you something.'

Sara felt a creeping dread, instinctively knowing bad news was coming. Tessa was about to speak when the front door opened.

'You're nothing but skin and bones,' Cathy chided. 'I knew you weren't eating enough up there.'

'It's good to see you, too, Mother.' Sara kissed her cheek. Eddie came up behind her, and she kissed his cheek, too. Her parents petted the dogs, cooing at them, and Sara tried not to notice that the greyhounds were getting a warmer welcome.

Eddie grabbed Sara's suitcase. 'I got this.' Before she could say anything else, he headed up the stairs.

Sara took off her sneakers as she watched her father leave. 'Is something—'

Cathy shook her head in lieu of an explanation.

Tessa kicked off her sandals. The freshly painted wall was scuffed where she had obviously done this many times before. She said, 'Mama, you need to tell her.'

Cathy exchanged a look with Tessa that raised the hair on the back of Sara's neck.

'Tell me what?'

Her mother started off with an assurance. 'Everybody's fine.'

'Except?'

'Brad Stephens got hurt this morning.'

Brad had been one of her patients, then one of Jeffrey's cops. 'What happened?'

'He got stabbed trying to arrest somebody. He's at Macon General.'

Sara leaned against the wall. 'Stabbed where? Is he all right?'

'I don't know the details. His mama's at the hospital with him now. I guess we'll get a phone call one way or another tonight.' She rubbed Sara's arm. 'Now, let's not worry until it's time to worry. It's in the Lord's hands now.'

Sara felt blindsided. 'Why would anyone hurt Brad?'

Tessa supplied, 'They think it had something to do with the girl they pulled out of the lake this morning.'

'What girl?'

Cathy cut off any further conversation on the matter. '*They* don't know anything, and *we* are not going to add to these rampant rumors.'

Sara pressed, 'Mama—'

'No more.' Cathy squeezed her arm before letting go. 'Let's remember the things we have to be thankful for, like both of my girls being home at the same time.'

Cathy and Tessa walked down the hall toward the kitchen, the dogs following them. Sara stayed in the foyer. The news about Brad had been brushed over so quickly that she hadn't had time to process it. Brad Stephens had been one of Sara's first patients at the children's clinic. She had watched him grow from a gawky teenager into a clean-cut young man. Jeffrey had kept him on a tight leash. He was more like a puppy than a cop – a sort of mascot at the station. Of course, Sara knew better than anyone else that being a cop, even in a small town, was a dangerous job.

She fought the urge to call the hospital in Macon and find out about Brad. An injured cop always brought a crowd. Blood was donated. Vigils were started. At least two fellow police officers stayed with the family at all times.

But Sara wasn't part of that community anymore. She wasn't the police chief's wife. She had resigned as the town's medical examiner four years ago. Brad's condition was none of her business. Besides, she was supposed to be on vacation right now. She had worked back-to-back shifts in order to get the time off, trading weekends and full moons in exchange for the Thanksgiving holiday. This week was going to be hard enough without Sara sticking her nose into other people's problems. She had enough problems of her own.

Sara looked at the framed photographs that lined the hallway, familiar scenes from her childhood. Cathy had put a fresh coat of paint on everything, but if the paint had not been recent, there would have been a large rectangle near the door that was lighter in color than the rest of the wall: Jeffrey and Sara's wedding picture. Sara could still see it in her head – not the picture, but the actual day. The way the breeze stirred her hair, which miraculously had not frizzed in the humidity. Her pale blue dress and matching sandals. Jeffrey in dark pants and a white dress shirt, ironed so crisp that he hadn't bothered to button the cuffs. They had been in the backyard of her parents' house, the lake offering a spectacular sunset. Jeffrey's hair was still damp from the shower, and when she put her head on his shoulder, she could smell the familiar scent of his skin.

'Hey, baby.' Eddie was standing on the bottom stair behind her. Sara turned around. She smiled, because she wasn't used to having to look up to see her father.

He asked, 'You get bad weather coming down?'

'Not too bad.'

'I guess you took the bypass?'

'Yep.'

He stared at her, a sad smile on his face. Eddie had loved Jeffrey like a son. Every time he spoke to Sara, she felt his loss in double measure.

'You know,' he began, 'you're getting to be just as beautiful as your mother.'

She could feel her cheeks redden from the compliment. 'I've missed you, Daddy.'

He took her hand in his, kissed her palm, then pressed it over his heart. 'You hear about the two hats hanging on a peg by the door?'

She laughed. 'No. What about them?'

'One says to the other, "You stay here. I'll go on a head."'

Sara shook her head at the bad pun. 'Daddy, that's awful.'

The phone rang, the old-fashioned sound of an actual ringing bell filling the house. There were two telephones in the Linton home: one in the kitchen and one upstairs in the master bedroom. The girls were only allowed to use the one in the kitchen, and the cord was so long from being stretched into the pantry or outside, or anywhere else there might be an infinitesimal bit of privacy, that it had lost all of its curl.

'Sara!' Cathy called. 'Julie is on the phone for you.'

Eddie patted her arm. 'Go.'

She walked down the hall and into the kitchen, which was so beautiful that she froze mid-stride. 'Holy crap.'

Tessa said, 'Wait till you see the pool.'

Sara ran her hand along the new center island. 'This is marble.' Previously, the Linton décor had favored Brady Bunch orange tiles and knotty pine cabinetry. She turned around and saw the new refrigerator. 'Is that Sub-Zero?'

'Sara.' Cathy held out the phone, the only thing in the kitchen that had not been updated.

She exchanged an outraged look with Tessa as she put the phone to her ear. 'Hello?'

'Dr. Linton?'

'Speaking.' She opened the door on the cherry wall cabinet, marveling at the antique glass panels. There was no answer on the phone. She said, 'Hello? This is Dr. Linton.'

'Ma'am? I'm sorry. This is Julie Smith. Can you hear me okay?'

The connection was bad, obviously a cell phone. It didn't help matters that the girl was speaking barely above a whisper. Sara didn't recognize the name, though she guessed from the twangy accent that Julie had grown up in one of the poorer areas of town. 'What can I do for you?'

'I'm sorry. I'm calling from work and I gotta be quiet.'

Sara felt her brow furrow. 'I can hear you fine. What do you need?'

'I know you don't know me, and I'm sorry to be calling

you like this, but you have a patient named Tommy Braham. You know Tommy, don't you?'

Sara ran through all the Tommys she could think of, then came up not with a face, but with a disposition. He was just another young boy who'd had myriad office visits for the sorts of things you would expect: a bead shoved up his nose. A watermelon seed in his ear. Unspecified belly aches on important school days. He stuck out mostly because his father, not his mother, had always brought him to the clinic, an unusual occurrence in Sara's experience.

Sara told the girl, 'I remember Tommy. How's he doing?'

'That's the thing.' She went quiet, and Sara could hear water running in the background. She waited it out until the girl continued, 'Sorry. Like I was saying, he's in trouble. I wouldn't have called, but he told me to. He texted me from prison.'

'Prison?' Sara felt her heart sink. She hated to hear when one of her kids turned out bad, even if she couldn't quite recall what he looked like. 'What did he do?'

'He didn't do anything, ma'am. That's the point.'

'Okay.' Sara rephrased the question. 'What was he convicted of?'

'Nothing as far as I know. He doesn't even know if he's arrested or what.'

Sara assumed the girl had confused prison with jail. 'He's at the police station on Main Street?' Tessa shot her a look and Sara shrugged, helpless to explain.

Julie told her, 'Yes, ma'am. They got him downtown.'

'Okay, what do they think he did?'

'I guess they think he killed Allison, but there ain't no way he—'

'Murder.' Sara did not let her finish the sentence. 'I'm not sure what he wants me to do.' She felt compelled to add, 'For this sort of situation, he needs a lawyer, not a doctor.'

'Yes, ma'am, I know the difference between a doctor and a lawyer.' Julie didn't sound insulted by Sara's clarification. 'It's just that he said he really needed someone who would listen to him, because they don't believe that he was with Pippy all night, and he said that you were the only one who ever listened to him, and that one cop, she's been really hard on him. She keeps staring at him like—'

Sara put her hand to her throat. 'What cop?'

'I'm not sure. Some lady.'

That narrowed things down enough. Sara tried not to sound cold. 'I really can't get involved in this, Julie. If Tommy has been arrested, then by law, they have to provide him with a lawyer. Tell him to ask for Buddy Conford. He's very good at helping people in these sorts of situations. All right?'

'Yes, ma'am.' She sounded disappointed, but not surprised. 'Okay, then. I told him I'd try.'

'Well . . .' Sara did not know what else to say. 'Good luck. To both of you.'

'Thank you, ma'am, and like I said, I'm sorry to bother you'uns over the holiday.'

'It's all right.' Sara waited for the girl to respond, but there was only the sound of a flushing toilet, then a dead line.

Tessa asked, 'What was that about?'

Sara hung up the phone and sat down at the table. 'One of my old patients is in jail. They think he killed somebody. Not Brad – someone named Allison.'

58

Tessa asked, 'Which patient was she calling about? I bet it's the boy who stabbed Brad.'

Cathy slammed the refrigerator door to express her disapproval.

Still, Tessa pressed, 'What's his name?'

Sara studiously avoided her mother's disapproving gaze. 'Tommy Braham.'

'That's the one. Mama, didn't he used to cut our grass?'

Cathy gave a clipped 'Yes,' not adding anything else to the conversation.

Sara said, 'For the life of me, I can't remember what he looks like. Not too bright. I think his father is an electrician. Why can't I remember his face?'

Cathy tsked her tongue as she spread Duke's mayonnaise onto slices of white bread. 'Age will do that to you.'

Tessa smiled smugly. 'You should know.'

Cathy made a biting retort, but Sara tuned out the exchange. She strained to remember more details about Tommy Braham, trying to place him. His father stuck out more than the son; a gruff, muscled man who was uncomfortable being at the clinic, as if he found the public act of caring for his son to be emasculating. The wife had run off – Sara remembered that at least. There had been quite a scandal around her departure, mostly because she had left in the middle of the night with the youth minister of the Primitive Baptist church.

Tommy must have been around eight or nine when Sara first saw him as a patient. All boys looked the same at that age: bowl hair cuts, T-shirts, blue jeans that looked impossibly small and bunched up over bright white tennis shoes. Had he had a crush on her? She couldn't remember. What stuck out the most was that he had been silly and a bit slow. She imagined if he'd committed murder, it was because someone else had put him up to it.

She asked, 'Who is Tommy supposed to have killed?'

Tessa answered, 'A student from the college. They pulled her out of the lake at the crack of dawn. At first they thought it was a suicide, then they didn't, so they went to her house, which happens to be that crappy garage Gordon Braham rents out to students. You know the one?'

Sara nodded. She had once helped her father pump the septic tank outside the Braham house while she was on a holiday break from college, an event that had spurred her to work doubly hard to get into medical school.

Tessa supplied, 'So, Tommy was there in the garage with a knife. He attacked Frank and ran out into the street. Brad chased after him and he stabbed Brad, too.'

Sara shook her head. She had been thinking something small – a convenience store holdup, an accidental discharge of a gun. 'That doesn't sound like Tommy.'

'Half the neighborhood saw it,' Tessa told her. 'Brad was chasing him down the street and Tommy turned around and stabbed him in the gut.'

Sara thought it through to the next step. Tommy hadn't stabbed a civilian. He had stabbed a cop. There were different rules when a police officer was involved. Assault turned into attempted murder. Manslaughter turned into murder in the first.

Tessa mumbled, 'I hear Frank got a little rough with him.'

Cathy voiced her disapproval as she took plates down from the cabinets. 'It's very disappointing when people you respect behave badly.'

Sara tried to imagine the scene: Brad running after Tommy, Frank bringing up the rear. But it wouldn't have just been Frank. He wouldn't waste his time pounding on a suspect while Brad was bleeding out. Someone else would have been there. Someone who had probably caused the whole takedown to go bad in the first place.

Sara felt anger spread like fire inside her chest. 'Where was Lena during all of this?'

Cathy dropped a plate on the floor. It shattered at her feet, but she did not bend to pick up the pieces. Her lips went into a thin line and her nostrils flared. Sara could tell she was struggling to speak. 'Don't you dare say that hateful woman's name in my house ever again. Do you hear me?'

'Yes, ma'am.' Sara looked down at her hands. Lena Adams. Jeffrey's star detective. The woman who was supposed to have Jeffrey's back at all times. The woman whose cowardice and fear had gotten Jeffrey murdered.

Tessa struggled to kneel down and help her mother clean up the broken dish. Sara stayed where she was, frozen in place.

The darkness was back, a suffocating cloud of misery that made her want to curl into a ball. This kitchen had been filled with laughter all of Sara's life – the good-natured bickering between her mother and sister, the bad puns and practical jokes from her father. Sara did not belong here anymore. She should find an excuse to leave. She should go back to Atlanta and let her family enjoy their holiday in peace rather than dredging up the collective sorrow of the last four years.

No one spoke until the phone rang again. Tessa was

closest. She picked up the receiver. 'Linton residence.' She didn't make small talk. She handed the phone to Sara.

'Hello?'

'I'm sorry to be bothering you, Sara.'

Frank Wallace always seemed to be making an effort when he said Sara's name. He had played poker with Eddie Linton since Sara was in diapers, and had called her 'Sweetpea' until he realized that it was inappropriate to address his boss's wife with such familiarity.

Sara managed a 'Hi' as she opened the French door leading onto the back deck. She hadn't realized how hot her face was until the cold hit her. 'Is Brad all right?'

'You heard about that?'

'Of course I heard.' Half the town probably knew about Brad before the ambulance had arrived on the scene. 'Is he still in surgery?'

'Got out an hour ago. Surgeons say he's got a shot if he makes it through the next twenty-four hours.' Frank said more, but Sara couldn't concentrate on his words, which were meaningless anyway. The twenty-four-hour mark was the gold standard for surgeons, the difference between explaining a death at the weekly morbidity and mortality meeting or passing off an iffy patient to another doctor to manage their care.

She leaned against the house, cold brick pressing into her back, as she waited for Frank to get to the point. 'Do you remember a patient named Tommy Braham?'

'Vaguely.'

'I hate to pull you into this, but he's been asking for you.'

Sara listened with half an ear, her mind whirring with possible excuses to answer the question she knew that he was going to ask. She was so caught up in the task that she hadn't realized Frank had stopped talking until he said her name. 'Sara? You still there?'

'I'm here.'

'It's just that he won't stop crying.'

'Crying?' Again, she had the sensation of missing an important part of the conversation.

'Yeah, crying,' Frank confirmed. 'I mean, a lot of them cry. Hell, it's jail. But he's seriously not right. I think he needs a sedative or something to calm him down. We got three drunks and a wife beater in here gonna break through the walls and strangle him if he don't shut up.'

She repeated his words in her head, still not sure she'd heard right. Sara had been married to a cop for many years, and she could count on one hand the number of times Jeffrey had worried about a criminal in his cells – and never a murderer, especially a murderer who had harmed a fellow officer. 'Isn't there a doctor on call?'

'Honey, there's barely a cop on call. The mayor's cut half our budget. I'm surprised every time I flip a switch that the lights still come on.'

She asked, 'What about Elliot Felteau?' Elliot had bought Sara's practice when she left town. The children's clinic was right across the street from the station.

'He's on vacation. The nearest doc is sixty miles away.'

She gave a heavy sigh, annoyed with Elliot for taking a week off, as if children would wait until after the holiday to get sick. She was also annoyed with Frank for trying to drag her into this mess. But mostly, she was annoyed with herself that she had even taken the call. 'Can't you just tell him that Brad's going to be okay?'

'It's not that. There was this girl we pulled out of the lake this morning.'

'I heard.'

'Tommy confessed to killing her. Took him a while, but we broke him. He was in love with the girl. She didn't want to give him the time of day. You know the kind of thing.'

'Then it's just remorse,' she said, though she found the behavior strange. In Sara's experience, the first thing most criminals did after they confessed was fall into a deep sleep. Their bodies had been so shot through with adrenaline for so long that they collapsed in exhaustion when they finally got the weight off their chests. 'Give him some time.'

'It's more than that,' Frank insisted. He sounded exasperated and slightly desperate. 'I swear to God, Sara, I really hate asking you this, but something's gotta help him get through. It's like his heart's gonna break if he doesn't see you.'

'I barely remember him.'

'He remembers you.'

Sara chewed her lip. 'Where's his daddy?'

'In Florida. We can't get hold of him. Tommy's all alone, and he knows it.'

'Why is he asking for me?' There were certainly patients she had bonded with over the years, but, to her recollection, Tommy Braham had not been one of them. Why couldn't she remember his face?

Frank said, 'He says you'll listen to him.'

'You didn't tell him I'd come, did you?'

'Course not. I didn't even want to ask, but he's just bad off, Sara. I think he needs to see a doctor. Not just you, but a doctor.'

'It's not because—' She stopped, not knowing how to finish the question. She decided to be blunt. 'I heard you took him down hard.'

Frank couched his language. 'He fell down a lot while I was trying to arrest him.'

Sara was familiar with the euphemism, code for the nastier side of law enforcement. Abuse of prisoners in custody was a subject she never broached with Jeffrey, mostly because she did not want to know the answer. 'Is anything broken?'

'A couple of teeth. Nothing bad.' Frank sounded exasperated. 'He's not crying over a split lip, Sara. He needs a doctor.'

Sara looked through the window into the kitchen. Her mother was sitting at the table beside Tessa. Both of them stared back at her. One of the reasons Sara had moved back to Grant County after medical school was because of the paucity of doctors serving rural areas. With the hospital downtown closed, the sick were forced to travel almost an hour away to get help. The children's clinic was a blessing for the local kids, but, apparently, not during holidays.

'Sara?'

She rubbed her eyes with her fingers. 'Is she there?'

He hesitated a moment. 'No. She's at the hospital with Brad.'

Probably concocting a story in her head where she was the hero and Brad was just a careless victim. Sara's voice shook. 'I can't see her, Frank.'

'You won't have to.'

She felt grief tighten her throat. To be at the station house, to be where Jeffrey was most at home.

65

Lightning crackled high up in the clouds. She could hear rain, but not see it yet. Out on the lake, waves crashed and churned. The sky was dark and ominous with the promise of another storm. She wanted to take it as a sign, but Sara was a scientist at heart. She had never been good at relying on faith.

'All right,' she relented. 'I think I have some diazepam in my kit. I'll come through the back.' She paused. 'Frank—'

'You have my word, Sara. She won't be here.'

Sara did not want to admit to herself that she was glad to leave her family, even if it meant going to the station house. She felt awkward around them, a piece of a puzzle that didn't quite fit. Everything was the same, yet everything was different.

She took the back way around the lake again, avoiding her old house that she had shared with Jeffrey. There was no way to get to the station without driving down Main Street. Thankfully, the weather had turned, rain dripping down in a thick, hazy curtain. This made it impossible for people to sit on the benches that lined the road or stroll up the cobblestone sidewalks. All the shop doors were tightly closed against the cold. Even Mann's Hardware had taken down their porch swing display.

She turned down a back alley that ran behind the old pharmacy. The paved road gave way to gravel, and Sara was glad that she was in an SUV. She had always driven sedans while she lived in Heartsdale, but Atlanta's streets were far more treacherous than any country road. The potholes were deep enough to get lost in and the constant flooding during the rainy season made the BMW a necessity. Or at least that's what she told herself every time she paid sixty dollars to fill up her gas tank.

Frank must have been waiting for her, because the back door to the station opened before Sara put the car in park. He unfolded a large black umbrella and came out to the car to walk her back to the station. The rain was so loud that Sara did not speak until they were inside.

She asked, 'Is he still upset?'

Frank nodded, fiddling with the umbrella, trying to get it closed. Sutures crisscrossed the knuckles of his right hand. There were three deep scratches on the back of his wrist. Defensive wounds.

'Christ.' Frank winced from pain as he tried to get his stiff fingers to move.

Sara took the umbrella from him and closed it. 'Do they have you on antibiotics?'

'Got a prescription for something. Not sure what it is.' He took the umbrella from her and tossed it into the broom closet. 'Tell your mama I'm sorry for taking you away your first day back.'

Frank had always seemed old to Sara, mostly because he was a contemporary of her father's. Looking at him now, she thought Frank Wallace had aged a hundred years since the last time she had seen him. His skin was sallow, his face etched with deep lines. She looked at his eyes, noticing the yellow. Obviously, he was not well.

'Frank?'

He forced a smile. 'Good to see you, Sweetpea.'

The name was meant to put up a barrier, and it worked. She let him kiss her cheek. His dominant odor had always been cigarette smoke, but today she smelled whisky and chewing gum on his breath. Instinctively, she looked at her watch. Eleven-thirty in the morning, the time of day when a drink meant that you were biding time until your shift ended. On the other hand, this wasn't like a usual day for Frank. One of his men had been stabbed. Sara probably would have had her share of alcohol in the same situation.

He asked, 'How you been holding up?'

She tried to look past the pity in his eyes. 'I'm doing great, Frank. Tell me what's going on.'

He quickly shifted gears. 'Kid thought the girl was into him. He finds out she's not and sticks her with a knife.' He shrugged. 'Did a real bad job covering it up. Led us right to his doorstep.'

Sara was even more confused. She must be mixing up Tommy with one of her other kids.

Frank picked up on this. 'You really don't remember him?'

'I thought I did, but now I'm not so sure.'

'He seems to think y'all have some kind of bond.' He saw Sara's expression and amended, 'Not in a weird way or anything. He's kind of young.' Frank touched the side of his head. 'Not a lot going on up there.'

Sara felt a flash of guilt that this boy she barely remembered had felt such a connection to her. She had seen thousands of patients over the years. There were certainly names that stuck out, kids whose graduations and wedding days she had witnessed, a couple whose funerals she had attended. Other than a few stray details, Tommy Braham was a blank.

'It's this way,' Frank said, as if she had not been in the station a thousand times. He used his plastic badge to open the large steel door that led to the cells. A blast of hot air met them.

Frank noticed her discomfort. 'Furnace is acting up.'

Sara took off her jacket as she followed him through the door. When she was a child, the local school had sent kids on field trips to the jail as a way of scaring them away from a life of crime. The Mayberry motif of open cells with steel bars had changed over long ago. There were six steel doors on either side of a long hallway. Each had a wire-mesh glass window and a slot at the bottom through which food trays could be passed. Sara kept her focus straight ahead as she followed Frank, though out of the corner of her eye, she could see men standing at their cell doors, watching her progress.

Frank took out his keys. 'I guess he stopped crying.'

She wiped away a bead of sweat that had rolled down her temple. 'Did you tell him I was coming?'

He shook his head, not stating the obvious: he hadn't been sure that Sara would show up.

He found the right key and glanced through the window to make sure Tommy wasn't going to be any trouble. 'Oh, shit,' he muttered, dropping the keys. 'Oh, Christ.'

'Frank?'

He snatched up the keys off the floor, uttering more curses. 'Christ,' he murmured, sliding the key into the lock, turning back the bolt. He opened the door and Sara saw the reason for his panic. She dropped her coat, the bottle of pills she'd shoved in the pocket before she left the house making a rattling sound as they hit the concrete.

Tommy Braham lay on the floor of his cell. He was on his side, both arms reaching out to the bed in front of him.

His head was turned at an awkward angle as he stared blankly up at the ceiling. His lips were parted. Sara recognized him now, the man he had become not much different from the little boy he'd once been. He'd brought her a dandelion once, and turned the color of a turnip when she'd kissed his forehead.

She went to him, pressing her fingers to his neck, doing a cursory check for a pulse. He had obviously been beaten – his nose broken, his eye blackened – but that was not the reason for his death. Both his wrists were cut open, the wounds gaping, flesh and sinew exposed to the stale air. There seemed to be more blood on the floor than there was inside of his body. The smell was sickly sweet, like a butcher's shop.

'Tommy,' she whispered, stroking his cheek. 'I remember you.'

Sara closed his eyelids with her fingers. His skin was still warm, almost hot. She had driven too slowly getting here. She shouldn't have used the restroom before leaving the house. She should have listened to Julie Smith. She should have agreed to come without a fight. She should have remembered this sweet little boy who'd brought her a weed he'd picked from the tall grass growing outside the clinic.

Frank bent down and used a pencil to drag a thin, cylindrical object out of the blood.

Sara said, 'It's an ink cartridge from a ballpoint pen.'

'He must have used it to . . .'

Sara looked at Tommy's wrists again. Blue lines of ink crossed the pale skin. She had been the coroner for Grant County before she'd left for Atlanta, and she knew what a repetitive injury looked like. Tommy had scraped and scraped with the metal ink cartridge, digging into his flesh until he found a way to open a vein. And then he had done the same thing to his other wrist.

'Shit.' Frank was staring over her shoulder.

She turned around. On the wall, written in his own blood, Tommy had scrawled the words *Not me.*

Sara closed her eyes, not wanting to see any of this, not wanting to be here. 'Did he try to recant?'

Frank said, 'They all do.' He hesitated, then added, 'He wrote out a confession. He had guilty knowledge of the crime.'

Sara recognized the term 'guilty knowledge.' It was used to describe details that only the police and the criminal knew. She opened her eyes. 'Is that why he was crying? He wanted to take back his confession?'

Frank gave a tight nod. 'Yeah, he wanted to take it back. But they all—'

'Did he ask for a lawyer?'

'No.'

'How did he get the pen?'

Frank shrugged, but he wasn't stupid. He could guess what had happened.

'He was Lena's prisoner. Did she give him the pen?'

'Of course not.' Frank stood up, walked to the cell door. 'Not on purpose.'

Sara touched Tommy's shoulder before standing. 'Lena was supposed to frisk him before she put him in the cell.'

'He could've hidden it in—'

'I'm assuming she gave him the pen to write his confession.' Sara felt a deep, dark hate burning in the pit of her stomach. She had been back in town for less than an hour and already she was in the middle of yet another one of Lena's epic screwups. 'How long did she interrogate him?'

Frank shook his head again, like she had it all wrong. 'Couple'a three hours. Not that long.'

Sara pointed to the words Tommy had written in his own blood. ' "Not me," ' she read. 'He says he didn't do it.'

'They all say they didn't do it.' Frank's tone told her his patience was running thin. 'Look, honey, just go home. I'm sorry about all this, but . . .' He paused, his mind working. 'I gotta call the state, start the paperwork, get Lena back in . . .' He rubbed his face with his hands. 'Christ, what a nightmare.'

Sara picked her coat up off the floor. 'Where is his confession? I want to see it.'

Frank dropped his hands. He seemed stuck in place. Finally, he relented, leading her toward the door at the opposite end of the hall. The fluorescent lights of the squad room were harsh, almost blinding, compared to the dark cells. Sara blinked to help her eyes adjust. There was a group of uniformed patrolmen standing by the coffee-maker. Marla was at her desk. They all stared at her with the same macabre curiosity they had shown four years ago: *How awful, how tragic, how long before I can get on the phone and tell somebody I saw her?*

Sara ignored them because she did not know what else to do. Her skin felt hot, and she found herself looking down at her hands so that she would not see Jeffrey's office. She wondered if they had left everything as it was: his Auburn memorabilia, his shooting trophies and family photographs. Sweat rolled down her back. The room was so stifling that she thought she might be sick.

Frank stopped at his desk. 'Allison Spooner is the girl he killed. Tommy tried to make it look like a suicide – wrote a note, stuck Spooner's watch and ring in her shoes. He would've gotten away with it but Le—' He stopped. 'Allison was stabbed in the neck.'

'Has an autopsy been performed?'

'Not yet.'

'How do you know the stab wasn't self-inflicted?'

'It looked—'

'How deep did it penetrate? What was the trajectory of the blade? Was there water in her lungs?'

Frank talked over her, an air of desperation to his voice. 'She had ligature marks around her wrists.'

Sara stared at him. She had always known Frank to be an honorable man, yet she would have sworn on a stack of Bibles that he was lying through his teeth. 'Brock confirmed this?'

He hesitated before shaking his head and shrugging at the same time.

Sara could feel herself getting angrier. She knew somewhere in the back of her mind that her anger was unreasonable, that it was coming from that dark place she had ignored for so many years, but there was no stopping it now – even if she wanted to. 'Was the body weighted down in the water?'

'She had two cinder blocks chained to her waist.'

'If she floated with both hands hanging down, livor mortis could have settled into her wrists, or her hands could have rested at an angle on the bottom of the lake, making it look to the untrained eye as if she'd been tied up.'

Frank looked away. 'I saw them, Sara. She was tied up.'

He opened a file on his desk and handed her a piece of yellow legal paper. The top was torn where it had been ripped away from the pad. Both sides were filled. 'He copped to everything.'

Sara's hands shook as she read Tommy Braham's confession. He wrote in the exaggerated cursive of an elementary school student. His sentence construction was just as immature: *Pippy is my dog. She was sick. She ate a sock. She needed a picture took of her insides. I called my dad. He is in Florida.* Sara turned the page over and found the meat of the narrative. Allison had spurned a sexual advance. Tommy had snapped. He'd stabbed her and taken her to the lake to help cover his crime.

She looked at both sides of the paper. Two pages. Tommy had ended his life in less than two pages. Sara doubted he'd understood half of it. The only time he'd used a comma was right before a big word. These, he printed in block letters, and she could see small dots where he had pressed the pen under each letter to make sure he'd spelled it correctly.

Sara could barely speak. 'She coached him.'

'It's a confession, Sara. Most cons have to be told what to write.'

'He doesn't even understand what he's saying.' She skimmed the letter, reading, ' "I punched Allison to *subdude*." ' She stared at Frank, disbelieving. 'Tommy's IQ is barely above eighty. You think he masterminded this fake suicide? He's less than one standard deviation from being classified as mentally disabled.'

'You got that from reading two paragraphs?'

'I got that from treating him,' Sara snapped. It had all come flooding back to her as she read the confession:

Gordon Braham's face when Sara suggested his son might be developing too slowly for his age, the tests Tommy had endured, Gordon's devastation when Sara told him his son would never mature past a certain level. 'Tommy was slow, Frank. He didn't know how to count change. It took him two months to learn how to tie his shoes.'

Frank stared back at her, exhaustion seeping from every pore. 'He stabbed Brad, Sara. He cut me in the arm. He ran from the scene.'

Her hands started shaking. Her body surged with anger. 'Did you think to ask Tommy why?' she demanded. 'Or were you too busy beating his face to a pulp?'

Frank glanced back at the officers by the coffee machine. 'Keep your voice down.'

Sara was not going to be silenced. 'Where was Lena when all this happened?'

'She was there.'

'I bet she was. I bet she was right there pulling everybody's strings. "The victim was tied up. She must have been murdered. Let's go to her apartment. Let's get everybody around me hurt while I walk away without so much as a scratch."' Sara could feel her heart shaking in her chest. 'How many people does Lena have to get injured – killed – before somebody stops her?'

'Sara—' Frank rubbed his hands over his face. 'We found Tommy in the garage with—'

'His father owns the property. He had every right to be in that garage. Did you? Did you have a warrant?'

'We didn't need a warrant.'

'Have the laws changed since Jeffrey was alive?' Frank winced at the name. 'Did Lena identify herself as a cop or just start waving her gun around?'

75

Frank didn't answer her question, which was answer enough. 'It was a tense situation. We did everything by the book.'

'Does Tommy's handwriting match the suicide note?'

Frank blanched, and she realized he hadn't asked the question himself. 'He probably forged it, made it look like the girl's.'

'He didn't have the intelligence to forge anything. He was slow. Is that not getting through to you? There's no way in hell Tommy could've done any of this. He wasn't mentally capable of plotting out a trip to the store, let alone a fake suicide. Are you being willfully blind? Or just covering for Lena like you always do?'

'Mind your tone,' Frank warned.

'This is going to catch her.' Sara held up the confession like a trophy. The shaking in her hands had gotten worse. She felt hot and cold at the same time. 'Lena tricked him into writing this. All Tommy wanted to do was please people. She pushed him into a confession and then she pushed him into taking his own life.'

'Now, hold on—'

'She's going to lose her badge for this. She should go to prison.'

'Sounds to me like you care a hell of a lot more about some punk kid than a cop who's fighting for his life.'

He could have slapped her face and the shock would have been less. 'You think I don't care about a cop?'

Frank sighed heavily. 'Listen, Sweetpea. Just calm down, okay?'

'Don't you *dare* tell me to calm down. I've been calm for the last four *years*.' She took her cell phone out of her

76

back pocket and scrolled through the contacts, looking for the right number.

Frank sounded scared. 'What are you going to do?'

Sara listened to the phone ring at the Georgia Bureau of Investigation's headquarters in Atlanta. A secretary answered. She told the woman, 'This is Sara Linton calling for Amanda Wagner.'

FOUR

Sara sat in her car in the hospital parking lot, staring out at Main Street. The facility had stopped accepting patients a year ago, but the building had looked abandoned long before that. Weeds sprouted in the ambulance bay. Windows on the upper floors were broken. The metal door that used to be propped open for smokers was bolted shut with a steel bar.

Guilt about Tommy Braham still weighed heavily on her – not just because she hadn't remembered him, but because in the space of a few seconds, she had taken his death and used it as a launching pad for her own revenge fantasy against Lena Adams. Sara realized now that she should have just let it play out on its own instead of inserting herself into the middle. A suicide in police custody automatically triggered an investigation by the state. Frank would have followed the chain of command, calling in Nick Shelton, Grant County's local field agent for the Georgia Bureau of Investigation. Nick would have talked to all the officers and witnesses involved. He was a good cop. In the end, he would have come to the same conclusion as Sara: that Lena had been negligent.

Unfortunately, Sara hadn't been patient enough to trust the process. She had unilaterally decided to be town coroner again, elbowing poor Dan Brock out of the way, taking her own photographs of the scene, doing sketches of Tommy's cell, before she allowed the body to be removed. She'd made copies of every sheet of paper she could find in the station house that referred to Tommy Braham. Even with all of this, calling Amanda Wagner, a deputy director with the GBI, was the worst of her transgressions. It was like swinging a sledgehammer at a thumbtack.

'Stupid,' she whispered, leaning her head into the steering wheel. She should be home right now looking at the marble tile her father had installed in the master bathroom, not waiting for someone straight from GBI headquarters to show up so she could unduly influence an investigation.

She leaned back against the seat, checking the clock on the dashboard. Special Agent Will Trent was almost an hour late, but she had no way of calling him. The trip from Atlanta was four hours – less if you knew you could flash your badge and talk your way out of a speeding ticket. She looked at the clock again, waiting out the flicker of 5:42 changing to 5:43.

Sara had no idea what she was going to say to him. She had talked to Will Trent probably a half dozen times while he worked a case involving one of Sara's patients at Grady's ER. She had shamelessly inserted herself into the investigation then, much as she was doing now. Will would probably start to wonder if she was some kind of crime scene voyeur. At the very least, he would question her obsession with Lena Adams. He would probably think that she was crazy.

'Oh, Jeffrey,' Sara whispered. What would he think of the mess she was getting herself into? What would he say about how awful being back in his adoptive town, the town he loved, made her feel? Everyone was so careful around her, so respectful. She should be grateful, but on some level, her skin crawled when she saw the pity in their eyes.

She was so damn tired of being tragic.

The roar of an engine announced Will Trent's arrival. He was in a beautiful old Porsche, black on black. Even in the rain, the machine looked like an animal ready to pounce.

He took his time getting out of the car, snapping the faceplate off the radio, removing the GPS receiver from the dash, and locking them both in the glove compartment. He lived in Atlanta, where you bolted your front door even if you were just going out to get your mail. Sara knew he could leave the Porsche sitting in the parking lot with the doors wide open and the worst thing that might happen is someone would come along and close them for him.

Will smiled at her as he locked the door. Sara had only ever seen him in three-piece suits, so she was surprised to find him dressed in a black sweater and jeans. He was tall, at least six-three, with a lean runner's body and an easy gait. His sandy blond hair had grown out, no longer the military cut he'd sported when they first met. Initially, Sara had taken Will Trent for an accountant or lawyer. Even now, she had a hard time reconciling the man with the job. He didn't walk with a cop's swagger. He didn't have that world-weary stare that let you know he carried a gun on his hip. Still, he was an excellent investigator, and suspects underestimated him at their own peril.

This was one of the reasons that Sara was glad that

Amanda Wagner had sent Will Trent. Lena would hate him on sight. He was too soft-spoken, too accommodating – at least on first blush. She wouldn't know what she was getting herself into until it was too late.

Will opened the car door and got in.

Sara said, 'I thought you'd gotten lost.'

He gave her a half-grin as he adjusted the seat so his head wasn't hitting the roof. 'I apologize. I actually *did* get lost.' He looked at her face, obviously trying to get a read off her. 'How are you doing, Dr. Linton?'

'I'm . . .' Sara let out a long sigh. She didn't know him very well, which, oddly, made it easier for her to be honest. 'Not so great, Agent Trent.'

'Agent Mitchell said to tell you she's sorry she couldn't make it.'

Faith Mitchell was his partner, a onetime patient of Sara's. She was currently on maternity leave, fairly close to her due date. 'How is she holding up?'

'With her usual forbearance.' His smile indicated the opposite. 'Excuse me for changing the subject so quickly, but how can I help you?'

'Did Amanda tell you anything?'

'She told me there was a suicide in custody and to get down here as fast as possible.'

'Did she tell you about . . .' Sara waited for him to fill in the blank. When he didn't, she prompted, 'My husband?'

'Is that relevant? I mean, to what's going on today?'

Sara felt her throat tighten.

Will asked, 'Dr. Linton?'

'I don't know that it's relevant,' she finally answered. 'It's just history. Everyone you meet in this town is going to know about it. They're going to assume that you do,

81

too.' She felt tears sting her eyes for the millionth time that day. 'I'm sorry. I've been so angry for the last six hours that I haven't really thought about what I'm dropping you in the middle of.'

He leaned up and pulled a handkerchief out of his back pocket. 'There's no need to apologize. I get dropped in the middle of stuff all the time.'

Aside from Jeffrey and her father, Will Trent was the only man Sara knew who still carried a handkerchief. She took the neatly folded white cloth he handed her.

Will repeated, 'Dr. Linton?'

She wiped her eyes, apologizing again. 'I'm sorry. I've been tearing up like this all day.'

'It's always hard to go back.' He said this with such certainty that Sara found herself really looking at him for the first time since he'd gotten into the car. Will Trent was an attractive man, but not in a way that you would quickly notice. If anything, he seemed eager to blend in with his surroundings, to keep his head down and do his job. Months ago, he'd told Sara that he'd grown up in the Atlanta Children's Home. His mother had been killed when he was an infant. These were big revelations, yet Sara felt like she knew nothing about him at all.

His head turned toward her and she looked away.

Will said, 'Let's try it this way: You tell me what you think I should know. If I have more questions, I'll try to ask them as respectfully as I can.'

Sara cleared her throat several times, trying to find her voice. She was thinking about her own recovery after Jeffrey's death, the year of her life she had lost to sleep and pills and misery. None of that mattered right now. What she needed to convey to Will was that Lena Adams had a long-standing pattern of risking other people's lives, of sometimes getting people killed.

She said, 'Lena Adams was responsible for my husband's death.'

Will's expression did not change. 'How so?'

'She got mixed up with someone . . .' Sara cleared her throat again. 'The man who killed my husband was Lena's lover. Boyfriend. Whatever. They were together for several years.'

'They were together when your husband died?'

'No.' Sara shrugged. 'I don't know. He had this hold on her. He beat her. It's possible that he raped her, but—' Sara stopped, not knowing how to tell Will not to feel sorry for Lena. 'She goaded him. I know this sounds horrible, but it was like Lena *wanted* to be abused.'

He nodded, but she wondered if he really understood.

'They had this sick relationship where they brought out the worst in each other. She put up with it until it stopped being fun, then she called in my husband to clean up her mess and . . .' Sara stopped, not wanting to sound as desperate as she felt. 'Lena painted a target on his back. It was never proven, but her ex-lover is the man who killed my husband.'

Will said, 'Police officers have a responsibility to report abuse.'

Sara felt a spark of anger, thinking he was blaming Jeffrey for not stepping in. 'She denied it was happening. You know how hard domestic violence is to prove when—'

'I know,' he interrupted. 'I'm sorry my words were unclear. I meant to say that the onus was on Detective Adams. Even when the officer is herself the victim of abuse, by law, it's her duty to report it.'

Sara tried to even out her breathing. She was getting so worked up about this that she must have seemed slightly crazy. 'Lena's a bad cop. She's sloppy. She's negligent. She's the reason my husband is dead. She's the reason Tommy is dead. She's probably the reason Brad got stabbed in the street. She gets people into situations, puts them in the line of fire, then backs away and watches the carnage.'

'On purpose?'

Sara's throat was so dry she could barely swallow. 'Does it matter?'

'I suppose not,' he admitted. 'I'm guessing Detective Adams was never charged with anything in your husband's murder?'

'She's never held accountable for anything. She always manages to slither back under her rock.'

He nodded, staring ahead at the rain-soaked windshield. Sara had turned off the engine. She had been cold before Will came, but now their combined body heat was warm enough to cloud the windows.

Sara chanced another look at Will, trying to guess what he was thinking. His face remained impassive. He was probably the hardest person to read that Sara had ever met in her life.

She finally said, 'This all sounds like a witch hunt on my part, doesn't it?'

He took his time answering. 'A suspect killed himself while in police custody. The GBI is charged with investigating that.'

He was being too generous. 'Nick Shelton is the Grant County field agent. I leapfrogged over about ten heads.'

'Agent Shelton wouldn't have been allowed to conduct

the investigation. He's got a relationship with the local force. They would've sent me or somebody like me to look into this. I've worked in small towns before. Nobody feels bad about hating the pencil pusher from Atlanta.' He smiled, adding, 'Of course, if you hadn't called Dr. Wagner directly, it might've taken another day to get somebody down here.'

'I'm so sorry that I dragged you away this close to a holiday. Your wife must be furious.'

'My . . . ?' He seemed puzzled for a second, as if he'd forgotten about the ring on his finger. He covered for it badly, saying, 'She doesn't mind.'

'Still, I'm sorry.'

'I'll live.' He turned her back to the matter at hand. 'Tell me what happened today.'

This time the words came much more easily – Julie's phone call, the rumors about Brad's stabbing, Frank's plea for her help. She finished with finding Tommy in the cell, seeing the words he had scrawled on the wall. 'They arrested him for Allison Spooner's murder.'

Will's eyebrows furrowed. 'They charged Braham with murder?'

'Here's the worst part.' She handed him the photocopy she'd made of Tommy's confession.

Will seemed surprised. 'They gave this to you?'

'I have a relationship – a past relationship.' She didn't really know how to explain why Frank had let her bulldoze her way through. 'I was the town coroner. I was married to the boss. They're used to showing me evidence.'

Will patted his pockets. 'I think my reading glasses are in my suitcase.'

She dug around in her purse and pulled out her own pair.

Will frowned at the glasses, but slid them on. He blinked several times as he scanned the page, asking, 'Tommy is local?'

'Born and raised.'

'How old is he?'

Sara couldn't keep the outrage out of her tone. 'Nineteen.'

He looked up. 'Nineteen?'

'Exactly,' she said. 'I don't know how they think he masterminded this. He can barely spell his own name.'

Will nodded as he turned back to the confession, his eyes going back and forth across the page. Finally, he looked at Sara. 'Did he have some kind of reading problem, like dyslexia?'

'Dyslexia is a language disorder. But, no, Tommy wasn't dyslexic. His IQ was around eighty. Intellectually disabled people test out at seventy or below – what used to be called retarded. Dyslexia has nothing to do with IQ. Actually, I had a couple of kids with it who ran circles around me.'

He gave his half-grin. 'I find that very hard to believe.'

She smiled back, thinking he didn't know the first thing about her. 'Don't get hung up on a couple of spelling mistakes.'

'It's more than a couple.'

'Think about it this way: I could sit across from a dyslexic all day and never know it. With Tommy, he could talk about baseball or football until the cows came home, but get him into more complex areas of thinking and he'd be completely lost. Concepts that required logic, or processing cause and effect, were incredibly difficult for him to grasp. You couldn't talk a dyslexic into a false confession any more easily than you could talk someone who had green eyes or red hair into saying they did something they didn't do. Tommy was incredibly gullible. He could be talked into anything.'

Will stared at her, not speaking for a moment. 'You think Detective Adams elicited a false confession?'

'Yes, I do.'

'Do you think she's criminally negligent?'

'I don't know the legal threshold. I just know that her actions led to his death.'

He spoke carefully, and she finally realized that he was interviewing her. 'Can you tell me how you reached that conclusion?'

'Other than the fact that he scrawled "Not me" in his own blood before he died?'

'Other than that.'

'Tommy is – was – very suggestible. It goes hand in hand with his low IQ. He didn't test low enough to be classified as severely disabled, but he had some of the same attributes: the desire to please, the innocence, the gullibility. What happened today – the note, the shoes, the botched cover-up. On the surface, it seems like the kind of thing a person who is slow or stupid might do, but it's all too complicated for Tommy.' She tried to listen to herself from Will's perspective. 'I know this sounds like I'm hell-bent on going after Lena, and obviously I am, but that doesn't mean that what I'm saying isn't scientific fact. I had a hard time treating Tommy because he would always say he had whatever symptom I asked him about, whether it was a headache or a cough. If I put it into his head the right way, he would've told me he had the bubonic plague.'

'So you're saying Lena should have recognized that Tommy was slow and . . . ?'

'Not badgered him into killing himself, for one.'

'And two?'

'Sought proper medical care for him. He was obviously stricken. He wouldn't stop crying. He wouldn't talk to anybody . . .' Her voice trailed off as she saw the hole in her argument. Frank had called Sara for help.

Instead of pointing out the obvious, Will asked, 'Isn't the prisoner the responsibility of the booking officer?'

'Lena is the one who put him there. She didn't frisk him – or at least didn't frisk him well enough to find the ink cartridge he used to kill himself with. She didn't alert the guards to keep a close eye on him. She just got the confession and walked away.' Sara could feel herself getting angrier by the second. 'Who knows how she left him emotionally. She probably talked him into thinking his life wasn't worth living. This is what she does over and over again. She creates these shitstorms and someone else always pays the price.'

Will stared out at the parking lot, his hands resting lightly on his knees. Though the hospital had closed, the electricity was still working. The parking lot lights flickered on. In their yellow glow, Sara could see the scar that ran down the side of Will's face and into his collar. It was old, probably from his childhood. The first time she'd seen it, she'd thought maybe he'd ripped the skin sliding into first base or failing at some daring feat on a bicycle. That was before she'd found out that he'd grown up in an

88

orphanage. Now, she wondered if there was more to the story.

Certainly, it wasn't Will Trent's only scar. Even in profile, she could see the spot between his nose and lip where someone or something had repeatedly busted the skin apart. Whoever had stitched the flesh back together hadn't done a very good job. The scar was slightly jagged, giving his mouth an almost raffish quality.

Will exhaled a breath of air. When he finally spoke, he was all business. 'They charged Tommy Braham with murder? Nothing else?'

'No, just murder.'

'Not attempted murder for Detective Stephens?' Will asked. Sara shook her head. 'Wasn't Chief Wallace also injured?'

Sara felt a blush work its way up her chest. She imagined Frank was calling it that even after the beating he gave Tommy in the middle of the street. 'The arrest report said murder. Nothing else.'

'The way I see it is that I have two issues here. One is that a suspect killed himself while he was in Detective Adams's custody, and two is that I'm not sure why she arrested Tommy Braham for murder based on his confession. And not just his confession, but any confession.'

'Meaning?'

'You don't just arrest someone for murder based solely on their confession. There has to be corroborative evidence. The sixth amendment gives a defendant the right to confront his accuser. If you're your own accuser and you recant your confession . . .' He shrugged. 'It's like a dog chasing its tail.'

Sara felt stupid for not making this connection hours

ago. She had been the county medical examiner for almost fifteen years. The police didn't necessarily need a cause of death to hold someone for suspicion of murder, but they needed the official finding that a murder had been committed before an arrest warrant was issued.

Will said, 'They had plenty of reason to hold Braham without the murder charge: assault with a deadly weapon, attempted murder, assault on a police officer during the course of duty, assault during the course of arrest, evading arrest, trespassing. These are serious felonies. They could hold him on any combination for the next year and no one would complain.' He shook his head, as if he couldn't grasp the logic. 'I'll need to get their reports.'

Sara turned around to the back seat and retrieved the copies she'd made. 'I'll have to wait for the drugstore to open in the morning so I can print the photographs.'

Will marveled at her access as he flipped through the pages. 'Wow. All right.' He skimmed the pages as he talked. 'I know you're convinced Tommy didn't kill this girl, but it's my job to prove it one way or another.'

'Of course. I didn't mean to . . .' Sara let her voice trail off. She *had* meant to influence him. That was the point of them being here. 'You're right. I know you have to be impartial.'

'I just need you to be prepared, Dr. Linton. If I find out Tommy did it, or can't find solid proof that he didn't, no one is going to care how he was treated in jail. They're going to think your Detective Adams saved them a lot of their tax dollars by avoiding a trial.'

Sara felt her heart sink. He was right. She had seen people in this town make assumptions before that weren't necessarily rooted in fact. They didn't embrace nuance.

He gave her an alternate scenario. 'On the other hand, if Tommy didn't kill this girl, then there's a murderer out there who's either very lucky or very clever.'

Again, Sara hadn't let herself think this far. She had been so concerned with Lena's involvement that it hadn't occurred to her that Tommy's innocence would point to another killer.

Will asked, 'What else did you find out?'

'According to Frank, both he and Lena saw marks on Spooner's wrists that indicated she was tied up.'

Will made a skeptical noise. 'That's really hard to tell when a body's been in the water that long.'

Sara did not revel in her feelings of vindication. 'There's a stab wound, or what they think is a stab wound, in her neck.'

'Is it possible that it was self-inflicted?'

'I haven't seen it, but I can't imagine anyone would kill themselves with a stab to the back of the neck. And there would've been a lot of blood, especially if her carotid was hit. We're talking high velocity, up and back, like a hose turned on full blast. I would guess you'd find anywhere from four to five pints of blood at the scene.'

'What about Spooner's suicide note?'

' "I want it over," ' Sara recalled.

'That's strange.' He closed the folder. 'Is the local coroner any good?'

'Dan Brock. He's a funeral director, not a doctor.'

'I'll take that as a no.' Will stared at her. 'If I transfer Spooner and Braham up to Atlanta, we lose another day.'

She was already a step ahead of him. 'I talked to Brock. He's happy to let me do the autopsies, but we'll have to start after eleven so we don't disturb anyone. He's got a funeral tomorrow morning. He's supposed to call me later with the exact time so we can coordinate the procedures.'

'Autopsies are done at the funeral home?'

She indicated the hospital. 'We used to do them here, but the state cut funding and they couldn't stay open.'

'Same story, different town.' He looked at his cell phone. 'I guess I should go introduce myself to Chief Wallace.'

'Interim Chief,' she corrected, then, 'Sorry, it doesn't matter. Frank's not at the station right now.'

'I've already left two messages for him about meeting up with me. Did he get called out?'

'He's at the hospital with Brad. And Lena, I imagine.'

'I'm sure they're taking some time to get their stories straight.'

'Will you go to the hospital?'

'They're going to hate me enough without me trampling into the hospital room of an injured cop.'

Sara silently conceded the point. 'So, what are you going to do now?'

'I want to go to the station and see where they were keeping Tommy. I'm sure they'll have an extremely hostile patrolman there who's going to tell me he just got on shift, doesn't know anything, and Tommy killed himself because he was guilty.' He tapped the file. 'I'll talk to the other prisoners if they haven't already let them go. I imagine Interim Chief Wallace won't show up until the morning, which will give me some time to go over these files.' He leaned up to get his wallet out of his back pocket. 'Here's my business card. It's got my cell number on the back.'

Sara read Will's name next to the GBI logo. 'You have a doctorate?'

He took the card back from her and stared at the printing. Instead of answering her question, he said, 'The numbers are good. Can you tell me where I can find the closest hotel?'

'There's one over by the college. It's not very nice, but it's fairly clean. It'll be quiet since the kids are on break.'

'I'll get supper there and—'

'They don't have a restaurant.' Sara felt a flash of shame for her small town. 'Everything's closed this time of night except the pizza place, and they've been shut down by the health department so many times that only the students will eat there.'

'I'm sure there are some snack machines at the hotel.' He put his hand on the door handle, but Sara stopped him.

'My mother made a huge dinner and there's plenty left over.' She took the file from him and wrote her address on the front. 'Crap,' she muttered, scratching through the street number. She had given her old address, not her parents'. 'Lakeshore,' she said, pointing at the street directly across from the hospital. 'Go right. Or left if you want the scenic route. It's just a big circle around the lake.' She wrote down her cell number. 'Call if you get lost.'

'I couldn't impose on your family.'

'I've dragged you all the way down here. You could at least let me feed you. Or let my mother feed you, which would be far better for your health.' Then, because she knew he was not a stupid man, she added, 'And you know I want to know what's happening on the case.'

'I don't know how late I'll be.'

'I'll wait up.'

FIVE

Will Trent pressed his face to the closed glass door of the station house. The lights were out. There was no one at the front desk. He rapped his keys on the door for a third time, thinking if he used any more pressure, the glass would break. The building overhang wasn't doing much to keep the rain off his head. His stomach was grumbling from hunger. He was cold and wet, and extremely irritated that he had been ordered to this small-town hellhole during his vacation.

The worst part about this particular assignment was that this was the first time in his working life that Will had ever asked for a whole week off from work. Back home, his front yard was torn up where he had been digging a trench around the sewer line from his house to the street. Tree roots had taken over the ninety-year-old clay pipe, and a plumber wanted eight thousand dollars to change it out to plastic. Will was digging the trench by hand, trying not to destroy the thousands of dollars worth of landscaping he'd planted in the yard over the last five years, when the phone rang. Not answering didn't seem like an option. He'd been expecting news from Faith – that her baby was finally coming or, even better, that it was already here.

But, no, it was Amanda Wagner, telling him, 'We don't say no to a cop's widow.'

Will had put a tarp over the trench, but something told

him his two days of digging would be erased by a mudslide by the time he got back home. If he ever made it back home. It seemed like he was destined to spend the rest of his life standing in the pouring-down rain outside this Podunk police station.

He was about to tap on the glass again when a light finally came on inside the building. An elderly woman headed toward the door, taking her time as she waddled across the carpeted lobby. She was large, a bright red prairie-style dress draping over her like a tent. Her gray hair was wrapped up in a bun on the top of her head, held there by a butterfly clip. A gold necklace with a cross dangled into her ample cleavage.

She put her hand on the lock, but didn't open it. Her voice was muffled through the glass. 'Help you?'

Will took out his ID and showed it to her. She leaned in, scrutinizing the photograph, comparing it with the man in front of her. 'You look better with your hair longer.'

'Thank you.' He tried to blink away the rain pouring into his eyes.

She waited for him to say something else, but Will held his tongue. Finally, she relented, unlocking the door.

The temperature inside was negligibly warm, but at least he was out from the rain. Will ran his fingers through his hair, trying to get the wet out. He stamped his feet to knock off the damp.

'You're making a mess,' the woman said.

'I apologize,' Will told her, wondering if he could ask for a towel. He took out his handkerchief and wiped his face. He smelled perfume. Sara's perfume.

The woman gave him a steely look, as if she could read what was going through Will's mind and didn't like it.

'You gonna just stand there all night sniffing your handkerchief? I got supper to make.'

He folded the cloth and put it back in his pocket. 'I'm Agent Trent from the GBI.'

'I already read that on your ID.' She looked him up and down in open appraisal, obviously not liking what she saw. 'I'm Marla Simms, the station secretary.'

'Nice to meet you, Ms. Simms. Can you tell me where Chief Wallace is?'

'Mrs.' Her tone was cutting. 'Not sure if you heard, but one of our boys was almost killed today. Struck down in the street while trying to do his job. We've been a little busy with that.'

Will nodded. 'Yes, ma'am, I did hear that. I hope Detective Stephens is going to be okay.'

'That boy has worked here since he was eighteen years old.'

'My prayers are with his family,' Will offered, knowing religion paid currency in small towns. 'If Chief Wallace isn't available, may I speak with the booking officer?'

She seemed annoyed that he knew such a position existed. Frank Wallace had obviously given her the task of stalling the asshole from the GBI. Will could almost see the wheels in her head turning as she tried to figure out a way around his question.

Will politely pressed, 'I know that the prisoners aren't left unattended. Are you in charge of the cells?'

'Larry Knox is back there,' she finally answered. 'I was about to leave. I already locked up all the files, so if you want—'

Will had tucked the file Sara had given him down the

96

front of his pants so that it wouldn't get wet. He lifted his sweater and handed Marla the file. 'Can you fax these twelve pages for me?'

She seemed hesitant to take the papers. He couldn't blame her. The file was warm from being pressed against his body. 'The phone number is—'

'Hold on.' She extracted a pen from somewhere deep inside her hair. It was plastic, a retractable Bic that you'd find in any office setting. 'Go ahead.'

He gave her his partner's fax number. The woman took her time writing it down, pretending to get the numbers mixed up. Will glanced around the lobby, which looked like every other small-town police station lobby he had ever walked into. Wood paneling lined the walls. Group photographs showed patrolmen in their uniforms, shoulders squared, jaws tilted up, smiles on their faces. There was a tall counter opposite the photographs, a gate filling in the space between the front part of the building and the back, where all the desks were lined up in a row. The lights were all off.

'All right,' she said. 'I'll fax them before I go.'

'Do you have an extra pen I can borrow?'

She offered him the Bic.

'I wouldn't want to take your last one.'

'Go ahead.'

'No, really,' he insisted, holding up his palms. 'I couldn't take—'

'There's twenty boxfuls in the closet,' she snapped. 'Just take it.'

'Well, all right. Thanks.' He tucked the pen into his back pocket. 'About the fax – I've numbered the pages, so if you can make sure all twelve go in the same order?'

She grumbled as she walked toward the gate. He waited as she bent over to find the release. There was a loud buzz and the click of a lock. Will found it strange that there was such a high level of security in the station, but small towns had found lots of inventive ways to spend Homeland Security money after 9/11. He had visited a jail once that had Kohler toilets in all the cells and nickel-plated fixtures on the sinks.

Marla busied herself in front of the row of office machines by the coffeemaker. Will took in the space. Three rows of three desks were in the center of the room. Tables with folding chairs lined the back wall. On the side of the building facing the street was a closed office door. There was a window looking out onto the squad room, but the blinds were tightly shut.

'Jail's in the back,' Marla advised. She stacked the pages on the table, giving him a careful eye. Will looked back at the office and something like panic seemed to take hold of Marla, as if she was afraid he would open the door.

'Through here?' he said, indicating a metal door in the back of the room.

'That's the back, isn't it?'

'Thank you,' he told her. 'I appreciate your help.'

Will let the door close before taking out Marla's pen and unscrewing the barrel. As he suspected, the ink cartridge inside was plastic. Sara had said the cartridge Tommy Braham used to cut open his wrists was metal. Will was guessing it came from a nicer pen than the Bic.

He reassembled the pen as he walked down the hall. Exit signs illuminated a tiled floor that was around sixty feet long and four feet wide. Will opened the first door he came to, a storage room. He checked over his shoulder before turning on the light. Boxes of paper clips and various office supplies lined the shelves, as did the twenty boxes of retractable Bic pens Marla had mentioned. Two tall stacks of yellow legal pads were beside the pens, and Will imagined the detectives coming into this closet, grabbing a pen and a legal pad so they could give suspects something to write their confessions with.

There were three more doors off the hallway. Two led to empty interrogation rooms. The setup was as you would expect: a long table with a metal eyebolt sticking out of the top, chairs scattered around. Two-way mirrors looked into each room. Will guessed you had to stand in the supply closet to see the first room. The other viewing room was behind the third door. He tried the knob and found it locked.

The door at the end of the hall opened and a cop in full uniform, including hat, came out. Will glanced over his shoulder, finding a camera in the corner that had tracked his progress down the hallway.

The cop asked, 'What do you want?'

'Officer Knox?'

The man's eyes narrowed. 'That's right.'

'You're the booker?' Will asked, surprised. The position of booking officer was a necessary but tedious job. They were responsible for processing all the newly arrested prisoners and in charge of their well-being while they were housed in the cells. Generally, this was the sort of job an old-timer was given, a light desk position that eased the transition into retirement. Sometimes it was given to a cop who was being punished. Will doubted that was the case with Knox. Frank Wallace wouldn't have left an aggrieved officer here to handle Will.

Knox was staring at him with open anger. 'You just gonna stand there?'

Will took out his badge. 'I'm Special Agent Trent. I'm with the GBI.'

The man took off his hat, showing a shock of carrot red hair. 'I know who you are.'

'I'm sure your chief has briefed you. We were called in as a matter of routine to investigate the suicide of Tommy Braham.'

'You were called in by Sara Linton,' he countered. 'I was standing right there when she did it.'

Will smiled at the man, because he had found that smiling at people when they thought you should be mad was a good way of bringing down some of the tension. 'I appreciate your cooperation in this investigation, Officer. I know how difficult things must be for you right now.'

'Do you now?' So much for the smiling. Knox looked like he wanted to punch Will in the throat. 'A good man is fighting for his life in that hospital over in Macon and you're worried about the piece of shit who stabbed him. That's what I see.'

'Did you know Tommy Braham?'

He was taken aback by the question. 'What does that matter?'

'I was just curious.'

'Yeah, I knew him. Had a screw loose in his head from the day he was born.'

Will nodded as if he understood. 'Can you take me to the cell where Tommy was found?'

Knox seemed to be really trying to think of a reason to say no. Will waited him out. Any cop would tell you that the best way to get someone to talk was to be quiet. There was a natural, human inclination to fill silence with noise. What most cops didn't realize was that they were just as susceptible to the same technique.

Knox said, 'All right, but I don't like you, and you don't like me, so let's not pretend anything otherwise.'

'Fair enough,' Will agreed, following him through the door, finding himself in a smaller hallway with yet another door. A bench was on one side with a row of gun lockers. Every jail Will had ever visited had the same setup. Rather wisely, weapons were not allowed back with the prisoners.

Knox indicated the lockers. 'Be sure to take out your clip and eject the round.'

'I don't have my gun on me.'

From the look Knox gave him, Will might as well have said he'd left his penis at home.

The man's lip curled in disgust. He turned around, walking toward the next door.

Will asked, 'You said you were here when Dr. Linton made her phone call. Were you just coming on shift?'

Knox turned. 'I wasn't here when the boy killed himself, if that's what you mean.'

'Were you on shift?' Will repeated.

He hesitated again, as if it wasn't already clear that he didn't want to cooperate.

Will said, 'I'm assuming you're not the regular booking officer. You're patrol, right?'

Knox didn't answer.

'Who was the booking officer this afternoon?'

He took his time answering. 'Carl Phillips.'

'I'll need to talk to him.'

He smiled. 'Carl's on vacation. Left this afternoon. Camping with his wife and kids. No phones.'

'When will he be back?'

'You'll have to ask Frank about that.'

Knox took out his keys and opened the door. To Will's relief, they were finally at the jail. Beside another large door was a viewing window showing another hallway, but this one had the familiar metal doors of jail cells. Just outside the cells was a sort of office for the officer in charge. To one side was a large filing cabinet. To the other was a built-in desk with six flat-screen monitors showing the inside of five of the cells. The sixth monitor had a game of solitaire going. Knox's supper, a home-made sandwich with chips, was laid out in front of a computer keyboard.

Knox said, 'Only got three people in here tonight,' by way of explanation.

Will checked the screens. One man was pacing his cell, the other two were curled up on their bunks. 'Where's the tape for the cameras?'

The cop rested his hand on the computer. 'Stopped recording yesterday. We've got a call in to get it fixed.'

'That's really strange that it stopped working right when you needed it.'

Knox shrugged. 'Like I said, I wasn't here.'

'Were any of the prisoners released after Braham was found?'

He shrugged. 'I wasn't in on that.'

Will took the answer as a tacit yes. 'Do you have the visitors' log?'

He opened up one of the filing cabinets and pulled out a sheet of paper, which he handed to Will. The form was lined with columns for names and times, the usual sort of paperwork you found in any jail in America. At the top of the page, someone had written in the date. The rest of the form was blank.

Knox said, 'Guess Sara didn't sign in.'

'Have you known her long?'

'She looked after my kids until she left town. How long have you known her?'

Will noticed a subtle change in the man's anger. 'Not long.'

'Looked like you knew her plenty well, sitting in the car with her for an hour like that in front of the hospital.'

Will hoped he didn't look as surprised as he felt. He had forgotten how insular and incestuous small towns could be. He pressed his luck. 'She's a lovely woman.'

Knox puffed out his chest. He was at least six inches shorter than Will, obviously trying to make up for it with bravado. 'Jeffrey Tolliver was the finest man I ever worked with.'

'His reputation is well known in Atlanta. It was out of respect for him that my boss sent me down here to look after his people.'

Knox narrowed his eyes, and Will realized the patrolman could take his words in many different ways, not least of all as a sign that Will planned to go light on the investigation out of respect for Jeffrey Tolliver. This seemed to relax Knox, so Will did not correct him.

Knox said, 'Sara just gets a little hot under the collar sometimes. Real emotional.'

Will would hardly describe Sara as someone ruled by her emotions. He didn't trust his ability to pull off a cliché like 'Women!' He simply nodded and shrugged at the same time, as if to say, 'What are you gonna do?'

Knox kept staring at him, trying to make up his mind.

'All right, then,' he finally said. He used a plastic card to open the last door. His keys were still in his hand, and he jangled them as he walked. 'This'n's a drunk sleeping it off. Came in about an hour ago.' He indicated the next cell. 'Meth head. He's coming down hard. Last time we tried to wake him, he near about knocked somebody's teeth out.'

'What about door number three?' Will asked.

'Wife beater.'

'I am not!' came a muffled shout from behind the door.

Knox silently nodded to Will. 'Third time he's been locked up for it. She won't testify—'

'Goddamn right!' the man screamed.

'He's covered in his own puke, so I'm gonna have to hose him down if you wanna talk to him.'

'I hate to ask . . .' Will shrugged. 'It might help expedite this so we can all get back to our lives. My wife's gonna kill me if I'm not home for the holiday.'

'Know whatcha mean.' Knox motioned Will to the next cell. The door was open. 'This is it.'

Tommy Braham's blood had been cleaned up, but the red stain on the concrete floor told the story. His feet would have been toward the door, head back. Maybe he was lying on his side, arm out in front of him. Will guessed from the circumference of the stain that Tommy had not just stopped at one wrist. He had cut open both to make sure the job was done right.

Will stepped into the cell, feeling a slight sense of claustrophobia. He took in the cinder-block-lined walls, the metal bed frame with its thin mattress. The toilet and sink were built as one stainless steel unit. The bowl looked clean, but the smell of sewage was pungent. Beside the sink was a toothbrush, a metal cup, and a small tube of toothpaste like the kind you'd get at a hotel. Will wasn't superstitious, but he was keenly aware that Tommy Braham had, in his misery, taken his life here less than eight hours ago. The feel of his death still lingered.

' "Not me," ' Knox said.

Will turned around, wondering what he meant.

Knox nodded toward the faded wall. 'That's what he wrote. "Not me." ' He took on a knowing tone. 'If it wasn't you, buddy, then why'd you kill yourself?'

Will had never found it useful to ask dead men to explain their motivations, so he threw the question back to Knox. 'Why do you think he kept insisting he didn't kill Allison Spooner?'

'Told you.' Knox touched the side of his head. 'Not right up here.'

'Crazy?'

'Nah, just stupider than shit.'

'Too stupid to know how to kill somebody?'

'Hell, I wish there was such a thing. Wouldn't have to keep such a close eye on the wife during that time of month.' He gave a loud laugh, and Will forced himself to join in, pushing away thoughts of Tommy lying on the floor of this cell, slicing and slicing the ink cartridge across his wrist, trying to draw blood. How long would it take before the flesh opened? Would the skin get hot from the friction? Would the metal ink cartridge start to get warm? How long would it take for enough blood to leave his body so that his heart stopped?

Will turned back to the faded letters on the wall. He didn't want to break this new, if false, camaraderie with Knox. 'Did you know Allison Spooner?'

105

'She worked at the diner. All of us knew her.'

'What was she like?'

'Good girl. Got the plates out fast. Didn't stand around yapping too much.' He looked down at the floor, shaking his head. 'She was good-lookin', too. I guess that's what caught Tommy's eye. Poor thing. She probably thought he was harmless.'

'Did she have any friends? A boyfriend?'

'I guess it was just Tommy. Never saw anybody else around her.' He shrugged. 'Not like I was paying attention. Wife don't like it when my eye wanders.'

'Did you see Tommy at the diner a lot?'

Knox shook his head. Will could see his compliance was waning.

'Can I talk to the wife beater?'

'I didn't touch her!' the prisoner screamed back, slamming his hand against the cell door.

'Thin walls,' Will noted. Knox was leaning against the door, arms crossed. His shirt pocket was bunched up, a silver pen clipped to the material. 'Hey, can I borrow your pen?'

Knox touched the clip. 'Sorry, this'n's the only one I got.'

Will recognized the Cross logo. 'Nice.'

'Chief Tolliver gave 'em to us the Christmas before he passed.'

'All of you?' Knox nodded. Will gave a low whistle. 'That must've been expensive.'

'They sure ain't cheap.'

'It takes a special cartridge, right? A metal one?'

Knox opened his mouth to respond, then caught himself.

106

Will asked, 'Who else got one?'

Knox's lip curled up in a sneer. 'Fuck you.'

'That's all right. I can ask Sara about it when I see her later.'

Knox stood up straight, blocking the door. 'You better be careful, Agent Trent. Last guy who was in this cell didn't end up too well.'

Will smiled. 'I think I can take care of myself.'

'That a fact?'

Will forced a grin. 'I hope so, because you seem to be threatening me.'

'You think?' Knox banged on the open cell door. 'You hear that, Ronny? Mr. GBI here says I'm threatening him.'

'What's that, Larry?' the wife beater shouted back. 'I can't hear nothing through these thick walls. Not a goddamn thing.'

Will sat in the interrogation room, trying to breathe through his mouth as he stared at the photocopied pages Sara had given him. Officer Knox had rescinded his offer to hose down the wife beater. Will had endured the man's stench for twenty minutes before giving up on interrogating him. In Atlanta, Ronny Porter would have sung his way to freedom, giving Will any information he had in order to get out of jail. Small towns were different. Instead of trying to cop a plea, Porter had defended every officer in the building. He'd even waxed poetic on Marla Simms, who apparently used to be his Sunday school teacher.

Will spread out the files, trying to put them into some sort of order. Tommy Braham's confession was hand-written, the copy dark from the yellow paper. He set that

107

aside. The police report was like every form Will had ever handled at the GBI. Boxes provided space for dates, times, weather, and other details of the crime, to be written in by hand. The suicide note had caught the light from the copier, the letters blurring.

There were two other pages that were photocopies of notepaper from a small pad, the sort of thing most cops carried in their back pocket. Four sheets of the smaller paper had been lined up to fit on one copied page. In all, there were eight pages that had been torn from the notepad. Will studied the positioning. He could see faint marks where the lined paper had been taped to a bigger sheet for copying. Instead of jagged edges at the top where the paper had been ripped from the spiral, there was a clean line as if someone had used scissors to cut them out. This he found strangest of all – not just because cops didn't tend to be neat, but because he had never in his career known a police officer to tear pages out of their notebook.

The arrest warrant was the last page in the pile, but this part of the process, at least, was computerized. All the spaces were printed in a typewriter font. The suspect's name was at the top, his address and home phone. Will found the lined box for Tommy's employer. He leaned over the form, squinting his eyes as he held his finger under the tiny letters. His mouth moved as he tried to sound out the word. Will was tired from the monotonous drive. The letters mixed around. He blinked, wishing there was more light in the room.

Sara Linton had been right about one thing. She had sat across from Will for a solid hour and not realized that he was dyslexic.

His phone rang, the noise startling him in the small space. He recognized Faith Mitchell's number. 'Hey, partner.'

'You were going to call me when you got there.'

'Things have been busy,' he said, which was sort of the truth. Will had always been bad with directions, and there were parts of Heartsdale between Main Street and the interstate that weren't on his GPS.

She asked, 'How's it going?'

'I'm being treated with the utmost respect and care.'

'I wouldn't drink anything unless it's in a sealed bottle.'

'Good advice.' He sat back in the chair. 'How're you holding up?'

'I'm about to kill somebody or myself,' she admitted. 'They're going to do the C-section tomorrow afternoon.' Faith was diabetic. Her doctors wanted to control the delivery so her health wasn't jeopardized. She started to give Will the details of the procedure, but he dazed out after she used the word 'uterus' the second time. He studied his reflection in the two-way mirror, wondering if Mrs. Simms was right about his hair looking better now that he'd let it grow out.

Finally, Faith wound down her story. She asked, 'What's this fax you sent me?'

'Did you get all twelve pages?'

He could hear her counting the sheets. 'I've got seventeen total. All from the same number.'

'Seventeen?' He scratched his jaw. 'Are some of them duplicates?'

'Nope. Got a police report, xeroxed field notes – pages are cut out of the notebook, that's weird. You don't take pages out of your field book – and . . .' He assumed she was reading Tommy Braham's confession. 'Did you write this?'

'Very funny,' Will said. He hadn't been able to make out the words when Sara had shown him the confession in the car, but even to Will, the looped, cartoonish shape of Tommy Braham's handwriting seemed off. 'What do you think?'

'I think this reads like one of Jeremy's book reports when he was in first grade.'

Jeremy was her teenage son. 'Tommy Braham is nineteen.'

'What is he, retarded?'

'You're supposed to call it "intellectually disabled" now.'

She made a snorting sound.

'Sara says his IQ was around eighty.'

Faith sounded suspicious, but she had been prickly the last time about Sara inserting herself into their case. 'How does Sara happen to know his IQ?'

'She used to treat him at her clinic.'

'Did she apologize for dragging you below the gnat line on your vacation?'

'She doesn't know it's my vacation, but, yes, she apologized.'

Faith was quiet for a moment. 'How's she doing?'

He thought not of Sara, but of the scent she had left on his handkerchief. She didn't strike him as the type of woman who would wear perfume. Maybe it was one of those fancy soaps that women used to wash their faces.

'Will?'

He cleared his throat to cover for his silence. 'She's

okay. She was very upset, but mostly I think she has a good reason.' He lowered his voice. 'Something doesn't feel right about any of this.'

'You think Tommy didn't kill the girl?'

'I don't know what I think yet.'

Faith went quiet; never a good sign. He had been partnered with her for over a year, and just when Will thought he was learning to read her moods, she had gotten pregnant and the whole thing went out of whack. 'All right,' she said. 'What else did Sara tell you?'

'Some stuff about the man who killed her husband.' Will knew that Faith had already gone behind Sara's back to find out the details. She didn't know about Lena Adams's involvement, or the fact that Sara believed Lena was responsible for Tolliver's death. Will stood up and walked into the hall, making sure Knox wasn't there. Still, he kept his voice low as he relayed the story Sara had told him about her husband's murder. When he finished, Faith let out a long breath of air.

'Sounds like Sara has a hard-on for this Adams woman.'

Will sat back down at the table. 'That's one way to put it.' He did not share the part of Sara's story that had stuck out the most. The entire time she spoke, she had not once uttered Jeffrey Tolliver's name. She had only referred to him as 'my husband.'

Faith offered, 'I think priority number one is tracking down this Julie Smith. She either saw the murder or heard about it. Do you have her cell phone number?'

'I'll get it from Sara later.'

'Later?'

Will ignored the question. Faith would want an explanation for why he was having dinner at Sara's house, and then she'd want a report on how it went. 'Where does – did – Tommy Braham work?'

She shuffled through the pages. 'Says here he was employed at the bowling alley. Maybe that's why he killed himself – to keep from having to spray Lysol in shoes all day.'

Will didn't laugh at the joke. 'They charged him with murder right off the bat. Not assault, not attempted murder, not resisting.'

'Where did they get murder? Am I missing the autopsy report? Lab reports? Forensic filings?'

Will laid it out for her. 'Brad Stephens is stabbed. He's airlifted to the hospital. The first thing Adams does is take Tommy Braham back to the station and get his confession for the Spooner girl's murder.'

'She didn't go to the hospital with her partner?'

'I'm assuming the chief did. He's been a no-show.'

'Did Braham have a lawyer present?' Faith answered her own question. 'No lawyer would let him make this confession.'

'A murder charge resonates more than assault. It could be political – get the town behind them so no one cares that a killer has killed himself.' Will had told Sara the same thing. If Tommy Braham was Allison Spooner's murderer, then people would assume justice had already been served.

Faith said, 'This confession is strange. He's got details out the wazoo until the murder. Then, it's taken care of in three lines. "I got mad. I had a knife on me. I stabbed her once in the neck." Not much of an explanation.' She added, 'And there would be a boat-load of blood from something like this. Remember

112

that case where the woman's throat was slit?'

Will cringed at the memory. Blood had sprayed everywhere – the walls, ceiling, floor. It was like walking into a paint booth. 'Allison Spooner was stabbed in the back of the neck. Maybe that's different?'

'That brings up another good point. One stab wound doesn't sound mad. That sounds very controlled to me.'

'Detective Adams was probably in a hurry to get back to the hospital. Maybe she was planning a follow-up interview. Maybe Chief Wallace was going to have a go at Tommy later.'

'That's not how you do it. If a suspect is talking, especially confessing, you get every detail.'

'They haven't shown much of an aptitude for policing so far. Sara thinks Adams is sloppy, that she plays it too loose. From what I'm seeing with the Spooner investigation, she's right about that.'

'Is she pretty?'

For a moment, Will thought she was asking about Sara. 'I haven't seen a picture yet, but the cop I spoke with said she was good-looking.'

'Young girl, college aged. The press is going to be all over this, especially if she's pretty.'

'Probably,' he acknowledged. Yet another motive for putting Allison Spooner's murderer behind bars as quickly as possible. 'The girl worked at the local diner. I gather a lot of the cops in the station knew her.'

'That could explain why they made such a quick arrest.'

'It could,' he agreed. 'But, if Sara is right and Tommy didn't kill the girl, then we've still got a murderer out there.'

'When is the autopsy?'

'Tomorrow.' Will didn't tell her that Sara had volunteered to do the procedure.

'It all seems very convenient,' Faith pointed out. 'Dead girl found in the morning, murderer arrested before noon, found dead in his cell before suppertime.'

'If Brad Stephens doesn't make it, they're probably not going to let Tommy Braham be buried in the city limits.'

'When are you going to the hospital?'

'I hadn't planned on it.'

'Will, a cop is in the hospital. If you're within a hundred miles, you go see him. You hang around and comfort his wife or his mother. You give blood. It's what cops do.'

Will chewed his lip. He hated hospitals. He had never understood why it was necessary to hang around them unless you had to.

'Isn't Brad Stephens a potential witness, too?'

Will laughed. Unless Stephens was a Boy Scout, he doubted the man would help shed any light on what happened yesterday. 'I'm sure he'll be as courteous as he is forthcoming.'

'You still have to go through the motions.' She paused before continuing. 'And since I'm being a cop, let me state the obvious: Tommy killed himself for the same reason he ran when they confronted him in the garage. He was guilty.'

'Or he wasn't, and he knew no one would believe him.'

'You sound like a defense lawyer,' Faith noted. 'What about the rest of this stuff? It looks like the first few pages of a novel.'

'What do you mean?'

'The handwritten notes from Spooner's crime scene. "Found on the shore approximately thirty yards from the

114

tide line and twelve feet from a large oak is a pair of white Nike Sport tennis shoes, sized women's eight. Inside the left, resting on the sole, which is blue with the word 'Sport' emblazoned where the heel rests, is a yellow-gold ring. . . ." I mean, come on. This isn't *War and Peace*. It's a field report.'

'Did you get the suicide note?'

' "I want it over." ' She had the same reaction as Will. 'Not exactly the "goodbye cruel world" you'd expect. And the paper is torn from a larger sheet. That's strange, right? You're going to write a suicide note and you tear it from another sheet of paper?'

'What else did you get? You said there were seventeen pages.'

'Incident reports.' She read aloud, 'Police were called to Skatey's roller rink on Old Highway 5 at approximately twenty-one hundred hours . . .' Her voice trailed off as she skimmed the words. 'All right. Last week, Tommy got into a fight with a girl whose name they didn't bother to get. He wouldn't stop shouting. He was asked to leave. He refused. The police came and told him to leave. He left. No one arrested.' Faith was quiet again. 'The second report involves a barking dog at the residence from five days ago. The last one is about loud music. This was two days ago. There's a note on the last page where the cop who took the report makes a reminder to follow up with Tommy's father when he gets back in town.'

'Who took the reports?'

'Same cop. Carl Phillips.'

That name was more than familiar. 'I was told Phillips was the booking officer on duty when all of this went down.'

'That doesn't make sense. You don't put a street cop on booking.'

'Either he's a really bad liar or they're afraid he's going to tell me the truth.'

'So, find him and figure it out for yourself.'

'I was told he's out camping with his wife and kids right now. No cell phone. No way to get in touch with him.'

'What an amazing coincidence. His name's Carl Phillips?'

'Right.' Will knew Faith was writing down the name. She hated when people tried to hide. He told her, 'Their security cameras in the cells aren't recording, either.'

'Did they tape the interview with Tommy?'

'If they did, I'm sure the film met with some kind of dropping accident involving electricity and water.'

'Shit, Will. You numbered these pages yourself, right?'

'Yeah.'

'One through twelve?'

'Right. What's going on?'

'Page number eleven is missing.'

Will thumbed through his originals. They were all out of order.

She asked, 'You're sure you numbered—'

'I know how to number pages, Faith.' He muttered a curse as he saw that the eleventh page was missing from his copies, too.

'Why would someone take out a page and send the incident reports instead?'

'I'll have to see if Sara—'

He heard a noise behind him. A cough, maybe a sneeze. He guessed that Knox was standing in the viewing room listening to everything that was being said.

'Will?'

He stood up, stacking the pages together, putting them back in the file. 'You still seeing your mom for Thanksgiving?'

She took her time answering, misinterpreting his meaning. 'You know I'd ask you to come if—'

'Angie's planning a surprise for me. You know how she loves to cook.' He walked into the hallway and stopped outside the storage room, where he rapped his knuckles on the door. 'Thank you for your help, Officer Knox.' The door didn't open, but Will heard feet shuffling on the other side. 'I'll let myself out.'

Faith didn't question him until he was in the squad room. 'You clear?'

'Give me another minute.'

'Angie loves to cook?' She gave a deep belly laugh. 'When's the last time you saw the elusive Mrs. Trent?'

Seven months had passed since Angie had made an appearance, but that was none of Faith's business. 'How's Betty doing?'

'I raised a child, Will. I think I can take care of your dog.'

Will pushed open the glass front door and walked into the drizzle. His car was parked at the end of the lot. 'Dogs are more sensitive than children.'

'You've obviously never spent time around a sullen eleven-year-old.'

He glanced over his shoulder. Knox, or at least a figure looking very much like Knox, was standing in the window. Will kept his gait slow, casual. He didn't speak again until he was safely inside the car. 'There's something else going on with this girl's murder, Faith.'

'What do you mean?'

'Call it gut instinct.' Will looked back up at the station. One by one, the lights went off in the front of the building. 'It's just convenient that the one person who could probably tell me the truth about what really happened is dead.'

SIX

Lena held Brad's hand. His skin felt cool. The machines in the room beeped and blipped and hummed, yet none of them could tell the doctors how Brad was really doing. She'd heard a nurse use the phrase 'touch and go' a few hours ago, but Brad looked the same to Lena. He smelled the same, too. Antiseptic, sweat, and that stupid Axe body wash he'd started using because of the TV commercials.

'You're going to be okay,' she told him, hoping her words were true. Every bad thing she'd thought about Brad today was ringing in her head like a bell. He wasn't street smart. He wasn't cut out for the job. He didn't have the skills to be a detective. Was Lena to blame for Brad's injuries because she had kept her mouth shut? Should she have told Frank that Brad shouldn't be on the force? Frank knew this better than anybody. Every week for the last two years he'd muttered something about firing Brad. Ten minutes before Brad was stabbed, Frank was chewing him out.

But was it really Brad's fault? Lena could see this morning's events like a movie playing endlessly in her head. Brad ran down the street. He told Tommy to stop. Tommy stopped. He turned. The knife was in his hands. The knife was in Brad's stomach.

Lena rubbed her hands over her face. She should be congratulating herself for getting Tommy Braham to confess. Instead, she couldn't get past the feeling that she had missed something. She needed to talk to Tommy again, pull out more details about his movements before and after the murder. He was holding out on her, which wasn't unusual in murder cases. Tommy didn't want to admit that he was a bad person. That much had been evident the entire interview. He had skirted around the gory details, and Lena had let him because she wanted – needed – to get to Brad to see if he was okay. Lena wasn't so exhausted that she couldn't see that Tommy had more to say. She just needed some sleep before she went at him again. She had to make sure that her part of the case, at least the part she could control, was airtight.

The biggest problem was that Tommy was so damn hard to talk to. Less than a minute into his interrogation, Lena had figured out the kid wasn't right in the head. He wasn't just slow, he was stupid. Eager to fill in whatever blanks Lena left open so long as she gave him a map and directions. She had promised him he could go home if he confessed. She could still see the confused look on his face when she'd taken him back to the cells. He was probably sitting on his bunk right now wondering how on earth he had gotten himself into this mess.

Lena was wondering the same thing. All the pieces had come together so quickly this morning that she hadn't had time to consider whether they really fit or if she was just forcing them into place. The stab wound in Allison Spooner's neck. The suicide note. The 911 call. The knife.

The stupid knife.

Lena's phone vibrated in her pocket. She ignored it the same way she had ignored everything around her since she had gotten to the hospital. Two hours with Tommy at the station. Two hours driving to Macon. More hours spent standing vigil outside Brad's room. She had given blood. She'd drunk too much coffee. Delia Stephens, his mother, was getting some air now. She only trusted Lena to stay with her son.

Why? Lena was the last person on earth the woman should trust with her boy.

She got some tissue out of the box and wet the edge in the cup of water by the bed. Brad was on a ventilator, and some dried saliva was caked around his mouth. His lung had collapsed. His liver was damaged. There was lots of internal bleeding. They were worried about infection. They were worried he would not make it through the night.

She wiped his chin, surprised to feel stubble. Lena had always thought of Brad as a kid, but the hair on his face, the size of his hand that she held in hers, reminded her that he was a grown man. He knew the risks that came with being a cop. Brad had been on the scene when Jeffrey died, the first responding officer. He never talked about it, but Brad was different after that day. More grown up. The chief's death was a grim reminder that none of them was impervious to the bad guys they arrested.

Her phone vibrated again. Lena took it out of her pocket and scrolled through the numbers. She had called her uncle Hank in Florida to let him know she was okay in case he saw something on the news. Jared had called her as she was putting Tommy Braham in the back of the car. He was a cop. He'd heard about the stabbing on his radio. She had told him two words, 'I'm okay,' then hung up before she started crying.

All of the other incoming calls on her phone were from

Frank. He had been trying to reach her for the last five hours. She hadn't seen him since he took off with Brad in the helicopter that had landed in the middle of the street. The look in his rheumy eyes had told a story she hadn't wanted to hear. And now he was worried that she was going to tell everyone what she knew.

He *should* be worried.

Her phone rang again as she held it in her hand, but Lena pressed the button until the device powered down. She didn't want to talk to Frank, didn't want to hear any more of his excuses. He knew what had gone wrong today. He knew that Brad's blood was on his hands just as much as it was on Lena's – maybe more so.

She should just quit. Her resignation letter was in her jacket pocket, had been for weeks. She had gotten Tommy's confession in record time. Let someone else get the details from him. Let another cop stare at Tommy Braham's slack-jawed face for another two hours trying to figure out what was going on in that tiny little brain of his. They could not fault Lena for her work. Jeffrey's ghost could not hold her here after what had happened today.

Delia Stephens came back into the room. She was a large woman, but she moved quietly around the bed, fluffing Brad's pillows, kissing his forehead. She stroked back her son's thinning blond hair. 'He loves being a police officer.'

Lena found her voice. 'He's very good at it.'

Delia had a sad smile on her face. 'He always wanted to please you.'

'He never failed to,' she lied. 'He's a good detective, Ms. Stephens. He's going to be back on the street in no time.'

Delia's eyes clouded with worry. She rubbed Brad's

shoulder. 'Maybe I can talk him into selling insurance with his uncle Sonny.'

'You'll have plenty of time to persuade him,' Lena's voice cracked. Her false optimism was fooling no one.

Delia stood up. She clasped her hands in front of her. 'Thank you for watching him. I always feel safer when he's with you.'

Lena felt dizzy again. The room was too small, too hot. 'I'm just gonna go to the bathroom for a second.'

Delia smiled, her gratefulness so apparent that Lena felt like a knife was being twisted in her chest. 'Take your time, sweetheart. You've had a long day.'

'I'll be right back.'

Lena kept her head up as she walked down the hallway. There were a couple of Grant County patrolmen standing vigil outside the ICU waiting room. Inside, she could see local Macon cops milling around. Frank Wallace was nowhere to be seen. More than likely he was bellied up at a bar trying to drink the bad taste out of his mouth. It was probably best for her not to see him right now. If he'd been standing in the hallway, she would've called him out on his drinking, his lies – everything that she'd been ignoring for the past four years. No more. After today, Lena's knee-jerk loyalty to the man was gone for good.

At least Gavin Wayne, the Macon chief of police, was there. He nodded as Lena walked by. A few weeks ago, he had talked to Lena about joining his force. She was picking up Jared from his shift because his truck was in the shop. Lena had liked Chief Wayne all right, but Macon was a huge, sprawling city. Wayne was more politician than policeman. He was nothing like Jeffrey, an obstacle that had seemed insurmountable when he'd mentioned a job.

Lena pushed open the door of the ladies' room, glad to find it empty. She turned on the cold faucet. Water ran through her hands. She had washed them a thousand times but the blood – Brad's blood as well as her own – was still stuck under her fingernails.

She had been shot in the hand. The bullet had taken a chunk of skin off the outside edge of her palm. Lena had doctored it herself, using the first aid kit at the station. Oddly, there hadn't been much blood. Maybe the heat of the bullet had cauterized the wound. Still, it took three overlapping Band-Aids to cover it up. At first the pain was manageable, but now that the shock had worn off, her whole hand throbbed. She couldn't have anyone at the hospital look at it. Gunshot wounds had to be reported. Lena would have to call in a favor for some antibiotics so she didn't get an infection.

At least it was her left hand. She reached toward the faucet with her good hand and added hot water to the cold. Lena felt filthy. She wet a paper towel, added some soap from the dispenser, and washed under her arms. She kept going, giving herself a whore's bath at the sink. How long had she been up? Brad's call about the body in the lake came around three this morning. The last time she'd checked a clock, it was coming up on ten in the evening. No wonder she was punch-drunk from exhaustion.

'Lee?' Jared Long stood in the doorway. He was dressed in his motorcycle patrol uniform. His boots were scuffed. His hair was a mess. Lena's heart jumped at the sight of him.

The words rushed from her mouth. 'You shouldn't be here.'

'My squad came over to donate blood.' He let the door

close behind him. It felt like forever as he crossed the room and took her into his arms. Her head rested on his shoulder. She fit into him like a puzzle being solved. 'I'm so sorry, baby.'

She wanted to cry, but nothing was left inside.

'I nearly died when I heard one of you got hurt.'

'I'm okay.'

He took her hand in his, saw the Band-Aids she had used to cover her wound. 'What happened?'

She pressed her face against his chest again. She could hear his heart beating. 'It was bad.'

'I know, baby.'

'No,' she said. 'You don't know.' Lena pulled back, still letting him hold her. She wanted to tell him what had really happened – not what the reports would say, not what the newspapers would be told. She wanted to confess her complicity, to unburden her soul.

But when she looked into his deep brown eyes, words failed.

Jared was ten years younger than she was. She thought of him as pure and perfect. He didn't have crow's feet or lines around his mouth. The only scar on his body came from a bad tackle during a high school football game. His parents were still happily married. His younger sister worshipped him. He was the exact opposite of Lena's type. The exact opposite of any man she had ever been with.

She loved him so much that it frightened her.

He said, 'Tell me what happened.'

She settled on half of the truth. 'Frank was drunk. I didn't realize how much until . . .' She shook her head. 'Maybe I just haven't been paying attention. He's been drinking a lot lately. He can usually handle it, but . . .'

'But?'

'I'm through,' Lena told him. 'I'm going to resign. I've got some vacation time coming. I just need to get my head clear.'

'You can move in with me until you figure out what to do.'

'I'm serious this time. I'm really quitting.'

'I know you are, and I'm glad.' Jared put his hands on her shoulders so he could look at her. 'But, right now, I just wanna take care of you. You've had a hard day. Let me be there for you.'

She relented easily. The thought of handing over the next few hours of her life to Jared seemed like the best gift in the world. 'You go first. I'll check in on Brad and then follow you in my car.'

He tilted up her chin and kissed her mouth. 'I love you.'

'I love you, too.'

He reached for the door just as it opened. Frank stood stock-still, staring at Jared as if he'd seen a ghost.

'Jesus Christ,' he whispered. She could smell the whisky on him from five feet away.

'Go,' Lena told Jared. 'I'll meet you back at the house.'

Jared wasn't so easily directed. He stood his ground, glaring at Frank.

'Please go,' she begged him. 'Jared. Please.'

He finally moved his gaze from Frank to Lena. 'You sure you're okay?'

'I'm fine,' she told him. 'Just go.'

Reluctantly, he left. Frank stared after him so long that Lena had to close the door before he would look away.

'What the hell are you doing?' Frank demanded. He had

to keep his hand on the wall to steady himself. 'How old is he?'

'It's none of your damn business.' Still, she told him, 'He's twenty-five.'

'He looks ten,' Frank countered. 'How long have you been seeing him?'

Lena wasn't in the mood to answer questions. 'What are you doing here, Frank? You can barely stand up straight.'

He wiped his mouth with the back of his hand.

'Did you drive here? Don't answer that.' She didn't want to think about how many lives he had risked climbing behind the wheel.

'Is the kid okay?'

He meant Brad. 'They don't know. He's stable for now. Have you had anything to drink today that didn't have alcohol in it?'

Frank's footing was off. He didn't go to the sink so much as fall into it.

Lena turned on the water for him. She had a flash of her childhood, her uncle Hank so drunk that he'd pissed himself. She tried to separate her emotions, to distance herself from the anger she was feeling. It didn't work. 'You smell like a bar.'

'I keep thinking about what happened.'

'Which part?' she asked, leaning down so that her face was close to his. 'The part where we didn't identify ourselves as cops or the part where we nearly shot a boy for holding up a letter opener?'

Frank gave her a panicked look.

'You didn't think I'd find out about that?'

'It was a hunting knife.'

'It was a letter opener,' she insisted. 'Tommy told me,

Frank. It was a gift from his grandfather. It was a letter opener. It looked like a knife, but it wasn't.'

Frank spit into the sink. Lena's stomach roiled at the dark brown color of his phlegm. 'It doesn't matter. He stabbed Brad with it. That makes it a weapon.'

'What did he cut you with?' Lena asked. Frank had been writhing on the floor of the garage, clutching his left arm. 'You were bleeding. I saw it. That's what set this whole thing in motion. I told Brad he cut you.'

'He did.'

'Not with a letter opener, and I didn't find anything else on him except a toy car and some chewing gum.'

Frank glanced at himself in the mirror. Lena stared at his reflection. He looked like he was two steps from falling into the grave.

She peeled off the Band-Aids on the side of her hand. The wound was red and raw. 'Your shot went wild. Did you even realize I was hit?'

His throat worked as he swallowed. He probably wanted a drink. By the looks of him, he needed it.

'What happened, Frank? You had your gun out. Tommy came for you. You pulled the trigger and shot me. How did you get cut on the arm? How did a hundred-thirty-pound wimp of a kid get past you with a goddamn letter opener?'

'I told you that he cut me with the knife. He was wrong about the letter opener.'

'You know, for a cop, you're a shitty liar.'

Frank braced himself on the sink. He could barely stand. 'Tommy doesn't mention a letter opener in his confession.'

Lena's voice was more like a snarl. 'Because I've got

about two drips of loyalty left for you, old man, and they've been circling the drain all damn day. Tell me what happened in that garage.'

'I don't know. I don't remember.'

'How did Tommy get past you? Did you black out? Did you fall?'

'It doesn't matter. He ran. That's the point. Everything that happened after that is on him.'

'We didn't identify ourselves in the garage. We were just three people pointing guns at his head.'

He glared at her. 'I'm glad to hear you admitting you did something wrong today, princess.'

Lena felt overwhelmed with fury, ready to do any kind of damage she could. 'When Brad shouted "Police," Tommy stopped. He turned around. He had the letter opener in his hand. Brad ran into it. Tommy didn't mean to stab him. I'll tell that to anyone who asks me.'

'He killed that girl in cold blood. You telling me you don't care about that?'

'Of course I care about that,' she snapped. 'Jesus, Frank, I'm not saying he didn't do it. I'm saying the minute Tommy gets a lawyer, you're screwed.'

'I didn't do anything wrong.'

'Let's hope the judge agrees with you, otherwise he'll invalidate the arrest, the confession, everything that came out of finding Tommy in that garage. That kid's gonna get away with murder because you can't stand up straight without a bottle of whisky in you.' She put her face inches from his. 'Is that how you want to be remembered, Frank? As the cop who let a killer get away because he couldn't stay off the booze while he was on the job?'

Frank turned on the faucet again. He splashed water on

his face, the back of his neck. She saw his hands were shaking again. His knuckles were busted up. There were deep scratch marks on his wrist. How hard had Frank hit Tommy that the boy's teeth had managed to break through Frank's leather gloves?

She said, 'It's your fault this went bad. Tommy got past you. I don't know what you were doing rolling on the floor, how your arm got cut, but I do know if you had done your job and stopped him at the door—'

'Shut up, Lena.'

'Screw you.'

'I'm still your boss.'

'Not anymore, you drunk, worthless bastard.' She reached into her pocket and pulled out her resignation. When he didn't take it, she threw it in his face. 'I'm done with you.'

He didn't pick up the letter. He didn't shoot back a stream of obscenities. Instead, he asked, 'Which pen did you use?'

'What?'

'Your pen that Jeffrey gave you. Is that the one you used?'

'Are you trying to guilt me into staying? You're going to tread on Jeffrey's memory so I'll stick around to help you clean up this mess?'

'Where's your pen?' When she didn't volunteer it, he started searching her coat, patting her pockets. She resisted, and he slapped her around, throwing her against the wall.

'Get away from me!' She shoved him back into the sink. 'What the hell is wrong with you?'

He looked her in the eye for the first time since he'd

walked into the room. 'Tommy killed himself in the cells.'

Lena put her hand to her mouth.

'He cut his wrists open with an ink cartridge. The metal kind that you use in good pens. Good pens like the ones Jeffrey gave us.'

Lena's hands wouldn't work for a few seconds. She found the pen where she always kept it – inside the spiral of the notebook in her back pocket. She twisted the barrel. The ballpoint didn't come out. 'Shit,' Lena hissed, unscrewing the cap. 'No . . . no . . .' The pen was empty. 'How did he get . . .' She felt sick with grief. Her stomach clenched. 'What did he . . .'

Frank asked, 'Did you frisk him before you put him in the cells?'

'Of course I—' Had she? Had Lena taken the time to pat him down or just thrown him into a cell as fast as she could so she could get to the hospital?

'It's a good thing he didn't attack anybody while he was back there. He already killed one person and stabbed a cop.'

She couldn't stand anymore. Her knees gave out. She sank to the floor. 'He's really dead? Are you sure?'

'He bled out.'

Lena put her head in her hands. 'Why?'

'What did you say to him?'

'I didn't . . .' She shook her head, trying to clear out the image of Tommy Braham lying dead. He had been upset when she'd locked him up, but suicidal? She didn't think so. Even as rushed as she was to get to the hospital, Lena would have said something to the booking officer if she thought Tommy needed to be watched. 'Why did he do it?'

131

'Must've been something you said.'

She looked up at Frank. He was paying her back now. She could tell it by the petty look in his eyes.

He added, 'At least that's what Sara Linton thinks.'

'What does Sara have to do with this?'

'I called her because Tommy, your prisoner, wouldn't calm down. I thought she could give him something to help. She was there when I found him.'

Lena knew she should be worried about her own hide, but all she could think about was Tommy Braham. What had gotten into him? What had pushed that stupid kid over the edge?

'She's got some bigwig from the GBI down here to look into the case. Knox has already dealt with him. He's figured out Tommy got the pen from one of us.'

Lena tasted something awful in the back of her throat. Tommy was her prisoner. He was in her care. Legally, he was her responsibility. 'Do they know the cartridge came from me?'

Frank dug around in his coat pocket. He tossed Lena a cardboard packet. She recognized the Cross logo. A new ink cartridge was wrapped in a plastic shell.

She asked, 'Did you just buy this?'

'I'm not that stupid,' he told her. 'I buy them online. You can't get the cartridges local.'

Everyone else did, too. It was a pain in the butt, but the gift meant a lot, especially now that Jeffrey was gone. Lena had a stack of ten cartridges in a box back home.

Frank said, 'We're both in trouble on this.'

Lena didn't respond. She was running through her time with Tommy, trying to figure out when he'd decided to take his own life. Had he said anything to her before she locked the cell door? Lena didn't think so. Maybe that was one of the many clues she had missed. Tommy had calmed down too quickly after she'd left the room to get him some tissues. She had taken him back to the cells shortly after. He'd been sniffling, but he'd kept his mouth shut, even as she shut the heavy metal door. They always said the quiet ones were the ones who had made up their minds. How had she missed that? How had she not noticed?

Frank said, 'We need to stick together, get our stories straight.'

She shook her head. How did she get into this mess? Why was it that the minute she crawled out of one pile of shit, she fell back into another one?

'Sara's out for blood. Your blood. She thinks she's finally found a way to punish you for what you did to Jeffrey.'

Lena's head shot up. 'I didn't do anything.'

'We both know different from that, don't we?'

His words cut straight through her. 'You're a bastard. You know that?'

'Yeah, well, back at you.'

Lena felt her hand stinging. She was gripping the plastic packet hard enough to cut into her skin. She tried to pry it open, but her nails were too short. She ended up biting the cardboard with her teeth and ripping it away from the plastic.

Frank asked, 'How solid is that confession?'

She jammed the new cartridge into her pen. 'Tommy admitted to everything. He put it on paper.'

'You better shout that to whoever listens or his daddy's gonna sue you for everything you have.'

She snorted. 'A fifteen-year-old Celica and an eighty-thousand-dollar mortgage on a sixty-thousand-dollar house? He can have the keys right now.'

'You'll lose your badge.'

'Maybe I should.' She gave up on the pen. She gave up on everything. Four years ago, Lena would have been scrambling for a way to cover this up. Now, all she wanted to do was tell the truth and move on. 'This doesn't change anything, Frank. Tommy was my responsibility. I'll take the consequences. But you'll have to take yours, too.'

'It doesn't have to be like that.'

She looked up at him, wondering at the sudden shift. 'What do you mean?'

'Tommy killed that girl. You think anybody's gonna care about some little retard murderer slitting his wrists in a jail cell?' Frank wiped his mouth with the back of his hand. 'He killed that girl, Lee. He stabbed her through the neck like he was taking down an animal. All because she wouldn't let him get his pecker off.'

Lena closed her eyes. She was so damn tired that she couldn't think. But she knew Frank was right. No one would care about Tommy's death. But that didn't mean it was okay. That didn't change what happened in the garage today, or fix the damage that had been done to Brad.

She told him, 'Your drinking is out of hand. I didn't say anything about Brad being unfit. Maybe he'll be okay or maybe my silence will end up meaning the death of him. I don't know. I'm not gonna watch the same thing happen to you. You're not fit for duty, Frank. You shouldn't be behind the wheel of a car, let alone carrying a gun.'

Frank knelt down in front of her. 'There's a hell of a lot more you could lose than just your shield, Lena. Think about that.'

'There's nothing to think about. I've made up my mind.'

'I could always put in a word with Gavin Wayne about your little boyfriend.'

'Be sure to brush the whisky off your breath before you do.'

'We both know the kind of trouble I could make.'

'Jared will know I made a mistake,' Lena said. 'And he'll know I stood up to take the consequences.'

'When did you turn so noble?'

She didn't answer, but the thought of Tommy Braham sitting in those cells, scraping away at his wrists with Lena's ink pen, made her feel like the least noble person on the planet. How had she managed to fuck up so much in so little time?

Frank pressed, 'Does your little boyfriend really know you, Lena? I mean, *really* know you?' His lips curled up in a smile. 'Think about all the things you've told me over the years. All those squad cars we sat in together. All those late nights and early mornings after Jeffrey died.' He showed his yellow teeth. 'You're a dirty cop, Lee. You think your boyfriend's gonna forgive that?'

'I'm not dirty.' She had stepped right up to the line many times, but Lena had never crossed it. 'I'm a good cop, and you know it.'

'You sure about that?' He sneered at her. 'Brad got stabbed while you were standing with your thumb up your ass. You talked a nineteen-year-old retard into killing himself. I got a witness in the next cell who will say anything I tell him to as long as I let him go back to his wife.'

Lena felt her heart stop in her chest.

'You think I'm just gonna walk away from my pension, lay down my gun and my shield, because you've developed a conscience?' He spat out a laugh. 'Trust me, girl, you don't want me to start telling people what I know about you, because by the time I shut up, you'll be lucky if you don't find yourself sitting on the wrong side of a jail door.'

'You wouldn't do that to me.'

'You strut around town like you're some hot piece of shit wearing your bad reputation on your sleeve. Wasn't that what Jeffrey was always warning you about? Too many burned bridges. Too many people in town with knives in their backs.'

'Shut up, Frank.'

'The thing about having a bad reputation is that folks will believe just about anything people say about you.' He sat back on his heels. 'The chief could've gotten away with murder because no one thought he was capable of doing anything bad. You think people feel that way about you? You think they trust your character?'

'You can't prove anything and you know it.'

'Do I need to?' He smiled again, his lips peeling back from his teeth. 'I've lived in this town all my life. People know me. They trust me – trust what I tell them. And if I say you're a dirty cop . . .' He shrugged.

Lena's chest was so tight she could barely breathe.

'Maybe I'll ask ol' Jared out for a beer,' Frank continued. 'I bet Sara Linton wouldn't mind tagging along, either. What do you think of that? The two of them together having a nice chat about you?' Lena stared her hate into him. Frank's rheumy eyes glared back. 'Don't forget what a son of a bitch I am, girlie. And don't for a minute think I won't throw your worthless ass under the bus to save mine.'

She knew he was serious. She knew the threat was as real and as dangerous as a ticking bomb.

Frank took out his flask. He carefully unscrewed the top and took a long drink.

Lena's voice was barely above a whisper. 'What do you want me to do?'

Frank smiled in a way that made her feel like she was something he'd just scraped off his shoe. 'Just stick to the truth. Tommy confessed to killing Allison. He stabbed Brad. Nothing else matters.' Frank shrugged again. 'You play by my rules until we're clear of this, and maybe I'll let you go over to Macon and be with your little boyfriend.'

'What else?' she asked. There was always something else.

He pulled a plastic evidence bag out of his pocket. Now that it was close up, Lena wondered how she'd ever thought it was real – the thick, dull blade, the fake leather handle. The letter opener.

He tossed the bag onto her lap. 'Get rid of it.'

SEVEN

Sara sat at the dining room table thumbing through a magazine while her sister and mother played cards. Her cousin Hareton had joined them half an hour ago, dropping by without a phone call as usual. Hare was two years older than Sara. They had always competed in everything, which was why he had made her go out into the pouring rain to look at his brand-new BMW 750Li. How he could afford such a luxurious car on a rural doctor's salary was beyond her, but Sara had made the appropriate noises because she didn't have the strength to do otherwise.

She loved her cousin, but sometimes it seemed as if his goal in life was to get on her nerves. He made fun of her height. He called her 'Red' just to annoy her. The worst part was that everyone thought he was charming. Even her own mother thought he walked on water – a particularly sore point considering Cathy did not extend this rose-colored view to her own children. The biggest problem Sara had with Hare was that he never came across a situation he couldn't make light of, which could be a heavy burden to those around him.

Sara finished her magazine and started over from the beginning, wondering why none of the pages looked familiar. She was too distracted to read and too smart to try to have a conversation with anyone at the table.

Especially Hare, who seemed determined to catch her eye.

Finally, she asked, 'What?'

He slapped a card down on the table. 'How's the weather up there, Red?'

Sara gave him the same look she'd given him thirty years ago when he'd first asked her that question. 'Balmy.'

He put down another card. Tessa and Cathy groaned. 'You're on vacation, Red. What's the problem?'

Sara closed the magazine, fighting the desire to tell him that she was sorry she wasn't more upbeat, but that she couldn't quite get the image out of her mind of Tommy Braham lying dead on the jailhouse floor. A quick glance at her mother told Sara that Cathy knew exactly what she was thinking.

'I'm expecting someone,' she finally confessed. 'Will Trent. He's an agent with the GBI.'

Cathy's eyes narrowed. 'What's a GBI agent doing here?'

'He's investigating the murder at the lake.'

'And the death at the police station.' Cathy spoke pointedly. 'Why is he coming to the house?'

'He missed supper. I thought you could—'

'Am I responsible for feeding strangers now?'

Tessa, as usual, didn't help matters. 'You're gonna be responsible for putting him up for the night, too.' She told Sara, 'The hotel's closed for remodeling. Unless he wants to drive forty-five minutes into Cooperstown, you'd better go straighten up the apartment over the garage.'

Sara held back the curse that came to her lips. Hare was leaning forward, chin resting in his hands, as if he was watching a movie.

Cathy shuffled through the cards again. The noise was

made louder by the tension. 'How does this man know you?'

'Police officers are always at the hospital.' Not technically a lie, but close enough.

'What's going on here, Sara?'

She shrugged, the gesture feeling so fake that she had trouble letting her shoulders drop back down. 'It's complicated.'

'Complicated?' Cathy echoed. 'That sure did happen fast.' She slapped the cards down on the table as she stood up. 'I guess I'll go tell your father to put some pants on.'

Tessa waited until their mother had left. 'You might as well tell her, Sissy. She'll get it out of you somehow.'

'It's none of her business.'

Tessa gave a shocked bark of laughter. *Everything* was their mother's business.

Hare picked up the cards. 'Come on, Red. Aren't you taking this a little too seriously? This is probably the most exciting thing that's happened to Brad Stephens in his entire life. The guy still lives with his mother.'

'That's not funny, Hare. Two people are dead.'

'A retard and a college student. The town mourns.'

Sara bit her tongue so that she wouldn't cut him in two.

Hare sighed as he shuffled the cards between his hands. 'All right. The thing about the girl in the lake was a cheap shot, but Tommy's fair game. People don't just up and kill themselves for no reason. He felt guilty for killing the girl. That's why he stabbed Brad. End of story.'

'You sound like a cop.'

'Well . . .' He put his hand to his chest. 'You know I *did* dress up as one for Halloween.' He turned to Tessa. 'Remember the thong?'

140

'That was my birthday party, not Halloween,' Tessa reminded him. She asked Sara, 'Why did you go to the jail in the first place?'

'Tommy needed . . .' She didn't bother to finish the sentence. 'I don't know why I went down there.' She stood from the table. 'I'm sorry. All right? I'm sorry I went to the station. I'm sorry for bringing this home. I'm sorry Mama's mad at me. I'm sorry I came here in the first place.'

Tessa began, 'Sissy—' but Sara left before she could say more.

Tears filled her eyes for the umpteenth time that day as she went down the hall and stood at the front door. She should go upstairs and talk to her mother. At the very least, Sara could try to come up with an explanation that would stop Cathy from worrying. Of course, Cathy would see right through any explanation Sara could come up with, because they both knew the truth: Sara was trying to get Lena in trouble. Her mother would take no joy in telling Sara that she might as well go outside and howl at the rain. She would be right – at least partially. Lena was good at lying, cheating, and doing whatever else it took to keep herself out of trouble. Sara was no match for the woman because she lacked the basic deviousness with which Lena approached every situation in her life.

And what about the dead girl? Sara was as bad as Hare. She had completely ignored Allison Spooner, treating her death as yet another springboard for attacking Lena. People around town who knew Allison were starting to talk. Tessa had been on the phone most of the afternoon and had the whole story for Sara by the time she got back from downtown. Allison was petite and cheery, the sort of girl with good country manners and a bright smile for strangers. She had worked at the diner during lunch and over the weekends. She must have a family somewhere, a mother and father who had just gotten the worst news a parent could ever hear. Surely they were on their way to Grant County right now, heavy hearts sinking further with every mile.

There were footsteps on the stairs behind her – Cathy, judging by the light tread. Sara heard her mother pause on the landing, then head toward the kitchen.

Sara let out a breath of air she hadn't realized she'd been holding.

'Sweetpea?' Eddie called from upstairs. He was listening to his old records, something he did when he was feeling melancholy.

'I'm all right, Daddy.' She waited for the squeaking floorboards to signal he was going back to his room. They took an awful long time.

She closed her eyes again. Her father put on some Bruce Springsteen, the needle skipping on the vinyl record as he found the right place. She could hear her mother moving around the kitchen. Plates and pans banged. Hare said something that must have been funny, because Tessa's laugh rang through the house.

Sara stared out at the street, rubbing her arms to fight the chill that had come over her. This was silly, she knew, to stand at the door waiting for a man who might not even come. As much as Sara did not want to admit it, she wanted more than information from Will. He was from her Atlanta life. He was a reminder that there was something else waiting for her.

And thank God he was finally here.

For the second time that day, Sara watched Will hide the various electronics in his Porsche. It seemed to take longer this time, or maybe she was more impatient. Finally, he got out of the car. He held the file she had given him over his head to shield himself from the rain as he ran up the driveway.

She started to open the door, then reconsidered. She didn't want him to think she'd been standing here waiting for him. Then again, if she was trying to be covert, she probably shouldn't have been staring at him through the window.

'Idiot,' she muttered, opening the door.

'Hi.' He shook the rain out of his hair, taking advantage of the cover of the front porch.

'You want me to—' She reached for the wet file in his hand. Sara suppressed a groan of disappointment. It was soaked through. Everything would be ruined.

'Here,' he said, lifting his sweater, untucking his undershirt. Sara saw the pages she'd given him pressed against his bare skin. She also saw what looked like a dark bruise fanning across his abdomen, disappearing into the waist of his jeans.

'What—'

He quickly pulled down his shirt. 'Thanks.' He scratched his face, a nervous habit she had forgotten about. 'I think we can just throw the folder away.'

She nodded, not knowing what to say. Will seemed at a loss for words, too. They stared at each other until the hall light snapped on.

Cathy stood in the kitchen doorway with her hands on her hips. Eddie came down the stairs. There was a brief moment of the most uncomfortable silence Sara had ever experienced in her life. She felt for the first time what a monumental mess she had made of the day. If she could've clicked her heels and gone back to the beginning, she would still be in Atlanta and her family would have been spared this awful situation. She wanted to melt into the floor.

The silence broke with her father. He held out his hand to Will. 'Eddie Linton. Glad we can give you respite from this rain.'

'Will Trent.' Will gave him a firm handshake.

'I'm Cathy,' her mother chimed in, patting Will on the arm. 'Goodness, you're soaked through. Eddie, why don't you see if you can find him something dry?' For some reason, her father chuckled to himself as he ran up the stairs. Cathy told Will, 'Let's get this sweater off before you catch a chill.'

Will looked as uncomfortable as any man would look if an overly polite sixty-three-year-old woman told him to undress in her foyer. Still, he complied, lifting his sweater over his head. He was wearing a long-sleeved black T-shirt underneath. It started to ride up when he lifted his arms and Sara reached out without thinking, holding down the shirt.

Cathy gave her a sharp look that made Sara feel like she'd been caught stealing.

'Mama,' Sara began, feeling a cold sweat coming on. 'I really need to talk to you.'

'We'll have plenty of time later, sweetheart.' Cathy looped her hand through Will's arm as she led him down the hall. 'You're from Atlanta, my daughter tells me?'

'Yes, ma'am.'

'What part? I have a sister who lives in Buckhead.'

'Uh . . .' He glanced back at Sara. 'Poncey-Highlands, it's near—'

'I know exactly where that is. You must live close to Sara.'

'Yes, ma'am.'

'Mother—'

'Later, honey.' Cathy shot her a cat's smile as she took Will into the dining room. 'This is Tessa, my youngest. Hareton Earnshaw is my brother's boy.'

Hare gave him a look of open appraisal. 'My, you're a tall drink of water.'

'Just ignore him,' Tessa advised as she shook Will's hand. 'Nice to meet you.'

Will started to sit in the closest chair, and Sara felt her heart drop in panic. Jeffrey's place.

Cathy was not completely devoid of a soul. 'Let's put you at the head of the table,' she suggested, tugging Will gently in the right direction. 'I'll be right back with your dinner.'

Sara sank down beside Will. She put her hand on his arm. 'I am *so* sorry.'

He feigned surprise. 'About what?'

'Thank you for pretending, but we don't have much time before—' Sara jerked her hand away. Her mother was already back with a plate of food.

'I hope you like fried chicken.'

'Yes, ma'am.' Will stared down at the full plate. There was enough food for half the town.

'Sweet tea?' Cathy asked. Sara started to stand, but her mother nodded toward Tessa to fetch a glass. 'Tell me how you know my daughter.'

Will held up his finger for a minute so that he could swallow a mouthful of butterbeans. 'I met Dr. Linton at the hospital.'

Sara could have kissed him for his odd adherence to formality. She explained, 'Mama, Agent Trent's partner was a patient of mine.'

'Is that right?'

Will nodded, taking a healthy bite of fried chicken. Sara couldn't tell if he was hungry or just desperate to have a reason not to speak. She chanced a look at Hare. For once in his miserable life, he was choosing to be silent.

'Is your wife in law enforcement, too?'

Will stopped chewing.

'I noticed your ring.'

He looked down at his hand. Cathy kept him trained in her sights. He chewed some more. Finally, he answered, 'She's a private investigator.'

'That must give you two a lot to talk about. Did you meet during the course of one of your investigations?'

He wiped his mouth. 'This food is very good.' Tessa put a glass of tea down in front of him. Will took a long drink, and Sara wondered if he was wishing there was something stronger in the glass.

Cathy kept up her subtle pressure. 'I wish my daughters had been interested in cooking, but neither one of them took to it.' She paused for a breath. 'Tell me, Mr. Trent, where are your people from?'

Sara fought the urge to drop her head into her hands. 'Mama, really. It's none of our—'

'That's all right.' Will wiped his mouth with his napkin. He told Cathy, 'I was raised in state care.'

'Bless your heart.'

146

Will didn't seem to know how to answer her. He took another long drink of tea.

Cathy continued, 'Mr. Trent, my youngest daughter reminded me that the hotel is closed for renovations. I hope you'll accept the offer of my home while you're here?'

Will choked on his tea.

'There's an apartment over the garage. I'm sorry to say it's not much, but I wouldn't feel right making you drive all the way over to Cooperstown in this weather.'

Will wiped the tea off his face. He looked to Sara for help.

She shook her head, helpless to stop the onslaught of her mother's southern hospitality.

The Linton home renovation had not extended to the laundry room. Sara had to go down the stairs into the unfinished part of the basement to get some clean towels for Will. The dryer was still running when she turned on the lights. She checked the towels. They were damp.

Sara turned the dryer back on. She started up the stairs, but stopped halfway and sat down. She had been acting pretty dimwitted throughout most of the day, but she wasn't crazy enough to offer herself up to her mother right now.

She rested her chin in her hand. Her cheeks had been beet red from the moment Cathy welcomed Will Trent into the house.

'Sis?' Tessa whispered from the top of the stairs.

'Quiet,' Sara admonished. The last thing she needed was more of her mother's attention.

Tessa gently pulled the door to. She held one hand

under her stomach and grabbed the railing with the other as she descended the stairs. 'You all right?'

Sara nodded, helping Tessa sit on the stair above her.

'I can't believe they didn't move the laundry room upstairs.'

'Her sanctuary?'

They both laughed. As teenagers, Tessa and Sara had studiously avoided the laundry room for fear of being ordered to help out. They'd both thought they were so clever until they realized their mother was actually enjoying the lack of company.

Sara placed her hand on her sister's stomach. 'Hey, what's this?'

Tessa grinned. 'I think it's a baby.'

Sara spanned both of her hands across the width. 'You're enormous.'

'I love it,' Tessa whispered. 'You wouldn't believe all the shit I've been eating.'

'You must be feeling it kick all the time now.'

'She's going to be a soccer player.'

'She?' Sara raised an eyebrow.

'I'm just guessing. Lem wants to be surprised.'

'We could go to the clinic tomorrow.' Elliot Felteau had bought Sara's practice, but she still owned the building. 'I can just pretend I'm doing something landlord-y over by the ultrasound machine.'

'I want to be surprised, too. Besides, I think you have enough on your plate right now.'

Sara rolled her eyes. 'Mother.'

Tessa chuckled. 'My God, that was epic. What a shakedown!'

'I can't believe how awful she was.'

'You kind of sprung him on her.'

'I thought . . .' Sara shook her head. What *had* she been thinking? 'Hare wasn't any help.'

'He's taking this harder than you think.'

'I doubt that.'

'Tommy used to cut his grass, too.' Tessa shrugged. 'You know how Hare is. He's been through a lot.'

Hare had lost many friends as well as his longtime lover to AIDS, but Sara thought she was the only person in her family who remembered that his casual attitude had predated the epidemic. 'I hope he didn't embarrass Will.'

'Will took care of himself just fine.'

Sara shook her head as she thought about the mess she had made. 'I'm sorry, Tess. I didn't mean to bring all of this to your doorstep.'

'What's "all this"?'

She thought about the question. 'A vendetta,' she admitted. 'I think I've finally found a way to get Lena.'

'Oh, honey, will it make a difference?'

Sara felt tears in her eyes. She didn't fight them this time. Tessa had seen her in much worse shape before. 'I don't know. I just want . . .' She paused for breath. 'I want her to be sorry for what she did.'

'Don't you think she's sorry?' Tessa tread carefully. 'As awful as she is, she loved Jeffrey. She worshipped him.'

'No. She's not sorry. She won't even accept that she's the reason Jeffrey died.'

'You can't really think that she knew that bastard boyfriend of hers was going to kill Jeffrey.'

'It's not what she *wanted* to happen,' Sara admitted. 'But it's what she *let* happen. Jeffrey would've never even known that the man existed but for Lena. She put him in our life. If someone throws a grenade, you don't say they're innocent because they never considered that it'd actually blow up.'

'Let's not talk about her anymore.' Tessa wrapped her arm around Sara's shoulder. 'All that matters is that Jeffrey loved you.'

Sara could only nod. This was the one truth in her life. She had known without a doubt that Jeffrey had loved her.

Tessa surprised her. 'Will's nice.'

Sara's laugh didn't sound very convincing, even to her own ears. 'Tess, he's married.'

'He was looking at you all googly-eyed at the table.'

'That was fear you saw.'

'I think he likes you.'

'I think your hormones are making you see things.'

Tessa leaned back on the stairs. 'Just prepare yourself for the first time being awful.' Sara's look must've given her away. Tessa's mouth dropped. 'Oh, my God. Have you already slept with somebody?'

'Shh,' Sara hissed. 'Keep your voice down.'

Tessa leaned forward. 'Why am I trekking all the way to the only pay phone in Oobie Doobie to call you if you're not gonna tell me about your sex life?'

Sara waved her away. 'There's nothing to tell. You're right. It was awful. It was too soon and he never called me again.'

'What about now? Are you seeing anybody?'

Sara thought of the epidemiologist from the CDC. The fact that this was the first time all week that she'd really considered the man said it all. 'Not really. I've been on a few dates, but . . . What's the point?' Sara threw up her hands. 'I'm never going to connect with anyone like that again. Jeffrey ruined me for everybody else.'

'You'll never know if you don't try,' Tessa countered. 'Don't deny yourself, Sara. Jeffrey wouldn't want that.'

'Jeffrey wouldn't want me to ever touch another man ever again and you know it.'

'You're probably right.' Still, she said, 'I think Will could be good for you.'

Sara shook her head, wishing Tessa would drop the subject. Even if Will was available – even if by some miracle he was interested – Sara would never date another cop again. She couldn't have a man leave her bed every morning not knowing whether or not he would come back in one piece that night. 'I told you. He's married.'

'Now, there's married and there's *married*.' Tessa had dabbled in more than her share of trysts before settling down. She'd practically had a revolving door to her bedroom. 'Where'd he get that scar on his lip?'

'I have no idea.'

'Makes you want to kiss his mouth.'

'Tess.'

'Did you know about him growing up in a home?'

'I thought you were in the kitchen when he talked about that.'

'I had my ear pressed to the door,' she explained. 'He eats like the kids at the orphanage.'

'What do you mean?'

'The way he sort of wraps his arm around his plate so no one can steal his food.'

Sara hadn't noticed, but now she realized it was true.

'I can't imagine growing up without parents. I mean—' She laughed. 'After tonight, it seems ideal, but it must've been hard for him.'

'Probably.'

'Ask him about it.'

'That would be rude.'

'Don't you want to know more about him?'

'No,' Sara lied, because of course she did. She wanted to know about the scars. She wanted to know how he had entered the system as an infant and never been adopted. She wanted to know how he could stand in a room full of people and still seem completely alone.

'The kids in my orphanage are so happy,' Tessa said. 'They miss their parents – there's no question about that. But, they get to go to school. They get three meals a day, clean clothes. They don't have to work. The other kids who still have parents are jealous.' She smoothed out her skirt. 'Why don't you ask Will what it was like for him?'

'It's none of my business.'

'Give Mama another go at him and you'll find out everything.' Tessa pointed her finger at Sara's chest. 'You have to admit she was at the top of her game tonight.'

'I don't have to admit anything.'

Tessa affected their mother's soft accent. 'Tell me, Mr. Trent, do you prefer boxers or briefs?' Sara laughed, and Tessa continued, 'Was your first sexual experience from a missionary position or more of a canine nature?'

Sara laughed so hard that her stomach ached. She wiped her eyes, thinking this was the first time she was actually happy to be home. 'I've missed you, Tess.'

'I've missed you, too, Sissy.' Tessa struggled to stand. 'But right now, I'd better go to the bathroom before I pee in my pants from all this laughing.' She made her way up the stairs, taking them one tread at a time. The door closed softly behind her.

Sara stared into the basement. Her mother's rocking chair and lamp were in a corner by a small window. The ironing board was out, ready to be used. Plastic containers along the back wall held all of Sara and Tessa's childhood mementos, at least the ones that her mother deemed worth keeping. Yearbooks, school photos, report cards, and class papers filled two boxes for each girl. Eventually, Tessa's baby would get her own box. She would have baby shoes and flyers from school plays and piano recitals. Or soccer trophies, if Tessa got her way.

Sara couldn't have children. An ectopic pregnancy while she was in medical school had taken away her ability. She'd been trying to adopt a child with Jeffrey, but that dream had disappeared the day he'd died. He had a son somewhere, a brilliant, strong young man who had never been told that Jeffrey was his real father. Jeffrey was just an honorary uncle, Sara an honorary aunt. She often thought about reaching out to the boy, but the decision was not hers. He had a mother and father who had done a very good job of raising him. Ruining that, telling him he had a father he could never talk to, seemed like an act of cruelty.

Except where Lena was concerned, Sara had an intense aversion to inflicting cruelty.

The dryer buzzed. The towels were ready enough, considering she had to walk outside in the pouring rain. She put on her jacket and left the house as quietly as she could. Outside, the rain had turned into a drizzle again. She glanced up at the night sky. Even with the dark clouds, she could see the stars. Sara had forgotten what it was like to be away from the lights of the city. The night was as black as coal. There were no sirens or screams or random gunshots piercing the air. There were only crickets and the occasional howl of a lonely dog.

Sara stood outside Will's door, wondering if she should knock. It was late. He might have already gone to sleep.

He opened the door just as she turned around. Will certainly wasn't looking at her all googly-eyed, as Tessa had stated. If anything, he seemed distracted.

'Towels,' she told him. 'I'll just leave them with you.'

'Wait.'

Sara held up her hand to keep the rain from pelting her in the eyes. She found herself staring at Will's mouth, the scar above his lip.

'Please come in.' He stepped back so she could walk through the door.

Sara felt an unexplained wariness. Still, she went inside. 'I am so sorry about my mother.'

'She should teach a class on interrogation at the academy.'

'I cannot apologize enough.'

He handed her one of the clean towels to wipe her face. 'She loves you very much.'

Sara hadn't expected his response. She supposed a man who had lost his mother at such a young age had a different perspective on Cathy's obtrusiveness.

'Did you ever—' Sara stopped. 'Never mind. I should let you get to sleep.'

'Ever what?'

'I mean . . .' Sara felt her cheeks redden again. 'Were you in foster homes? Or . . .'

He nodded. 'Sometimes.'

'Good ones?'

He shrugged. 'Sometimes.'

Sara was thinking about the bruise on his belly – not a bruise at all, but something far more sinister. She had seen her share of electrical burns in the morgue. They left their own distinct mark, like a dusting of gunpowder that got under the skin and never washed away. The dark branding on Will's body had faded with time. He'd probably been a child when it happened.

'Dr. Linton?'

She shook her head by way of apology. Instinctively, her hand went to his arm. 'Can I get you anything else? I think there's some extra blankets in the closet.'

'I've got some questions for you. If you have a few minutes?'

She had forgotten the reason she'd come up here in the first place. 'Of course.'

He indicated the couch. Sara sank into the old cushion, which nearly swallowed her. She looked around the room, seeing it as Will might. There was nothing fancy about the space. A galley kitchen. A tiny bedroom with an even tinier bathroom. The shag carpet had seen better days. Buckled wood paneling covered every vertical surface. The couch was older than Sara. And it was big enough for two people to comfortably lie down on, which was why Cathy had moved it from the den to the upstairs apartment when Sara turned fifteen. Not that Sara had boys lining up to lie on the couch with her, but Tessa, three years younger, had.

Will put the towels on the kitchen counter. 'Can I get you some water?'

'No, thank you.' Sara indicated the apartment. 'I'm so sorry we couldn't offer you better accommodations.'

He smiled. 'I've stayed in a lot worse.'

155

'If it's any consolation, this is actually nicer than the hotel.'

'The food's better anyway.' He gestured toward the opposite end of the couch. There was really nowhere else for him to sit. Still, he asked, 'May I?'

Sara bent her legs up underneath her as he sat on the edge of the cushion. She crossed her arms, suddenly aware that they were alone in the same room together.

The uncomfortable silence was back. He played with his wedding ring, twisting it around his finger. She wondered if he was thinking about his wife. Sara had met the woman once at the hospital. Angie Trent was one of those vivacious, life-of-the-party types who never left the house without her makeup on. Her nails were perfect. Her skirt was tight. Her legs would have given the Pope second thoughts. She was about as different from Sara as a ripe peach was from a Popsicle stick.

Will clasped his hands together between his knees. 'Thank you for dinner. Or, thank your mother. I haven't eaten like that in . . .' He chuckled, rubbing his stomach. 'Well, I'm not sure I've ever eaten like that in my life.'

'I'm so sorry she questioned you like that.'

'It's no bother. I'm sorry for imposing.'

'It's my fault for bringing you down here.'

'I'm sorry the hotel was closed.'

Sara cut to the chase, afraid they would spend the rest of the night trading inconsequential apologies. 'What questions did you have for me?'

He paused another few seconds, staring openly. 'The first one is kind of delicate.'

She tightened her arms around her waist. 'All right.'

'When Chief Wallace called you earlier today to come

help Tommy . . .' He let his voice trail off. 'Do you always keep diazepam on you? That's Valium, right?'

Sara couldn't look him in the eye. She stared down at the coffee table. Will had obviously been working here. His laptop was closed, but the light was pulsing. Cables connected the machine to the portable printer on the floor. An unopened packet of colored folders was beside it. A wooden ruler was on top alongside a pack of colored markers. There was a stapler, paper clips, rubber bands.

'Dr. Linton?'

'Will.' She tried to keep her voice steady. 'Don't you think it's time you started calling me Sara?'

He acquiesced. 'Sara.' When she didn't speak, he pressed. 'Do you always have Valium with you?'

'No,' she admitted. She felt such shame that she could only look at the table in front of her. 'They were for me. For this trip. In case . . .' She shrugged the rest of her answer away. How could she explain to this man why she would need to drug herself through a family holiday?

He asked, 'Did Chief Wallace know that you had the Valium?'

She tried to think back on their conversation. 'No. I volunteered to bring it.'

'You said you had some in your kit?'

'I didn't want to tell him they were for—'

'It's all right,' he stopped her. 'I'm really sorry that I had to ask such a personal question. I'm just trying to figure out how it happened. Chief Wallace called you to help, but how would he know that you'd be able to?'

Sara looked up at him. Will stared back, unblinking. There was no judgment in his gaze, no pity. Sara couldn't remember the last time someone had looked at her and really seen her. Certainly not since she'd gotten into town this morning.

She told him, 'Frank thought I could talk to Tommy. Talk him down, I guess.'

'Have you helped prisoners in the jail before?'

'Not really. I mean, I got called in a couple of times when there was an overdose. Once, someone had a burst appendix. I transferred them all to the hospital. I didn't really treat them at the jail. Not medically.'

'And on the phone with Chief Wallace—'

'I'm sorry,' Sara apologized. 'Could you call him Frank? It's just—'

'You don't have to explain,' he assured her. 'On the phone before, when you said that you didn't really remember Tommy Braham, that there was no connection with him. Did you feel like Frank was trying to push you into coming to the station?'

Sara finally saw where this was going. 'You think he called me after the fact. That Tommy was already dead.' She remembered Frank looking through the cell door window. He had dropped his keys on the floor. Had that all been an act?

'As you know, time of death isn't an exact science,' Will said. 'If he called you right after he found Tommy—'

'The body was still warm,' she remembered. 'But the temperature inside the cells was hot. Frank said the furnace was acting up.'

'Had you ever known it to act up before?'

She shook her head. 'I haven't stepped foot in that station in over four years.'

'The temperature was normal when I was there tonight.'

Sara sat back on the couch. These were people who had

worked with Jeffrey. People she had trusted all of her life. If Frank Wallace thought Sara was going to cover something up, he was sadly mistaken. 'Do you think they killed him?' She answered her own question. 'I saw the blue ink from the pen. I can't imagine they held Tommy down and scraped it across his wrists. There are easier ways to kill someone and make it look like a suicide.'

'Hanging,' he suggested. 'Eighty percent of custodial suicides are achieved by hanging. Prison inmates are seven times more likely to kill themselves than the general population. Tommy fits just about every part of the profile.' Will listed it out for her. 'He was unusually remorseful. He wouldn't stop crying. He wasn't married. He was between the ages of eighteen and twenty-five. This was his first offense. He had a strong parent or guardian at home who would be angry or disappointed to learn of his incarceration.'

She admitted, 'Tommy was all of those things. But why would Frank postpone finding the body?'

'You're well respected here. A prisoner killed himself in police custody. If you say there's nothing hinky about it, then people will believe you.'

Sara couldn't argue with him. Dan Brock was a mortician, not a doctor. If people got it into their heads that Tommy had been killed at the jail, then Brock would be hard-pressed to disprove the rumor.

'The cartridge from the pen that Tommy used,' Will began. 'Tonight, Officer Knox told me that your husband gave them all pens for Christmas one year. That's a very thoughtful thing to do.'

'Not exactly,' Sara said before she could catch herself. 'I mean, he was busy, so he asked me to . . .' She waved her hand, dismissing her words. She had been so annoyed with Jeffrey for asking her to track down the pens, as if her life was less busy than his. She passed this off by telling Will, 'I'm sure there are things you ask your wife to do for you when you're tied up.'

He smiled. 'Do you remember where you got the pens?'

Sara felt another wave of shame crashing down. 'I asked Nelly, my office manager at the clinic, to find them online. I didn't have time to . . .' She shook her head, feeling like a heel. 'I might be able to find the credit card receipt if it's important. This was over five years ago.'

'How many did you get?'

'Twenty-five, I think? Everyone on the force got one.'

'That's a lot of money.'

'Yes,' she acknowledged. Jeffrey hadn't given her a budget, and Sara's idea of an expensive gift had a higher price tag than Jeffrey's. It all seemed so silly now. Why had they wasted days being angry at each other? Why had it mattered so much?

Will surprised her, saying, 'Your accent is different down here.'

She laughed, taken off guard. 'Do I sound country?'

'Your mother has a beautiful accent.'

'Cultured,' Sara said. Except for tonight, she had always loved the sound of her mother's voice.

He surprised her again. 'You've kind of been dragged into the middle of this case, but in a lot of ways, you've put yourself there on your own.'

She felt a blush brought on by his candor.

His expression was soft, understanding. She wondered if it was genuine or if he was using one of his interviewing techniques. 'I know this sounds forward, but I'm

160

assuming you had me meet you at the hospital in plain view of Main Street for a reason.'

Sara laughed again, this time at herself, the situation. 'It wasn't that calculated. It must seem that way now.'

'I'm staying at your house. People are going to see my car parked on the street. I know how small towns work. They're going to think something's going on between us.'

'But there's not. You're married and I'm—'

His smile was more of a wince. 'The truth isn't much help in these types of situations. You must know that.'

Sara looked back at his office supplies. He had separated the rubber bands by color. Even the paper clips were turned in the same direction.

Will said, 'Something is going on here. I'm not sure if it's what you think, but something's not right at that station house.'

'What is it?'

'I don't know yet, but you need to prepare yourself for some bad reactions.' He spoke carefully. 'Cases like this, where the police get questioned. They don't like that. Part of the reason they're good at their jobs is because they think they're right about everything.'

'I'm a doctor. Trust me, it's not just cops who feel that way.'

'I want you to be prepared, because when we get to the end of this, whether I find out Tommy was guilty, or Detective Adams screwed up, or if I find out nothing was wrong at all, people are going to hate you for bringing me down here.'

'They've hated me before.'

'They're going to say you're dragging your husband's memory through the mud.'

'They don't know anything about him. They have no idea.'

'They'll fill in the blanks themselves. It's going to get a lot harder than it is now.' He turned his body toward her. 'I'm going to make it harder. I'm going to do some things on purpose to get them mad enough to show their hand. Are you going to be okay with that?'

'What if I say no?'

'Then I'll find another way to do it that doesn't upset you.'

She could see that his offer was genuine, and felt guilty for questioning his motives before. 'This isn't my home anymore. I'm leaving in three days no matter what happens. Do what you have to do.'

'And your family?'

'My family supports me.' Sara wasn't certain about a lot of things these days, but this, at least, was true. 'They may not agree with me, but they support me.'

'All right.' He looked relieved, as if he'd gotten the hard part out of the way. 'I need to get Julie Smith's phone number from you.'

Sara had anticipated the request. She took a sheet of folded paper out of her pocket and handed it to Will.

He pointed to the Princess phone beside the couch. 'Is this the same line as the house?'

She nodded.

'I wanted to make sure the caller ID was the same.' He picked up the phone and stared at the rotary dial.

Sara rolled her eyes. 'My parents don't exactly embrace technology.'

He started spinning the dial, but the rotary slipped out from under his finger in the middle of the number.

'Let me,' she offered, taking the phone before he could protest. She spun the dial, the motion coming back to her more quickly than she wanted to admit.

Will put the receiver to his ear just as an automated squawk blared down the line. He held the phone between them so they both could hear the recorded voice advising the caller that the line he was trying to reach had been disconnected.

Will put the phone back on the hook. 'I'll have Faith do a trace tomorrow. My bet is that it was a throwaway phone. Do you remember anything else about Julie? Anything she said?'

'I could tell that she was calling from a bathroom,' Sara told him. 'She said that Tommy had texted her that he was in jail. Maybe you can get the transcript from his phone?'

'Faith can do that, too,' he offered. 'What about Julie's voice? Did she sound young? Old?'

'She sounded really young and really country.'

'Country how?'

Sara smiled. 'Not like me. At least I hope not. She sounded more like the wrong side of the tracks. She used the word "you'uns."'

'That's mountain talk.'

'Is it? I'm not up on dialects.'

'I had an assignment in Blue Ridge a while back,' he explained. 'Do you hear that word around here much?'

She shook her head. 'Not really. Not that I can remember.'

'All right, so we've got someone young, probably a transplant from north Georgia or Appalachia. She told you that she was Tommy's friend. We'll dump his phone line and see if they've ever called each other.'

'Julie Smith,' Sara said, wondering why it had never occurred to her that the girl might be using an alias.

'Maybe the phone taps will give us something.'

Sara indicated the photocopies she'd made. 'Were these helpful?'

'Not in the way you're thinking.' He thumbed through the pages. 'I asked the station secretary, Mrs. Simms, to fax these to Faith. Can you look at them for me?'

Sara glanced through the pages. There were handwritten numbers at the top. She stopped on the eleventh page. Someone had written the number twelve in the corner. The two was backward. 'Did you number these?'

'Yes,' he said. 'When I got them back from Mrs. Simms, one of the pages was missing. Page eleven. The page right after Detective Adams's field report.'

Sara thumbed back to the second page. The two was written the correct way. She checked the third and fifth page. Both numbers were facing the correct direction. The pen had been pressed so hard that the paper felt embossed.

He asked, 'Can you remember what's missing?'

Sara went through them again, concentrating on the content instead of the numbering. 'The 911 transcript.'

'You're sure?'

'There was another page from Lena's notebook. It was taped on the sheet of paper by itself. She wrote down the contents of the 911 call.'

'Can you remember what it said?'

'I know that it was a woman's voice. I can't really remember the rest.'

'Did they trace the number she called from?'

'I didn't see anything indicating they had.' She shook her head. 'Why can't I remember what else it said?'

'We can get it from the call center.'

'Unless they managed to lose it.'

'It's no big deal,' he told her. 'You got the file from Frank, right?'

'From Carl Phillips.'

'The booking officer?'

'Yes. Did you talk to him tonight?'

'He's gone on vacation with his family. No idea when he'll be back. No phone. No cell. No way to get in touch with him.'

Sara felt her mouth drop open.

'I doubt he's really gone. They're probably keeping him away from me. He might even be at the station tomorrow, hiding in plain sight.'

'He's the only African American on the force.'

Will laughed. 'Thanks for the tip. That narrows things down considerably.'

'I can't believe they're doing this.'

'Cops don't like to be questioned. They circle their wagons, even if they know it's wrong.'

She wondered if Jeffrey had ever done anything like this. If he had, it was only because he wanted to be the one to clean out his own house. He would never let someone come in and do his job for him.

Will asked, 'Where did you make the copies?'

'At the front of the room.'

'The copier that's on the table by the coffeemaker?'

'That's right.'

'Did you get some coffee?'

'I didn't want to dawdle.' Everyone had been staring at her like she was a monster. Sara's only goal had been to make the copies and get out of there as soon as possible.

'So, you're standing by the copier waiting for the pages to come out. That looked like an old machine. Does it make a noise?'

She nodded, wondering where this was going.

'Like a whirring or a clunking?'

'Both,' she answered, and she could hear the sound in her head.

'How much coffee was left in the pot? Did anyone come up?'

She shook her head. 'No. The pot was full.' The machine was older than the copier. She could smell the grounds burning.

'Did anyone talk to you?'

'No. No one would even look at—' She saw herself standing by the copier. The machine was old, the kind you had to feed the pages into one at a time. She had read the file to keep from staring aimlessly at the wall. 'Oh.'

'What do you remember?'

'I skimmed the 911 transcript while I was waiting for the copier to warm up.'

'What did it say?'

She could see herself standing back in the station reading the files. 'The woman called it a possible suicide. She said she was worried her friend had done something.' Sara narrowed her eyes, trying to force the memory to come. 'She was worried Allison was going to kill herself because she'd gotten into a fight with her boyfriend.'

'Did she say where she thought Allison was?'

'Lover's Point,' she recalled. 'That's what town people call it. It's the cove where Allison was found.'

'What's it like?'

'A cove.' Sara shrugged. 'It's romantic if you're out for a walk, but not in the pouring rain and cold.'

'Is it secluded?'

'Yes.'

'So, according to this caller, Allison got into a fight with her boyfriend. The caller was worried Allison was suicidal. The caller also knew she was going to be at Lover's Point.'

'It was probably Julie Smith. Is that what you're thinking?'

'Maybe, but why? The caller wanted to bring attention to Allison's murder. Julie Smith was trying to help Tommy Braham get away with murder. They seem to have opposite goals.' He paused. 'Faith is trying to track her down, but we're going to need more than a disconnected number to find her.'

'Frank and Lena are probably thinking the same thing,' Sara guessed. 'That's why they hid the transcript. They either don't want you to talk to her or they want to talk to her first.'

Will scratched his cheek. 'Maybe.' He was obviously considering another option. For her part, Sara could not get past Marla Simms hiding information in a formal investigation. The old woman had worked at the station longer than anyone could remember.

Will sat up on the couch. He thumbed through the pages on the coffee table. 'Mrs. Simms took it upon herself to send some extra information. I had Agent Mitchell scan these in so I could print them out.' He found what he was looking for and handed it to Sara. She recognized the form, a two-page incident report. Patrolmen filled out dozens of these a week to notate cases where they had been called in but no arrest had been made. They were useful to have in case something bad happened later, sort of like a progress report on a person or an area of town.

Will said, 'These are incident reports documenting Tommy's run-ins with the law.' He indicated the pages in Sara's hands. 'This one talks about a girl he got into a screaming match with at the roller rink.'

She saw there was a yellow dot in the corner of the report.

He asked, 'Did you ever know Tommy to have a temper?'

'Never.' Sara checked through the other incident reports. There were two more, each two stapled pages, each with a dot from a colored marker in the corner. One was red. The other was green.

She looked back up at Will. 'Tommy was pretty even-keeled. Kids like that tend to be very sweet.'

'Because of their mental state?'

Sara stared at him, thinking back on their conversation in the car. 'Yes. He was slow. Very gullible.'

Much like Sara.

She handed a different report back to Will, showing it to him upside down. She pointed to the middle of the page where Carl Phillips had described the incident. 'Did you read this part?'

She watched Will's eyes go to the red dot. 'The barking dog. Tommy started screaming at his neighbor. The woman called the cops.'

'Right.' She took the third report and handed it to him in the right direction. 'Then there's this.'

Again, his eyes went not to the words, but to the colored dot. 'Loud music reported a few days ago. Tommy yelled at the officer.'

She was silent, waiting for him to send out another feeler.

He took his time, finally asking, 'What are you thinking?'

She was thinking he was incredibly clever. Sara looked at the folders, the markers. He color-coded everything. His penmanship was awkward, like a child's. He'd written the number two backward, but not with any consistency. He couldn't tell whether a page was upside down or not. Sara might not have even noticed under different circumstances. Hell, she *hadn't* noticed the last time she'd spent time with him. He'd been in her home. She had watched him work and never realized there was a problem.

He joked, 'Is this some kind of test?'

'No.' She couldn't do this to him. Not like this. Maybe not ever. 'I was looking at the dates.' She shuffled through the forms to give herself something to do. 'All the incidents happened within the last few weeks. Something must have set him off. Tommy didn't have a temper until recently.'

'I'll see what I can find.' He took back the pages and stacked them on the table. He was nervous, and he was not stupid. He had spent a lifetime looking for cues, searching for tells and ticks, so that he could keep his secret hidden.

Sara put her hand on his arm. 'Will—'

He stood up, moving out of her reach. 'Thank you, Dr. Linton.'

Sara stood, too. She fumbled for something to say. 'I'm sorry I couldn't help more.'

'You've been great.' He walked to the door and held it open for her. 'Please thank your mother for her hospitality.'

Sara left before she was pushed out. She got to the bottom of the steps and turned around, but Will had already gone inside.

'Good Lord,' Sara mumbled as she walked across the wet grass. She'd actually managed to make Will feel more uncomfortable than her mother had.

The distant sound of a car came from up the road. Sara watched a police cruiser roll by. This time, the cop behind the wheel did not tip his hat at her. In fact, he seemed to glare at her.

Will had warned her this would happen, that the town would turn against her. Sara hadn't thought the time would come so quickly. She laughed at herself, the circumstances, as she crossed the driveway and went into the house. Will might have trouble reading the words on a page, but he was pretty damn good at reading people.

EIGHT

Jason Howell paced back and forth across his tiny dorm room, the shuffling of his feet blending with the shushing of the rain outside his window. Papers were strewn across the floor. His desk was cluttered with open books and empty Red Bull cans. His ancient laptop made a sound like an exhausted sigh as it went to sleep. He needed to be working, but his brain was spinning in his head. Nothing could hold his attention for more than a few minutes – not the broken lamp on his desk or the emails flooding his inbox and certainly not the paper he was supposed to be working on.

Jason rested his palm just below the keyboard on the laptop. The plastic was hot to the touch. The fan that cooled the motherboard had started clicking a few weeks ago, around the same time he'd nearly gotten a third-degree burn on his legs from keeping the computer on his lap. He guessed there was something bad happening between the battery and the charger plugged into the wall. Even now there was a slight tinge of burning plastic in the air. Jason grabbed the plug but stopped short of yanking it out of the socket. He chewed the tip of his tongue as he stared at the snaking electrical cord in his hand. Did he want the machine to overheat? A dead laptop was a life-altering catastrophe. Maybe his work would be lost, his footnotes and research and the last year of his life melting into one giant lump of stinking plastic.

And then what?

He didn't have any friends left. Everyone in the dorm avoided him when he walked down the hall. Nobody talked to him in class or asked to borrow his notes. He hadn't been out for a drink in months. Except for his professors, Jason couldn't recall one meaningful conversation he'd had with anyone since before Easter break.

Anyone but Allison, but that didn't count. They weren't really talking lately. All they did was end up screaming at each other about the stupidest things – who was supposed to order the pizza, who forgot to shut the door. Even the sex was bad. Confrontational. Mechanical. Disappointing.

Jason couldn't blame Allison if she hated him right now. He couldn't do anything right. His paper was a mess. His grades had started to slip. He was running out of money from his grandfather's trust. Papa had left him twelve thousand dollars to supplement Jason's scholarships and loans for school. At the time, the number had seemed enormous. Now that Jason was a year into his graduate program, it seemed like a pittance. And that pittance was getting smaller every day.

No wonder he was so depressed he barely had the strength to raise his head.

What he really wanted was Allison. No, scratch that – he wanted the Allison he had known for one year and eleven months. The one who smiled when she saw him. The one who didn't burst into tears every five minutes and yell at him for being a bastard when Jason asked her why she was sad.

'*Because of you,*' she would say, and who wanted to hear that? Who wanted to be blamed for somebody else's misery when you were knee-deep in your own?

And Jason *was* miserable. It radiated off him like the heat lamp over the french fries at McDonald's. He'd lost track of the last time he'd showered. He couldn't sleep. Nothing could make his brain shut down long enough for rest. As soon as he lay down, his eyelids started going up and down like a lazy yo-yo. Darkness tended to bring it all fresh into his mind, and before long that monster weight of loneliness started pressing on his chest so that he felt like he couldn't breathe.

Not that Allison cared. He could be dead right now for all she knew. He hadn't seen another human being since the dorm cleared out for Thanksgiving break three days ago. Even the library had closed early on Sunday, the last stragglers clawing at the steps as the staff finally locked the doors. Jason had watched them go from his window, wondering if they were going to be alone, if they had anyone to spend their holiday with.

Except for the constant hum of the Cartoon Network and Jason's occasional mumblings to himself, the place was completely silent. Even the janitor hadn't shown his face in days. Jason probably wasn't supposed to be in the building. The heat had been turned off when the last students left. He was sleeping in his warmest clothes, holed up under his winter coat. And the one person who was supposed to care about this evidently didn't give a shit.

Allison Spooner. How had he fallen in love with a girl who had such a stupid name?

She had called him like crazy for days, and then yesterday – nothing. Jason had watched his phone light up each time with her caller ID and each time he hadn't answered it. Her messages were all the same: *'Hey, call me.'* Would it kill her to say something else? Would it kill her to say that she missed him? He had conversations in his head where he asked her these questions and she said, 'You know what? You're right. I should be a better girlfriend.'

Conversations. More like fantasies.

For three days, all the phone did was ring. He started to worry that Allison's caller ID would get etched into the screen on his phone. He'd watched the bars for the battery indicator disappear one by one. With each bar, he told himself he would answer the phone if she called before the next one disappeared. Then it would blink off with no call and he'd say the next one. Then the next one. Finally, the phone had turned itself off while he was sleeping. Jason had panicked as he searched for the charger. He'd plugged it into the wall and – nothing.

Her silence was loud and clear. You didn't give up on somebody like that if you loved them. You kept calling. You left messages that said something more deep and personal than *'Hey, call me.'* You apologized. You didn't send a stupid IM every twenty minutes saying 'where r u?' You banged on their door and yelled at the top of your lungs for them to please, please see you.

Why had she given up on him?

Because he didn't have any balls. That's what she had told him the last time they talked. Jason wasn't man enough to do what needed to be done. He wasn't man enough to take care of her. Maybe she was right. He *was* afraid. Every time they talked about what they were going to do, he felt like his intestines were squeezing up on him. He wished that he had never talked to that asshole from town. He wished that he could take it all back – everything they had done over the past two weeks. Allison acted like she was fine with it, but he knew she was afraid, too. It wasn't too late. They could back out of this. They could pretend like it didn't happen. If only Allison would see that there was no good way out. Why was Jason the only person in this whole damn mess who seemed to be cursed with a conscience?

Suddenly, there was a noise outside. He threw open the door and went into the hallway. Jason stood in the dark, glancing around like a madman. No one was there. No one was watching him. He was just being paranoid. Considering the number of Red Bulls he'd chugged and the two bags of Cheetos that were sitting like a brick in his stomach, it was no wonder he was feeling wired.

Jason went back into his room. He opened the window to let in some air. The rain had slacked off, but the sky hadn't given up the sun in days. He checked his bedside clock, unsure whether it was morning or night. Midnight was only a few minutes away. A stiff wind was blowing, but he had been holed up inside for so long that he welcomed fresh air, even if it was cold enough to make his breath appear as a cloud in front of his face. Outside, he could see the empty student parking lot. In the distance, a dog barked.

He sat back down at his desk. He stared at the lamp by his laptop. The neck was broken. The shade dangled from two wires, hanging its head as if in shame. The light cast weird shadows in the room. He had never liked the dark. It made him feel vulnerable and lonely. It made him think about things he didn't want to think about.

Thanksgiving was a few days away. Last week, Jason

had made the usual call to his mother, but she wasn't interested in seeing him. She never was. Jason was from his mother's first marriage, to a man who'd gone out for beer one day and never come back. Her second husband made it clear from the start that Jason wasn't his son. They had three daughters who barely knew Jason existed. He wasn't invited to family get-togethers. He didn't get invitations to weddings or holidays. His mother's only connection to him was through the U.S. Postal Service. She mailed a check for twenty-five dollars every birthday and Christmas.

Allison was supposed to make things different. They were supposed to spend all of their holidays together. They were supposed to create their own family. That's what they'd done for the last year and eleven months. They went to movies or ate Chinese food while the rest of the planet was holed up with relatives they didn't like, eating food they didn't enjoy. That was their thing – they were two against the world, filled with combined glee because they had each other. Jason had never known what it was like to be inside something good. He was always on the outside, his face pressed against the glass. Allison had given him that, and now she had taken it away.

He didn't even know if she was still in town. She might have gone home to visit her aunt. Maybe she had run off with another guy. Allison was attractive. She could do a hell of a lot better than Jason. He wouldn't be surprised if she was screwing some new guy right now.

A new guy.

The thought cut him like a knife. Their legs and arms entangled, her long hair draped across another guy's chest. Probably it was a hairy chest, the kind of chest that men had, not a concave, pasty white chest that hadn't changed since junior high school. This new guy would have balls the size of grapefruits. He would pick Allison up in his arms and take her like a beast whenever he wanted.

How could she be with another guy? Jason knew from the first time they kissed that he was going to marry her. He'd given her that ring with the promise that as soon as all of this was over, he'd buy her a better one. A real one. Had Allison forgotten that? Could she really be that cruel?

Jason chewed at his tongue, rolling it around with his front teeth until he tasted blood. He stood up and started pacing again. The broken lamp traced his movements in an eerie shadow that swung back and forth across the wall. Six paces one way. Six paces back. The shadow hesitated, stopped and started, clinging to Jason like a bad dream. He raised his hands, hunched his shoulders, and the shadow grew into a monster.

Jason dropped his hands, thinking he was going to freak himself out if he didn't stop this.

If he could just get through Thanksgiving, all of this would be over. He and Allison would be rich, or at least not as poor. Tommy would be able to buy enough equipment to start his own gardening business. Allison would be able to quit her job at the diner and concentrate on school. Jason would . . . What would Jason do?

He would buy Allison that ring. He would block that other guy and his stupid hairy chest from his mind, and he and Allison would go on and live their lives together. They could get married. Have children. They'd both be scientists, doctors. They could buy a new house, new cars, leave the air-conditioning on sixty all summer if they wanted to. The last three months would be a distant memory, something they would talk about in ten, fifteen years when it was all behind them. They would be at a dinner party. Allison would've had a little too much to drink. Talk would turn to wild college days, and her eyes would sparkle in the candlelight as she looked at Jason, a smile tugging at her lips.

'Oh, we can top that,' she would say, and proceed to shock them all with the crazy mess they had gotten themselves into over the last few weeks.

That's what it would end up being – a party story, like the one Jason told about the first time his papa took him duck hunting and Jason had accidentally maimed two decoys.

He needed to finish his paper for that to happen. He couldn't just settle for a degree now. He had to be the best, the top in his class, because Allison didn't say it, but she liked having nice things. She liked the idea of being able to go into a store and buy whatever she wanted. She hated having to balance her checkbook down to the last penny every month. Jason wasn't going to be the kind of husband who asked how much a pair of shoes cost or why she needed another black dress. He was going to be the kind of husband who made so much money that Allison could fill ten closets with designer clothes and there would still be money left over to go to Cancún or St. Croix or wherever it was filthy rich people went on their private jets for the holidays.

Jason rested his fingers on the keys but did not type. He felt feverish. Guilt had always been a problem for him. There was no punishment that anyone could mete out that was worse than the distress brought on by Jason's own disappointment in himself. And he *should* be disappointed. He should be feeling horrified by what he had done. He should have protected Allison from all of this, told her that no matter how much money was involved, it wasn't worth it. He'd endangered her. He'd gotten Tommy mixed up in it, too, because Tommy was stupid enough to go along with anything as long as you pushed him in the right direction. Jason was responsible for both of them. He was supposed to protect his friends, not push them into oncoming traffic. Were their lives really worth so little? Was that what it boiled down to at the end of the day, twenty-something years of life for less money than what a janitor brought home?

'No,' he said, the sound of his voice drowned out by the howling rain. He couldn't let all of them get dragged down into this. Allison was wrong. Jason had balls. He had balls enough to do the right thing.

Instead of working on his paper, he opened his Internet browser. A quick search brought him to the right place. He found the contact information buried in the site map. Jason clicked on the icon to write new mail, but changed his mind. He didn't want this traced back to him. It was the coward's way out, but Jason would rather be an honest coward than a jailed whistle-blower. There was no denying his culpability in all of this – extortion, fraud, who knew what else. The feds would be involved. This might even count as attempted murder.

Jason opened up the Yahoo account he used for porn and pasted the contact address into the email. He spoke aloud as he wrote, 'I don't know if you are the right person to talk to about this, but there is something seriously wrong going on at your Grant County . . .' Jason's voice trailed off as he searched for the right word. Was it a site? A location? Facility?

'Hey.'

Jason jerked up his head, surprised. 'You scared the crap out of me.' He fumbled for the mouse to close the browser.

'You all right?'

Jason glanced nervously at the computer. 'What are you doing here?' The stupid email program was asking if he wanted to save. Jason moved the mouse again to minimize the page. It still asked if he wanted to save.

'What are you writing?'

'School stuff.' Instead of hitting Save, Jason pressed the Delete key. The program closed down. He could hear the laptop's fan clicking, trying to cool the processor enough to complete the request. His dissertation flashed up, then disappeared. The screen went black.

'Shit,' he whispered. 'No, no, no . . .'

'Jason.'

'Just give me a minute.' Jason tapped the space bar, trying to wake the computer. Sometimes that's all it took. Sometimes, it just needed to know he was paying attention.

'You asked for this.'

'Wha—' Jason pitched forward, his jaw snapping shut as his face slammed into his computer. The plastic was hot against his cheek. Dark liquid pooled around the keys. He had the crazy thought that the computer was injured, bleeding.

Wind gusted in from the open window. Jason tried to cough. His throat wouldn't comply. He coughed again. Something wet and thick came out of his mouth. He stared at it, thinking it looked like a piece of pork. Pink flesh. Raw meat.

Jason gagged.

He was staring at his tongue.

TUESDAY

NINE

Will felt like a thief as he sneaked across the Linton yard and climbed into his Porsche. At least the driving rain gave him an excuse to keep his head down and move quickly. He jammed the key in the lock and was inside the car before he realized there was something trapped under his windshield wiper. Will groaned. He pushed open the door and tried to reach around to the wiper, but his arm wasn't long enough. His sleeve was nearly soaked through by the time he got out of the car again to retrieve the plastic sandwich bag.

Someone had left him a note. The paper was folded in two, safe inside the plastic. Will glanced around, trying to see up and down the street. No one was milling about, which was unsurprising, considering the awful weather. There were no parked cars with the engines running. Will unzipped the bag. He caught a whiff of a familiar scent.

Fancy soap.

He stared at the folded piece of paper, wondering if Sara was playing some kind of joke. He'd paced the floor of her family's romper room half the night, replaying in his mind the last five minutes of their conversation. She hadn't said anything, really. Or had she? There was definitely a look in her eyes. Something had changed between them, and it wasn't a good change.

Other than Will's wife, there were only two people in

his life who knew about his dyslexia. Both of them had found their own special ways to make him miserable about it. Amanda Wagner, his boss, threw out occasional bon mots about him being professionally incompetent at best and mentally incapacitated at worst. Faith was more well-meaning, but she was too nosy for her own good. Once, she'd peppered Will with so many questions about the disorder that he'd stopped talking to her for two whole days.

His wife, Angie, was a combination of both responses. She had grown up with Will, helped him write school assignments and work on papers and fill out applications. She'd been the one who reviewed his reports and made sure he didn't sound like a backward chimp. She was also prone to dangling her help in exchange for things she wanted. And they were never good things. At least not good for Will.

In their own way, all three women made it clear that they thought something was wrong with him. Something not quite right with his head. With the way he thought. With the way he handled things. They didn't pity him. He was pretty sure Amanda didn't even like him. But they treated him differently. They treated him like he had a disease.

What would Sara do? Maybe nothing. Will wasn't even sure if she had figured it out. Or he could just be fooling himself. Sara was smart – that was part of the problem. She was a hell of a lot smarter than Will. Had he tripped up? Did she have some kind of special doctor's tool to trap unsuspecting morons? He must have said something or done something that had given himself away. But what?

Will glanced back at the Linton home to make sure no one was watching him. Sara had developed a weird habit of lurking behind closed doors. He unfolded the notebook paper. There was a smiley face at the bottom.

Did she think he was a child? Was she out of gold stars?

He pressed his fingers to his eyes, feeling like an idiot. There was nothing sexy about a barely literate thirty-five-year-old man.

He looked back at the note.

Thankfully, Sara didn't write in cursive. She didn't write like a doctor, either. Will put his finger under each letter, moving his lips as he read. 'Fun . . .' His heart did a weird double beat in his chest, but quickly he realized his mistake. 'Funeral.' He knew the next word, and numbers had never been a problem for him.

He stared back at the front door. The window was clear. He checked the note again. 'Funeral home 11:30.'

And a smiley face, because apparently she thought he was intellectually disabled.

Will stuck his key into the ignition. Obviously, she was talking about the time for the autopsies. But was this also some kind of test to see how well he could read? The thought of Sara Linton examining him like a lab rat made him want to pack his bags and move to Honduras. She would feel sorry for him. Worse, she might try to help him.

'Hello?'

Will jumped so hard he slammed his head into the ceiling. Cathy Linton was standing outside his car with a pleasant look on her face. She had a large umbrella over her head. She motioned for him to roll down the window.

'Good morning, Mr. Trent.' She was all smiles again, but he had fallen for her sweet-southern-lady crap once before.

'Good morning, Mrs. Linton.'

Her breath was visible in the cold. 'I hope you slept well.'

He looked back at the house, wondering why this was the only time Sara wasn't lurking behind the door. 'Yes, ma'am. Thank you.'

'I just went for my walk. Exercise is the best way to start the morning.' She smiled again. 'Won't you come in and have some breakfast with us?'

His stomach rumbled so loudly he was sure the car was shaking. The energy bar he'd found at the bottom of his suitcase this morning hadn't exactly hit the spot. A woman like Cathy Linton would know how to make a good biscuit. There would be butter and ham. Probably grits. Eggs. Sausage patties. It was like she was inviting him into the woods to visit her cottage made of candy.

'Mr. Trent?'

'No, ma'am. I need to get to work, but I appreciate it.'

'Dinner, then.' She had a way of saying things that sounded like a suggestion at first but ended up being a strict order. 'I hope the apartment wasn't too horrible last night.'

'No, ma'am. It was fine.'

'I'll just slip up there later and do some dusting. Eddie and I haven't used the place since the girls were here. I cringe to think of the state it must be in.'

Will thought about the dirty clothes he'd left piled on the couch. He'd packed in Atlanta thinking he'd wash everything at the hotel. 'That's all right. I—'

'Nonsense.' She tapped her hand on the car door like a judge passing down an edict. 'I can't have you breathing in all that dust.'

He knew there was no way to stop her. 'Just . . . uh . . . Just ignore my mess. Please. I'm sorry.'

Her smile changed to something much kinder than he'd seen before. He could see now where Sara got her beauty. Cathy reached into the car and gently rested her hand on his arm. Sara had touched him on the arm a lot last night. They were obviously a touchy-feely kind of family, which was just as foreign to Will as if they were from Mars.

She squeezed his arm. 'Dinner's at seven-thirty sharp.'

He nodded. 'Thank you.'

'Don't be late.' Her smile changed back to the one he was more familiar with. She winked at him before turning on her heel and walking back toward the house.

Will rolled up his window. He put the car in gear and headed up the road, too late remembering that he was going in the wrong direction. Or maybe not. Sara had told him that Lakeshore was just a big circle. Will had lately gone around in enough circles to last a lifetime, but he wasn't going to risk driving past the Linton home again.

The road was empty, he assumed because of the early hour. Will was timing his arrival at the police station so that he'd get there before most of the cops came on shift. He wanted to look eager and alert. He wanted them to feel like he was stepping on their toes.

He slowed his car as he rounded a curve. The road was more like a stream, rainwater flooding across the asphalt. He maneuvered the Porsche into the opposite side of the street to keep his floorboards from flooding. Will had spent ten years of his life and a chunk of his savings restoring the 9-11 by hand. Most of that time, he was bent over manuals and schematics, trying to figure out how the car was supposed to work. He'd learned to weld. He'd learned to do body work. He'd learned that he wasn't particularly fond of either.

The engine was solid, but the gears were temperamental. He felt the clutch slip as he downshifted. Once he was out of the floodwaters, he idled the car, thinking he'd let the undercarriage drain, wondering if such a thing was even possible. Up ahead, a blue mailbox with an Auburn University logo painted on it rocked in the strong wind. He recalled the first house number Sara had written on the outside of the folder when she was giving him directions to her parents' house. Will had always been good at remembering numbers.

In Atlanta, Sara lived in the old dairy factory, one of those industrial complexes that had been turned into luxurious lofts back during the real estate boom. He'd remarked then that the place didn't really seem like her type of home. The lines were too hard. The furniture too sleek. He had imagined she lived somewhere warm and welcoming, more like a cottage.

He had been right.

The Auburn mailbox belonged to a shotgun-style, one-story home with plants overflowing in the front yard. Sara had lived on the lake, and the sky was just light enough so that Will could see the glorious aspect of her backyard. He wondered what Sara's life had been like when she lived here. She didn't strike him as the kind of wife who would have dinner and a dry martini waiting when her husband got home, but maybe occasionally she had filled the role out of kindness. There was something about her that indicated a tremendous capacity for love.

The porch light came on. Will put the car in gear and continued around the lake. He missed the turnoff for Main

Street and had to back up. He felt his wedding ring on his hand, making a mental note that the turn would be on that side. Over the years, he had trained his mind to recognize his watch, not the ring. Probably because the watch was more permanent.

Will had met Angie Polaski when he was eight years old. Angie was three years older, thrown into the system because her mother had overdosed on a nasty combination of heroin and speed. While Diedre Polaski lay comatose in the bathroom, Angie was being looked after by her mother's pimp in the bedroom. Finally, someone had called the police. Diedre was put on life support at the state hospital, where she remained to this day, and Angie was sent to the Atlanta Children's Home for the remaining seven years of a childhood that had already been lost. Will had fallen in love with her on sight. At eleven, she'd had a chip on her shoulder and hell in her eyes. When she wasn't giving boys handjobs in the coat closet, she was beating the snot out of them with her unsurprisingly quick fists.

Will had loved her for her fierceness, and when her fierceness had worn him down, he had clung to her for her familiarity. Last year, she had married him on a dare after years of empty promises. She cheated on him. She pushed him to the breaking point, then sank her claws into his flesh and yanked him back. His relationship with Angie was more akin to a twisted hokey pokey. She was in Will's life. She was out. She was in. She was shaking him all about.

Will found Main Street after a couple of wrong turns. The rain wasn't coming down in sheets anymore, so he could make out the small shops lining the road. One place was obviously a hardware store. The other looked like a shop to buy ladies' clothing. Directly across from the station was a dry cleaners. Will thought about his dirty laundry piled on the couch. Maybe he could find time to sneak back and get it. He usually wore a suit and tie to work, but he hadn't had a lot of options this morning. There was just one T-shirt and a pair of boxers left. His jeans were clean enough to last another day. The sweater was the one he wore last night. The cashmere blend hadn't responded well to the rain. He felt the material tighten every time he flexed his shoulders.

Will pulled into the farthest space from the front door, backing in so that the Porsche was facing the street. Catty-corner to the station, he saw a low office building with glass brick on the front. The faded sign out front had a teddy bear holding some balloons. Probably a daycare center. A squad car rolled down the street but didn't stop, going ahead through the gates of what must have been the college. Will's was the only car in the lot. He supposed Larry Knox was inside the station, or maybe they'd given him a relief when Will left last night. Either way, he wasn't going to spend the next twenty minutes standing in the rain outside the locked door.

He dialed Amanda Wagner's number, holding out slim hope that she wasn't in the office yet.

His luck took a nasty turn. Amanda answered the phone herself.

'It's Will,' he said. 'I'm outside the station house.'

Amanda never gave anyone the benefit of the doubt, not least of all Will. 'Did you just get there?'

'I got in last night.' He felt a slight bit of relief. In the back of his mind, he'd been worried that Sara would call

Amanda and ask that Will be taken off the case. She would want the best the GBI had to offer, not a functional illiterate with a suitcase full of dirty laundry.

Amanda's tone was clipped. 'Run it down for me, Will. I haven't got all day.'

He told her Sara's story: that she had gotten a call from Julie Smith, then Frank Wallace. That she had gone to the jail and found Tommy Braham dead. He didn't tell her about Sara's beef with Lena Adams, instead skipping ahead to the Cross pens that Jeffrey Tolliver had given his staff. 'I'm pretty sure the ink cartridge Braham used came from one of those pens.'

'Good luck finding out whose.' Amanda picked at the same thread Will had spotted. 'There's no way of knowing exactly when Tommy Braham died – before or after Frank Wallace called Sara.'

'We'll see what the autopsy brings. Dr. Linton is going to do it.'

'There's a bright spot in a bleak day.'

'It's good to have someone down here who knows what they're doing.'

'Shouldn't that be you, Will?'

He let the remark go unanswered.

She asked, 'What's your impression on the Allison Spooner homicide?'

'I'm fifty-fifty. Maybe Tommy Braham did it. Or maybe her killer's assuming he got away with murder.'

'Well, figure it out and get back here fast, because they're not going to like you very much if you prove he's innocent.'

She was right. One thing cops hated more than bad guys was being proven wrong about the bad guys. Will had seen an Atlanta detective nearly go into convulsions as he argued that the DNA exonerating his suspect had to be wrong.

Amanda told him, 'I called Macon General this morning. Brad Stephens had to be taken back into surgery. They missed a bleeder the first time.'

'Is he all right?'

'Prognosis is guarded. They're keeping him sedated for the time being, so he's not going to talk to anyone anytime soon.'

'I'm pretty sure he's not going to remember anything useful except that his fellow officers saved his life.'

'Be that as it may, he's still a cop. You need to go over there at some point and share in the camaraderie. Donate some blood. Buy him a magazine.'

'Yes, ma'am.'

'What's your game plan?'

'I'm going to rattle some cages this morning and see if anything falls out. Faith is working on the paper trail for Julie Smith and Carl Phillips. Talking to them is my priority, but we've got to find them first. I want to check out the lake where Spooner was found, then go see the garage where she lived. It feels like her murder is at the center of this. Whatever they're hiding from me goes back to her death.'

'You don't think they're tap-dancing because of the suicide?'

'They might be, but my gut is telling me something else is going on.'

'Ah, your famous women's intuition.' Amanda never missed an opportunity to insult him. 'What about Adams?'

'I'll keep her close by.'

'I met her once. She'll be a hard nut to crack.'

'So I hear.'

'Loop me in at the end of the day.'

She hung up the phone before Will could respond. He rubbed his fingers through his hair, wondering if the damp was from the rain or his own sweat.

For the second time that morning, Will jumped when someone knocked on the window of his car. This time the knocker was an older black man, and he stood at the passenger door, grinning at Will's reaction. He made a rolling motion with his arm. Will leaned over and opened the door.

'Come in out of the rain,' Will offered, thinking the man was the first nonwhite face he'd seen since he'd arrived in Grant County. He didn't want to make assumptions, but he would've bet half his paycheck that the African Americans in town didn't make a habit of approaching investigators outside the police station.

The man groaned as he climbed into the bucket seat. Will saw that he walked with a cane. His leg was stiff, and bent awkwardly at the knee. Rain dripped from his heavy coat. A slight mist clung to his salt-and-pepper beard. He wasn't as old as Will had first thought – maybe early sixties. When he spoke, his voice was like sandpaper scratching through gravel.

'Lionel Harris.'

'Will Trent.'

Lionel took off his glove and they shook hands. 'My father was named Will. Short for William.'

'Me too,' Will told him, though his birth certificate said no such thing.

Lionel pointed up the street. 'Daddy worked at the diner for forty-three years. Old Pete closed it down back in oh-one.' He rubbed his hand along the leather dashboard. 'What year is this?'

Will assumed he meant the car. 'Seventy-nine.'

'You do all the work yourself?'

'Is it that obvious?'

'Nah,' he said, though he'd found the kink in the leather under the handle of the glove box. 'You did a good job, son. Real good job.'

'I take it you're interested in cars?'

'My wife would tell you I'm too interested for my own good.' He glanced pointedly at Will's wedding ring. 'You known Sara long?'

'Not too long.'

'She took care of my grandson. He had asthma real bad. She'd rush over in the middle of the night to help him. Sometimes she'd still be in her pajamas.'

Will tried not to think of Sara in her pajamas, though he imagined from Lionel's story that they were probably not the ones his mind had conjured.

'Sara's from good people.' He ran his finger along the trim on the door, which, thankfully, Will had done a better job covering. Lionel seemed to agree. 'You learned from your mistakes. Got a good fold on this corner here.'

'It took me half the day.'

'Worth every minute,' he approved.

Will felt foolish even as he asked, 'Your son isn't Carl Phillips, is he?'

Lionel gave a deep, satisfied laugh. ' 'Cause he's black and I'm black—'

'No,' Will interrupted, then, 'Well, yes.' He felt uncomfortable even as he explained, 'There doesn't seem to be much of a minority population around here.'

'I guess coming from Atlanta, you've had a bit of a culture shock.'

He was right. In Atlanta, Will's white skin made him a minority. Grant County stood as a stark contrast. 'I'm sorry.'

'That's all right. You aren't the first person to do that. Carl goes to my church, but I don't know him other than that.'

Will tried to steer the conversation away from his own stupidity. 'How do you know I'm from Atlanta?'

'License plate says Fulton County.'

Will smiled patiently.

'All right, you got me,' Lionel relented. 'You're here to look into that stuff with Tommy?'

'Yes, sir.'

'He was a good kid.'

'You knew him?'

'I saw him in town a lot. He's the kind of kid got thirty different jobs – mowing lawns, walking dogs, hauling trash, helping people move house. Just about everybody in town knew him.'

'How do people feel about him stabbing Brad Stephens?'

'About how you'd expect. Confused. Angry. Torn between thinking there was some mistake and thinking . . .' His voice trailed off. 'He was a bit tetched in the head.'

'He'd never been violent before?'

'No, but you never know. Maybe something set him off, turned on the crazy.'

In Will's experience, people were either prone to violence or not. He didn't think Tommy Braham was an exception. 'Do you think that's what happened – he just snapped?'

'I don't know what to think about nothin' anymore, and that's the God's honest truth.' He gave a weary sigh. 'Lord, I feel old today.'

'The weather gets into your bones,' Will agreed. He'd broken his hand many years ago, and every time it got cold like this, his fingers ached. 'Have you lived here all your life?'

Lionel smiled again, showing his teeth. 'When I was a boy, people called where we lived Colored Town.' He turned to Will. 'Can you believe that? Colored Town, and now I live on a street with a bunch of professors.' He gave a deep laugh. 'A lot's changed in fifty years.'

'Has the police force?'

Lionel stared openly at Will, as if he was trying to decide how much to say. Finally, he seemed to make up his mind. 'Ben Carver was chief when I left town. I wasn't the only young black man who thought it was a good idea to leave while the gettin' was good. Joined the army and got this for my trouble.' He knocked on his leg. There was a hollow sound, and Will realized the man wore a prosthetic. 'Laos. Nineteen and sixty-four.' Lionel paused for a minute as if to reflect on the loss. 'There was two kinds of living for people back then, just like there was two kinds of law under Chief Carver: one for black and one for white.'

'I heard Carver retired.'

Lionel nodded approvingly. 'Tolliver.'

'Was he a good cop?'

'I never met the man, but I can tell you this: A long while back, my father was working at the diner when a lady professor from the college got killed. Everybody saw a black face and made their assumptions. Chief Tolliver spent the night at Daddy's house just to make sure he woke up the next morning.'

'It was that bad?'

'Chief Tolliver was that good.' Lionel added, 'Allison was a good girl, too.'

Will got the feeling that they had finally reached the point of Lionel's impromptu visit. 'You knew her?'

'I own the diner now. You believe that?' He shook his head as if he still could not believe it himself. 'I came back a few years ago and took it off Pete's hands.'

'Is business good?'

'It was slow at first, but most days now we're full up. My wife works the books. Sometimes my sister pitches in but it's better if she doesn't.'

'When was the last time you saw Allison?'

'Saturday night. We're closed on Sundays. I guess except for Tommy, I was one of the last people to see her alive.'

'How was she?'

'Same as usual. Tired. Glad to be getting off work.'

'What sort of person was she?'

His throat worked, and he took a few moments to collect himself before he could continue. 'I never hire kids from the college. They don't know how to talk to people. They just know how to type into their computers or their phones. No work ethic and nothing's ever their fault no matter how red-handed you catch 'em. Except for Allison. She was different.'

'How so?'

'She knew how to work for a living.' He pointed to the open gates at the end of Main Street. 'Not a kid in that school knows how to do an honest day's work. This economy is their wake-up call. They're gonna have to learn the hard way that a job is something you earn, not something you're given.'

Will asked, 'Did you know much about Allison's family?'

'Her mama was dead. She had an aunt she didn't talk about much.'

'Boyfriend?'

'She had one, but he never bothered her at work.'

'Do you know his name?'

'She never mentioned him except in passing, like I'd ask what she was going to do over the weekend and she'd say she was going to study with her boyfriend.'

'He never called her or dropped by? Not even once?'

'Not even once,' he confirmed. 'She was mindful that I was paying for her time, you see. I never saw her on her cell phone. She never had her friends come in and take up her time. It was work for her, and she knew that she had to take care of business.'

'Did she make a good living?'

'Hell no.' He laughed at what must have been a surprised look on Will's face. 'I don't pay much and my customers are cheap – mostly old men and cops, sometimes students from the school who think it's funny to run out on the bill. Or, try to run out. Pretty stupid thinking you're gonna stiff the check in a room full of cops.'

'Did she carry a purse or book bag with her?'

'She had this pink book bag with a tassel on the zipper. Left it in her car when she was at work. Except her wallet. She wasn't one'a them primpin' girls, can't stay away from a mirror.'

'Was there anyone suspicious hanging around her? Customers who were too attentive?'

'I would've taken care of that myself. Not that I'd need to. That girl was street-smart. She knew how to take care of herself.'

'Did she carry a weapon? Maybe pepper spray or a pocket knife?'

'Not that I ever saw.' He held up his hands. 'Now, don't get the impression she was hard. She was a real sweet girl, one'a them who just wanted to go along to get along. She didn't take to confrontation, but she stood up for herself when it mattered.'

'Had her attitude changed lately?'

'She seemed a little more stressed than usual. She asked me a couple of times could she study when we were slow. Don't get me wrong – I'm an easy man to work for so long as you do your job. I let her crack open her books when we weren't busy. I made sure she had a hot meal before she went home.'

'Do you know what kind of car she drove?'

'Old Dodge Daytona with Alabama plates. You remember those? Based on the Chrysler G platform. Front-wheel drive, kind of low to the ground.'

'Four door?'

'Hatchback. The pistons were blown. She kept the trunk tied down with a bungee cord. I think it's a '92, '93.' He tapped his head. 'Mind ain't as good as it used to be.'

'What color?'

'Red, you could say. Mostly it's primer and rust. Spits out smoke from the tailpipe every time she cranks it.'

'Where did she park?'

'Behind the diner. I checked this morning. It's not there.'

'Did she ever walk home from work?'

'Sometimes when the weather was good, but it ain't been good in a long while, and she wasn't making her way home.' He pointed behind them. 'The lake's back there. Behind the station. Behind the diner.' He pointed across the street. 'When she walked home, she always went that way, out the front door.'

'Do you know Gordon Braham?'

'I believe he works for the power company. He also dates the woman who works at the five and dime across from the diner. They come in for lunch every couple'a three days.'

'You seem to know a lot about people.'

'This is a small town, Mr. Trent. Everybody knows a lot about everybody else. That's why we live here. Cheaper than cable TV.'

'Who do you think killed Allison?'

Lionel didn't seem surprised by the question, but he gave the expected answer. 'Police say it was Tommy Braham.'

'What do you say?'

He looked at his watch. 'I say I'd better go fire up the grill before the breakfast crowd comes in.' He put his hand on the door, but Will stopped him.

'Mr. Harris, if you think somebody—'

'I don't know what to think,' he admitted. 'If Tommy

didn't do it, then why'd he stab Brad? And why'd he kill himself?'

'You don't think he did it.' Will wasn't asking a question.

Lionel gave another weary sigh. 'I guess I'm a bit like old Chief Carver. There's good people and there's bad people. Allison was good. Tommy was good. Good people can do bad things, but not that bad.'

He started to leave again.

'Can I ask you—' Will waited for him to turn back around. 'Why did you come to talk to me?'

'Because I knew Frank wouldn't be knocking on my door. Not that I've been able to tell you much, but I wanted to say something on the girl's behalf. She ain't got nobody speaking up for her right now. It's all about Tommy and why'd he do it, not about Allison and what a good girl she was.'

'Why do you think Chief Wallace wouldn't want to talk to you?'

'Meet the new boss, same as the old boss.'

Will knew he didn't mean Jeffrey Tolliver. 'Ben Carver?'

'Frank and Ben – they were cut from the same cloth. White cloth, if you catch my drift.'

'I think I do.'

Lionel still had his hand on the door handle. 'When I got back to town after Daddy died, I saw a lot of people had changed. On the outside, I'm talking – not on the inside. You gotta go through a special kind of hell or a special kind of love to change who you are inside. Outside's a whole different story.' He rubbed his beard, probably thinking about the gray in it. 'Now, Miss Sara, she got prettier. Her daddy Mr. Eddie got more hair sprouting out of his eyebrows. My sister got older and fatter, which ain't never a good combination for a woman.'

'And Frank?'

'He got careful,' Lionel said. 'I may not be living in Colored Town anymore, but I still remember what it feels like to have that man's foot on my neck.' He pulled the handle on the door. 'You get you a heat gun and work it just the tiniest little bit around that leather on your glove box and you'll be able to get that kink out.' He picked up his leg so he could get out of the car. 'Just a tiny bit, though. Too much heat, and you'll burn a hole right through.' He stared his meaning into Will. 'Not too much heat, son.'

'I appreciate your advice.'

Lionel struggled to get out of the Porsche, finally gripping the roof and pulling himself up. He steadied himself on the cane and held out his hand, giving Will a gymnast's finish and a 'tah-dah,' before gently closing the door.

Will watched Lionel lean heavily on the cane as he made his way up the street. He stopped in front of the hardware store to talk to a man who was sweeping debris from the sidewalk. The rain had died down, and they seemed to be taking their time. Will imagined they were talking about Allison Spooner and Tommy Braham. In a place as small as Grant County, there wouldn't be anything else to occupy people's minds.

An old Cadillac pulled into the parking lot. Even from a distance, the gospel music hummed in Will's ears. Marla Simms parked her car as far from Will's as she could. She checked her makeup in the mirror, arranged her glasses –

did all of the things that made it obvious she was ignoring him – before getting out of the car.

He walked across the lot to meet her, putting as much cheer into his voice as he could manage. 'Good morning, Mrs. Simms.'

She tossed him a wary look. 'No one's here yet.'

'I see that.' He held up his briefcase. 'I thought I'd go ahead and get set up. If you wouldn't mind bringing me the evidence from the lake and anything collected from Tommy Braham's person?'

Marla didn't bother to acknowledge him as she threw back the bolt on the door. She turned on the lights and walked into the lobby. Again, she leaned over the gate and buzzed herself through. Will caught the door before it latched closed.

'Cold in here,' Will said. 'Something wrong with the furnace?'

'The furnace is fine,' she said defensively.

'Is it new?'

'Do I look like I work for the furnace company?'

'Mrs. Simms, I'd be lying if I didn't say that you look like you know everything that goes on in this station, if not the entire town.'

She made a grumbling noise as she took the carafe from the coffeemaker.

'Did you know Tommy Braham?'

'Yes.'

'What was he like?'

'Slow.'

'What about Allison Spooner?'

'Not slow.'

Will smiled. 'I should thank you, Mrs. Simms, for those

incident reports you sent to my partner last night. It shows an interesting pattern with Tommy. He'd had some trouble with his temper lately. Is that what you wanted me to know?'

She gave him a look over her glasses, but her mouth stayed closed as she walked to the back of the room. Will watched her push open the heavy steel door. She'd left him alone in the dark.

He went to the fax machine and checked under the table, giving Marla Simms the benefit of the doubt. There were no loose pages underneath, no 911 transcript that had fallen through the cracks. He opened the copier and saw the glass staring back at him. Something sticky was in the center. Will used his thumbnail to pry off the substance, which would transfer to every copy made on the machine. He held it up to the light. Glue, maybe? Gum?

He flicked it into the trashcan. None of the copies Sara had made for him yesterday showed a mark. Maybe someone else had used the machine after her and unwittingly transferred the gum onto the glass.

The office on the side of the squad room was empty, just as he'd thought. Will tried the knob. The door was unlocked. He went in and opened the blinds, giving him a nice view of the desks where the detectives sat. There were nail holes in the walls. In the slim ray of light coming through the outside window, he could see the shadows where photographs had once been. The desk was empty but for a telephone. All the drawers were cleaned out. The chair squeaked when he sat down.

If he was the betting type, Will would have put ten bucks on this being Jeffrey Tolliver's old office.

He opened his briefcase and set out his files. Finally, the

overhead lights flickered on. Will saw Marla through the glass in the wall. She stared at him, mouth open. With her tight bun and dirty glasses, she looked like one of those beady old ladies from a Gary Larson comic strip. Will plastered a smile on his face, tossed her a wave. Marla gripped the handle of the carafe so hard he could almost feel her desire to smash the glass into his face.

Will reached into his pocket and found his digital recorder. Every cop in the world kept a spiral notebook in which to record details of their investigations. Will did not have that luxury, but he'd learned to compensate.

He checked the window for Marla before putting the recorder to his ear and pressing play. The volume was low, and he heard Faith's voice reading Tommy Braham's confession. Will had not wasted the entire night worrying about his schoolgirl crush on Sara Linton. He'd prepared himself for the day by reading every single word in the reports and listening to Tommy Braham's confession over and over again until he had memorized almost every word. He listened to the whole thing again in the office, the cadence of Faith's voice so familiar that he could have spoken along with her.

Her tone was dispassionate, offering no inflection. ' "I was in Allison's apartment. This was last night. I don't know what time. Pippy, my dog, was sick. It was after I took her to the doctor. Allison said she would have sex with me. We started to have sex. She changed her mind. I got mad. I had a knife on me. I stabbed her once in the neck. I took the extra chain and lock and drove her to the lake. I wrote the note so people would think she had killed herself. Allison was sad. I thought that would be reason enough." '

There were murmurs in the squad room. Will glanced up to find a couple of uniformed cops staring at him in disbelief. One of them started toward the office, probably to confront him, but his partner stopped him.

Will leaned back in the chair, hearing the squeak again. He took out his cell phone and called Faith. She picked up on the fourth ring. Her hello was more like a grunt.

'Did I wake you up?'

'It's seven-thirty in the morning. Of course you woke me up.'

'I can call back.'

'Just gimme a minute.' He heard her moving around. She yawned so loudly that Will felt his own jaw twitching to open. 'I pulled up some info on Lena Adams.'

'And?'

She yawned again. 'Let me get to my laptop.'

Will couldn't stop his own yawn. 'I'm sorry I got you out of bed.'

'You've got me until four this afternoon. That's when I meet my doctor at the hospital.'

Will started talking so she wouldn't explain the procedure again. 'That's great, Faith. I guess your mom is driving you. She must be excited. What about your brother? Have you called him?'

'You can shut up now. I'm at my computer.' He heard keys being tapped. 'Salena Marie Adams,' Faith said, probably reading from the woman's personnel file. 'Detective first grade. Thirty-five years old. Five-four and a hundred and twenty pounds.' Faith mumbled a curse. 'God, that's enough to make me hate her right there.'

'What about her history?'

'She was raped.'

Will was taken aback by her abruptness. He'd been expecting date of birth, maybe some commendations. Sara had said that she suspected Lena had been raped by her ex-boyfriend, but he'd been under the impression no formal charges had been filed. He asked Faith, 'How do you know that?'

'The case came up when I cross-referenced her file. You really should Google more.'

'When did it happen?'

'Ten years ago.' He heard her fingers pecking the keyboard. 'Her file is pretty clean. She's worked some interesting cases. You remember that south Georgia pedophile ring awhile back? She and Tolliver broke it open.'

'Does she have any black marks?'

'Small-town forces don't air their dirty laundry on paper,' Faith reminded him. 'She took some time off the job six years ago. She worked security at the college less than a year, then went back on the job. That's all I've got on her. Have you found anything else?'

'I had an interesting conversation with the man who runs the diner this morning.'

'What did he say?'

'Not a whole lot. Allison was a good kid. Hard worker. He didn't know much about her personal life.'

'Do you think he killed her?'

'He's sixty-something years old with a fake leg.'

'A real fake leg?'

Will thought about Lionel knocking on the prosthesis, the hollow sound. 'I'll see if I can confirm it, but he was putting on quite an act if the leg is real.'

'You never know with those small towns. Ed Gein was a babysitter.'

Faith was never one to miss an opportunity to compare a kindly old man to one of the twentieth century's most notorious serial killers.

She said, 'Spooner's background check didn't offer much, either. She's got a bank account with eighteen dollars and change. She must be a cash-and-carry gal. The only checks she's written in the last six months are to the college and the campus bookstore. The statements are delivered to the Taylor Drive address. Other than that, she's got no credit cards. No utilities in her name. No credit history. No cell phone on record. No car.'

'The old guy at the diner says she drove a Dodge Daytona with Alabama plates.'

'It must be registered in someone else's name. Do you think the locals know about it?'

'I don't know. My source also says that Allison had a pink book bag she kept in the car when she was working.'

'Hold on a second.' Faith was obviously doing something on her computer. 'All right, I'm not finding any BOLOs for the car coming out of Grant County or any towns in the vicinity.' If Frank Wallace knew about Allison's car, he would have posted a 'be on the lookout' to all neighboring counties.

Will said, 'Maybe they already know where the car is but they don't want me to find it.'

'I'm posting a BOLO around the state right now. Your chief will have to tell his boys to look for it during their briefing this morning.'

'It's an old car. Allison's lived here a couple of years without changing the plates.'

'College town. Wouldn't be odd to have cars with out-of-state tags. The only reason not to register a car is because it's not insured,' Faith pointed out. 'I'd buy that. This girl was living on the margins. She barely made a blip on the radar.'

Will saw that the squad room was filling up. The crowd of cops had gotten bigger. A more fearful man might call them a growing mob. They kept stealing looks at Will. Marla was pouring them coffee, glaring at him over her shoulder. And then, as if on cue, they all looked toward the front door. Will wondered if Frank Wallace had deigned to make an appearance, but quickly saw this was not the case. A woman with olive skin and curly, shoulder-length brown hair joined the group. She was the smallest in the bunch, but they parted for her like the Red Sea.

Will told Faith, 'I think Detective Adams has decided to grace us with her presence.'

'How does she look?'

Lena had spotted him. Her eyes burned with hatred.

He said, 'She looks like she wants to rip out my throat with her teeth.'

'Be careful. You know you have a weakness for bitchy, spiteful women.'

Will didn't bother to argue. Lena Adams had the same color skin and hair as Angie, though she was obviously of Latin descent, whereas Angie's origins were vaguely Mediterranean. Lena was shorter, more athletic. There was none of Angie's womanliness about her – Lena was too cop for that – but she was an attractive woman. She also seemed to share Angie's talent for stirring things up. Several of the cops were staring at Will with open hostility now. It wouldn't be long before someone grabbed a pitchfork.

Faith asked, 'What's this email from you?' She answered her own question. 'Julie Smith. All right, I'll see if I can trace the number. The warrant for Tommy Braham's phone records shouldn't be a problem considering he's dead, but I may need an official cause of death before we get access.'

Will kept his eyes on Lena. She was saying something to the group. Probably telling them to check their weapons. 'Can you fudge that a little? Julie Smith told Sara that Tommy texted her from jail. The transcript might help find out who she is. Maybe Amanda can call in some favors.'

'Oh, great. Just who I want to talk to first thing in the morning.'

'Can you get her to rush through a search warrant for the garage, too? I want to show the locals what proper procedure looks like.'

'I'm sure she'll fall over herself trying to accommodate your requests.' Faith gave a heavy groan. 'Anything else you want me to ask her?'

'Tell her I want my testicles back.'

'They're probably already at the bronzer.'

Lena took off her jacket and threw it on a desk. 'I need to go.' Will hung up the phone just as the detective stomped toward the office.

Will stood up. He gave one of his winning smiles. 'You must be Detective Adams. I'm so glad to finally meet you.'

She stared at the hand he offered. He thought for a minute she might rip it off.

'Is there something wrong, Detective?'

She was obviously so angry she could barely speak. 'This office—'

'I hope you don't mind,' Will interrupted. 'It was empty, and I want to make sure I stay out of your way.' His hand was still extended between them. 'We're not to that point yet where you can't shake my hand. Are we, Detective?'

'We passed that point the minute you sat behind that desk.'

Will dropped his hand. 'I was expecting Chief Wallace.'

'Interim Chief,' she corrected, just as raw as Sara on the subject. 'Frank's at the hospital with Brad.'

'I heard Detective Stephens had a rough night, but he seems all right this morning.'

She didn't answer him, which was just as well. Her accent was full of south Georgia twang, and anger made her words blend like cake batter.

Will indicated the chair. 'Please have a seat.'

'I'll stand.'

'Hope you don't mind if I sit.' The chair squeaked as he settled back in it. Will steepled his fingers together. He noticed that a pen was clipped to Lena's breast pocket. It was silver, a Cross just like the one Larry Knox had clipped to his shirt last night. Will glanced at the group of officers who were milling around the coffee machine. They all had pens clipped to their chest pockets, too.

Will smiled. 'I'm sure your chief already told you why I'm here.'

He saw her eye twitch. 'Tommy.'

'Right, Tommy Braham, and by extension, Allison Spooner. I hope we can wrap this up quickly. I'm sure we'd all rather have this off our plate going into Thanksgiving.'

'This good-guy bullshit isn't really going to work with me.'

'We both have badges, Detective. Don't you think you should try to cooperate so we can get to the truth of this matter?'

'You know what I think?' She crossed her arms high on her chest. 'I think you're down here where you don't belong, sleeping in places you have no right, and trying to get a lot of good people into trouble for shit that's beyond their control.'

There was a loud knock at the open door. Marla Simms stood ramrod straight, a medium-sized cardboard box gripped between her hands. She walked to the desk and dropped the box with a thud in front of Will.

'Thank you,' he told her retreating back. 'Mrs. Simms?' She didn't turn, but she stopped. 'If you don't mind, I need the audiotape of the 911 call reporting Allison Spooner's alleged suicide.'

She left without acknowledging the request.

Will looked over the top of the box, eyeing the contents. There were several plastic evidence bags, obviously taken from the scene of Allison Spooner's death. A pair of white sneakers was in one. Streaks of mud went up the sides and stuck into the treads.

The ring and watch mentioned in Lena's report were in the other bag. He studied the ring, which was cheap, the sort of thing you gave a girl when you were fifteen and spending fifty dollars on a piece of jewelry from the locked display at Walgreens was a big deal.

He held up the ring. 'I gave my wife one of these when we were kids.'

Lena's nasty look resembled the same one Angie had shown Will when he'd given her the ring.

He pulled another bag out of the box. There was a

closed wallet inside. Will managed to pry it open through the plastic. He found a photo of an older woman beside a young girl and another photograph of an orange cat. There were some bills in the cash compartment. Allison Spooner's student ID and driver's license were tucked in the back sleeves.

Will looked at the girl's picture. Faith had guessed right. Allison was very pretty. She also looked younger than her given age. Maybe it was her size. She seemed delicate, almost fragile. He flipped back to the photograph of the older woman, realizing now that the girl beside her was Allison Spooner. The picture had obviously been taken a few years ago. Allison looked like a teenager.

He asked Lena, 'Is this all you found in the wallet?' He listed it out for her. 'Two photos, forty bucks, the license, and student ID?'

She was staring at the open wallet in his hands. 'Frank catalogued it.'

Not exactly an answer, but Will knew that he'd need to choose his battles. He saw there was one more evidence bag in the box. He guessed it contained the contents of Tommy Braham's pockets. 'Gum, thirty-eight cents, and a metal Monopoly game piece of a car.' He looked back up at Lena. 'He didn't have a wallet on him?'

'No.'

'Cell phone?'

'Is there one in the bag?'

Her combative answers were telling him more than she realized. Will asked, 'What about his clothes and shoes? Any blood on them? Any stains?'

'Per protocol for a suicide in custody, Frank sent them to the lab. Your lab.'

'The Central GBI lab in Dry Branch?'

She nodded.

'What about the sheath?'

She seemed confused.

'In Tommy's confession, he said he had a knife on him when he killed Allison. I imagine he had a sheath on his belt? A knife sheath?'

She shook her head. 'He probably got rid of it.'

'He doesn't mention in his confession what kind of knife he used.'

'No, he doesn't.'

'Did you find any knives in the house where Tommy lived?'

'We can't search his house without a warrant or permission from his father, who's the owner of the property.'

Well, at least she knew the law. That she was choosing to follow it now was a bit of a mystery. 'Are you assuming Tommy used the same knife to stab Detective Stephens that he used to kill Allison Spooner?'

Lena was silent for a few seconds. She had conducted enough interviews to recognize what a corner felt like when it was pressing against your back. 'I've found in my career that it's better not to make assumptions about what a suspect will and will not do.'

'That's a valuable lesson for any officer,' he allowed. 'Any reason why the Spooner evidence wasn't sent to Central?'

She hesitated again. 'I assume because the case is closed.'

'You're sure about that?'

'Tommy ran from the police. He stabbed a police officer. He confessed to the crime. He killed himself

216

because he couldn't take the guilt. I'm not sure how you do it in Atlanta, but down here we generally stop throwing money at an investigation once it's closed.'

Will rubbed the back of his neck. 'I really wish you'd sit down. This is going to take a while and I don't think I can keep looking up at you without getting a crick.'

'What's going to take a while?'

'Detective Adams, perhaps you don't comprehend the import of this investigation. I'm here to interview you about the death of a prisoner who was in your custody, in your jail, in your town. In addition to that, a young woman was murdered. A police officer was badly wounded. This isn't going to be a quick chat over coffee and doughnuts, not least of all because I've been advised not to take any food from y'all that isn't sealed in a container.' He smiled. She didn't smile back. 'Would you please sit down so we can talk to each other like rational people?' She still didn't move, and Will took it a step further. 'If you'd rather go to one of the interrogation rooms instead of being in your dead chief's office, then I'd be more than happy to accommodate you.'

Her jaw tightened. They had a long, drawn-out staring match that Will nearly lost. Lena was hard to look at. Her pain and exhaustion showed on every line of her face. Her eyes were swollen, the whites shot through with red. Her hand was resting on the chair in front of her, yet still she swayed, as if her knees wanted to give out.

Finally, she said, 'Yes.'

'Yes, what?'

'Yes, I think you're the enemy.' Still, she pulled out the chair and sat down.

'I appreciate your candor.'

'Whatever.' She kept opening and closing her fist. He saw two flesh-colored Band-Aids wrapped around the palm of her hand. Her fingers looked swollen.

He asked, 'That happen yesterday?'

She didn't answer.

Will took a red folder out of his briefcase and left it unopened on the desk. Lena glanced down nervously. 'Would you like a lawyer present?'

'Do I need one?'

'You should know better than to ask an investigator for legal advice, Detective. How about your union rep?'

She gave a short, sharp laugh. 'We don't have unions down here. We barely have uniforms.'

He should have remembered. 'Do I need to remind you of your Miranda rights?'

'No.'

'Should I mention that lying to a state investigator during the course of an active investigation is a felony that can result in fines and imprisonment up to five years?'

'Didn't you just do that?'

'I guess I did. Where was she stabbed?'

He'd caught her off guard. 'What?'

'Allison Spooner. Where was she stabbed?'

'Here.' She put her hand to the back of her neck, her fingers resting a few inches from the spine.

'Was that the only wound?'

She opened her mouth, then closed it. Finally, she answered, 'As you said, Frank noticed ligature marks around her wrist.'

'Did you notice them?'

'The body was in the water for a long time. I'm not sure what I saw except for the knife wound in the neck.'

The detail bothered him, mostly because it was the first point where Frank Wallace's story didn't dovetail with Lena's. 'Have you found Spooner's car?'

'She doesn't have one.'

'That strikes me as odd.'

'It's a college town. Kids walk everywhere or drive their scooters.' Lena shrugged. 'If they need to go somewhere, they can usually bum a ride.'

'Could Allison have a car without you knowing about it?'

'Not at the school. They'll tow you if you take up two spaces. They're really good about policing the campus. And, there aren't a lot of places around town to ditch a car, either. I can put out a BOLO at the morning briefing if you want, but it's a dead end. This isn't Atlanta. If people see abandoned cars, they call the police.'

Will studied Lena, trying to read any deceit. 'What about Allison's boss at the diner? Have you talked to him?'

'Lionel Harris. Frank said he talked to him last night. He doesn't know anything.'

Either Frank had lied or Lena was making things up as she went along.

Will asked, 'How does Mr. Harris look for the murder?'

'He's got one leg and he's older than Jesus.'

'I'll take that as an unlikely.' Will opened the red folder. The photocopy of Tommy Braham's confession was on top. He saw a flash of recognition in Lena's eyes. 'Take me through it.'

'Which part?'

He knew she was expecting him to get straight to the point – the stabbing, what went down outside the garage.

He went the opposite direction, hoping to throw her off. 'Let's start with you bringing Tommy Braham into the station and work our way forward. Did he say anything in the car?'

'No.'

Will hadn't yet seen the booking pictures or the crime scene photos Sara had taken of Tommy Braham in the cell, but he knew that a cop had been stabbed while two other able-bodied officers were at the scene. He hazarded a guess about what happened next. 'What condition was Tommy in at this time?'

She stared at him blankly.

'Did he fall down a couple of times during the arrest?'

Again, she took her time. 'You'll have to ask Frank about that. I was tending to Brad.'

'You saw Tommy in the car. What kind of state was he in?'

Lena pulled a spiral-bound notebook out of her back pocket. She slowly flipped to the pages she wanted. Will saw the paper was taped back into the notebook and assumed these were the originals Sara had photocopied last night.

Lena cleared her throat. 'I brought in the suspect, Thomas Adam Braham, at approximately eight-thirty yesterday morning.' Lena scrutinized him. 'You're not going to take notes?'

'Why, do you want to let me borrow your pen?'

Her composure cracked just a tiny bit, and Will saw what he had been looking for from the minute Lena walked into the room. No matter what she thought about Tommy Braham, she was upset about his death. Not upset because it might get her into trouble, but upset because he was a human being who had been in her care.

Will said, 'I've already read your notes, Detective. Tell me the parts that aren't on the pages.'

She started picking at the Band-Aid.

'Who did the death notifications?'

'I did.'

'On both Spooner and Braham?'

She nodded. 'Elba, where Allison's from, is a small town. The detective I talked to went to school with her. He says her mother died eight years ago. The father's unknown. There's an aunt, Sheila McGhee, but she's not home much. She works for a crew that's remodeling roach motels along the Panhandle. The detective's going to try to track her down. I left a message on her answering machine, but she won't hear it until she gets home or calls to check her messages.'

She was actually sounding like a detective now. Will asked, 'No cell phone?'

'Not that I can find.'

'Was there an address book in Allison's apartment?'

'We didn't have time to do a search.' Her tone became clipped again. 'A lot was going on yesterday. My partner was bleeding to death in the street.'

'I'd like to know when Ms. McGhee returns your call.'

She nodded.

'What about Tommy's relations?'

'There's just his dad, Gordon. I talked to him early this morning, told him what happened.'

'How did he take it?'

'No father wants to hear that his son's confessed to murder.'

221

'How did he take the suicide?'

'About how you'd expect.' Lena looked down at her notes, though Will could tell she was buying time to collect herself. 'Gordon's driving up from Florida right now. I don't know how long that'll take. Seven, maybe eight hours.'

Will wondered where Frank Wallace was in all of this, and why the hardest parts of the case had fallen to Lena. He asked, 'Did you know Allison Spooner?'

'Half the town did. She worked at the diner down the street.'

'Did *you* know her?'

'I never met her.'

'You don't go to the diner?'

'Why does that matter?' She wasn't looking for an answer. 'Tommy laid it all out. You've got his confession right in front of you. He said that he wanted to have sex with her. She didn't. So he killed her.'

'How long did it take for him to confess?'

'He dicked around for about an hour, then I got it out of him.'

'Did he offer an alibi? Initially, I mean.'

'He said he was at the vet. He's got this dog, Pippy. She swallowed a sock or something. Tommy took her to the emergency vet over on Conford. The office staff can't vouch for him being there the entire time.'

'Does he have a car?'

'A green Chevy Malibu. It's at the shop. Tommy said the starter's been acting up. He dropped the keys in the lockbox at Earnshaw's yesterday morning.'

Will hadn't been expecting that. 'Earnshaw?'

'Sara's uncle.'

'Is there security footage of the lot?'

'No, but I called the garage. The car is there.' She shrugged. 'Tommy could've left it there after he killed Allison.'

'Have you searched the car?'

'I planned on doing that today.' Her tone indicated that Will was the major obstacle standing between her and doing her job.

Will didn't back down. 'How did Tommy know Allison?'

'She rented space from his dad – a converted garage apartment.' Lena looked at her watch.

'What was Tommy like?'

'Stupid,' she told him. 'Slow in his thinking. I'm sure Sara's already told you all about it.'

'According to Dr. Linton, Tommy's IQ was around eighty. He wasn't bright, but he held down a job at the bowling alley. He was a good kid. Good except for the trouble he'd been in lately.'

'I'd call murder a bit more than trouble.'

'I was referring to the incident reports.'

She hid her surprise well, but he could see the flicker of a question in her eyes.

'There are three reports detailing altercations over the last month. Mrs. Simms was kind enough to provide them.' She remained silent, so he asked, 'You knew about them, right?'

Still, Lena didn't respond. Will slid the incident reports across the desk so she could see them.

She skimmed the summaries. 'Small problems. He obviously had a temper.'

'Who told you to arrest Tommy for Allison's murder?'

'Frank—' She looked like she wanted to take back the word. 'Frank and I discussed it. It was a joint decision.'

At least he knew what she looked like when she was lying. The bad news was that her lying face looked a lot like her honest one. 'When did you first hear there was a body in the lake?'

'Brad called me around three yesterday morning. I woke everybody else up, started the investigation.'

'Have you talked to any of Allison's teachers at school?'

'They're all off for Thanksgiving break. I've got phone numbers for them, but I haven't made any calls yet. Most of them are local. They're not going anywhere. I was going to track them down this morning, but . . .' She held out her arms, indicating the space between them.

'What else were you going to track down?' He listed out her plans so far. 'Talk to the teachers. Maybe talk to the office staff at the vet. Look at Tommy's car. Try to track down Allison's known associates. I guess you'd get that through the school, maybe Lionel Harris?'

She shrugged. 'Maybe.'

'Were you planning on talking to Tommy again? Had he lived, I mean.'

'Yes.'

'Why?'

'I wanted to get his confession on tape. He was a compelling witness against himself.'

'But everything else made sense to you – his motivations, stabbing her in the neck?'

'There were things I wanted to clear up. Obviously, I wanted to find the murder weapon. I assume it's in his garage somewhere. Or his car. He must have taken Allison to the lake. There would have been trace evidence.

Stop me if any of this reminds you of something you might have read in a textbook when you were in GBI school.'

'That's a good word to use for it – "textbook."' He pointed out, 'Seems like a lot of work for a case you considered closed. Isn't that what you told me a few minutes ago, that it was closed?'

She stared at him again. Will knew she was waiting for him to ask about the 911 call.

He said, 'You must be tired.'

'I'm fine.'

'You've had a pretty tough couple of days.' He indicated her field notes. 'You got Brad's call around three a.m. yesterday. Suspected suicide. You went to the lake. Found Spooner was dead, possibly murdered. Went to Spooner's house and your boss got hurt, your partner got stabbed. You arrested Tommy. Got his confession. I'm sure you were at the hospital all night.'

'What's your point?'

'Was Tommy a malicious person?'

She didn't equivocate. 'No.'

'Did he show any anger during your interrogation?'

She was silent again, gathering her thoughts. 'I don't think he planned to hurt Brad. But he *did* stab him. And he killed Allison, so . . .'

'So?'

She crossed her arms again. 'Look, we're just going in circles here. What happened to Tommy was bad, but he confessed to killing Allison Spooner. He stabbed my partner. Frank was hurt.'

Will carefully weighed her words. She obviously believed Tommy was guilty of killing Allison Spooner.

225

She got sketchier when she talked about Brad Stephens being stabbed and Frank Wallace getting cut.

Lena checked her watch again. 'Are we finished here?'

She was very good at this, but she couldn't keep it up forever. 'The lake is behind the station, right?'

'Right.'

'Between the college and Lover's Point.'

'Not exactly between.'

'Do you think I can borrow a jacket?'

'What?'

'A raincoat. Jacket. Whatever you have.' Will stood up from the desk. 'I'd like for us to go for a walk.'

The rain had turned unrelenting, dark clouds rolling across the sky, tossing down buckets of water that all seemed to fall directly on Will's head. He was wearing a police-issue jacket meant for a man with considerably more girth than Will carried. The sleeves hung down past his thumbs. The hood fell into his eyes. The reflective panels on the back and front slapped against him with every step.

Will had always had trouble finding clothes that fit, but usually the opposite was the problem: short cuffs, tight seams stretching against his shoulders. He had been expecting Lena to offer him one of her own coats as a sort of joke. Apparently, she had come up with a better idea. Will stared down at the stitching on the breast pocket as they made their way around the lake. The jacket belonged to Officer Carl Phillips.

He stuck his hands into the pockets as the wind picked up. He could feel some latex gloves, a measuring tape, a plastic pen, and a small flashlight. At least he hoped it was a small flashlight. Despite Lena's worst intentions, the jacket was nice, a North Face rip-off with tons of zippered pockets and enough insulation to keep the wind out. Will had the brand-name version back at home. He hadn't brought it because in Atlanta, cold weather never lasted more than a few days, and even then, the sun came up to burn off the chill. The thought of the jacket hanging in his closet gave him a longing to be back home that surprised him.

Lena stopped, turning back toward the police station. She raised her voice to be heard over the rain. 'The college is back there, past the station.'

Will guessed they had been walking for about fifteen minutes. He could barely make out a bunch of buildings resting in the curve of the lake just beyond the police station.

Lena said, 'There's no reason for Allison to walk this way.'

'Where's Lover's Point?'

She pointed in the opposite direction. 'That cove about a half mile away.'

Will followed the line of her finger to the indentation in the shoreline. The cove was smaller than he'd thought it would be. Or perhaps the distance made it seem that way. Large boulders were scattered along the shore. He imagined people built campfires when the weather was better. It looked like the kind of place a family might pull up a boat to for a long picnic.

'Are we just going to stand here?' Lena had her hands deep in her pockets, head down against the wind. Will didn't need ESP to figure out she didn't want to be out here in the pouring rain. It was so cold by the water that he had to fight to keep his teeth from chattering.

He asked, 'Where are the roads again?'

She gave him a look that said she wasn't going to play this game much longer. 'There.' She pointed into the distance. 'That's the fire road. It hasn't been used in years. We checked it when we pulled the body out of the lake. Nothing's there.'

'That's the only egress from here to Lover's Point, right?'

'Like I showed you on the map back at the station.'

Will had never been good with maps. 'That place over there.' He pointed to an area just past the cove. 'That's the second road that people normally use to get to the cove, right?'

'Empty, like I told you. We checked it, all right? We're not total morons. We checked for cars. We checked for tire tracks, footprints. We checked both roads and neither one of them showed any signs of use.'

Will tried to get his bearings. The sun wasn't doing much to help light the way. The sky was so dark that it could've been nighttime instead of smack in the middle of morning. 'Where's the residential area?'

She pointed across the lake. 'That's where Sara lives. Her parents. Over here' – she pointed farther along – 'all of this shoreline, including where we're standing, belongs to the State Forestry Division.'

'Do people take their boats out?'

'There's a dock at the campus for the rowing teams. A lot of the homeowners go boating during the summer. No one would be stupid enough to be out here in this rain.'

'Except us.' Will put as much cheer into his voice as he could muster. 'Let's keep going.'

She trudged along ahead of him. Will could see her

sneakers were soaked. The running shoes he had found in the back of his car weren't faring much better. Allison's shoes, or at least the ones found near her body, were dirty, but not caked in mud. If she had walked along the shore, the terrain had been a lot harder than the red Georgia clay that was sliding out from under his feet.

Will had checked the weekly weather report last night on his computer. Temperatures had been lower the morning Allison was found, but the same rain they were seeing now had been pounding down the night before. It was a good time to kill somebody. Trace evidence on the shore would be lost. The cold water would make guessing when the murder occurred next to impossible. Except for the 911 caller, no one would have known there was a body in the lake.

Lena slipped in the mud. Will reached out, catching her before she fell into the water. She was so light that he could almost pick her up with one hand.

'Christ.' She braced her hand against a tree. She was breathing hard. He realized she had been walking fast to keep a few paces between them.

Will asked, 'Are you okay?'

She pushed away from the tree, a look of determination on her face. Will watched her feet as she picked her way across the large roots and fallen branches that riddled the shoreline. He had no way of knowing whether or not Allison had made her way to Lover's Point along this same route. His goal was to get Lena Adams out of the station, out of her element, so that she would talk to him. Between the pounding rain and the rough going, he was thinking that it might be wise to set the bar lower. For instance, he could aim not to let them both freeze to death.

Lena was so certain that Tommy Braham had killed Allison Spooner – just as certain as Sara was that Tommy had not. Will felt caught in the middle, and was mindful that it would be wrong to let either woman influence his thinking. He supposed for Lena the question of Tommy's innocence carried with it a lot more guilt than she wanted to shoulder. To believe otherwise would mean that the kid had killed himself for nothing. That she had given him the means – and the motivation – to take his life. For Sara's part, admitting Tommy was a murderer would mean admitting that Lena wasn't as ruthless as she wanted to believe.

Will didn't feel the rain let up so much as hear it. The constant tapping of water against leaves died down to a gentle whisper. He heard a bird, a bunch of crickets. Up ahead, a large tree blocked the path. Thick roots jutted into the air, earth dripping from the tendrils. Lena lifted herself up and over. Will followed her, looking around, trying to get his bearings again. They were near the fire road. At least he thought they were.

'There,' she said, pointing to a pile of stacked logs. 'That's the end of the road.' She took off her hood. Will followed suit. Two strips of earth about the width of the front end of a car lined the road for about ten feet, then gave way to thick forest. He understood why Lena was convinced the road was untraveled. You'd need a bulldozer to get through.

She told him, 'The road on the other side is the one most people use, but it's about a hundred yards west of the cove. I told you, we had to clear out a path to get the emergency vehicles back here.'

Will guessed they hadn't been looking for tire tracks on

the way to a suicide. They had probably destroyed any evidence of another car out by the cove. He asked, 'If Allison didn't have a car, how did she get here?'

Lena stared at him. 'Tommy brought her here.'

'But you just said you checked for cars.'

'He had a scooter. He could've used that.'

Will agreed, but he couldn't see Tommy balancing a dead body on the handlebars while he maneuvered his way through the forest. 'Where was she before Tommy killed her?'

'Home, waiting to be killed.' She stamped her feet to fight the cold. 'All right. The school library closed at noon on Sunday. She could've been there.'

'What about work?'

'The diner's closed on Sunday.'

'Would Allison go this way to get home?'

Lena shook her head. 'She would go through the woods across from the station. She'd be home in ten minutes.'

At least she was being honest about that. Lionel Harris had told Will the same thing. He asked, 'So, why was Allison here?'

Lena dug her hands into her pockets as the breeze picked up.

'Detective?'

'She was here because Tommy brought her here.' She started walking again, trudging through the mud. Her shoes made a sucking sound with every step.

Will's stride was twice Lena's. He caught up with her easily. 'Let's profile our killer.'

She snorted a laugh. 'You believe in that shit?'

'Not really, but we've got some time on our hands.'

'This is stupid.' She slipped again, but caught herself. 'Are you really going to make me walk all the way to the cove?'

If Will could make her do anything, it would be for her to tell the truth. That didn't seem to be an option, so he said, 'Let's do the profile.'

'Sure,' she muttered, pushing forward. 'He's a retarded kid between the ages of nineteen and nineteen and a half who drives a green Chevy Malibu and lives with his father.'

'Let's take Tommy out of this for just a minute.'

She gave him a wary look.

Will asked, 'What took place?'

Lena picked her way around another fallen tree.

'What took place?' he repeated.

She let her reluctance hang on every word. 'You mean the murder?'

'Right. What happened?'

'Allison Spooner was stabbed in the neck Sunday night or early Monday morning.'

'Was it messy?'

She shrugged, but then said, 'Probably. There's all kinds of stuff in the neck. Arteries and veins. There would've been a lot of blood, which explains why Tommy had a bucket and sponge at Allison's apartment. He was trying to clean up the mess.'

'Why did it happen?'

She laughed, incredulous. 'This is profiling?'

Will's version, at least. He didn't share Lena's certainty. She was so sure she was right about Tommy Braham that she hadn't considered the possibility that a savage killer might be sharpening his knife for the next victim. 'Why

232

did the killer decide to kill? Anger? Opportunity? Money?'

'He killed her because she wouldn't have sex with him. Did you actually read his confession?'

'I thought we were going to take Tommy out of this.' She shook her head, and Will tried again, 'Just humor me, Detective. Let's say there's some mystery killer out there who wanted Allison dead. Other than Tommy Braham.'

'That's quite a fantasy considering he admitted to doing it.'

He took her elbow to help her over a large puddle. 'Did the murderer bring the weapon to the scene?'

Lena seemed to consider the question. 'Maybe. He also had the cinder blocks, the chain, and lock.'

Will assumed the blocks and chain had been planted at the scene ahead of time, but now didn't seem like a good time to bring up the theory. 'So, this was premeditated.'

'Or, these were things lying around his house.' She added, 'On Taylor Drive.'

Will didn't rise to the bait. If Allison was killed at the lake rather than the garage, then Lena's whole theory about Tommy's guilt started to break down. He asked, 'Was the killer angry?'

'The wound in her neck is pretty violent.'

'But not furious. That's controlled. Deliberate.'

'He probably freaked out when he got a mouthful of blood back in his face.' She jumped over a puddle. 'What else?'

'Let's look at what we know: Our killer is organized. Not opportunistic. Has good knowledge of the area. He knows Allison. He drives a car.'

She nodded. 'I'd buy that.'

'Go over the sequence of events.'

Lena stopped. They were about thirty feet away from the cove. 'All right. Tommy, or your mystery guy, kills Allison, brings her here.' She squinted her eyes. 'Probably he lays her down on the shore. He wraps the chains around her waist, ties her to the cinder blocks, then tosses her into the water.'

'Tosses her how?'

Lena stared at the cove. Will could almost hear her mind working. 'He would have to carry her. She was found about fifteen feet out in the water, where the bottom drops off. The cinder blocks were heavy. Maybe he would've floated her out to the water, then bolted the chain and blocks around her. That makes more sense. There's no way she could have been thrown in the water from the shore and ended up there.'

Will kept leading her along. 'So, the killer walks her into the water, then chains her down. It was cold that night.'

'He'd need waders or something. He'd have to get back into his car to drive away. What's the point of disposing of the body in water if you're going to take the lake with you back into the car?'

'Being in the water wouldn't necessarily be a bad idea.'

'Right. He would've been covered in blood.'

'Our killer didn't want the body found. He walked her out to the deep end so she'd stay there. He weighted her down.'

Lena was silent again, but he knew she was too smart not to be thinking the same thing he was.

Will said it for her. '*Someone* wanted the body found. There was the call to 911.'

'Maybe one of Tommy's neighbors saw something.'

'And followed him to the lake, watched him dump the body, and . . .'

'You think he had an accomplice?'

'What do you think?'

'I think at best we've got a material witness. We'll need to talk to her at some point, but why does this matter when the guy who admitted to killing Allison is dead?'

Will looked around. They were standing in mud up to their ankles. The earth was darker here, turning almost black as it dipped into the water. Allison's shoes had black mud on them, not red clay.

Will asked, 'Did Tommy mention whether or not Allison had a boyfriend?'

'Don't you think we'd be talking to him right now if he had?'

Will saw a fat squirrel scamper up a tree, tail twitching. Several twigs had been snapped in two. The ground covering was bent down. He heard a car in the distance. 'Is there a road close by?'

'About a mile out.' She pointed in the direction of the noise. 'There's a divided highway.'

'Any residences?'

Lena pressed her lips together. She wouldn't look at him.

'Detective?'

She stared down at the ground, knocked some mud off her shoe. 'Tommy lived out that way.'

'So did Allison Spooner.' Will glanced back at the lake. The water was churning. The wind coming off the water was like ice against his skin. 'Have you ever heard the name Julie Smith?'

Lena shook her head. 'Who is she?'

235

'Did Tommy mention any friends? Either his or Allison's?'

'That wasn't the focus of the interview.' Her tone was terse. 'I was trying to get him to confess to murder, not give me his life story.'

Will kept his eyes on the lake. He was looking at this the wrong way. Their killer was smart. He knew that water would get rid of trace evidence. He knew to walk the body into the deeper part of the lake. He had probably lured Allison out here after careful deliberation. The wet terrain, the mud and underbrush, all would serve to help cover his tracks.

Will rolled up the legs of his jeans. His shoes were already soaked, so he didn't bother to take them off before walking into the lake. The cold water sloshed into his sneakers.

'What are you doing?'

He went out a few feet and scanned the shoreline, studying the trees, the underbrush.

Lena had her hands on her hips. 'Are you crazy? You're going to get hypothermia.'

Will studied each tree, each branch, each section of weeds and moss. His feet were completely numb by the time he found what he was looking for. He walked toward a large oak that was leaning away from the shore. Its knotty roots coiled into the lake like an open fist. At first, Will had thought he was seeing a shadow on the bark, but then he remembered you had to actually have sun or some other source of light to cast a shadow.

Will stood in front of the tree, his shoes sinking into the silt at the bottom of the water. The tree was deciduous, its bony canopy reaching up at least a hundred feet overhead.

The trunk was about three feet around and bowed away from the water. Will wasn't an arborist, but there were enough oaks around Atlanta so that he knew their red-brown furrows of bark turned the color of charcoal as the tree aged. The scaly bark had absorbed the rain like a sponge, but there was something else Will had noticed from his vantage point in the water. He scraped at a small section of bark with his fingernails. The wood left a wet, rust-colored residue. He rolled the grit between his fingers, squeezing out the moisture.

Blood really was thicker than water.

'What is it?' Lena asked. She kept her hands in her pockets as she leaned out into the water.

Will remembered the flashlight in his jacket pocket. 'Look.' He traced the light along a dark stain that sprayed up the trunk. He thought about what Sara had said about Allison's injury, that there would be a high-velocity spray, like a hose turned on full blast. Four to five pints of blood. That was over half a gallon.

Will said, 'She must have been facedown on the ground, just shy of the water. Her blood spattered up and back in an arc. You can see the dispersement is thicker here at the base of the tree, closer to her neck. Then it starts to dissipate at the top.'

'That's not—' Lena stopped. She saw it now. He could see from her shocked expression.

Will glanced up at the sky. The clouds were letting loose a few drops at a time. They hadn't been given much of a reprieve. It didn't matter. Short of scrubbing the bark, there was no way to completely clean the tree. The wood had absorbed the mark of death the same way it would absorb smoke from a fire.

Will asked, 'You still think our murderer is a nineteen-year-old boy who lives with his father?'

The wind whipped off the lake as Lena stared at the tree. Tears came into her eyes. Her voice shook. 'He confessed.'

Will quoted Tommy's words back to her. ' "I got mad. I had a knife on me. I stabbed her once in the neck." ' He asked, 'Did you find blood in the garage?'

'Yes.' She wiped her eyes with the heel of her hand. 'He was cleaning it up when we got there. I saw a bucket, and there was . . .' Her voice trailed off. 'There was blood on the floor. I saw it.'

Will rolled down the legs of his jeans. His shoes were sinking into the mud at the base of the tree. He saw there was a new color mixed in with the soil, a deep rust that soaked into the mesh on the toe of his sneaker.

Lena saw it, too. She fell to her knees. She stuck her fingers deep into the ground and grabbed a fistful of earth. The soil was soaked, but not just with rainwater. She let the dirt fall back to the ground. Her hand was dark red, streaked with Allison Spooner's blood.

TEN

Lena pressed a wet paper towel to her neck. She was sitting with her back against the stall of the locker room toilet. A patrolman had tried to come in while she was dry-heaving. He'd left without saying a word.

She'd never had a strong stomach. Her uncle Hank used to say that Lena didn't have the guts for the kind of life she was living. He wouldn't have taken any pleasure in seeing that he was right.

'Oh, God,' she whispered, as close to a prayer as she'd come in a long while. What had that stupid kid gotten himself into? What else had she missed?

She closed her eyes. Nothing made sense right now. Nothing was fitting together the same way it had yesterday morning.

He did it. Lena knew Tommy had killed Allison. People didn't confess to murder unless they were guilty. Even without that, less than fifteen minutes after they pulled the girl out of the lake, they had found Tommy in Allison's apartment going through her things. Wearing a black ski mask. He ran when they confronted him. He stabbed Brad, even if it was with a letter opener. Lena had seen him stab Brad with her own eyes. She had listened to Tommy's confession. She had watched him write down everything in his own stupid words. And he had killed himself. The guilt had gotten to him and he had sliced open his wrists because he knew what he had done to Allison was wrong.

So why was Lena doubting herself?

Suspects lied all the time. They never wanted to confess to all the horrors they'd committed. They split hairs. They admitted to rape but not murder. They admitted to punching but not beating, stabbing but not killing. Was it as simple as that? Had Tommy lied about killing Allison in the garage because he'd wanted to make the crime seem more understandable, more spur of the moment?

Lena pressed her head against the wall.

That stupid profile Will Trent came up with kept coming back to her. Cold. Calculated. Deliberate. That wasn't Tommy. He wasn't smart enough to think of all the variables. He would've had to plan ahead, get the cinder blocks and chains ready, carry them out to the lake ahead of time. Even if Tommy got the blocks after the fact, he would've had to anticipate the blood, and plan on the rain covering his tracks.

All that blood. The ground was soaked in it.

Lena scrambled to her knees and held her head over the toilet. Her stomach clenched, but nothing was left to come up. She sat back on her heels, staring at the back of the tank. The cool white porcelain stared back. This was her stall, and only her stall. This toilet was the one piece of ground she had managed to stake out solely for herself in the unisex locker room. The urinals were stained like old-lady teeth. The other two stalls were disgusting. They reeked of excrement no matter how many times they were cleaned. This morning, it didn't seem to stop there. The whole place reeked of shit. And it was all coming from the top down.

Lena wiped her mouth with the paper towel. Her hand was throbbing where she'd been shot. She was probably getting an infection. The skin felt hot down to her wrist. She squeezed her eyes shut. She wanted to be away from here. She wanted to be back in bed with Jared. She wanted to go back to yesterday and shake Tommy Braham until he told her the truth about what really happened. Why was he in Allison's apartment? Why was he going through her things? Why was he wearing the ski mask? Why did he run? And why, in God's name, did he kill himself?

'Lena?' Marla Simms's creaky voice was just above a whisper. 'Can I have a minute?'

Lena pressed herself up to standing. It was not lost on her that the only spot she could call her own in this entire godforsaken place was the toilet.

Marla stood with a folded sheet of paper in her hands. 'You all right?'

'No,' she said, because there was no use lying. She need only glance in the mirror to see the truth. Her hair was disheveled. Her face was red and blotchy. She was punch-drunk with lack of sleep and her nerves were so raw that she felt like she was vibrating even standing dead still.

'Agent Trent wanted this.' Marla held out the sheet of paper between her fingers, giving Lena a meaningful look, as if they were two spies passing a briefcase in front of the Kremlin. 'He didn't see it last night.'

Lena had to tug the sheet before Marla would release it. She recognized her own handwriting. The copied page was from her notebook. The transcript she had made of the 911 call. She tried to pick out the words but her eyes blurred. 'I thought he asked for the tape?'

'If he wants more than this, then he's going to have to

drive down to Eaton to get it.' She tucked her hands into her wide hips. 'And you can tell him from me that I'm not his personal secretary. I don't know who he thinks he is, ordering people around.'

He was the man who was going to shut down this force if they didn't do everything he said. 'Have you talked to Frank this morning?'

'I'm guessing he came by last night. My files were a mess when I got here.'

Lena already knew Frank had stolen Tommy's phone and taken the photograph from Allison's wallet, but this new information sent a chill straight to her chest. 'Which files?'

'All of them. I don't know what he was looking for, but I hope he found it.'

'You gave Trent those incident reports.'

'What of it?'

'Why?'

'No one wants to speak ill of the dead, but I'll come on out and say it to whoever asks. Tommy wasn't acting right lately. He was getting into trouble, yelling at people, threatening them. Don't get me wrong. He was a good boy when he was little. Had those precious little blond curls and pretty blue eyes. That's what Sara's remembering. But she doesn't know what he was like lately. I think something just clicked in his head. Maybe it was there all along and we just didn't notice. Didn't want to notice.' Marla shook her head in a tight half-circle. 'This is just a mess. A grade-A, certified pile of doo.'

Lena focused on Marla for the first time. The old woman wasn't one of her biggest fans. At best, she managed a nod for Lena when she walked through the door in the morning. Most times, she never bothered to look up from her desk. 'Why are you talking to me? You never talk to me.'

Marla bristled. 'Excuse me for trying to help.' She turned on her heel and stomped out.

Lena watched the door slowly close on its hinges. The room felt small, claustrophobic. She couldn't stay here all day, but her instinct to hide from Will Trent was hard to overcome. Larry Knox had told Frank that Will was a suit, not a cop. Lena's first impression had been the same. With his cashmere sweater and metrosexual haircut, Will looked like he'd be more at home behind a desk, clocking out at five and going home to the wife and kids. The old Lena would have dismissed him as a fraud, not on her level and not deserving of the badge.

That old Lena had been burned so many times by her snap judgments that she'd practically self-immolated. Now, she could look past her knee-jerk reaction and see the truth. Will had been sent down by a deputy director who was a heartbeat away from the top job. Lena had met Amanda Wagner many years ago. She was a tough old bitch. There was no way Amanda would've sent her second string down here, especially at the request of Sara Linton. Will was probably one of the best investigators on her team. He had to be. In less than two hours, he had shattered Lena's case against Tommy Braham into tiny pieces.

And now she had to go back out there and face him again.

Lena's feet still ached from the long trek through the forest. Her shoes were soaking wet. She went to her locker. The combination left her mind as soon as she turned the dial. She pressed her forehead against the cool metal. Why was she still here? She couldn't keep this up with Will Trent. There were so many lies and half-truths dangling out there that she couldn't remember them all. He kept laying traps, and with each one, she felt herself getting closer and closer to falling in. She should go home before she said too much. If Trent wanted to stop her, he would have to do it with handcuffs.

The combination came into her head. Lena spun the dial, opening the locker. She looked at her rain jacket, her toiletries, the various crap she'd collected over the years. There was nothing here she wanted except the extra pair of sneakers she kept in the bottom. She started to close the locker but stopped at the last minute. Inside a box of tampons was a picture of Jared that had been taken three years ago. He was standing outside Sanford Stadium at the University of Georgia. The place was packed. Georgia was playing LSU. There was a crowd of students around him, but he was the only one looking back at the camera. Looking back at Lena.

This picture was the moment that she had fallen in love with him – outside that noisy stadium, surrounded by drunken strangers. Lena had actually managed to capture on film that exact moment when everything in her life had changed. Who would be around to capture it when it all changed back?

Probably the booking officer who took her mugshot.

The door popped open. Four patrolmen came in, so lost in conversation that they barely acknowledged Lena. She tucked Jared's picture into her back pocket. Her socks were soaking wet, but she slid on her spare sneakers anyway. She just wanted to get out of here. She would walk through the squad room, right past Will Trent, get into her car and go home to Jared.

Lena would start packing tonight. She'd be one of those people who left her house key in the mailbox for the bank. Her car was in good shape. She had enough in savings to last her three months, four if Jared didn't expect her to help out with rent. She would move in with him and try to get over this, try to find a way to live her life without being a cop.

If she wasn't in jail for obstructing an investigation. If she wasn't convicted of negligence. If Gordon Braham didn't sue her into the ground. If Frank didn't fill Jared's ear with poison. Poison Jared would believe, because the great thing about lying was people believed it so long as the lie was close enough to the truth.

Lena slammed the locker closed, pressing her hand against the cool metal.

One of the patrolmen said, 'You let that GBI asshole slip and hit his head, we're not going to shed any tears.'

They were all suiting up, pulling on their heavy rain gear. Will had taken photographs and samples from the bark and soil by the tree, but he had ordered a full-scale search of the woods. He wanted more photographs, drawings, diagrams. He wanted to make sure the force knew that they had made a mistake. That Lena had made a mistake.

'Fucking retard,' another cop said.

Lena didn't know if he meant Will or Tommy. Either way, she managed some false bravado. 'Wish he was a little smarter so he knew how stupid he was.'

They were all laughing when she left the locker room. Lena pulled on her jacket. She walked through the squad room with more swagger than she felt. She had to get her composure back. She had to steel herself against the next barrage of questions from Will Trent. The fewer answers she gave him, the better off she would be.

The paper Marla had given her was in her hand. Lena skimmed the words as she walked so she wouldn't have to talk to anybody. She stopped as she reached the front door. She read the transcript again. The words were in her handwriting, but the last few lines from the call were missing. The caller had mentioned that Allison had gotten into a fight with her boyfriend. Why was that part taken out?

She glanced at Marla behind the front desk. Marla stared back, one eyebrow raised above her glasses. She was either still pissed or sending Lena a message. It was hard to tell. Lena looked at the transcript again. The last part was gone, the cut clean so that you would never know it was missing. Had Marla taken a shot at tampering with police evidence? Frank had gone through her files last night. Why would he edit the transcript without telling Lena? Christ, she had her notebook in her back pocket with the original transcript. All Trent had to do was ask her to see it and Lena would be looking at an obstruction charge for tampering with evidence.

The front door opened before Lena could reach it. Will Trent had obviously grown impatient waiting outside.

'Detective,' he said by way of greeting. He'd changed back into his dress shoes and shed Carl Phillips's jacket. He looked as eager as she was reticent.

Lena handed him the paper. 'Marla told me to give you this. She said you'd have to track down the audio from Eaton yourself.'

Will called to Marla at the desk. 'Thank you, Mrs. Simms.' He took the paper from Lena's hand. His eyes scanned back and forth. 'You heard the call, right?' He looked up. 'You made the transcript from the audio?'

'They dictated it to me from the screen. The audiotapes are stored off-site. They're not hard to get.' Lena held her breath, praying that he would not ask her to track them down.

'Any idea who made the call?'

She shook her head. 'It was a woman's voice. The number was blocked and she wouldn't leave her details.'

'Did you make this copy for me?'

'No. Marla handed it to me.'

He pointed at a black dot on the page. 'You've got some gum on the glass in your copier.'

Lena wondered why the hell he was telling her this. Will Trent was like no cop she had ever seen. He had a habit of skirting around the real questions, making random comments or observations that seemed to lead nowhere until suddenly it was too late and she felt the noose tighten around her neck. He was playing chess and she was sucking at checkers.

Lena tried her own diversion. 'We should get out to the crime scene if you want to be back in time for the autopsies.'

'Weren't we just at the crime scene?'

'We don't know for a fact what happened. Tommy could've lied. That happens in Atlanta, right? Bad guys lie to the cops?'

'More often than I'd like.' He slipped the transcript into his briefcase. 'What time are the procedures supposed to start?'

'Frank said eleven-thirty.'

'This was when you talked to him last night?'

Lena tried to remember the answer she had given Will the first time he'd asked this question. She had talked to Frank twice. Both times he had drilled her on Tommy's confession. Both times he had renewed his threat to tear down her life if she didn't cover his drunk ass.

Lena cast out a nonanswer, hoping Will would bite. 'It's like I told you before.'

He held open the front door for her. 'Any idea why the press isn't all over this?'

'The press?' She would have laughed if she hadn't been standing up to her knees in shit. 'The paper's closed for the holiday. Thomas Ross always goes skiing this time of year.'

Will laughed good-naturedly. 'You gotta love small towns.' A cold wind made him have to put his shoulder into closing the glass door. He tucked his hands into his jeans pockets. The cuffs of his pants were still wet. 'Let's take your car.'

She felt uncomfortable having him in her Celica, so she nodded toward Frank's Town Car. Lena pulled her key chain from her pocket. The county was on a tight budget and they both were supposed to share the car.

She pressed the button to unlock the doors.

Will didn't get in. Instead, he scowled at the smell that wafted through the morning air. 'Smoker?'

'Frank,' she said. The stink was worse than usual. He must have chain-smoked the whole trip to and from Macon last night.

Will asked, 'This is Chief Wallace's car?'

She nodded.

'Where's Chief Wallace if this is his car?'

Lena managed to swallow the bile in her throat. 'He took a cruiser to the hospital.'

Will didn't comment, though she wondered if he'd made a mark in his book. Frank had taken the cruiser so he wouldn't get stopped along the way. Speeding during a nonemergency situation was illegal, but it was the sort of illegal cops danced around all the time.

Will asked, 'Can you drive a stick?'

It was her turn to scowl. Of course she could drive a stick.

Will said, 'Let's take my car.'

'Are you kidding me?' Lena had heard about the Porsche before she'd made it to the station this morning. The whole town was talking about it – what it must've cost, why a state investigator would be driving it, and, more important, that it was parked in front of the Linton house all night.

Will didn't wait to see if she followed as he walked toward the opposite end of the lot. He talked as he made his way to the car, his leather briefcase swinging gently at his side. 'I'm curious about Allison Spooner. You said she's from Alabama?'

'Yes.'

'And she's a student at Grant Tech?'

Lena was careful with her answer. 'She's registered at the school.'

Will turned to her. 'So, that means she's a student?'

'It means she's registered. We haven't talked to her teachers yet. We don't know if she was actively attending classes. We get a lot of calls from parents this time of year wondering why they're not getting report cards.'

He asked her again, 'Do you think Allison Spooner dropped out?'

She tried a new strategy. 'I think that I'm not going to tell you something unless I know it's the absolute truth.'

He gave one of his quick nods. 'Fair enough.'

Lena waited for another question, another insinuation. Will just kept walking, his mouth closed. If he thought this new technique was going to break her, he was dead wrong. Lena had been dealing with silent disapproval her entire life. She had made an art out of ignoring it.

She tucked her head down against the cold. Her mind kept going back to her earlier conversation with Will. She had been so furious about him being in Jeffrey's office that she hadn't really paid attention to what he was saying at first. But then he had pulled out Allison's wallet and she had seen that the third photograph was missing.

The picture showed Allison sitting beside a boy who had his arm around her waist. An older woman sat on her left, some distance between them. They were all on a bench outside the student center. Lena had stared at the photo long enough to remember the details. The boy was around Allison's age. He had been wearing the hood of his sweatshirt pulled down low on his head but she could tell he had brown hair and eyes. A smattering of a goatee was on his weak chin. He was chubby the way most of the guys at Grant Tech tended to be, from too many days spent in classrooms and nights wasted in front of video games.

The woman in the photograph was obviously from the poor part of town. She was in her forties, maybe older. Past a certain age, it was difficult to tell with hard-looking women. The good news was that they stopped aging. The bad news was that they already looked ninety. Every line on her face said she was a smoker. Her bleached-blonde hair was so dry it looked more like straw.

Also missing from evidence was Tommy's cell phone. Frank had handed it to Lena in the street. He'd found it in Tommy's back pocket when he frisked him before putting him into the back of the squad car. She had sealed the phone in a plastic bag, written out the details, and logged it into evidence.

And at some point last night, both the photo from Allison's wallet and Tommy's phone had gone missing.

There was only one person who could've hidden the evidence, and that was Frank. Marla said he'd gone through her files. He had probably doctored the 911 transcript, too. But why? Both the picture and the call brought up the possibility of Allison having a boyfriend. Maybe Frank was trying to track down the kid before Will Trent found him. Frank had told Lena that they both should stick to the truth, or at least a close version of it. Why was he going behind her back and looking for another suspect?

Lena wiped her eyes with her hand. The wind was cutting, making her nose run, her eyes water. She had to carve out ten, fifteen minutes alone so she could think this through. Will's presence made it impossible for her to do anything but worry about the next question that would come out of his mouth.

'Ready?' Will asked. They had reached the Porsche. The car was an older model than Lena thought. There was no remote to unlock the door. Will did the honors, then handed her the key.

Lena felt a new wave of nervousness wash over her. 'What if I crash this thing?'

'I'd really appreciate it if you didn't.' He reached in and tucked his briefcase behind the front seat.

Lena couldn't move. This felt like a trap but she couldn't see the reason.

'Is there a problem?' Will asked.

Lena gave in. She climbed into the bucket seat, which was more like a recliner. With her feet stretched toward the pedals, the back of her calves were only a few inches off the floorboard.

Will opened the passenger door. She asked, 'You don't have a car from the job?'

'My boss wanted me to get here as soon as possible.' He had to let the seat back before he got into the passenger's side of the car. 'It adjusts on the front,' he told Lena. She reached down and dragged herself closer to the steering wheel. Will's legs were about ten feet longer than hers. Lena was practically pressed into the steering wheel by the time her feet found the clutch and gas.

For his part, Will couldn't get his seat right. He pushed it to the end of the track, then cranked it down as low as it would go so his head wouldn't hit the roof. Finally, he folded himself into the car like a piece of origami. She waited for him to buckle in, chancing a look at him. He was fairly average except for his height. He was lean, but his shoulders were broad, muscled, like he spent a lot of time at the gym. His nose had obviously been broken at some point in his life. Faint scars were on his face, the sort of damage you got from fighting with your fists.

No, he definitely was not Amanda Wagner's second string.

'All right,' Will said, finally settling into the seat.

She reached toward the ignition, but there wasn't one.

'It's on the other side.'

She found the ignition on the left-hand side of the steering wheel.

Will explained, 'It's from Le Mans racing. So you can start the engine with one hand while you change the gears with the other.'

She was extremely right-handed and it took a few tries before she managed to get the key to turn. The engine roared to life. The seat vibrated underneath her. She could feel the clutch pushing back against the ball of her foot.

Will stopped her. 'Can you give her a few minutes to warm up?'

Lena took her foot off the pedal. She stared across the street. He'd parked on the far side of the lot, the nose of the car facing out. She had a clear view to the children's clinic across the way. Sara's clinic. She wondered if he had parked here on purpose. He seemed to be very deliberate about everything he did. Or maybe her paranoia was such that she couldn't watch his chest rise and fall without thinking it was part of some master plan to trip her up.

Will asked one of his random questions. 'What do you think about the 911 call?'

She told him the truth. 'It bothers me that it came from a blocked number.'

'She called in a fake suicide. Why?'

Lena shook her head. The caller was the last thing on her mind right now. 'Tommy might have talked to her. She could be a co-worker. An accomplice. A jealous girl-friend.'

'Tommy didn't strike me as a player.'

No, he hadn't. During the interrogation, Lena had asked him to be explicit because she wasn't sure he really knew what sex was.

Will asked, 'Did Tommy say anything about dating anyone?'

She shook her head.

'We can ask around. At the very least, the girl who called in the fake suicide knew something wasn't right. She was obviously laying down a foundation for Tommy's defense.'

Lena's head jerked around. 'How so?'

'The phone call. She said Allison got into a fight with her boyfriend. That's why she was worried she'd committed suicide. She didn't say anything about Tommy.'

Lena felt every ounce of blood in her body freeze. Her hand gripped the steering wheel. Frank's amended transcript didn't mention a boyfriend. Will must have already contacted the call center in Eaton. So why had he asked Marla for the audio?

To set a trap. And Lena had just fallen right into it.

Will's tone of voice was even. 'Obviously, we'll need to find the boyfriend. He'll probably be able to lead us to the caller. Did Allison have any photographs in her apartment? Love letters? A computer?'

Photographs. Did he know about the missing picture? Lena's throat felt so raw that she couldn't swallow. She shook her head.

Will took his briefcase from behind the seat. He snapped open the locks. She could hear a high-pitched alarm in her ears. Her chest was tight. Her vision blurred. She wondered if this was what a panic attack felt like.

'Hmm,' Will mumbled, rifling through the case. 'My

reading glasses aren't in here.' He held out the transcript. 'Do you mind?'

Lena's heart shook against her rib cage. Will held the paper in his hand, the edge fluttering in the air blowing out from the heater.

Her voice was barely a whisper. 'Why are you doing this?'

Fear saturated her every word. Will stared at her for a long while – so long that she felt as if her soul was being peeled away from her body. Finally, he gave one of his patented nods, as if he'd made a decision. He put the transcript back in his case and snapped the locks shut.

'Let's go to Allison's.'

Taylor Drive was less than ten minutes from the station, but the trip seemed to take hours. Lena felt so panicked that she slowed down a couple of times, thinking she was going to be sick. She needed to concentrate on Frank, to figure out how many nails he could put in her coffin, but she was thinking about Tommy Braham instead.

He had died on her watch. He was her prisoner. He was her responsibility. She hadn't patted him down when she put him in the cells. She had assumed because he was slow that he was without guile. Who was the stupid one now? Lena thought the kid was capable of murder but considered him so harmless that she'd let him walk into a cell with a sharp object hidden on his person. Frank was right – she was lucky Tommy didn't turn the weapon on someone else.

When had Tommy taken the ink cartridge out of her pen? He must have known when he did it that he was going to use it for something bad. By the time he finished writing his confession, Tommy was in tears. The Kleenex box was empty. Lena had left him alone for no more than half a minute to get more tissues. When she came back into the room, his hands were under the table. She had wiped his nose for him like he was a child. She had soothed him, rubbed his shoulder, told him everything was going to be okay. He seemed to believe her. He'd blown his nose, dried his eyes. She had thought at the time that Tommy had resolved himself to his fate, but maybe the fate he had decided on was a lot different from the one that Lena had imagined.

Was it sympathy for Tommy or her instinctual need for self-preservation that had kept Lena from getting rid of the letter opener he had used on Brad Stephens? Last night, she had thought about tossing it over one of the thousands of concrete bridges between here and Macon. But she hadn't. It was still wrapped in its bag, buried under the spare tire in the trunk of her car. Lena hadn't wanted it in the house. Now, she didn't like that it was so close to the station. Frank had doctored paperwork. He'd broken the chain of custody. He'd tampered with evidence. She wouldn't put it past the old man to rummage through her car.

Christ. What else was he capable of?

She took a right onto Taylor Drive. The rain had come in torrents last night, washing away the blood on the street. Still, she could see it in her mind's eye. The way Brad had blinked away the rain. The way his skin had already started to turn gray by the time the helicopter landed.

Lena steered the car onto the far side of the road and stopped. 'This is where Brad was stabbed.'

Will asked, 'Where's Spooner's apartment?'

She pointed up the road. 'Four houses, left-hand side.'

He stared straight down the street. 'What's the number?'

'Sixteen and a half.' Lena put the car into gear and rolled past the scene of Brad's stabbing. 'We got the address from the college. We came here to see if there was a roommate or landlord we could talk to.'

'Did you have a warrant to search the house?'

He had asked the question before. She gave him the same answer. 'No. We didn't come to search the house.'

She waited for him to ask something else, but Will was silent. Lena wondered if what she had told him was the truth. If Tommy hadn't been in Allison's apartment, they still would have found a way to get into the garage. Gordon Braham was out of town. Knowing Frank, he would've broken the lock and gone into Allison's apartment anyway. He would have made some comment about how it was better to ask for forgiveness than permission. No one would have minded a simple breaking and entering when a young girl from the college had been murdered.

Will asked, 'Did you canvass the neighbors?'

Lena stopped the car in front of the Braham house. 'Patrol did. No one saw anything different from what happened.'

'And what exactly *did* happen?'

'Brad was stabbed.'

'Tell me from the beginning. You pulled up here . . .'

She tried to take a breath. Her lungs would only fill to half capacity. 'We approached the garage—'

'No,' he interrupted. 'Go back to the very beginning. You drove up to the scene. Then what?'

'Brad was already here.' She didn't tell him about the pink umbrella or Frank's screaming fit.

'You got out of the car?' Will prodded. He really was going to make her go through this step-by-step.

She opened her door. Rain splattered her face with lazy, fat drops. Will had gotten out of the car, too. She told him, 'The rain had died down. Visibility was good.' She started up the driveway. Will was beside her with his briefcase in his hand. At the top of the hill, she could see that the garage was marked with yellow crime scene tape. Frank must have come back last night. Or maybe he had sent patrol to mark the space so it looked like they were taking this seriously. There was no telling anymore what he was doing or why.

Will opened his briefcase and pulled out a sheet of paper. 'The search warrant came in while you were getting your coat.'

He handed the document to Lena. She saw it had been issued by a judge out of Atlanta.

He asked, 'What next? I take it the garage door was closed when you approached?'

She nodded. 'We were standing about here. All three of us. The lights were out. There weren't any cars in the driveway or on the street.' She pointed to the scooter. Mud was caked around the plastic fenders. 'The lock and chain appeared to be the same.' Lena stared at the scooter, feeling good about the debris lodged in the tires. Tommy could have gone to the woods on the scooter. They wouldn't be able to find tracks, but the mud on the wheels would match the mud around the lake.

'Detective?'

Lena turned around. She had missed his question.

'Did you knock on the front door of the house?'

She glanced back at the house. The lights were still off. There was a small bouquet of flowers propped against the door. 'No.'

Will leaned down and opened the garage's metal door. The noise as it rolled up was deafening, a loud clanging that must have been heard by half the neighborhood. Lena saw the bed, the table, the scattered papers and magazines. There was a small pool of blood where Frank had fallen by the mouth of the entrance. Ice glazed the top. The cut in his arm was deeper than she thought. There was no way the letter opener had done the damage. Had he stabbed himself?

Will asked, 'Is this how you found the garage?'

'Pretty much.' Lena crossed her arms over her chest. She could feel the cold seeping in through her jacket. She should have come back to the scene after getting Tommy's confession and searched Allison's things for more clues to back up Tommy's story. It was too late for that now. The best thing Lena could do for herself was to start thinking like a detective instead of acting like a suspect. The murder weapon was probably in here. The scooter was a good lead. The stain by the bed was an even better one. Tommy could've hit Allison in the head, then taken her into the woods to kill her. Maybe his plan was to drown her by the lake. The girl had come to, and he'd stabbed her in the back of the neck. Tommy had lived in Grant County all his life. He'd probably been to the cove hundreds of times. He would know where the bottom dropped in the lake. He would know to take the body out deep so that she wouldn't be easily found.

Lena exhaled. She could breathe now. This was making

sense. Tommy had lied to her about how he'd killed Allison, but he *had* killed her.

Will cleared his throat. 'Let's go back a few steps. All three of you were standing here. The garage was closed. The house looked empty. Then what?'

Lena took a minute to regain her composure. She told him about Brad seeing the masked intruder inside, the way he had circled the building before they fanned out to confront the suspect.

Will seemed to be only half listening as she laid out the events. He stood just under the garage door with his hands behind his back, scanning the contents of the room. Lena was telling him about Tommy refusing to lower the knife when she noticed that Will was focusing on the brown stain by the bed. He walked into the garage and knelt down for a better look. Beside him was the bucket of murky water she had seen yesterday. The crusty sponge was beside it.

He looked up at her. 'Keep going.'

Lena had to think to find her place. 'Tommy was behind that table.' She nodded to the table, which was crooked.

Will said, 'That door isn't exactly quiet when it rolls up. Did he already have the knife in his hand?'

Lena stopped, trying to remember what she'd said the first time Will asked her the question. He wanted to know if Tommy had a sheath on his belt where he kept a knife. He wanted to know if it was the same knife that had killed Allison Spooner.

She said, 'When I saw him, he already had the knife in his hand. I don't know where it came from. Maybe the table.' Of course it had come from the table. There was a partially opened envelope there, the kind of junk mail that contained coupons nobody used.

'What else did you notice?'

She indicated the bucket of brown water by the bed. 'He'd been cleaning. I guess he hit her in the head or knocked her out here. He put her on the scooter and—'

'He didn't mention cleaning up in his confession.'

No, he hadn't. Lena hadn't even thought to ask him about the bucket. All she had been thinking about was Brad, and how gray his skin had looked the last time she'd seen him. 'Suspects lie. Tommy didn't want to admit how he did it. He made up a story that painted him in a better light. It happens all the time.'

Will asked, 'What happened next?'

Lena swallowed, fighting the image of Brad that kept popping into her head. 'I approached the suspect from the right.'

Will had opened his briefcase on the bed. 'Your right or his?'

'My right.' She stopped talking. Will had taken some kind of field kit out of his briefcase. She recognized the three small glass bottles he took out of the plastic pouch. He was going to do a Kastle-Meyer test on the stain.

Will didn't prompt her to continue the story. He took a clean swab from the kit. He opened the first bottle and used the dropper to wet the cotton tip with ethanol. He touched the swab to the stain, gently rolling it so that the brown substance would transfer. He added the reagent, phenolphthalein, from the second bottle. Lena held her breath as he used the last dropper to add hydrogen peroxide to the mix. She had studied the procedure in class, performed it a hundred times herself. If the brown

261

stain was human blood, the tip of the swab would rapidly turn bright pink.

The swab didn't turn.

Will started to pack the kit back up. 'What happened next?'

Lena had lost her place. She couldn't take her eyes off the stain. How could it not be blood? It had the same shape, the same color, as a bloodstain. Tommy was in Allison's apartment, going through her things. He was dressed like a burglar. He was standing two feet away from her blood with a knife in his hand.

Not a knife. A letter opener.

And not Allison's blood.

Will prodded her to continue. 'So, you flanked Tommy on your right. Interim Chief Wallace was on your right?'

'My left, your right.'

'Is this when you identified yourself as police officers?'

Lena held her breath. She would have to lie to him. There was no way she could say she didn't remember, because that would be taken as an admission that she hadn't followed the most basic procedure when confronting a suspect.

'Detective?'

Lena let out a slow breath. She tried to muster some sarcasm. 'I know how to do my job.'

He gave a solemn nod. 'I hope so.' Instead of jamming his foot down harder, he let up. 'Tell me what happened next.'

Lena continued the story as Will walked around the garage. The space was small, but there wasn't one inch that he didn't study at some point. Every time he stopped to examine an item more closely – the bracing along the back wall, a strip of metal jutting out from the track for the garage door – her heart skipped.

Still, she told him about Tommy running into the street, Brad chasing him. The stabbing. The LifeFlight's arrival. Lena finished, 'The helicopter took off, and I went to the car. Tommy was already inside, handcuffed. I took him to the station. You know the story from there.'

Will scratched his jaw. 'How much time would you say elapsed between when Tommy knocked you to the floor and when you were able to regain your footing?'

'I don't know. Five seconds. Ten.'

'Did you hit your head?'

Lena's head still ached from the bruise. 'I don't know.'

Will was at the back of the room. 'Did you notice this?'

She had to force herself to walk into the garage. She followed his pointing finger to a hole in the wall. It was round with jagged edges, about the size of a bullet. Without thinking, Lena looked back at the front of the garage where Frank had been standing. The trajectory matched up. There were no casings on the floor. She hoped to God Frank had thought to look behind the garage. The bullet hadn't stopped after grazing her hand and punching a hole in the metal siding. It was out there somewhere, probably buried in mud.

Will asked, 'Did anyone fire their weapons?'

'Mine wasn't fired.'

He looked at the Band-Aids on the side of her hand. 'So, you were here on the floor.' He walked to the bed, standing where she had fallen.

'That's right.'

'You stood up and saw that Frank Wallace was on the ground. Was he facedown? On his side?'

263

'On his side.' Lena followed Will as he slowly walked to the front of the garage. She stepped over magazines that had scattered in the struggle. She saw a flash of an older model Mustang clinging to the side of a racetrack.

Will pointed to the jagged metal sticking out from the garage door track. 'This looks dangerous.'

He opened his briefcase again. With a steady hand, he used a pair of tweezers to pull a few threads of light tan material from the sharp metal. Frank's coat was tan, a London Fog he'd been wearing for as long as Lena had known him.

Will handed her the K-M test kit. 'I'm sure you know how to do this.'

Her hands trembled as she took the kit. She went through the same procedure Will had followed, using the dropper to add the reagent. When the tip of the swab turned bright pink, Lena didn't think either of them was too surprised.

Will turned back around and looked at the garage. She could almost hear his mind working. For Lena's part, she had the benefit of her own involvement to paint a picture of the truth. Tommy had shoved the table toward Lena. Frank had panicked, or startled, or something – for whatever reason, he'd ended up pulling the trigger on his gun. The shot had gone wild, taking a chunk out of Lena's hand. Frank had dropped the gun. The Glock's recoil had probably been unexpected. Or maybe he was so drunk by then that his balance was off. He'd pitched to the side, cutting open his arm on the sharp metal that jutted out from the track for the door. He'd fallen to the floor. He was clutching his arm by the time Lena had gotten up. By then, Tommy was running down the driveway with the letter opener in his hand.

Keystone Kops. They were a fucking joke.

How many drinks had Frank had yesterday morning? He was sitting in the car with his flask while Lena was watching Allison being dragged from the lake. He'd taken three or four swigs on the drive over. What about before then? How many drinks did it take him just to get out of bed these days?

Will was silent. He took back the swab, the bottles, and put everything back in its proper place. She waited for him to say something about the scene, about what had really happened. Instead, he asked, 'Where's the bathroom?'

Lena was too confused to answer anything other than 'What?'

'The bathroom.' He indicated the open space, and Lena realized that he was right. The room was just one big box. There was no bathroom. There wasn't even a closet. The furnishings were Spartan, nothing more than a bed that looked like it had been bought from a military supply store and a folding table of the sort they used at church bake sales. There was a small television in the corner with aluminum foil on the antennae and a Playstation jacked into the front. Instead of a chest of drawers, there were metal shelves bolted to the walls. T-shirts spilled over. Jeans. Baseball hats.

Will said, 'What did Tommy say about why he was wearing a ski mask?'

Lena felt like she had swallowed a handful of gravel. 'He said he had it on because it was cold.'

'It's pretty cold in here,' Will agreed. He put the kit in his briefcase. Lena flinched when he snapped the locks shut. The sound echoed like a gunshot. Or a cell door closing.

The car magazines. The dirty sheets on the bed. The lack of even the most basic facilities. There was no way Allison Spooner had lived in this desolate garage.

Tommy Braham had.

ELEVEN

Brock's Funeral Home was housed in one of the oldest buildings in Grant County. The Victorian castle, complete with turrets, had been built in the early 1900s by the man in charge of maintenance at the railroad yard. That he had used funds embezzled from the railroad company was a matter later settled by the state prosecutor. The castle had eventually been auctioned on the courthouse steps to John Brock, the local mortician.

Sara had heard from her grandpa Earnshaw that everyone in town had breathed a sigh of relief when the Brocks left Main Street – especially the butcher who'd had the unfortunate luck of being their next-door tenant. The basement and first floor of the Victorian had been turned into a funeral parlor, while the top floor was reserved for the family.

Sara had grown up with Dan Brock. He'd been an awkward, serious boy, the sort of child who was more comfortable around adults than children his own age. She witnessed firsthand the relentless teasing Dan had experienced in grade school. Bullies had latched onto him like piranha and had not stopped until junior high, when Dan shot past six feet tall. As the tallest girl in her class, then the tallest person in school but for Dan, Sara had always appreciated having him around.

And yet, she still couldn't look at him without seeing

the gangly ten-year-old boy girls had screeched at on the bus for having dead people's cooties.

A funeral was just letting out as Sara pulled into the parking lot. Death was a brisk business, even in the worst economies. The old Victorian was well cared for. The paint was fresh and there was a new tile roof. Sara watched the mourners leaving the house, preparing to make the short trek to the burial.

There was a marble headstone at the cemetery with Jeffrey's name on it. Sara had his ashes back in Atlanta, but his mother had suddenly found her religion and insisted on a proper funeral. The church was so full during the service that the back doors were opened so the people lining the steps could hear the preacher's voice. People walked to the cemetery rather than drive behind the hearse.

Those closest to Jeffrey had each put something in the coffin that reminded them of their friend, their boss, their mentor. There was an Auburn football program with Jeffrey on the cover supplied by his boyhood friends. Eddie had added a hammer Jeffrey used to help him build a shed in the backyard. Her mother had put in her old frying pan because she'd taught Jeffrey how to fry chicken with it. Tessa provided a postcard he had sent her from Florida. He had always loved teasing her. The postcard read, *Glad you're not here!*

A few weeks before Jeffrey had been killed, Sara had given him a signed first edition of MacKinlay Kantor's *Andersonville.* Sara had a hard time letting the book go, even though she knew she had to. She couldn't let the ground cover Jeffrey's coffin of memories without her own contribution. Dan Brock had sat with her in the living room of her house for hours until she was ready to relinquish the book. She had looked at each page, touched her fingers to the spots where Jeffrey's hands had rested. Dan had been patient, quiet, but when the time came for him to go, he was crying as hard as Sara.

She took a tissue out of the glove compartment and wiped her eyes. She was going to end up bawling like a baby if she let her mind continue along this track. Her jacket was on the seat beside her but Sara didn't bother to put it on. She found a clip in the pocket and pulled back her hair. She checked the frizzy mess in the mirror. She should've put on some makeup this morning. The freckles across her nose were more pronounced. Her skin looked pale. Sara pushed away the mirror. It was too late to do anything about it now.

The last car pulled into the funeral procession. Sara jumped out of her SUV, barely missing a deep puddle. The rain was beating down and she covered her head with her hands in futility. Brock stood in the doorway, waving to her. His hair looked a bit thinner on the top, but with his three-piece suit and lanky frame, Dan Brock looked much as he had in high school.

'Hey there.' He gave her a quick smile. 'You're the first one here. I told Frank we'd start around eleven-thirty.'

'I thought I could get a head start laying everything out.'

'I think I may have beat you to that.' He gave her a smile that seemed reserved for mourners. 'How you holding up, Sara?'

She tried to return the smile, but was unable to answer the question. She'd skipped the pleasantries at the jail yesterday when Brock showed up to claim Tommy

Braham's body, and she felt a little awkward around him now. As usual, Brock smoothed over the moment.

'Aw, come here.' He grabbed her in a bear hug. 'You're looking great, Sara. Really good. I'm so glad you came back for the holiday. Your mama must be happy.'

'My father is, at least.'

He kept his arm around her and led her into the house. 'Let's get out of this inclement weather.'

'Wow.' She stopped at the door, glancing around the wide central hallway. Her parents weren't the only ones who'd been remodeling lately. The staid décor of the house had been considerably updated. The heavy velvet drapes and dark green carpeting had been replaced with Roman shades and a muted Oriental rug that covered beautiful hardwood floors. Even the viewing rooms had been updated so they no longer resembled formal Victorian parlors.

Brock said, 'Mama hates it, so I must've done something right.'

'You've done a lovely job,' she told him, knowing Brock probably hadn't gotten many compliments.

'Business has been good.' Brock kept his hand on her back as he led her down the hall. 'I'll have to admit, I'm real torn up about Tommy. He was a good kid. He cut my grass for me.' Brock stopped walking. He looked down at Sara, his attitude changed. 'I know people think I'm naïve, give folks too much of the benefit of the doubt, but I can't see him doing any of this.'

'Killing himself or killing the girl?'

'Both.' Brock chewed his bottom lip for a moment. 'Tommy was a happy kid. You know what he was like. Never had a cross word for anybody.'

Sara was circumspect. 'People can surprise you.'

'Maybe with their ignorance, thinking just because the kid was slow that his brain just snapped one day and he went on a rampage.'

'You're right.' Tommy was disabled. He wasn't psychotic. One had nothing to do with the other.

'The thing that gets me is, she wasn't killed bad. Not like in a fury.'

'What do you mean?'

He tucked his hand between the buttons of his vest. 'You'd just expect more, is all.'

'More?'

His demeanor changed back just as quickly. 'Listen to me. You're the doctor here. You'll see for yourself, and probably find a lot more than I ever could.' He put his hand on her shoulder. 'It's really good to have you back, Sara. And I want you to know that I'm real happy for you. Don't listen to what anybody else says.'

Sara didn't like the sound of that. 'Happy about what?'

'Your new fella.'

'My new—'

'Whole town's buzzing about it. Mama was on the phone all last night.'

Sara felt her face turning red. 'Brock – Dan. He's not really—'

'Shh,' Brock warned. She heard shuffling on the stairs above them. He raised his voice. 'Mama, I'm gonna go to the cemetery now to help Mr. Billingham's people. Sara'll be downstairs working, so don't you go and bother her. You hear?'

Audra Brock's voice was frail, though the old biddy would probably outlive them all. 'What'd you say?'

He raised his voice again, cutting to the chase. 'I said leave Sara alone.'

There was something like a 'humph,' then more shuffling as she made her way back to her room.

Brock rolled his eyes, but his good-natured smile was still on his face. 'Everything downstairs is the same as when you left it. I should be back in an hour or so to lend you a hand. Should I put a sign on the door for your fella?'

'He—' Sara stopped herself. 'I'll do it.'

'My office is still in the kitchen. I spiffed it up a bit. Lemme know what you think about it.' He gave her a wave before leaving through the front door.

Sara walked to the back of the house. She had left her purse in the car so she didn't have a paper or pen to leave Will a note. The Victorian's kitchen had always served as the office. Brock had finally taken out the old sink and washboard, making the space more conducive to the business of managing death. The coffin display was built into the breakfast nook. Catalogues of flower arrangements were artfully spread out on a mahogany table. Brock's desk was glass and steel, a very modern design considering he was the oldest soul she had ever met.

She took a Post-it off his blotter and started to write Will a note, then stopped herself. Frank was planning to make an appearance. What could she put on this small square of paper that would tell Will where to go without making Frank suspicious?

Sara tapped the pen to her teeth as she walked to the front door. She finally settled on 'down stairs,' writing it as two words, each on its own line. To make it as clear as possible, she drew a large, downward-pointing arrow. That might not do any good, though. Every dyslexic was different, but there were certain characteristics that the majority of them shared. Primary among these was a lack of any sense of direction. It was no wonder Will had gotten lost driving down from Atlanta. Making a phone call wouldn't have helped matters. Telling a dyslexic to turn right was about as useful as telling a cat to tap-dance.

Sara pressed the note to the glass on the front door. She had agonized over the message this morning, writing it six different times, signing it, not signing it. The smiley face had been a last-minute addition, her way of trying to let Will know that everything was okay between them. A blind man could've seen how upset he was last night. Sara felt horrible for embarrassing him. She had never been a smiley face person, but she'd drawn two eyes and a mouth at the corner of the note before sticking it in a baggie under his windshield, hoping that he would take it the right way.

It seemed wildly inappropriate to leave a smiley face on the front door of a funeral home, but she drew a small figure – two eyes and a curved mouth – thinking at least she'd get points for consistency.

The floorboards overhead creaked, and Sara trotted quickly back toward the kitchen. She left the basement door wide open and took the stairs two at a time to avoid Brock's mother. There was a burglar door at the bottom of the landing. Black metal bars and a mesh screen kept anyone from breaking into the embalming area. You wouldn't think that a person would want to come down here unless they had to, but many years ago, a couple of kids from the college had busted open the old door in their quest to steal some formaldehyde, a popular choice for cutting powder cocaine. Sara assumed the combination on the keypad hadn't changed. She entered 1-5-9 and the door clicked open.

Brock kept the area immediately across from the door empty so that no one would accidentally glance through the mesh screen and see something they should never have to see. The buffer zone continued down the long, well-lit hallway. Storage shelves contained various chemicals and supplies with the labels all turned toward the wall so the viewer would not know what he was looking at. Small shoe boxes filled the last metal cabinet; cremains no one had ever bothered to pick up.

At the end of the hall, Brock had posted a sign that Sara recognized from the hospital morgue: *Hic locus est ubi mors gaudet succurrere vitae.* Roughly translated, 'This is the place where death delights to teach the living.'

The swinging doors to the embalming suite were propped open with old bricks from the house. Artificial light bounced off the white tile walls. While the upstairs had been drastically changed, the downstairs looked exactly the same as Sara remembered. There were two stainless steel gurneys in the middle of the room with large industrial lights spring-mounted above them. A work-station stood at the foot of each gurney, plumbing connected at the ends to help evacuate the bodies. Brock had already laid out the autopsy tools – the saws, the scalpels, the forceps, and scissors. He was still using the pruning shears Sara had bought at the hardware store to cut through the breastbone.

The back of the room was wholly devoted to the funeral business. Beside the walk-in freezer was a rolling tray containing the metal trocar that was used to pierce and clean out organs during the embalming process. Neatly tucked into the corner was the embalming machine, which looked like a cross between a buffet-style coffee warmer and a blender. The arterial tube hung limply in the sink. Heavy rubber gloves were laid out on the basin. A butcher's apron. A pair of construction goggles. A splatter mask. An industrial-sized box of roll cotton for stopping leaks.

Incongruously, there was a hair dryer and a pink makeup kit opened on top of the cotton box. Pots of foundation and various shades of eyeshadows and lip glosses were inside. The logo for 'Peason's Mortuary makeup' was embossed on the inside of the lid.

Sara took a pair of disposable surgical gloves from the box mounted on the wall. She opened the freezer door. A gust of cold air met her. There were three bodies inside, all zipped into black bags. She checked the tags for Allison Spooner.

The bag unzipped with the usual hassle, catching on the bulky black plastic. Allison's skin had taken on the waxy, iridescent tone of death. Her lips were blackish blue. Pieces of grass and twigs were stuck to her skin and clothing. Small contusions pebbled her mouth and cheeks. Sara slipped on the surgical gloves and gently folded back the girl's bottom lip. Teeth marks cut into the soft flesh where Allison's face had been pressed into the ground. The wound had bled before she died. The killer had held her down in order to kill her.

Carefully, Sara turned Allison's head to the side. The rigor had already dissipated. She could easily see the gaping stab wound at the back of the girl's neck.

Brock was right. She wasn't killed bad. There was no fury written on the body, just a deadly, precise incision.

Sara pressed her fingers to the top and bottom of the wound, stretching the skin to reconstruct its probable position at the time of injury. The knife would have been thin, approximately half an inch wide, probably no more than three and a half inches long. The blade had gone in at an angle. The bottom of the incision appeared curved, which meant that the knife had been twisted to ensure maximum damage.

Sara pulled up the girl's jacket, matching the slice in the material to the wound in the neck. Lena was right about this, at least. The girl had been stabbed from behind. Sara guessed the killer had been right-handed, and very sure of himself. The blow would have been as swift as it was deadly. The hilt of the knife had bruised the skin around the injury. Whoever had killed Allison had not hesitated in driving home the blade, then twisting it for effect.

This was not the work of Tommy Braham.

Sara zipped back the bag with the same difficulty. Before she left the freezer, she put her hand on Tommy's leg. Obviously, he couldn't feel the pressure – it was too late for Sara to give him comfort – but it made her feel better knowing that she was going to be the one to take care of him.

She slipped off the gloves and tossed them into the trash as she made her way to the back of the basement. There was a small windowless room that, in the Victorian's early days, was meant to store wine. Red bricks lined the walls and wrapped around the floor and ceiling. Brock used the space as an office, despite the fact that the temperature was much cooler inside. Sara grabbed the jacket hanging by the door, then quickly changed her mind when she smelled Brock's aftershave.

The desk was empty but for the autopsy forms and an ink pen. Brock had put together two packets for the procedures. He'd stuck Post-it notes on each with the name, date of birth, and last known address for each victim.

Georgia law required a medical autopsy to be performed only under certain circumstances. Violent death, death in the workplace, suspicious death, sudden death, unattended death, and surgical death all required further investigation. For the most part, the information gathered was always the same: legal name, aliases, age, height, weight, cause of death. X rays were taken. The stomach contents would be examined. Organs were weighed. Arteries, valves, and veins were explored. Contusions were noted. Traumas. Bite marks. Stretch marks. Lacerations. Scars. Tattoos. Birthmarks. Every detail, remarkable or not, that was found on or in the body had to be noted on the corresponding form.

Sara had hooked her reading glasses on her shirt before getting out of the car. She slipped them on and started on the forms. Most of the paperwork would have to be filled out after the procedures, but every label attached to a specimen or sample had to have her name, the location, and the proper date and time. In addition to that, every form had to have the same information at the bottom along with her signature and license number. She was halfway through the second packet when she heard someone knocking at the metal door.

'Hello?' Will's voice echoed through the basement.

Sara rubbed her eyes, feeling as if she'd just woken from a nap. 'I'll be right there.' She pushed herself back from the desk and walked toward the stairs. Will was standing on the other side of the security door.

She pushed open the latch. 'I guess my notes worked.'

He gave her a careful look, almost like a warning.

Sara waved him back to the autopsy suite.

'Quite a spread,' Will told her, taking in the room. His hands were in his pockets. She saw that his jeans were wet and muddy at the hem.

She asked, 'How did it go this morning?'

'The good news is that I found out where Allison was killed.' He told her about his walk in the forest. 'We were lucky the rain didn't wash it all out.'

'Blood is five times more dense than water. It would take weeks for the soil to filter it out, and I'd bet that water oak will hold on to it for years.' Sara explained, 'The plasma would break down, but the proteins and globulin would remain in an indefinite colloidal stage.'

'That's exactly what I was thinking.'

She smiled. 'What's the bad news?'

He leaned his hand on the gurney, then thought better of it. 'I executed a search warrant on the wrong property and tainted some evidence.'

Sara didn't speak, but her expression must have conveyed her surprise.

'Tommy lived in the garage, not Allison. The search warrant Faith got listed the garage address. Anything I found is tainted. I doubt a judge would let it through in court.'

She suppressed a rueful laugh. At least he was seeing firsthand how Lena managed to screw up everything and everyone around her. 'What did you find?'

'Not a lot of blood, if that's what you mean. Frank Wallace was cut while he was standing at the front of the garage. The stain on the floor by the bed was probably from Tommy's dog, Pippy, trying to hork up a sock.'

Sara winced. 'Do you still think Tommy did this? His confession doesn't line up with the facts.'

'Lena's been working on the theory that Tommy took Allison out to the woods on his scooter and murdered her there. I suppose he was sitting on the cinder blocks the way you'd put a kid on some phone books at the kitchen table.'

'That sounds completely believable.'

'Doesn't it just?' He scratched his jaw. 'Have you examined Allison's body yet?'

'I took a preliminary look at the wound. The attacker was behind her. Most knife injuries to the throat are from behind, but usually the blade is drawn across the front of the throat, oftentimes resulting in a partial decapitation. Allison was stabbed from behind with the blade going into the neck from the rear, the trajectory going toward the front of the throat. It was one thrust, very calculated, almost like an execution, then the killer twisted the blade just to make sure.'

'So, she died from the stab wound?'

'I can't say for sure until I have her on the table.'

'But you have an idea.'

Sara had never liked giving her opinion unless she had strong medical fact to support it. 'I don't want to make assumptions.'

'It's just us down here. I promise I won't tell anybody.'

She was only vaguely aware that she was relenting much more easily than she should have. 'The angle of the wound was designed to deliver a quick death. I haven't cut her open yet, so I'm not sure—'

'But?'

'It looks like the carotid sheath was cut, so we're talking an instant interruption of the common carotid and more than likely the internal jugular. They're branched together like this.' She lined up the index fingers of both her hands. 'The carotid's job is to carry oxygenated blood at a rapid speed from the heart into the head and neck. The jugular is a vein. It's gravity fed. It collects the deoxygenated blood from the head and neck and sends it back to the heart via the superior vena cava, where it's oxygenated again and the whole process starts all over. You follow?'

Will nodded. 'Arteries are the water supply, veins are the drain. It's a closed system.'

'Right,' she agreed, giving him points for the plumbing analogy. 'All arteries have a little muscle spiraling around them that relaxes and contracts to control blood flow. If you cut an artery in two, sever it, the muscle contracts, curling up like a broken rubber band. That helps stanch the blood flow. But, if you slice open the artery without cutting it in two, the victim dies from exsanguination, usually very quickly. We're talking seconds, not minutes. The blood shoots out, they panic, their heart beats faster, blood shoots out faster, and they're dead.'

'Where is the carotid?'

She put her fingers alongside her trachea. 'You've got one carotid on each side, mirror images. I'll have to excise the wound, but it appears that the knife followed this route, entering near the sixth cervical vertebra and traveling along the angle of the jaw.'

He stared at her neck. 'How hard is that to hit from behind?'

'Allison is very small framed. Her neck is the width of

my palm. There's so much going on in the back of the neck – muscles, blood vessels, vertebrae. You would have to pause, to take a second, to aim so that you hit the exact spot. You couldn't go straight in from the back. You'd have to go from the back toward the side. With the right knife, at the right angle, the odds are pretty good that you'll end up opening both the carotid and the jugular.'

'The right knife?'

'I'm guessing it had a three-and-a-half- to four-inch blade.'

'So, we're talking about a kitchen knife?'

He obviously wasn't good with measurements. She showed him the distance using her finger and thumb. 'Three and a half inches. Think about the size of her neck. Or my neck, for that matter.' Sara kept the measurement between her fingers and held her hand to her neck. 'If the blade had been any longer, it would've exited the front of the neck.'

He crossed his arms. She couldn't tell if he was pleased or annoyed with the visual aids. He asked, 'How wide do you think the blade was?'

She narrowed the space between her thumb and finger. 'Five-eighths? Three-quarters? The skin is elastic. She must have struggled. The incision is wider at the bottom, so the killer jammed in the knife to the hilt, then twisted the blade to make sure he was doing maximum damage. I'm sure it wasn't over an inch wide.'

'That sounds like a large folding knife.'

Sara thought he was right based on the bruise from the hilt, but she told him, 'I really need to look at the wound in a better setting than inside the freezer.'

'Was it serrated?'

'I don't think so, but really, let me get into the wound and I can tell you everything you need to know.'

He chewed his lip, obviously thinking about what she had told him. 'It takes less than two pounds of pressure to penetrate skin.'

'As long as the knife is pointed and sharp and the blade is forcefully thrust.'

'Sounds like something a hunter would know how to do.'

'Hunter, doctor, mortician, butcher.' She felt the need to add, 'Or anyone with a good search engine. I'm sure you can find all kinds of anatomical diagrams on the Internet. Whether they're accurate is up for debate, but whoever did this was showing off his skills. I hate to keep banging the same drum, but Tommy had an IQ of eighty. It took him two months to learn how to tie his shoes. Do you really think that he committed this crime?'

'I don't like to speculate.'

She gave him his own words. 'It's just us down here. I won't tell anyone.'

Will didn't give in as easily as Sara had. 'Was Tommy a hunter?'

'I doubt Gordon would've let him have a gun.'

Will took a moment before asking his next question. 'Why not drown her? She was standing by a lake.'

'The water must have been close to freezing. There was the chance of a struggle. She could've yelled. My house is – was – across the lake from Lover's Point, but sometimes when the wind was right, I could hear music playing, kids laughing. Certainly, any number of people would have heard a young girl screaming for her life.'

'Wouldn't it be easier to cut the front of the throat instead of going in through the back?'

She nodded, saying, 'If you cut the trachea, the victim wouldn't be able to speak, let alone yell for help.'

Will pointed out, 'Women tend to use knives.'

Sara hadn't considered the possibility, but she was grateful his mind was moving off Tommy. 'Allison was small. A woman could have overwhelmed her, then carried her to the water.'

'Was the killer left-handed? Right-handed?'

'Well—' Sara was going to ask if it mattered to someone who could not tell the difference, but answered him instead. 'I'm assuming right-handed.' Sara held up her right hand. 'The attacker would have been at a superior position, standing above her, possibly straddling her, when the blade went in.' She paused. 'This is why I don't like to make assumptions. I need to check her stomach and lungs. If we find lake water, then that means she was probably facedown in the water when he stabbed her.'

'Knowing whether she was in the water or in the mud when she was stabbed will be instrumental to my investigation.'

She furrowed her brow. 'Are you being a smart-ass, Agent Trent?'

'Based on how you asked that question, I think my answer should be no.'

Sara laughed. 'Good call.'

'Thank you, Dr. Linton.' He looked around the embalming suite and gave a shiver. 'It's cold down here. Aren't you cold?'

She realized he was wearing the same clothes from

yesterday but for the black T-shirt, which he'd changed for a white one. 'Didn't you bring a coat?'

He shook his head. 'I'm in an awful situation with my clothes. I need to borrow your mom's washer and dryer tonight. Do you think she'll mind?'

'No. Of course not.'

'Have you heard from Frank Wallace today?'

She shook her head.

'It's starting to annoy me that he hasn't bothered to show up. Does he normally let Lena do all the heavy lifting?'

'I don't know how they work together now. She used to go back and forth between Frank and my husband, whoever needed her at the time.'

'I'm just wondering if she's reporting back to Frank or if they're both doing their own thing.' Will gestured toward the gurneys. 'Can I help you with anything?'

'What's your squeamish level?'

'I don't like rats and I'm bad around vomit.'

'I think we're safe on both points.' Sara wanted to get started so she wasn't here past midnight. 'Can you help me get Allison onto the table?'

The joking camaraderie from before quickly turned into a more serious collaboration. They worked in silence, rolling the gurney into the freezer, lifting the body in unison. There was a scale in the floor. The digital readout already took the gurney into account. Sara rolled the bed onto the plate. Allison Spooner had weighed 102 pounds.

When Sara put on a pair of surgical gloves, Will followed suit. She let him help unzip the body bag and roll the girl left, then right, to slide the black plastic out from

284

under her. He held one end of the measuring tape so she could get the girl's height.

Will said, 'Sixty-three inches. Five foot three.'

'I need to write this down.' Sara knew there was no way she could remember all these numbers. There was a whiteboard mounted to the back wall over the counter. Sara used the marker hanging on a string to record Allison's height and weight. To be thorough, she then added age, sex, race, and hair color. The girl's eyes were open, so she noted that her eye color was brown.

When Sara turned around, she found Will looking at the numbers. Sara had used abbreviations that even a reading person would have trouble understanding. She pointed to the letters. 'Date of birth, height, weight—'

'I got it,' he said. His tone was as close to curt as she'd ever heard.

Sara resisted the urge to talk about the elephant in the room, to tell him that it was foolish for him to be ashamed. He had spent a lifetime hiding his dyslexia, and she wasn't going to fix that by confronting him about it in the basement of the funeral home. Not to mention that it was none of her business.

She walked to the tall locker beside the office, assuming Brock still kept his supplies in the same place. 'Crap,' she mumbled. The camera and all its pieces were laid out on velvet cloths covering two shelves. She picked up a lens. 'I'm not sure I know how this thing goes together.'

'Mind if I try?' Will didn't wait for her response. He picked up the lens and twisted it onto the camera, then bolted on the lights, the flash, and the metal guide that recorded depth. He pressed several buttons until the LCD display blinked on, then scrolled through all the icons until he found the one he was looking for.

Sara had two degrees and a board certification under her belt, but hell would have frozen over before she would've been able to figure out anything to do with the camera. Curiosity broke her earlier resolve. 'Have you ever been tested?'

'No.' He stood behind Sara, holding the camera in front so she could see. 'Zoom here,' he said, flicking the toggle.

'You could probably—'

'This is macro.'

'Will—'

'Super macro.' He kept talking over her until she gave up. 'Here's where you adjust for color. This is light. Anti-shake. Red-eye.' He clicked through the features like a photography instructor.

Sara finally relented. 'Why don't I point and you shoot?'

'All right.' His back was stiff, and she could tell that he was irritated.

'I'm sorry I—'

'Please don't apologize.'

Sara held his gaze for a few moments longer, wishing she could fix this. There was nothing to say if he wouldn't even let her apologize.

She told him, 'Let's start.'

Sara directed him around the table as he photographed Allison Spooner head to toe. The warm-up jacket. The stab wound that went through to her neck. The sliced material where the knife had cut through. The teeth marks on the inside of her lip.

She folded back the torn jeans, exposing the knee. There

was a half-moon-shaped tear, the skin hanging on by a flap. A dark bruise outlined the area of impact. 'This kind of laceration comes from blunt trauma. She fell very hard on her knee, probably with her full weight, definitely on something hard, like a rock. The impact busted open the skin.'

'Can we look at the wrists?'

The jacket had bunched up around the girl's hands. Sara pushed up the material.

He took a few photographs. 'Ligature marks?'

Sara leaned down for a closer look. She checked the other wrist. The veins were an iridescent blue. Lines of red shot through the skin where clots held the blood in place.

She explained, 'Bodies start to float anywhere from two hours to two days after they're in the water. Decomposition starts quickly – as soon as the heart and lungs stop, the body turns on itself. Bacteria leaks out of the intestines. Gases build up, causing buoyancy. The cinder blocks would have kept her from floating to the surface. The cold water would've retarded decomposition. I don't know what the temperature of the lake was, but we can assume it was close to freezing. She was probably facedown, her hands hanging in front of her. Livor mortis settled into her fingertips, pooled up into her wrists. I suppose you could mistake the discoloration for ligature marks. It would've been dark that time of morning.' Sara couldn't make any more excuses for Frank. 'Honestly, I thought Frank was lying to me when he said it the first time.'

'Why lie about that?' Will asked. 'The stab wound is evidence enough that something was seriously wrong.'

'You'll have to ask Frank.'

'I've got a lot of questions for him if he ever shows up.'

'He's probably with Brad. Frank has known him since he was a kid. We all have.'

Will only nodded.

Sara put the ruler by Allison's wrist so he could take a photograph. When he was finished, she turned the hand over. There was a faint scar along the crease of the wrist. She checked the other hand. 'She tried to kill herself before. A razor, maybe a sharp knife. I'd say within the last ten years.'

Will studied the raised white lines. 'What was Tommy like?'

She was surprised by the question because her focus was on Allison. Sara hadn't slept much last night. She'd had a lot of time to think about Tommy. 'He was cheerful,' she told Will. 'I don't think there was ever a time I didn't see him smile. Even when he felt bad.'

'Did you ever see him angry?'

'No.'

'Did he have many broken bones or bruises?'

She shook her head, knowing where this was going. 'Gordon was very gentle with him. The only time I saw him angry was when Tommy ate a whole jar of paste.'

Will smiled fondly. 'I used to eat paste.' He held the camera at his side. 'I wonder if it tastes as good as it used to.'

Sara laughed. 'I wouldn't recommend finding out. Tommy was sick for days.'

'You didn't tell me Lena was raped.'

The observation came out of nowhere. Sara was taken off guard, which was probably what he had intended. 'It was a long time ago.'

'Faith found it on the Internet.'

She busied herself over by the back counter, finding a roll of brown paper under the cabinet so she could lay out the clothes. 'Does it matter?'

'I don't know. It bothers me that you left it out.'

Sara spread out the paper. 'A lot of women have been raped.' She looked up when he didn't respond. 'Don't feel sorry for her, Will. She's so good at making people feel sorry for her.'

'I think she regrets what happened to Tommy.'

Sara shook her head. 'You can't expect good from her. She's not a normal person. There's no kindness in her.'

He spoke carefully, staring his meaning into Sara. 'I've met a lot of people in my life who were truly unkind.'

'Still—'

'I don't think Lena's completely devoid of a soul. I think she's angry, and self-destructive, and feeling trapped.'

'I used to think that, too. And I felt sorry for her. Right before she got my husband killed.'

There wasn't much more Sara could say after that. She unbuttoned Allison's shirt and continued to undress the girl. Will changed out the memory card and took photographs when she asked him to. She didn't ask for his help when she draped a clean white sheet over Allison's body. Their companionable silence was a distant memory. The tension was so great that Sara felt herself getting a headache. She was angry with herself that it mattered. Will Trent was not her friend. His dyslexia, his quirky sense of humor, his dirty clothes – none of this was her concern. All she needed for him to do was get his job done and then go back to his wife.

Out in the hall, the metal door slammed shut. Moments later, Frank Wallace came into the room carrying a cardboard box. He was wearing a long trench coat and a pair of leather gloves. His hair was wet from the rain.

Will said, 'Chief Wallace. It's nice to finally meet you. I was beginning to think you were avoiding me.'

'You wanna tell me why you've got half my guys out chasing their tails in the pouring rain?'

'I assume you've heard that we found the crime scene where Allison Spooner was stabbed.'

'You test that blood yet? Could be an animal for all I know.'

Will told him, 'Yes, I tested it on scene. It's human blood.'

'All right, so he killed her in the woods.'

'It appears so.'

'I called off the search. You can bring in your own team if you wanna comb through six inches of mud.'

'That's a very good idea, Chief Wallace. I think I will call in a team.'

Frank was obviously finished with Will. He dropped the box at Sara's feet. 'Here's all the evidence we've got.' She held her breath until he backed away. He smelled rancid, a combination of mouthwash, sweat, and tobacco.

Will said, 'I hope you don't mind, Chief Wallace. I've got Detective Adams re-canvassing the neighborhood and checking with Allison's teachers from school.'

'Do whatever you want,' Frank grunted. 'I'm finished with her.'

'Is there a problem?'

'You wouldn't be here if there wasn't.' Frank coughed into his gloved hand. Sara winced at the sound. 'Lena screwed this whole thing up top to bottom. I'm not covering for her anymore. She's a bad cop. Her work's sloppy. She managed to get somebody killed.' He gave Sara a meaningful look. 'Somebody else.'

She felt hot and cold at the same time. Frank was saying all the things that she wanted to hear – all the things she knew in her heart – but the words sounded dirty coming from his mouth. He was exploiting Jeffrey's death, while Sara was trying to avenge it.

Will said, 'Lena told me you spoke with Lionel Harris last night?'

Suddenly, Frank seemed nervous. 'Lionel doesn't know anything.'

'Still, he might have some personal information about Allison.'

'Lionel's daddy raised him right. He knows better than to be sniffing around a little white girl from the college.'

Sara felt her mouth open in surprise.

Frank shrugged off her shock. 'You know what I'm saying, Sweetpea. There's not a lot that a sixty-three-year-old black man has in common with a twenty-one-year-old white girl. At least not if he knows what's good for him.' He nodded toward Allison. 'What did you find?'

Sara couldn't find her voice to answer him.

Will provided, 'Knife wound to the neck. There's no definitive cause of death yet.'

Will caught Sara's eye. She nodded her complicity, though she still felt shocked by what Frank had said. He had never talked this way around her parents. Eddie would have shown Frank the door if Cathy hadn't beaten him to it. Sara wanted to chalk it up to his exhaustion. He certainly looked worse than he had the day before. Every item of clothing he wore, from his cheap suit to his trench coat, was wrinkled as if he had slept in it. His skin sagged off his face. His eyes glistened in the light. And he still hadn't taken off his leather gloves.

Will broke the moment. 'Chief Wallace, have you completed your report yet on the incident in the garage?'

Frank's jaw clenched tighter. 'I'm working on it.'

'Can you run it through for me now? Just the highlights. I'll get the details when you turn in your report.'

Frank's voice was gruff, making it clear he didn't like being questioned. 'Tommy was in the garage with a knife in his hand. We told him to put it down. He didn't.'

Sara waited for more, but it was Will who prompted, 'And then?'

Frank gave another sloppy shrug. 'The kid panicked. He pushed Lena out of the way. I went to help her. He came toward me with the knife, cut my arm. Next thing I know, Tommy's tearing down the driveway. Brad went after him. I told Lena to go, too.' He stopped. 'She sure took her time.'

'She hesitated?'

'Lena usually runs the other way when there's a fire.' He glanced at Sara, as if he expected her to agree. In Sara's experience, the opposite was true. Lena stood as close to the fire as she could. It was the best vantage point from which to watch people burn.

Frank continued. 'She trotted after them. Brad ended up being the one to pay for it.'

Will leaned against the counter, one hand resting on the edge. His interview style was certainly unusual. Put a beer in his hand and he could be talking football around a barbecue. 'Did anyone discharge their weapon?'

'No.'

Will nodded slowly, drawing out his next question. 'When you opened the garage door, did Tommy already have the knife in his hand?'

Frank leaned down and pulled an evidence bag out of the cardboard box. 'This knife.'

Will didn't take the bag, so Sara did. The hunting knife was serrated on one side and sharp on the other. The hilt was large. The blade was at least five inches long and an inch and a half wide. It was a miracle Brad was still alive. Without thinking, she blurted out, 'This isn't the knife that was used on Allison.'

Will took the weapon from Sara. He gave her a look that Tommy Braham had probably gotten every day of his life. He told Frank, 'This looks new.'

Frank gave the knife a cursory glance. 'So?'

'Was Tommy a knife enthusiast?'

Frank crossed his arms again. There was a bead of sweat on his forehead. Even with the colder temperature in the basement, he seemed to be burning up in the coat and gloves. 'Obviously, he had at least two. Like the doc said. This isn't the same one that was used on the girl.'

Sara would have melted into the floor if she had the power.

Will asked, 'What made you suspect Tommy was involved in Allison's murder? Other than the knife in his hand?'

'He was in her apartment.'

Will didn't offer any information to the contrary, but Sara saw that he'd managed to get a question answered. If Lena had talked to Frank, then she hadn't mentioned that Tommy lived in the garage, not Allison.

Frank's patience had obviously run out. 'Listen, son, I've been doing this a long time. There's two reasons a man does this to a woman: sex and sex. Tommy already confessed. What's the point of all this?'

Will smiled. 'Dr. Linton, I know you haven't done a full exam on Allison Spooner, but are there any signs of sexual assault?'

Sara was surprised to find herself back in the conversation. 'Not that I can see.'

'Were her clothes torn?'

'There was a tear in the knee of her jeans where she fell. Her jacket was cut by the knife.'

'Are there any other significant wounds except for the one in her neck?'

'Not that I've found.'

'So, Tommy wanted to have sex with Allison. She told him no. He didn't tear her clothes. He didn't try to force her anyway. He puts her on his scooter and takes her out to the lake. He stabs her once in the neck. And then he dumps her in the lake with the chains and cinder blocks, writes a fake suicide note, and goes back to clean up her apartment. Is that about right, Chief Wallace?'

Frank lifted his chin. Hostility radiated off him like heat from a fire.

Will said, 'The note is what's bothering me. Why not just dump her in the lake and leave it at that? It's doubtful anyone would have found her. The lake is pretty deep, right?' He looked at Sara when Frank did not answer. 'Right?'

She nodded. 'Right.'

Will seemed to be waiting for an answer from Frank that wasn't going to come. Sara waited for him to ask about the

911 call, the boyfriend. Will didn't. He just kept leaning against the counter, waiting for Frank to say something. For his part, Frank seemed to be scrambling for an explanation.

He finally came up with 'The kid was retarded. Right, Doc?'

Sara told him, 'I wish you wouldn't use that word. He—'

'It is what it is,' Frank interrupted. 'Tommy was stupid. You can't reason with stupid. He stabbed her once? So what. He left a note? So what. He was retarded.'

Will let Frank's words hang for a few seconds. 'You knew Allison, right? From the diner?'

'I seen her around.'

'Have you found her car yet?'

'No.'

Will smiled. 'Did you process Tommy's car?'

'I hate to break the news to you, Einstein, but the retard confessed. End of story.' He looked at his watch. 'I can't stick around jerking you off for the rest of the day. I just wanted to make sure you had all the evidence.' He nodded to Sara. 'You can reach me on my cell if you need me. I gotta get back to Brad.'

Will didn't protest the abrupt departure. 'Thank you, Chief. I appreciate your cooperation.'

Frank couldn't figure out if he was being sarcastic or not. He ignored the comment, telling Sara, 'I'll let you know about Brad,' before stomping out of the room.

Sara wasn't sure what to say. Will had let all the important questions go unanswered. Jeffrey's style of interviewing had been much more aggressive. Once he had Frank on the ropes, he would've never let the man walk out of the room. She turned to Will. He was still leaning against the counter.

She wasn't going to ignore the hundredth elephant that had just walked into the room. 'Why didn't you ask Frank about the boyfriend?'

He shrugged. 'An answer doesn't really matter if it's a lie.'

'I admit he was being an ass, but he was also being forthcoming.' She snapped off her gloves and tossed them into the trashcan. 'Did it occur to you that he has no idea Lena's been doctoring all this evidence?'

Will scratched his jaw. 'I've found that people tend to hide things for different reasons. They don't want someone else to look bad. They think they're doing the right thing, but they're really not. They're actually hindering an investigation.'

Sara had no idea where this was going. 'I've known Frank for a long time. Despite that stupid, ignorant thing he said about Lionel, he's not a bad man.'

'Sweetpea.'

She rolled her eyes. 'I know it seems like I'm too close—'

'Those were nice gloves he was wearing.'

Sara found herself holding her breath. 'I walked right into that, didn't I?'

'Tommy took a beating.'

She sighed. Sara's instinct had been to protect Frank. She'd never considered that Will would see this for what it was – hiding evidence. 'Frank's hand was cut up pretty badly. They must've sutured him at the hospital.'

'I don't imagine they asked very many questions.'

'Probably not.' Even at Grady, cops were given a free pass on suspicious injuries.

'How dangerous is a gunshot wound if it grazes your hand?'

'Who was shot?'

Will didn't answer. 'Let's say your hand was grazed. You didn't get medical attention. You had a first aid kit to clean it out yourself, then you slapped some Band-Aids on it. What are the chances of getting an infection?'

'Extremely high.'

'What are the symptoms?'

'It depends on the type of infection, whether or not it gets into the bloodstream. You could be looking at anything from fever and chills to organ failure and brain damage.' She repeated her question. 'Who was shot?'

'Lena.' Will held up his hand and pointed to the palm. 'Here on the side.'

Sara felt her heart sink, though not for Lena. She was more than capable of taking care of herself. 'Frank shot her?'

He shrugged. 'It's likely. Did you see the cut on his arm?'

She shook her head again.

'I think he ripped it open on some metal that was sticking out of the garage door.'

Sara put her hand on the counter, needing the support. Frank had stood right in front of her and said that Tommy had cut him with the knife. 'Why would he lie about that?'

'He's an alcoholic, right?'

She shook her head, but this time it was more from her own confusion. 'He never drank on the job before. At least not that I ever saw.'

'And now?'

'He was drinking yesterday. I don't know how much, but I smelled it on him when I got to the station. I just assumed that he was shaken up because of Brad. That generation . . .' She let her voice trail off. 'I guess I glossed it over because Frank's from a time when it was all right to take a couple of drinks during the middle of the day. My husband would've never tolerated it. Not while Frank was on duty.'

'A lot has changed since he died, Sara.' Will's voice was gentle. 'This isn't Jeffrey's police force anymore. He's not here to keep them in line.'

She felt tears come to her eyes. Sara wiped them away, laughing at herself. 'God, Will. Why am I always crying around you?'

'I'm hoping it's not my aftershave.'

She laughed halfheartedly. 'What now?'

Will knelt down and started rummaging through the box of evidence. 'Frank knows Allison has a car. Lena didn't. Lena knows Allison didn't live in the garage. Frank doesn't.' He found a woman's wallet and opened the clasp. 'It's odd that they're not working together on this.'

'Frank made it clear he's finished with her. My personal vendetta aside, he has ample reason to cut her loose.'

'I gather they've been through a lot. Why cut her off now?'

Sara couldn't think of an answer. Will was right. Lena had done a lot of things in her career that Frank had covered for. 'Maybe this is just the last straw. Tommy is dead. Brad was badly injured.'

'I talked to Faith on the ride over. There's no Julie Smith

that she can find. The cell phone number you gave me was for a throwaway purchased at a Radio Shack in Cooperstown.'

'That's about forty-five minutes away.'

'Tommy and Allison must've had throwaways, too. Neither one has a record of a phone. We'll need their numbers before we can track back where the phones were purchased, but that's not going to make much of a difference, I think.' He held up the knife Frank had given them. 'This doesn't appear to have blood on it. Would they clean it during surgery?'

'They'd throw iodine on it, but they wouldn't clean it like this.' She studied the weapon. 'You'd expect blood around the hilt.'

'You would,' he agreed. 'I'm going to have the local field agent do a lab run for me. Can I leave some samples here so he can take everything when you're done?'

'Nick Shelton?'

'You know him?'

'He worked with my husband all the time.' She offered, 'I'll call him when I'm finished.'

Will held up the suicide note and stared at the words. 'I don't understand this.'

'It says "I want it over."'

He gave her a sharp look. 'Thank you, Sara. I know what it says. What I don't understand is who wrote it.'

'The killer?' she tried.

'Possibly.' Will sat back on his heel, staring at the line of text that ran along the top section of the paper. 'I'm thinking there's two people out there – the killer and the 911 caller. The killer did his thing with Allison, and the caller is trying to get him in trouble for it. And then Julie

Smith was trying to get Tommy off the hook by enlisting your help.'

'It sounds a lot like you've taken him off your list of suspects.'

'I thought you didn't like to make assumptions.'

'I'm fine when other people do it.'

Will chuckled, but he kept his gaze on the note. 'If the killer wrote this, who's he telling he wants it over?'

She knelt down to look over his shoulder. 'The handwriting doesn't look like Tommy's.' She pointed to the 'I' at the beginning of the sentence. 'See this? In Tommy's confession, he used a formal capital with—' Sara realized how useless her words were to him. 'Okay, think about it this way: if the first stroke of the "I" is like a stem, and there are branches ... Well, not branches, more like bars ...' She let her voice trail off. Trouble visualizing the shape of letters was at the core of his language problem.

'It's frustrating,' Will agreed. 'If only he had written something easier. Like a smiley face.'

Sara was saved a response by Will's phone ringing.

'Will Trent.' He listened for at least a solid minute before saying, 'No. Keep canvassing. Tell him I'll be there in a few minutes.' He closed the phone. 'This day just keeps getting worse.'

'What's wrong?'

'That was Lena. We've got another dead body.'

TWELVE

Will followed Sara in his car as she drove to the campus. He was starting to recognize landmarks, houses with fences and play sets that were familiar enough for him to remember the turns. The campus was new territory, and like most schools, it seemed to follow no particular design. Buildings had been added on when the money was there to construct them. Consequently, the campus sprawled over several acres like a hand with too many fingers.

He had spent all morning with Lena Adams, and he thought he could read her mood by now. Her tone on the telephone had been strained. She was getting to the breaking point. Will wanted to press her a little harder but there was no way he could have Lena meet him at the crime scene right now. Sara had made it obvious that she wasn't going to be in the same room with the woman she believed killed her husband. Right now, Will needed Sara's forensic eye more than he needed Lena's confession.

He dialed Faith's number as he steered his car around the curve of the lake. Will saw the boathouse Lena had pointed out to him earlier. Canoes and kayaks were stacked up against the building.

'You've got me for three more hours,' Faith said by way of greeting.

'We've got a second victim. They think his name is Jason Howell.'

'That's good news.' Faith was hardly the optimistic type, but she was right. A new victim meant a new crime scene, a new set of clues to follow. They had absolutely no useful information on Allison Spooner. The aunt was nowhere to be found. Allison hadn't made any connections at home or school. The only person who seemed to mourn her loss was Lionel Harris from the diner, and he was hardly a close friend. But Jason Howell's death would surely open up new leads. A second body meant a second course of investigation. Find one detail, one person or friend or enemy, that tied together both Allison Spooner and Jason Howell, and usually that detail could lead to the murderer. Even the most careful killer made mistakes. Two crime scenes meant twice as many mistakes.

Faith told him, 'You're going to have a hard time getting a warrant for all the names of the students in that dorm building.'

'I hope the college will be compliant.'

'I hope this baby comes out clutching a bag full of gold.'

She had a point. Colleges were notorious for their desire for privacy. 'Where are we on the warrant for Allison's room?'

'You mean the real one?' She seemed to be enjoying this. 'I faxed it to the station about ten minutes ago. There's no landline to the Braham house, so that's a dead end. Did you get anything from the autopsy?'

He told her about Allison's injury. 'It's unusual that the killer stabbed her through the back of the neck instead of slicing through the front.'

'I'll run it through ViCAP right now.' She meant the FBI's Violent Criminal Apprehension Program, a database designed to detect similarities in criminal behavior. If

Allison's killer had used this method before, ViCAP would have a record of the case.

Will asked, 'Can you give Nick Shelton a call, too? He's the local field agent here. Sara knows him. I want him to run some stuff to the Central lab for me. Sara's going to let him know when she's got everything ready.'

'What else?'

'I still need that audiotape of the 911 call. I want Sara to listen to the voice and see if it belongs to our Julie Smith.'

'Can you say a sentence that doesn't have "Sara" in it?'

Will scratched his jaw, his fingers finding the scar that ran down his face. He felt jittery again, much as he'd felt when he'd been talking to Sara in the basement of the funeral home.

She said, 'You know that Charlie is at Central this week?'

'No.' Charlie Reed was on Amanda's team. He was the best forensics guy Will had ever worked with. 'Central's an hour away from here.'

'You want me to give him a call and see if he can come out?'

Will thought about the garage, the crime scene in the woods. He was working two cases now – one against Lena Adams and Frank Wallace and another against the man who had killed Allison Spooner and possibly their new victim. 'I told the local chief I was bringing out a team. Might as well follow through on it.'

'I'll give him a call,' Faith offered. 'ViCAP shows no similar hits on a killer using a knife to cut from the rear through the carotid sheath, the carotid, the jugular, or the carotid and jugular. I cross-referenced the twist, too. No MO matches.'

'I guess that's good news.'

'Or really bad news,' she countered. 'That's a clean kill, Will. You don't do that your first time out. I have to agree with Sara on this one. I don't see your retarded kid doing this.'

'Intellectually disabled.' Now that Sara had pointed it out, the word was starting to grate. Will supposed he should feel some solidarity with Tommy Braham since they both had a problem. 'Call me when you hear from Charlie.'

'Will do.'

Will closed his phone to end the call. Ahead, Sara's SUV took a turn up a circular drive that led to a three-story brick building. She parked behind a campus patrol car at the front entrance. The rain was still unrelenting. She pulled up the hood of her jacket before running up the steps to the entrance.

Will got out of his car and ran up after her, his shoes kicking up puddles. His socks hadn't dried since he'd stepped into the lake this morning. They were in the process of rubbing a large blister on his heel.

Sara waited for him in a small alcove between two sets of glass doors. The sleeves of her jacket were dripping wet. She knocked on the doors. 'No one is in the patrol car out front.' She cupped her hands to the glass. 'Is someone supposed to be here?'

'The security guard was told to remain in the building until we got here.' Will punched a few buttons on the keypad by the door. The LCD screen remained blank. He turned around, trying to find a camera.

'Back door's open.'

Will looked through the glass. The building was wider

than it was deep. A set of stairs faced the front door. A long hallway shot off to the side. At the back of the building, an exit sign glowed softly over the open fire door.

Sara asked, 'Where are the police?'

'I told Lena not to call anyone.'

Sara turned to look at him.

'She got the call on her cell phone. Apparently, the campus police have her as an after-hours contact.'

'She didn't call Frank?'

'No. Funny, right?'

' "Funny" isn't the word I'd use.'

Will didn't respond. Sara's personal ties were clouding her view. She wasn't looking at this as a criminal investigation. With two suspects, you always worked one against the other to see who would flip first to get the better deal. Self-preservation generally won out over loyalty. The garage where Tommy lived painted a grim story for Frank and Lena. At this point, it was just a matter of who would talk first.

Sara looked back through the glass door. 'Here he is.'

Will saw a small black man making his way up the hall. He was young and skinny, the shirt of his uniform puffing out like a woman's blouse. He gripped his cell phone close to his chest as he approached them. With the other hand, he waved his key card over a pad by the door. The lock clicked open.

Sara rushed in. 'Marty, are you all right?'

Will could see why she was worried. The man's face was ashen.

'Dr. Linton,' the man said. 'I'm sorry. I was just outside trying to catch my breath.'

'Let's sit down.' Sara helped him to a bench by the door. She kept her arm around his shoulders. 'Where's your inhaler?'

'I just used it.' He reached his hand out to Will. 'Sorry for my state. I'm Marty Harris. I think you met my grandfather this morning.'

'Will Trent.' Will shook his hand. The man's grip was weak.

Marty waved his phone in the air. 'I was talking to Lena about what happened.' He coughed. The color was slowly returning to his face. 'I'm sorry, it just got me worked up again.'

Will leaned his back against the wall. He tucked his hands into his pockets. He had figured out a long time ago that showing his irritation tended to get the exact opposite result he was looking for. 'Can you tell me what you told Detective Adams?'

He coughed a few more times. Sara rubbed his back. 'I'm all right now,' he told her. 'It's just hard to recollect is all. I've never seen anything like that in my life.'

Will fought to keep his patience. He looked up and down the hallway. The lights were still off, but his eyes were adjusting. There wasn't a camera on the front door. He guessed the entrance keypad was meant to catch students and visitors going into the building. There was a camera over the fire exit in the back, though, and he could see it was tilted up toward the ceiling.

'It was like that when I got here,' Marty told him. He put his phone in his shirt pocket and pushed his glasses up his nose.

'When was that?'

'About thirty minutes ago, I guess.' Marty looked at his

watch. 'It seems like it's been a lot longer than that.'

'Can you tell me what happened?'

He patted his hand to his chest. 'I was making my rounds. I do that every three hours. With the students gone for the holiday, I wasn't checking the dorms. We do drive-bys to make sure the front and back doors are okay, but we don't go in.' He coughed into his hand before continuing. 'I was at the library when I noticed one of the windows on the second floor was open. The second floor to this building.' He paused for breath. 'I figured the wind must've pulled it open. Those old windows never shut tight. With the rain, there'd be a lot of water damage if I didn't do something about it.' He paused again. Will could see he was sweating despite the fact that the building was cold. 'I went up there and saw him, and . . .' He shook his head. 'I called the emergency number.'

'Not 911?'

'We got a direct number we're supposed to call if something happens on campus.'

Sara explained, 'The dean doesn't like bad publicity.'

'Can't get more bad than this.' Marty gave a harsh laugh. 'Lord, what was done to that boy. The smell is the worst part. I don't think I'll ever get it out of my breath.'

Will asked, 'Did you come in through the front door or the back door?'

'Front.' He indicated the fire exit. 'I know I shouldn't'a gone out the back, but I needed air.'

'Was the back door locked?'

He shook his head.

Will saw the red warning signs plastered all around the door. 'Does the alarm go off when it's opened?'

'Students usually bypass the alarm the first week they're

307

here. We can't keep up with them. The minute we hook it up, they disconnect it again. Lots of engineers and computer folks in this place. They look at it as a challenge.'

'They bypass the alarm for fun?'

'It's easier to get to the library that way. The back entrance for the cafeteria is there, too. They're not supposed to go through the loading docks because of safety concerns, but they sneak back through anyway.'

Will pointed to the camera mounted over the door. 'Is that the only camera in the building?'

'No, sir, and like I said, it was tilted up like that when I got here. There's another one on the second floor that's been tilted up, too.'

Will saw how easy it would be to get into the building undetected. As long as you knew where the camera was, you could stand underneath it and use a broom handle or something similar to push it up, then go on your merry way. Still, he asked, 'Do you have footage from the cameras?'

'Yes, sir. It's all sent to a central building on campus. I don't have the key, but my boss, Demetrius, is on the way. Should be here in an hour or two.' He told Sara, 'He's in Griffin with his daddy's people.'

Will asked, 'What about exterior cameras?'

'The cold got to 'em. They're all out. Half are frozen solid, the rest cracked like walnuts. We had one fall on a student's car the other day. Broke the back windshield.'

Will rubbed his jaw. 'Does anyone else know the cameras are out?'

He thought about it. 'Demetrius, the dean, maybe some other people if they happened to look up. Some of the damage is pretty obvious even from the ground.'

'I saw the keypad by the door. Is that the only way to get in through the front?'

'Yeah, and I already checked the logs. I can run a system diagnostic on the keypad. No one's been in or out the front door since Saturday afternoon. The only key card not scanned out belongs to Jason Howell. The room he's in is registered to that name, too.' He told Sara, 'I don't know why he'd stay here. Heat's off. Campus is shut down. Library closed at noon on Sunday. I thought this place was deserted.'

'It's not your fault,' Sara told him, though Will had some issues about the man opening the exit door. She redeemed herself by asking, 'Do you think you could get a list of all the students in this dorm? It might be good if Agent Trent had them.'

'That's not a problem at all. I can print them up for you right now.'

Will asked, 'Do you remember what you touched upstairs?'

'Nothing. The door was open a little. I got this feeling, like this really bad feeling. I pushed open the door with my foot and saw him and . . .' He looked down at the ground. 'I wish I could take a pill to forget all this.'

Will said, 'I'm sorry to push you, Mr. Harris, but do you remember if the lights were on or off?'

'All the switches are downstairs.' He pointed to a set of light switches by the stairs. They were high up, probably to discourage students from flicking them on and off at will. 'I turned on the lights before I went up, but then I turned them all back off like I found them.'

'Thank you for your time, Mr. Harris.' Will nodded toward the stairs, indicating he was ready to go.

Sara stood up, but she didn't leave. 'Did you know Jason?'

'No, ma'am. I'd seen that girl at the diner – Allison. You know how Grandaddy is, had her running around every second she was on the clock. I'd smile at her but we never talked. Something like this happens, and you realize you need to be paying more attention to the people around you. I'd hate to think there was something I could've done to stop all this.'

Will could tell the man was genuinely distressed. He put his hand on Marty's shoulder. 'I'm sure you did everything you could do.'

They walked back to the stairs. Sara reached into her jacket pocket and pulled out two pairs of paper booties to cover their feet. Will slipped them on, watching her do the same. She pulled on a latex glove and reached up, flipping the light switch. Light came down the stairwell.

Will went first. The right way to do this would be to send in a team to clear the building, but Will knew that the killer was long gone. Bodies didn't smell when they were fresh.

The building was old, but solid, with an institutional feel that wasn't exactly welcoming. The stairs went straight up to the third floor, creating a wind chamber for cold air. Will looked down at the black rubber treads. They would need to be checked for traces of blood. He hoped Faith had managed to get in touch with Charlie Reed. Their killer was smart, and he knew how to cover his tracks. But he didn't have the benefit of a giant lake to wash away his presence this time. If anyone could find trace evidence, it was Charlie.

The view at the top of the second-floor landing was

familiar: a long hallway lined with closed doors, but for one. At the end of the hall was a cased opening, the inside obscured by shadows.

'Bathrooms,' Sara guessed.

Will turned around and found the security camera mounted high in the corner by the stairs. The lens pointed up toward the ceiling. Jason's killer had probably pressed himself along the stair railing, stood on the bottom step leading to the third floor, and used something to push up the camera.

'You smell that?'

Will took a shallow breath. 'He's been here a while.'

Sara had come prepared. She reached into her pocket and pulled out a paper mask. 'This should help.'

Will was torn between his need to be a gentleman and his need to not throw up. 'Do you only have one?'

'I'll be okay.'

She continued down the hall. Will slipped on the mask. The air got marginally more breathable. Jason Howell's room was closer to the bathroom than the stairs. Their footsteps echoed around them, bouncing off the walls. The closer they got, the stronger the smell became. Will saw that the students all had bulletin boards on their doors. Papers were pinned on top of photographs and messages. The board on Jason's door was empty.

Sara put the back of her hand to her nose. 'God, that's bad.'

She took a breath through her mouth before going into the room. Will stood in the doorway. He held his breath as the smell of death washed over him.

The kid was lying on his back, bloodshot eyes staring at the ceiling. His face was swollen, almost crimson. His nose was broken. Dried blood circled his nostrils and mouth. One hand dangled to the floor. The thumb was cut. The tip of the pinky finger hung by a few threads.

'Looks like a match.' Sara had found Jason's student ID hanging from the closet door. She showed the picture to Will. Even with all the damage, there was no mistaking the resemblance.

Oddly, Jason was clothed in layers – a pair of sweatpants over pajama bottoms; several shirts, a terry cloth housecoat, and a zippered jacket. His body was swollen from the early signs of decomposition. Gases filled his stomach. The skin on his hands was turning green. His shoes were loosely tied but his feet were so swollen that the laces cut into his socks.

Knife wounds punctured his chest. The blood had dried in thick chunks around the material of his jacket. More blood was on the floor, smeared in a streak to the desk opposite the bed. The computer, the notebooks and papers scattered around, were all covered in blood and pieces of brain matter.

Sara put her hand to the boy's wrist. The check for a pulse was routine, though hardly necessary. 'I count eight stab wounds to the chest, three more to the neck. The bacteria from the gut is what's causing the smell. His bowel was pierced. He's filled with toxins.'

Will asked, 'How long do you think he's been dead?'

'Judging by the rigor mortis, at least twelve hours.'

'You think we're looking at the same killer?'

'I think whoever killed Jason knew him. This is hatred.' She pressed her fingers to one of the wounds in Jason's neck, stretching the skin back into place. 'Look at this. There's the same twist at the bottom that I saw on

Allison.' She checked the other wounds on the neck. 'All of them are the same. The killer plunged in the blade, then twisted it to make sure he hit the mark. You can see bruising from the hilt. I'd guess the same type of knife was used. I'll have to get them both on the table, but it's an educated guess that this is the work of the same killer.'

'Jason was a lot bigger than Allison. He wouldn't be as easy to overpower.'

Gently, she slid her hand under the back of the head. 'The skull is fractured.' When she pulled her hand back, it was sticky with blood.

'Window's closed,' he pointed out. A sizable puddle covered the floor under the sash. Marty had been in the room after all.

Sara had noticed, too. 'He did you a favor. The rain could've flooded the floor and washed away the trace.'

'Charlie's not going to be happy.' Will realized he hadn't told her that a team was coming. 'He's our forensics guy. He'll probably want to keep the body here until he's processed the scene.'

'I'll let Brock know. Do you want me to do the autopsy?'

He thought he might be stepping on her toes. 'If it's not too much of an imposition.'

'I'll do whatever you want.'

Will didn't know what to say. He was used to the women in his life making things more difficult, not easier. 'Thank you.'

She asked, 'Do you think Jason was Allison's boyfriend?'

'They're close in age. They go to the same school. They both ended up dead by the same killer's hand. I think it's not a big leap.' Will asked, 'Assuming you hate to hypothesize, what do you think happened here?'

Sara changed into fresh gloves, telling him, 'I assume Jason was at the computer when he was hit with something. Statistically, we can guess a baseball bat. I'll know pretty quickly. There will be splinters in his scalp.' She pointed to spatter on the wall that Will hadn't noticed before. Unlike the oak tree by the lake, the white walls of the dorm showed clear signs of the violence that was done. 'Medium velocity. I don't think the blow was meant to kill him. The killer wanted to stun him.' She pointed to the red streaks on the floor. 'He was dragged over to the bed and stabbed, but it doesn't make sense.'

'Why?'

She looked under the bed. 'There should be a lot more blood than this.' She indicated a fleshy chunk on the desk. 'Obviously, he bit off his tongue—'

Will gagged. 'Sorry. Keep going.'

'Are you sure?'

His voice sounded unnaturally high even to him. 'Yes. Please keep going.'

She gave him a careful look before continuing. 'It's not uncommon with blows to the back of the head for the victim to bite their tongue. Usually it doesn't come clean off, but it explains the volume of blood on the keyboard. His mouth would've been engorged with blood.' She indicated the wall above the desk. 'The spatter here is what you'd expect from the baseball bat making contact with the head, but over by the bed is a different story.'

'Why?'

'From the position of the wounds, I can tell that major arteries were hit in the chest and neck.' Sara explained,

'Think about it this way – Jason's on the bed. We assume he's conscious because of the defensive wounds on his hand. He almost lost his finger. He must've grabbed the knife by the blade. His heart would've been pounding like crazy.' She patted her fist to her chest, mimicking the quick beat. 'Spray, spray, spray. All over the wall.'

Will looked at the wall. She was right. Except for two splotchy-looking stains close to the body, the white paint was hardly marked at all.

Sara suggested, 'Maybe the killer was wearing something like a clean suit. He could've put down plastic. He'd have to cover the room, tape the walls. This was really planned.'

'I think that's a little complicated.' Will had yet to meet a killer who was that fastidious. 'Most killers keep it simple. They're opportunistic.'

'I wouldn't call taking a couple of cinder blocks, a padlock, and a chain to the middle of the woods opportunistic.'

'I just think you're making this too complicated. Couldn't the killer cover Jason's body with something and stab him underneath?'

Sara looked at the body. 'The stab wounds are closely patterned. I don't know. What are you talking about? Plastic?' She nodded to herself. 'The killer could've covered him in plastic. Look at the floor. There's a drip line here.'

Will saw the line. It was irregular, following the shape of the bed.

She said, 'Plastic doesn't absorb. The line wouldn't be thin like that. It would come off in sheets.'

'Sheets.'

Sara leaned down and checked the bed. 'Fitted sheet, top sheet.'

'Blanket?' Will asked. The kid had been freezing cold. It didn't make sense that he'd go to bed without a blanket.

Sara opened the closet door. 'Nothing.' She started on the drawers. 'I think you're right. It must have been something absorbent that—'

Will walked down the hallway to the bathroom. The lights were off, but he found the switch by the door. The fluorescents flickered overhead. Green light bounced off the blue tiles. Will had never lived in a dorm, but he'd shared a communal bathroom with fifteen other boys until he was eighteen years old. They were all the same: sinks in the front, showers in the back, toilets on the side.

He found a wadded-up blanket in the first stall. Blood coated the blue cotton, making it stiff as cardboard.

Sara came up behind him.

He told her, 'Simple.'

Will looked for the house with the swing set that marked the turn on Taylor Drive. Though the route was familiar, he was loath to take it. Searching Allison Spooner's room was a necessary chore, but Will's instincts told him that Jason Howell's dorm room held more promising leads. Unfortunately, Will wasn't a crime scene technician. He didn't have the credentials or equipment to process such a complicated scene. He would have to wait for Charlie Reed and his team to drive over from the Central GBI lab. Two students were already dead and Will had no idea what was motivating the killer. Time was definitely not on his side.

Still, there were procedures to be followed. He had

dropped by the station to pick up the warrant to search the Braham house. While he was there, he'd sent Faith the list Marty Harris had printed out of all the students in the dorm. She didn't have time to do all the background checks, but she was going to get started on them now and send the rest of the list to Amanda's secretary before she went to the hospital.

The police station had been oddly quiet. Will guessed they were all either on the street or at the hospital with Brad Stephens, who was still in a medically induced coma. Still, something was going on. The patrolmen milling around the desks hadn't glared at Will with the expected hatred. Marla Simms had handed him the fax without having to be asked. Even Larry Knox had stared at the floor as he walked to the coffee machine to refill his cup.

There were two cars parked in front of the Braham house. One was a police cruiser. The other was a four-door Ford pickup. Will parked behind the truck. Exhaust drifted up from the tailpipe. He could see two figures in the cab. Lena Adams was in the passenger seat. A man was behind the wheel. His window was down, even though the rain hadn't let up. He held a cigarette in his hand.

Will went to the driver's side. His hair was plastered to his head. He was freezing. His socks were still soaking wet.

Lena made the introductions. 'Gordon, this is the agent from Atlanta I told you about. Will Trent.'

Will shot her a glance that he hoped conveyed his intense level of irritation. Lena was being investigated for her part in Tommy's death. She had no business talking to his father. 'Mr. Braham, I'm so sorry to be meeting you under these circumstances.'

Gordon held the cigarette to his mouth. He was crying openly, tears streaming down his face. 'Get in.'

Will climbed into the back seat. There were a couple of fast-food bags on the floor. Work orders with the Georgia Power logo were stacked in an open briefcase on the seat opposite. Even with the open window, smoke hung in the air like a shroud.

Gordon stared ahead at the road. Raindrops popped against the hood of the truck. 'I can't believe my boy would do any of this. It's not in his nature to be hurtful.'

Will knew there was no use wasting time with kindness. 'Can you tell me what you know about Allison?'

He took another hit off the cigarette. 'Paid her rent on time. Kept the house clean. I gave her a discount for doing the laundry, looking after Tommy.'

'Did he need looking out for?'

Gordon glanced at Lena. 'He knows, right?'

Will answered, 'I know that he was slow, Mr. Braham. I also know that he held down several jobs and was well respected in town.'

The man looked down at his hands. His shoulders shook. 'He did, sir. He worked real hard.'

'Tell me about Allison.'

Gordon's composure came back slowly, but his shoulders were still slumped. When he moved the cigarette to his mouth, it looked as if his hands were weighted down. 'Was she raped?'

'No, sir. There were no signs of that.'

He let out a ragged, relieved breath. 'Tommy had a crush on her.'

'Did she feel the same way?'

318

He shook his head. 'No. And he knew it. I taught him early on to be careful around girls. Look but don't touch. He never had any trouble. Girls saw him like a puppy dog. They didn't see that he was a man.' He repeated himself, 'He was a man.'

Will gave him some time before asking, 'Allison was living in the house?'

He lit a new cigarette off the old one. Will could feel the smoke clinging to his wet hair and clothes. He made an effort not to cough.

Gordon said, 'She rented the garage at first. I didn't want to let her. That's no place for a girl to be living. She started talking about discrimination, said she had lived in worse, so I told her fine. I figured she'd move out in a month.'

'How long had she been renting from you?'

'Almost a year. She didn't want to live in the dorm. Said all the girls there were boy crazy, staying up too late. She knew how to flirt to get what she wanted, though. Had Tommy wrapped around her little finger.'

Will didn't address the tone of blame in the father's voice. 'She wasn't living in the garage, though.'

He didn't answer immediately. 'That was Tommy. He said it wasn't right for her to be out there when it was so cold, having to run back and forth to get to the bathroom in the middle of the night. He changed rooms with her. I didn't know until after the fact.' He blew out a dark plume of smoke that wreathed around his head. 'I told you, she had him wrapped around her finger. I should've put my foot down, paid more attention to what was going on.' He inhaled sharply, fighting his emotions. 'I knew he had a crush on her, but he'd had crushes before. He liked the attention she was giving him. He didn't have a lot of friends.'

Will knew he couldn't tell the man details about an active case, especially one that could result in a nasty lawsuit. But he felt for the father, wished he could give him some words of comfort about his son. Instead, he asked, 'Did you spend much time at home?'

'Not much. Mostly, I'm at my girlfriend's house. Tommy didn't know, but we were planning on getting married in the spring.' He exhaled sharply. 'I was gonna ask him to be my best man once I got back from Florida.'

Will gave the man a few minutes to collect himself. 'Did you know Allison's boyfriend?'

'Jay. James.'

Will guessed, 'Jason?'

'That's right.' He wiped his nose with the back of his hand. 'He wasn't around much. I didn't let her have anybody sleep over. Wasn't right for a girl that age to be fooling around.'

'Did Tommy know Jason?'

He shook his head, but said, 'I guess. I don't know. I wasn't involved in his life as much as when he was little. He was grown. He had to figure out how to be on his own.' His breath caught as he tried to inhale some smoke. 'I know my son. He would never hurt anybody. I know what he did to Brad, but that's not my boy. I didn't raise him that way.'

Lena cleared her throat. 'I saw what happened, Gordon. Tommy was running, but then he turned around. Brad didn't have time to slow down. I don't think your son meant to stab him. I think it was an accident.'

Will chewed the inside of his cheek, wondering if she

was lying to help the man feel better or telling the truth.

Gordon seemed to have the same question. He wiped his eyes again. 'Thank you. Thank you for telling me that.'

Will asked, 'Was Tommy acting differently lately?'

He swallowed hard. 'Frank called me a week ago about some mess he'd gotten into. One of the neighbors got mad at him. He never yelled at people before. Never had a temper. I sat him down and talked to him. He said they were giving him grief about Pippy barking too much.' Gordon blew out some smoke. 'He loved that stupid dog.'

'Did he drink?'

'Never. He hated the taste of beer. I tried to get him used to it, thought we could sit around on Saturdays, have some brews and watch the game together, but it never took. He got bored. Basketball was his sport. He couldn't keep up with all the rules for football.'

'Did he have any friends? Was anyone giving him trouble lately?'

'He never met a stranger,' Gordon answered. 'But I don't think there was anybody specific he was close to. Like I said, he was into Allison, and she was sweet to him, but more like you'd be with a little brother.'

'Did they hang out much?'

'I wasn't here to see it. He talked about her a lot. I won't deny that.'

'When is the last time you spoke with your son?'

'I guess the night he . . .' Gordon didn't finish the sentence. He took a hit off his cigarette. 'He called because he needed permission to use the credit card. He thought Pippy swallowed one of his socks. I told him to take her to the vet.'

'We haven't found his cell phone.'

'I made him get one of those pay-as-you-go deals. He had a good job. He was a hard worker. He didn't mind paying his own way.' Gordon flicked his cigarette out into the street. 'I can't be here anymore. I can't go into that house. I can't see his things.' He told Lena, 'You can go on in there. Take whatever you like. Burn the place down. I don't care.'

Will opened the door, but he didn't leave. 'Did Tommy collect knives?'

'I never let him near knives. I don't know where he got one. Do you?'

Will answered, 'No, sir.'

Gordon shook out another cigarette from the pack. 'He liked to take things apart,' the man said. 'I'd get to work and try to write my service orders and the pen wouldn't work. Tommy would take the springs out. I'd find a bunch of them in his pockets when I was doing laundry. Tore up the motor in the dryer once. I thought it was something to do with his problem, but Sara told me he was playing me. He liked practical jokes. Liked trying to make people laugh.' Gordon wasn't finished. He glanced into the rearview mirror, looking Will in the eye. 'I knew early on he was different. I knew I wasn't gonna have that kind of life with him, the kind of life fathers have with sons. But I loved him, and I raised him right. My boy is not a murderer.'

Lena put her hand on Gordon's arm. 'He was a good man,' she told him. 'He was a very good man.'

Gordon put the car in gear, making it clear he didn't want to continue the conversation. Will and Lena got out. They watched the Ford drive up the street.

The rain had slacked off, but Lena still pulled the hood

of her jacket up to cover her head. She took a deep breath and let it go slowly. 'Tommy didn't kill Allison.'

Will had figured that out a while back, but he was surprised to hear the admission. 'What brought about this epiphany?'

'I've spent most of the day talking to people who knew him. The same as I would have done if Tommy was still alive.' She crossed her arms. 'He was a good kid. He ended up in trouble the same way a lot of good kids do – he was at the wrong place at the wrong time. And he had a knife in his hands.'

'I think you mean that he was in the right place at the wrong time. Tommy was in *his* apartment. His garage apartment.'

She didn't contradict him. 'He stabbed a police officer.'

'Accidentally, from what I've heard.'

'Accidentally,' she agreed. 'And we had no legal right to go into that garage. Brad got the address, but it's not on the building. I led us here. I was the one who said that the garage was Allison's apartment. That's why Brad looked in the window. That's what started everything.' She took a shallow breath. He could tell she was scared, but determined. 'How does this work? Do I make a statement? Do I write out a confession?'

Will tried to figure out her grand scheme. It couldn't be this easy. 'Let's back up a second. What are you confessing to?'

'The false search of the apartment. I guess that's breaking and entering. My negligence led to a police officer being injured. Two officers. I elicited a false confession. I'm the one who walked Tommy back to the cells. I'm the one who didn't frisk him. The ink cartridge

323

was from my pen. I had some extra ones, so I changed it out, but Tommy got the cartridge from me. And we both know I've been dicking you around all day.' She gave a forced laugh. 'So, that's obstruction of justice, right?'

'Right,' he agreed. 'Are you willing to put all that on paper?'

'I'll let you tape it.' She pulled the hood off her head and looked up at Will. 'What am I looking at? Jail time?'

'I don't know,' he admitted, but the truth was she had skated a thin line. Her negligence wasn't willful. The false confession had been taken in good faith. She was cooperating now, even if she'd been recalcitrant before. She wasn't shifting blame. 'In the immediate term, I imagine you'll be suspended pending a review of my investigation. You'll have to go in front of the board. They might come down on you hard or they might not. Your pension is probably gone. If it's not, you could take a hit on years of service, get a period of unpaid leave. If they don't pull your badge, this is going to be on your record until you die. Finding someone to hire you might prove difficult. And Gordon Braham might bring a civil suit against you.'

None of this seemed to surprise her. She reached into her pocket. 'Do I give you my badge now?'

'No,' Will told her. 'I'm not in charge of that part. I just file my report. There's bound to be some political involvement with your city council and various other civilian boards. As for whether or not you're suspended pending the outcome, I would assume Chief Wallace is the one who gets to decide what to do with you.'

She gave a rueful laugh. 'I think he's already decided.'

Will felt oddly conflicted. He knew that Lena had

screwed up, but she wasn't alone in this debacle. The evidence in the garage told a story that she could use to get herself out of this mess, or at least lessen some of the pain. He felt compelled to ask, 'Are you sure about this?'

'Tommy was my prisoner. He was my responsibility.'

Will couldn't argue the point. 'Why did you call Marty Harris after you talked to me?'

She hesitated, and he saw some of her old slyness come back. 'I wanted to know the details.'

'Which were?'

She gave him a halfhearted account of the same story Will had heard from Marty Harris an hour ago. She told Will, 'I got Jason's contact information and called his mother. She lives in West Virginia. She didn't seem too concerned that the police were calling about her son.'

'How were you sure about the victim's identity?' Will realized the answer before he finished the sentence. 'You went to the school.' She must have called Will from the building, a detail Lena had seen fit to leave out. 'Well?' he asked.

'I was already there checking Allison's school records when Marty called me.' She shrugged. 'I needed to see if it was the same killer.'

'And?'

'I don't know. It makes sense. Jason was Allison's boyfriend. They both turn up murdered within a day of each other. Tommy doesn't fit into the puzzle anymore.'

That at least explained part of her sudden turnaround. Tommy was dead before Jason was killed. Lena would know that he was innocent of the first crime because he couldn't have committed the second one. 'Did you close the window in Jason's dorm?'

'I used a glove. I didn't want the rain to wash away any trace. I also covered my shoes and hair. I was careful, but you can get my rule-out samples at the station. They should be on file with the GBI.'

Will wasn't going to waste time berating her. 'What did you find out at the school? You said you were going through Allison's records.'

She took out her spiral-bound notebook and thumbed to the right page. 'Allison was taking four courses this semester. I won't bore you with the details – chemistry stuff. I managed to talk to three of her professors. One on the phone and two in person. They say Allison was a good student, kept her head down, did her work. They never noticed her hanging out with a particular group. She was a bit of a loner. Her attendance was perfect. No missed days. Her grades were A's and high B's. Campus security didn't know her name. She's never filed a report with them or been the subject of a report.'

'What about the fourth teacher?'

'Alexandra Coulter. She's out of town for the holiday. I left a message on her cell and home.'

'Any other known associates?'

'None of them knew about Jason, but it makes sense. He was a couple of years ahead of her, taking graduate classes. She was undergrad. They wouldn't mix except outside of class. She didn't have friends. I tossed around the name Julie Smith because you brought it up earlier. She's not a student.'

'Did you get a warrant for searching Allison's records?'

'No one asked for one, so I didn't volunteer.' She added, 'I also talked to Tommy's boss at the bowling alley. I showed him Allison's picture. He says he's seen her around with another kid – male, dark hair, chubby, obviously Jason Howell. Tommy was giving them free games, but the manager put a stop to it when he found out.'

'At least we know they've all met each other,' Will said. 'What else?'

'There aren't any Julie Smiths in town. I checked the phone directory. There are four Smiths – three in Heartsdale, one in Avondale. I called all four numbers. None of them know a Julie or are related to a Julie. Are you going to tell me who she is?'

'No,' Will said, but only because he didn't know the answer himself. 'Have you heard from Allison's aunt yet?'

'Nothing. I called the Elba detective a few minutes ago. He seemed annoyed to hear from me again, said he'd call when he had something to say.'

'Annoyed because he thought you were pushing him?'

'He doesn't strike me as the type who likes a woman telling him what to do.'

He should try Will's job. 'What else?'

'I've talked to the neighbors, everybody but Mrs. Barnes, who lives there.' She pointed at the yellow ranch house across the street. There was an old Honda Accord parked by the mailbox. 'There's no mail in the box, her newspaper's been taken in, and her car isn't in the carport, so I assume she's out doing chores.'

'What about the Accord?'

'I looked in the windows. It's spotless. I can run the tag through the computer.'

'Do that,' he told her. 'What did the other neighbors say?'

'Exactly what our guys found when they canvassed the street yesterday. Tommy was great. Allison was quiet. None of them socialized; this is a pretty old street. Not a lot of kids.'

'Any criminal activity?'

'Not a lot. There are two foreclosures. The kid at the end of the block was caught joyriding in his mama's Cadillac two weeks ago. Two houses over, there's an ex–crack addict living with his grandparents. He's been clean as far as we know. Three doors the other way is a Peeping Tom who's in a wheelchair. He doesn't get out as much as he used to since his father took the ramp off the front porch.'

'And this seemed like such a nice neighborhood.'

'Only two people were home when Brad got stabbed.' She pointed to a house two doors down from the Barnes residence. 'Vanessa Livingston. She was late for work because her basement flooded. She was waiting on her contractor and looking out the window right when Brad was stabbed.'

'And she saw . . . ?'

'Exactly what I saw. Brad was chasing after Tommy. Tommy turned. He had the knife here.' She held her hand at her waist. 'Brad was stabbed.'

'And the second neighbor?'

'Scott Shepherd. Professional gambler, so he's on the computer all day. He didn't see anything until after the fact. Brad on the ground. Me beside him.'

'Frank apprehending Tommy?'

She pursed her lips. 'You want to talk to Shepherd?'

'Is he going to tell me that Frank was beating Tommy or is he going to tell me that he can't remember?'

'He told me that he didn't see Frank. He went into the house and called the station.'

'Not 911?'

'Scott's a volunteer fireman. He knows the direct number for the station.'

'Lucky for you.'

'Yeah, I feel really lucky right now.' Lena flipped her notebook closed. 'That's all I've got. Gordon says there's a spare key under the mat. I guess I should go home and call around for a lawyer.'

'Why don't you help me instead?'

She held his gaze. 'You just told me I'm going to lose my badge.'

'You've still got it in your pocket, right?'

'Don't bullshit me, man. There's only two other days in my life I can think of that were worse than this one – the day my sister died and the day I lost Jeffrey.'

'You're a good detective when you want to be.'

'I don't think that's going to matter anymore.'

'Then what've you got to lose?'

Will walked up the driveway, listening for Lena's steps behind him. He didn't really need her help, but Will hated to be lied to. Frank Wallace was knee-deep in this crap, and seemed content to let one of his officers take the fall for his own bad leadership. Will didn't feel any loyalty to Lena, but the thought of a drunk, crooked cop running this town's police force did not sit well with him.

Will found the key under the front doormat. He was opening the door when Lena joined him on the porch steps.

He asked, 'Have you heard anything about Detective Stephens?'

'No change. I guess that's good.'

'Why didn't you call Chief Wallace about the body in the dorm?'

She shrugged. 'Like you said, I'm only a good cop when I choose to be.'

Will pushed open the front door. Lena went in first. Her hand was high on her side, a motion she probably didn't realize she'd made. Will had seen Faith take this same stance many times. She'd been a beat cop for ten years. There were some things your muscles couldn't unlearn.

The living room was right off the entrance. The furniture was old and sad, duct tape keeping the stuffing in the cushions. The carpet was an orange shag that went into the hallway. Will could feel it clinging to his shoes as he walked back to the kitchen. The carpet gave way to yellow linoleum. Gordon hadn't bothered to update anything except the stainless steel microwave that rested on top of an old Formica table.

'Dishes,' Lena said. Two plates, two forks, and two glasses were in the drainer in the sink. Allison had shared a meal with someone before she died, then cleaned up after herself.

Lena pulled a paper towel from the roll and covered her hand so she could open the refrigerator. There was a line of blue painter's tape down the middle. Store-brand sodas filled each shelf. There was no food except for a dried-up orange and a Jell-O pudding cup. Lena opened the freezer. The same taped line split the compartment, but the moisture had weakened the adhesive. One side was stacked full of frozen dinners. The other had a box of Popsicles and some ice cream sandwiches.

Will used the edge of his palm to raise the lid on the

kitchen trashcan. He saw two empty boxes of Stouffer's French bread pizza. 'I'll ask Sara about stomach contents.'

'Tommy would've had more time to digest.'

'True.' He used the toe of his shoe to push open a pair of louvered doors, expecting to find a pantry but finding a toilet, small shower, and even smaller sink. The bathroom was by the back door. He assumed this was the toilet tenants used when they rented the garage. It certainly looked like a young man had used the facilities. The sink was filthy. Hair clogged the shower drain. Towels were strewn on the floor. A pair of dingy-looking briefs was wadded up in the corner. There was one sock on the floor, a footie that went up to the ankle. Will imagined the other sock was slowly making its way through Pippy's digestive track.

Will realized Lena wasn't behind him anymore. He walked through the dining room, which had a glass table and two chairs, and found her in a small study off the family room. The room looked hastily abandoned. Stacks of papers lined the floor – magazines, old bills, news-papers. Gordon must have been using this as a dumping ground for all the paperwork associated with his life. Lena checked the desk drawers. From what Will could see, they were piled with more invoices and receipts. The lone bookshelf in the room was bare and dusty except for a plate that contained a moldy, unrecognizable piece of food. A glass was beside it, the liquid dark and murky.

The carpet showed tracks from a vacuum cleaner but it still had the same grungy feel as the rest of the house. There was an ancient-looking computer monitor on the top of the desk. Lena pressed the power button, but nothing happened. Will leaned down and saw that the thing was not connected to a power supply. Or a computer.

Lena noticed this, too. 'He probably took the computer to Jill June's. That's his girlfriend.'

'Did you see a laptop in the garage?'

She shook her head. 'Could Tommy even use one?'

'He probably ran the machines at the bowling alley. That's all computer controlled.' Will shrugged because he didn't know for certain. 'Gordon disconnected the landline. I doubt he was springing for Internet service.'

'Probably.' Lena opened the last drawer in the desk. She held up a sheet of paper that looked like a bill. 'Fifty-two dollars. This place must be better insulated than it looks.'

Will guessed she had found a power or gas bill. 'Or Allison kept the heat turned down. She grew up poor. She was willing to live in the garage. She probably wasn't big on wasting money.'

'Gordon's pretty cheap himself. This place is a dump.' She dropped the bill on the desk. 'Moldy food on the shelf. Dirty clothes on the floor. I wouldn't walk through this carpet with my shoes off.'

Will silently agreed. 'The bedrooms are probably upstairs.'

The design of the house was a typical split-level, with the stairs running off the back of the family room. The railing was coming loose from the wall. The carpet was worn to the backing. At the top of the stairs, he saw a narrow hallway. Two open doors were on one side. A closed door was on the other. At the mouth of the hall was a bathroom with pink tile.

Will glanced into the first room, which was empty but for some papers and other debris stuck into the orange shag carpet. The next room was sparsely furnished, slightly larger than the first. A basket of folded clothes was on the bare mattress. Lena pointed to the empty closet, the opened drawers in the chest. 'Someone moved out.'

'Gordon Braham,' Will supplied. He looked at the basket of neatly folded clothes. For some reason it made him sad that Allison had done the man's laundry before she died.

Lena slipped on a latex glove before trying the last room. Her hand went up to her gun again as she pushed open the door. Again, there were no surprises. 'This must be Allison's.'

The room was cleaner than the rest of the house, which wasn't saying much. Allison Spooner hadn't been the neatest woman on the planet, but at least she managed to keep her clothes off the floor. And there were a lot of them. Shirts, blouses, pants, and dresses were packed so tightly into the closet that the rod bowed in the middle. Clothes hangers were hooked on the curtain rod and the trim over the closet door. More clothes were draped over an old rocking chair.

'I guess she liked clothes,' Will said.

Lena picked up a pair of jeans in a pile by the door. 'Seven brand. These aren't cheap. I wonder where she got the money.'

Will could hazard a guess. The clothes he'd worn as a kid generally came from a communal pile. There was no guarantee you'd find a good fit, let alone a style you liked. 'She probably had hand-me-downs all her life. First time away from home, making her own money. Maybe it was important to her to have nice things.'

'Or maybe she was shoplifting.' Lena tossed the jeans

back onto the pile. She continued the search, lifting the mattress, sliding her hand between clothes, picking up shoes and putting them back in place. Will stood in the doorway, watching Lena move around the room. She seemed more sure of herself. He wanted to know what had changed. Confession was good for the soul, but her newfound attitude couldn't be solely traced back to her revelation about Tommy. The Lena he'd left this morning was ready to burst into tears at any moment. The one thing she was sure about was Tommy's guilt. Something else had been weighing her down, but now it was gone.

Her certainty was making him suspicious.

'What about that?' Will pointed to the bedside table. The drawer was cracked open. Lena used her gloved hand to open it the rest of the way. There was a pad of paper, a pencil, and a flashlight inside.

'You ever read Nancy Drew?' he asked, but she was ahead of him. Lena used the pencil to shade the paper on the pad.

She showed it to Will. 'No secret note.'

'It was worth a try.'

'We can toss this place, but nothing's jumping out at me.'

'No pink book bag.'

She stared at him. 'Someone told you Allison had a pink book bag?'

'Someone told me she had a car, too.'

'A rusted red Dodge Daytona?' she guessed. She must have heard about the BOLO Faith put on the car this morning.

'Let's try the bathroom,' he suggested.

He followed her up the hallway. Again, Will let her

conduct the search. Lena opened the medicine cabinet. There was the usual array of lady things: feminine aids, a bottle of perfume, some Tylenol and other pain relievers as well as a brush. Lena opened the packet of birth control pills. Less than a third of the pills remained. 'She was current.'

He looked at the prescription label on the birth control. The logo at the top was unfamiliar. 'Is this a local pharmacy?'

'School dispensary.'

'How about the prescribing doctor?'

She checked the name and shook her head. 'No idea. Probably from her hometown.' Lena opened the cabinet under the sink. 'Toilet paper. Tampons. Pads.' She checked inside the boxes. 'Nothing that shouldn't be here.'

Will stared at the open medicine cabinet. Something was off. There were two shelves and space at the bottom of the cabinet that served as a third. The middle shelf seemed devoted to medication. The birth control packet had been wedged in between the Motrin and Advil bottles, which were shoved to the far end of the shelf close to the hinge. The Tylenol was on the opposite side, also shoved to the end. He studied the gap, wondering if there was another bottle that was missing.

'What is it?' Lena asked.

'You should get your hand looked at.'

She flexed her fingers. The Band-Aids were looking ragged. 'I'm fine.'

'It looks infected. You don't want it getting into your bloodstream.'

She stood up from the cabinet. 'The only doctor in town rents space at the children's clinic. Hare Earnshaw.'

'Sara's cousin.'

'He wouldn't exactly welcome me as a patient.'

'Who do you normally see?'

'That's not really any of your business.' She pulled back the cheap mini-blind on the window. 'There's a car parked in Mrs. Barnes's driveway.'

'Wait for me outside.'

'Why do you—' She stopped herself. 'All right.'

Will walked behind her down the hall. When he stopped outside Allison's room, Lena turned. She didn't say anything, but continued down the stairs. Will didn't think there was anything of note in the girl's room. Lena had done a thorough search. What struck Will the most was what was missing: There was no laptop. No schoolbooks. No notebooks. No pink backpack. No sign that a college student was living here except for the enormous amount of clothing. Had someone taken Allison's school things? More than likely, they were in her Dodge Daytona, whereabouts unknown.

Will heard the front door open and close. He looked out the window and saw Lena heading down the driveway toward the cruiser. She was on her cell phone. He knew she wasn't calling Frank. Maybe she was looking for a lawyer.

He had more pressing things to think about right now. Will went to the bathroom and used the camera on his cell phone to take a picture of the medicine cabinet. Next, he went downstairs to Tommy Braham's bathroom. Will stepped over the towels and underwear to get to the medicine cabinet. He opened the mirrored door. An orange plastic pill bottle was the only thing inside. Will leaned in. The words on the label were small. The light was bad. And he was dyslexic.

He used his phone to take another picture. This time, he sent the image to Faith with three question marks in the message.

Sara had kept his handkerchief again. Will looked around for something to use so his fingerprints wouldn't get on the bottle. Tommy's underwear and dirty sock were not an option. Will rolled off some toilet paper from the roll stuck on the back of the toilet and used it to pick up the bottle. The cap wasn't securely screwed down. He opened the top and saw a handful of clear capsules with white powder inside. Will shook one into his hand. There was no writing on the side, no pharmaceutical logo or maker's mark.

In movies, cops always tasted the white powders they found. Will wondered why drug dealers didn't leave piles of rat poison lying around just for this particular reason. He put the bottle on the edge of the sink so he could photograph the capsule in his hand. Then he took a closer shot of the prescription label and sent both images to Faith.

As a rule, Will stayed away from doctors. He couldn't read them his insurance information when he called to make an appointment. He couldn't fill out their forms while he was sitting in the waiting room. One time, Angie had been kind enough to give him syphilis and he'd had to take a regimen of pills four times a day for two weeks. Consequently, Will knew what a prescription label looked like. There was always an official logo from the pharmacy at the top. The doctor's name and date were listed, the Rx number, the patient's name, the dosage information, the warning stickers.

This label seemed to have none of those things. It wasn't even the proper size – he'd guess it was half the usual height and shorter in length. There were plenty of numbers typed across the top, but the rest of the information was written in by hand. A cursive hand, which meant Will didn't know if he was staring at heroin or acetaminophen.

His phone rang. Faith asked, 'What the hell is that?'

'I found it in Tommy's medicine cabinet.'

' "Seven-nine-nine-three-two-six-five-three," ' she read. '"Tommy, do not take any of these" is written across the middle in cursive. Exclamation point at the end. The "do not" is underlined.'

Will said a silent prayer of thanks that he hadn't tasted the white powder. 'Is the handwriting feminine?'

'Looks like it. Big and loopy. Slanted to the right, so she's right-handed.'

'Why would Tommy have a bottle of pills that said don't take them?'

'What about the three letters at the bottom? Looks like "H-O-C" or "H-C-C" . . . ?'

Will stared at the fine print in the corner of the label. The words were so blurry that his head started to ache. 'I have no idea. The last photo is as tight as I can get. I'm going to get Nick to take it to the lab with the other stuff. Anything on Jason Howell?'

'He's worse than Allison, if that's possible. No phone. No street address, just a PO box at the school. He's got four thousand dollars in a savings account out of a bank in West Virginia.'

'That's interesting.'

'Not as much as you'd think. The amount's been going down slowly over the last four years. I'd guess it's some kind of college fund.' She told him, 'He also has a car registered in his name. Ninety-nine Saturn SW. Green. I already put out a BOLO.'

That was at least something. 'I'll check at the school to see if it's there. How are the background checks going on all the students who lived in Jason's dorm?'

'Slow and boring. None of these kids even have parking tickets. My mother had gotten me out of a DUI and a shoplifting charge by the time I was that age.' She laughed. 'Please promise me you won't remind me of that when my children get into trouble.'

Will was too shocked to promise anything. 'Did you track down the 911 audio?'

'They said they'd email it to me but it hasn't shown up yet.' Her breath was short, and he guessed she was walking through the house. 'Let me do a computer search for those initials on the pill bottle.'

'I'll ask Gordon if his son was taking any medication.'

'Are you sure you should do that?'

'Meaning?'

'What if Tommy was selling illegal drugs?'

Will had a hard time imagining Tommy Braham as a drug kingpin. Still, he admitted, 'Tommy knew everybody in town. He was always walking the streets. It'd be a perfect cover.'

'What does the dad do for a living?'

'I think he's a lineman for Georgia Power.'

'How are they living?'

Will glanced around the crappy kitchen. 'Not very well. Gordon's truck is about ten years old. Tommy was living in a garage without a toilet. They were renting out a room to help make ends meet. The house must have been really 'nice thirty years ago, but they haven't done much to keep it that way.'

'When I did the sweep on Tommy, I found a checking account at the local bank. His balance was thirty-one dollars and sixty-eight cents. Did you say the dad was in Florida?'

He saw where she was going with this. Florida was the beginning of a major drug corridor that went from the Keys up into Georgia and on to New England and Canada. 'This doesn't strike me as a drug thing.'

'That knife wound to the neck sounds gang to me.'

Will couldn't deny she was right.

Faith asked, 'What else do you have?'

'Detective Adams has seen fit to accept her part in Tommy Braham's suicide.'

For once, Faith didn't have a quick comeback.

'She said that Tommy didn't kill Allison, and it's her fault he managed to kill himself in custody, and that she'll take all the blame.'

Faith made a thinking noise. 'What's she hiding?'

'What *isn't* she hiding?' Will countered. 'She's lied and covered up so much that it'd be like pulling a piece of string on a ball of yarn.' He went into the kitchen, hoping to find a plastic bag. 'Allison had a lot of nice clothes.'

'What was she studying in college?'

'Chemistry.'

'How do you manage to dress yourself in the morning?' Faith sounded frustrated by his slowness. 'Chemistry? Synthesizing chemicals to produce more complex products, like turning pseudoephedrine into methamphetamine?'

Will found a box of Ziplocs in the last drawer he

checked. 'If Allison was cooking meth, or shooting it, she was being careful about it. She didn't have any needle marks. There aren't any pipes or drug paraphernalia around the house or in the garage. Sara will do a tox screen as part of the autopsy, but I'm not buying it.'

'And Tommy?'

'I'll have to call Sara.' He waited for her to say something snarky about his using Sara's name too many times.

Miraculously, Faith let the opportunity pass. 'There's no H-O-C or H-C-C in Grant County. I'll try the number at the top of the label. Eight digits. Too long for a zip code, too short for zip-plus-four. One digit too many for a phone number. One too little for Social Security. Let me plug it in and see if I get anything.' Will sealed the pill bottle in the plastic bag as he waited for the results.

Faith groaned. 'My God, does every single search have to turn up porn?'

'It's God's gift to us.'

'I'd rather have a live-in nanny,' she countered. 'I'm not finding anything. I can make some phone calls around the state. You know how some of the yokels are slow to enter their case files into the network. I'm just waiting around for Mama to come pick me up and take me to the hospital.'

'I'd appreciate anything you feel like doing.'

'If I watch one more home-remodeling show, I'm going to come down there and hope someone puts a knife in the back of my neck. And I've got the worst gas. I feel like—'

'Well, I should go now. Thanks again for your help.' Will closed his phone to end the call. He locked up the house and put the pill bottle in his Porsche.

Lena was still on the phone, but she got off when she saw Will. 'Honda belongs to a Darla Jackson. She's on parole for kiting some checks two years ago. She's already paid it off. The charge will roll off her sheet in January.'

'Did you talk to her?'

Lena glanced over his shoulder. 'I think we're about to get our chance.'

He turned around. An elderly woman was making her way down the driveway of the house across the street. She leaned heavily on a walker with a wire basket on the front. Bright yellow tennis balls were stuck on the back legs. The front door to her house opened, and a woman dressed in a pink nurse's uniform called, 'Mrs. Barnes! You forgot your coat!'

The old woman didn't seem concerned, though she was wearing nothing more than a thin housedress and slippers. The wind was blowing so hard that the hem kicked up as she navigated the steep drive. Fortunately, the rubber soles of her terry cloth slippers kept her from sliding down the concrete.

'Mrs. Barnes!' The nurse jogged down the driveway with the coat. She was a big girl with broad shoulders and ample cleavage. She was out of breath when she finally caught up to the old woman. She wrapped the coat around her shoulders, saying, 'You'll catch your death out here.'

Lena approached the women. 'Mrs. Barnes, this is Agent Trent from the Georgia Bureau of Investigation.'

Mrs. Barnes did everything but wrinkle her nose. 'What do you want?'

Will felt like he was back in third grade and being yelled at for various schoolboy atrocities. 'I'd like to talk to you about Allison and Tommy, if you have a minute.'

'It seems like you've already made up your mind about that.'

Will glanced back at her mailbox, remembering the street number from one of the incident reports. 'Someone from your house called the police about Tommy's dog barking. Your name wasn't on the report.'

'That was me,' the nurse volunteered. 'I look after Mrs. Barnes in the evenings. Usually I'm not here until seven, but she needed help with some chores and I didn't have anything better to do.'

Will hadn't realized how late in the day it was. He checked his cell phone and saw it was almost three o'clock. Faith had a little over an hour left before she went to the hospital. He asked the nurse, 'You're here every night?'

'Every night but Thursday, and I get the last Sunday of the month off.' Will had to slow down her words in his head to understand what she was saying. The woman had more of a twang than anyone Will had yet to meet in Grant County.

Lena took out her pen and notebook. She asked the nurse, 'Can you tell me your name?'

'Darla Jackson.' She reached into her pocket and pulled out a business card. Her fingernails were bright red press-ons that complemented her caked-on makeup. 'I work out of the E-Med Building over on Highway 5.'

Lena pointed to the ancient Accord parked in front of the house. She already knew the answer, but she asked, 'Is that yours?'

'Yes, ma'am. It ain't much, but it's paid for. I pay all my bills on time.' She gave them a meaningful look, and Will gathered that Mrs. Barnes didn't know about the bad checks.

Lena handed Will the card. He looked down at it for a

few seconds before asking Darla, 'Why did you call the police about Tommy?'

She opened her mouth to answer, but Mrs. Barnes took over, directing her words toward Will. 'That boy never did anybody any harm. He had the sweetest heart and the most gentle disposition.'

Will put his hands in his pockets, feeling like the cold was going to snap his fingers in two. He needed to find out more about Tommy's sudden mood change in case Faith was right about the drugs he'd found in the kid's medicine cabinet. 'The incident report says that Tommy was yelling at someone. I take it that was you, Ms. Jackson?' The nurse nodded, and Will wondered why Darla's name hadn't been listed in the report. It seemed odd that the cop hadn't recorded it along with all the other details. 'Can you tell me what happened?'

'Well, first off, I didn't know he was retarded,' she said, almost like an apology. 'As a registered nurse, I try to be more compassionate with people of special needs, but that dog was just yapping its head off and Mrs. Barnes was trying to go to sleep—'

'I have terrible insomnia,' the old woman interjected.

'I guess I let my temper get the best of me. I went over there to tell him to quiet it down, and he told me he couldn't and I said that I'd call the pound if he didn't find a way and they'd make that dog real quiet. As in dead quiet.' She seemed embarrassed. 'Next thing I know, I hear this loud noise. I look out the front window and it's cracked. You can see I put some tape on it.' Will looked up at the house. The glass in the window had a crooked silver line of tape along the bottom. 'That wasn't in the report.'

Mrs. Barnes took over. 'Lucky for us it was Carl Phillips

they sent. I taught him in the fifth grade.' She put her hand to her chest. 'We all agreed it was best to handle this with Gordon when he got back from Florida.'

Will asked the nurse, 'You're here every night. Does that include Sunday night and last night?'

'Yes. I've been up with Mrs. Barnes for the last three days. Her new medication has been giving her an awful time with her insomnia.'

'It's true,' the woman agreed. 'I can't even get my eyes to close.'

'Did you see anything happening over at the house? Cars coming and going? Did Tommy use his scooter for anything?'

'The bedroom's at the back of the house,' Darla explained. 'We were both back there all night on account of it's close to the toilet.'

'Darla, please,' Mrs. Barnes warned. 'There's no need for them to hear about that.'

Lena asked, 'Did either of you know Allison Spooner? She lived across the street in Tommy's house.'

They both became more circumspect. Darla offered, 'I saw her around.'

'Did you see her boyfriend?'

'Sometimes.'

'Did you know his name?'

Darla shook her head. 'He was in and out a lot. I heard them screaming sometimes. Arguing. Struck me as the type of boy with a temper.'

In Will's experience, teachers were pretty good at making accurate snap judgments of people. He asked, 'What about you, Mrs. Barnes?'

'I saw him once or twice' was all she offered.

'Did you ever hear him fighting with Allison?'

She touched her fingers to her ear. 'I don't hear very well.'

Will thought she was being uncharacteristically polite, since she'd certainly heard the dog barking. Of course, not many people wanted to speak ill of the dead. He imagined Mrs. Barnes would've had plenty to say about Allison Spooner last week. 'Have you seen her car in the driveway recently?'

'Gordon asked her to park it in the street because it was leaking oil,' Mrs. Barnes said. 'I haven't seen it there in a while. At least not this weekend.'

'Me neither,' Darla confirmed.

'What about the boyfriend's car? Did you notice what he was driving?'

Both women shook their heads. Again, Darla spoke. 'I'm not good with those things. It was a station wagon. Green or blue. I know that's not real helpful.'

He asked, 'Did Allison ever have any friends come around? Men or women?'

Darla offered, 'Just that boyfriend. He was a beady-eyed little thing.'

Will felt a drop of rain hit the top of his head. 'Did you ever talk to him?'

'No, but I can spot a loser a mile away.' She gave a shockingly rough laugh. 'I sure have dated plenty of 'em in my life.'

'The point is,' Mrs. Barnes interjected, 'Tommy did not hurt that girl.' She glared at Lena. 'And you know that.'

Lena said, 'I do.'

That shut her up. She glanced back at the nurse. 'I think I should go now.'

Will started, 'Mrs. Barnes—'

She cut him off. 'My son is a lawyer. Any more questions you have for me should be directed to him. Come, Darla. It's time for my show.'

With that, she twisted the walker and began the slow climb back up her driveway. Darla shrugged an apology before she followed.

Will said, 'I don't think I've ever had an elderly woman in a walker lawyer up to me before.'

There was a buzzing in the air, like a bunch of cicadas decided to start singing at the same time. The rain didn't fall so much as turn into a light mist. Will blinked, feeling beads of water forming on his eyelashes.

Lena asked, 'What now?'

'I guess that's up to you.' Will looked at his phone again to check the time. Charlie would be here soon. 'You can go back to the college with me or you can go look for a lawyer.'

She didn't have to think about her answer. 'My car or yours?'

THIRTEEN

They'd barely left Taylor Drive when the sky opened up. Visibility was short. Lena kept the speedometer just below thirty as she navigated the flooded streets. The cold was making her injured hand ache. She flexed her fingers, trying to get some blood circulating. There was definitely an infection. She felt hot and cold at the same time. A slow ache was building in the back of her head.

Still, she felt better than she'd felt in a long time. Not just because she'd taken responsibility for Tommy, but because she had found a way to get herself free one last time. And it *would* be the last time. Lena was going to do things the right way from now on. She wasn't going to take shortcuts. She wasn't going to take risks.

Frank couldn't fault her for falling on her own sword, and if he did, then he could go screw himself. Will Trent had figured out everything that happened in the garage, but he couldn't prove it without Lena and Lena wasn't going to talk. That was her leverage over Frank. That was her ticket to freedom. If Frank wanted to drink himself to death, if he wanted to risk his life out on the street, then that was on him. She washed her hands of it.

The death of Tommy Braham was the only thing that still weighed on her. She needed to talk to a lawyer about how to handle things with the county, but she wasn't going to fight them. She deserved to be punished. Tommy was her prisoner. Lena had just as good as handed him the means to take his life. Working the system, finding a loophole, was out of the question. Maybe Gordon Braham would sue her or maybe not. All Lena knew was that she was finished with this town. As much as she loved being a cop, as much as she craved the adrenaline rush, the feeling that she was doing a job that hardly anybody else in the world wanted to do – or could do – she had to move on.

Will shifted in the seat beside her. He'd been standing in the rain half the day. His sweater was wet. His jeans had never really dried. You could say a lot of things about the man, but you couldn't claim he wasn't determined.

She asked, 'When are we going to do this? My confession, I mean.'

'Why the rush?'

She shrugged. He wouldn't understand. Lena was thirty-five years old and she was looking at having to start her life back over again from scratch in the worst job market since the Great Depression. She just wanted to get it over with. The not knowing was the hard part. She was getting out, but how much blood was she going to have to leave on the table?

He told her, 'You can still work a deal.'

'You have to have something valuable to get a deal.'

'I think you do.'

She didn't acknowledge the fact. They both knew taking down Frank would make her landing a lot softer. But Frank had leverage Will didn't know about. For this to work, Lena had to keep her mouth closed. It was too late to back out now.

He said, 'Tell me about the drug situation in town.'

349

The question surprised her. 'There's not much to say. Campus security handles most of the small infractions at the school – pot, a little coke, a tiny bit of meth.'

'What about in town?'

'Heartsdale is pretty upscale. Rich people are much better at hiding their addictions.' She slowed down as she came to the red light on Main Street. 'Avondale is all right, about what you'd expect – mostly middle-class people, working moms smoking meth after they put the kids to bed. Madison is the sore spot. Very poor. High unemployment, one hundred percent federal lunch assistance for all the kids. We've got a couple of small gangs running meth. They tend to kill each other, not civilians. There's not much money in the police budget for setting up sting operations. We catch them when we can, but they're like cockroaches. You take out one and there are ten more waiting to take their place.'

'Do you think Tommy might have been dealing drugs?'

Her laugh was genuine. 'Are you kidding me?'

'No.'

'Absolutely not.' She shook her head, vehement. 'If he was, Mrs. Barnes would've beat Nurse Darla to the phone. There were too many people in his life who were watching him too closely.'

'What about Allison? Could she have been using?'

Lena considered the question more seriously. 'We haven't uncovered anything that says drugs with her. She was barely getting by, living in a dump of a house. Her grades were good. She hadn't missed a day of school. If she was selling drugs, she was doing a bad job, and if she was using drugs, she was holding on pretty well.'

'All good points.' He changed the subject. 'It's really

convenient that Jason Howell died before we could question him.'

She stared up at the light, wondering if she should just run it. 'I guess the killer was afraid he would talk.'

'Maybe.'

'Did Sara find anything?'

'Nothing remarkable.'

Lena glanced at Will. He was good at leaving things out.

He shrugged. 'We'll see what she finds in the autopsies.'

The light finally turned. Lena wrenched the wheel to the side. The back tires slipped as she pressed on the gas. 'Listen, I know you're sleeping with her.'

Will gave a surprised laugh. 'All right.'

'It's not a bad thing,' she allowed, even though it hurt her to admit it. 'I knew Jeffrey. I worked with him most of my career. He wasn't the kind of guy who went around sharing his feelings, but with Sara, everyone knew the score. He'd want her to find somebody. She's not the type of person who's good at being alone.'

He didn't speak for a few seconds. 'I guess that's a nice thing for you to say.'

'Yeah, well, I'm not holding my breath for her to say anything nice about me.' Lena turned the windshield wipers on high as rain slammed into the car. 'I'm sure she's told you a lot of stories.'

'What would she tell me?'

'Nothing good.'

'Is she right?'

It was Lena's turn to laugh. 'You're always asking questions that you already know the answer to.' Her cell phone started ringing, filling the car with the opening lines of Heart's 'Barracuda.' She checked the caller ID. Frank. Lena sent the call to voice mail.

Will asked, 'Why does the school have your direct number to call when there's a problem?'

'I know a lot of the guys on the security staff.'

'From when you worked there before?'

She was about to ask him how he'd found out about that, but Lena didn't think she'd get much of an answer. 'No, I know them from working as the liaison. The guys who were there when I was are all gone.'

'Frank sure does let a lot of the job fall to you.'

'I can handle it,' she said, but then realized that didn't matter anymore. From now on, the only early morning phone calls that came to her house were going to be wrong numbers.

'What's the security setup on campus? The same as when you were there?'

'It changed a lot after Virginia Tech.'

Will was familiar with the college massacre, the deadliest in American history.

She explained, 'You know how institutions are – they're reactive, not preventative. The bulk of the murders at Virginia Tech took place in the engineering building, so all the other schools tightened down security around their classrooms and labs.'

'The first victims were killed in their dorm.'

'It's hard to police that. Students have to have key cards to get in and out, but it's not a foolproof system. Look at what they did at Jason's dorm. How stupid is that to cut a fire alarm?' Her phone started ringing again. Frank. Lena sent it to voice mail.

'Someone's trying to get in touch with you.'

'You're right.' Lena realized she was starting to talk like Will Trent. Maybe that wasn't a bad thing considering he was running circles around her. She slowed the car to fifteen miles per hour as the rain rocked the car. Water flooded across the road, making the asphalt look rippled. The windshield wipers couldn't keep up. She slowed the car to a stop, saying, 'I can't see in front of me. Do you want to drive?'

'I can't do any better than you. Let's wait it out and talk about our murderer.'

Lena put the car in park. She stared at the whiteness ahead. 'Do you think we're looking at a serial killer?'

'You have to have at least three victims on three different occasions for it to qualify as a serial.'

Lena turned in her seat to face him. 'So, we've got to wait for a third body?'

'I hope it doesn't come to that.'

'What about your profile?'

'What about it?'

She tried to remember his earlier questions. 'What took place? Two kids murdered, both with knives, both while they were alone. Why did it happen? The killer planned it out. He brought the knife. He knew the victims, probably knew Jason better than Allison because he was obviously furious when he killed him.'

Will continued, 'He has a car. He knows the town, the topography of the lake and the placement of the cameras in the dorm. So, he's someone who went to the school or goes to the school now.'

She shook her head, laughing at herself. 'This is the problem with profiles. You could be talking about me.'

'It's possible a woman committed these crimes.'

Lena gave him a tight smile. 'I was with my boyfriend Jared last night and with you all day.'

'Thanks for the alibi,' Will told her. 'But I'm being serious. Allison was small. A woman could have over-powered her. A woman could have floated her out into the lake, then chained her down with the cinder blocks.'

'You're right,' she admitted. 'Women like knives. It's more personal.' Lena had carried a knife herself a few years ago.

Will asked, 'Who are the women we've come up against on this case?'

She listed them out. 'Julie Smith, whoever she is. Vanessa Livingston, the woman whose basement was flooded. Alexandra Coulter, one of Allison's professors. Allison's aunt Sheila, who hasn't returned my calls yet. Mrs. Barnes from across the street. Darla the nurse with the long red nails.'

'Mrs. Barnes gives Darla a pretty tight alibi. She says she was up with her all night both nights.'

'Yeah, well, my uncle Hank says he never sleeps, but every time I stay over I hear him snoring like a freakin' chainsaw.' Lena took out her notebook. Heat rushed through her body, but not from the infection in her hand. She kept her notebook angled away from Will as she thumbed past the 911 transcript, then quickly went to the page where she'd recorded Darla's details. 'The cell number of the 911 caller is a 912 area code. Darla's is a 706.'

'Did her accent sound unusual to you?'

'Kind of trashy, but she's obviously pulled herself up.'

'She didn't sound Appalachian to you, did she?'

Lena stared at him openly. 'She sounded like everyone I

354

grew up with in south Georgia. Where are you getting Appalachia?'

'Do you know any women in town who moved down from the mountains in the last few years?'

She guessed this was another bit of information he was going to keep to himself. Two could play at that game. 'Now that you mention it, we had some hillbillies a while back but they loaded up their truck and moved to Los Angeles.'

'Beverly Hills?' He chuckled appreciatively before throwing out one of his sudden subject changes. 'You should have your hand looked at.'

Lena looked down at her injured palm. Her skin was sweating so badly that the Band-Aids were peeling off. 'I'll be all right.'

He told her, 'I talked to Dr. Linton about gunshot wounds today.'

'You two kids know how to have fun.'

'She says the probability of an untreated gunshot wound getting infected is very high.'

No shit, she wanted to say. Instead, she told him, 'Let's go back to the profile.'

He hesitated long enough to let her know he wasn't happy about letting someone else change the subject. 'What's the sequence of events?'

Lena tried to wrap her brain around the question. 'We already went through what happened to Allison. With Jason, I guess the killer came into the dorm, moved the cameras, stabbed him, then left.'

'He covered Jason's body with a blanket. He knew there would be a lot of blood.'

That was new. 'Where was the blanket?'

'I found it in the bathroom at the end of the hallway.'

'You should check the drains, the—' She stopped herself. Will would know to do all of these things. He didn't need her help. 'There were four questions for the profile, right?'

'The last one is, you have to ask yourself who would have done these things in this order for these reasons.'

'Allison was killed before Jason. She could've been a warning that Jason didn't heed.'

'Jason was holed up in his dorm room. We don't even know if he heard about the murder.'

'So, the killer is antsy, worried that the message hasn't gotten through.' A thought occurred to her. 'The suicide note. The killer left it as a warning. "I want it over."'

'Right,' he agreed, and she assumed he'd figured this out a while ago without telling her.

Still, she said, 'It would make sense that the killer would be angry with Jason for not taking Allison's death as a warning. He was stabbed at least eight or nine times. That speaks to a lot of anger.'

Will looked up at the sky. 'Rain's let up.'

Lena sat up in the seat, sliding the gear into drive. She rolled the car slowly forward. The road was still flooding. Streams of water gushed back toward Main Street. 'Both Allison and Jason were students. They could be mixed up in something to do with the school.'

'Like what?'

'I don't know. A grant. There's all kinds of government money going in and out of there. Defense spending. The engineering school works on medical devices, nano-technology. The polymer labs are testing all kinds of adhesives. We're talking hundreds of millions of dollars.'

'Would a grad student have access to the money?'

She thought about it. 'No. The doctoral candidates might, but the grad students basically do shitwork around the labs and the undergrads can't wipe their own asses without getting permission. I used to date a guy who was in one of the master's programs. They're not involved in anything remotely interesting.'

They had reached Jason Howell's dorm. There were two black vans parked outside. They each had the GBI logo on their doors and CRIME SCENE UNIT emblazoned in white on the sides. Despite herself, Lena felt excited, like a bloodhound who'd caught a scent. The sensation quickly faded. She had spent countless hours at this school studying for a degree that she would probably never get to use. At best, her education would go toward being one of those annoying people who point out everything they get wrong on *CSI*.

Will looked at his cell phone. 'I need to make a quick call to my partner, if you don't mind.'

'Sure.' Lena parked the car. The rain was still pounding down, and she bolted from the car and ran up the steps, holding down the hood of her jacket with both hands.

Marty was sitting inside reading a magazine. She knocked on the door. He jerked up his head, his glasses tilting on his nose. He buzzed her in with his card.

He said, 'You look bad.'

Lena was taken aback by the comment. She ran her fingers through her hair, feeling a damp that hadn't come from the rain. 'It's been a long day.'

'For you and me both.' Marty sat back on the bench. 'I'll be glad when it's over.'

'Anything happening?'

'They got three men upstairs. Two more went over to the parking decks. The guy in charge, he's got a handlebar mustache like he's outta the circus. He found some car keys up in the room and drove around clicking the alarm until it went off.'

Lena nodded her approval, thinking the guy was pretty smart for a circus freak.

Marty admitted, 'I never checked the parking decks. He was parked on the third level by the ramp.'

Lena gave him a pass. 'I never checked the decks when all the kids were gone, either.'

'Uh-oh. Here he comes.' Marty reached over and pressed his key card against the pad.

Will pushed open the door, stamping his feet on the floor. 'Sorry,' he apologized. 'Mr. Harris, thank you for giving us your time today. I'm sorry we're taking you away from your family.'

'Demetrius told me to stay here as long as you need me.'

'Can you tell me who was on shift last night?'

'Demetrius. He's my boss. We've been switching back and forth so we each get some time off for the holiday.' He put down the magazine. 'He doesn't remember anything, but he'll be happy to talk to you whenever you want.'

Lena thought there were more important things for Will to work on right now. 'Marty told me that one of your people found Jason's car over in the deck. They're looking at it now.'

Will smiled. She could almost feel his relief. 'That's good. Thank you, Mr. Harris.'

He offered, 'Demetrius is at the office pulling all the security tapes for you. I can drive you over if you want.'

Will glanced at Lena. Staring at videotaped footage for

hours on end hoping to find two seconds of a clue was the kind of mind-numbing work that could make you want to put a bullet in your head. Lena wanted to be at that car combing through the carpet fibers, looking for traces of blood or fingerprints, but there was no point.

She volunteered, 'I'll go look at the tapes if you want.'

'It's not going to be fun.'

'I think I've had enough fun lately.'

Lena sat in the interrogation room at the police station where she had talked to Tommy Braham two days before. She had rolled in the television cart with the old VCR and newer digital equipment that they sometimes used to record interviews. The film from the campus security cameras was a combination of both – digital for the outside cameras and regular VCR tape for inside. Demetrius, the chief of security, had given her everything he had.

As far as Lena knew, she was the only person in the station right now except for Marla Simms, who never left her desk, and Carl Phillips, who was back in the cells working as booking officer for the night. Carl was a big guy who didn't take a lot of crap off anybody, which was why Frank had stuck him with booking duty. Carl was incredibly honest. Frank was doing everything he could to keep the man away from Will Trent.

Lena had already gotten the story from Larry Knox, who gossiped like a woman. She knew Carl had protested kicking out some of the more talkative prisoners in the cells after Tommy's body was found. Frank had told Carl to leave if he didn't approve, and Carl had taken him up on the offer. The only prisoners Frank hadn't let go were either comatose or stupid. Top among this last designation was Ronald Porter, a twat of a man who'd beaten his wife so many times that her face had caved in. Frank had found a way to bully Ronny into keeping quiet. He was trying to push Carl around. He was lying to Will Trent. He was hiding evidence, probably postponing the delivery of the audio from the 911 tape. He thought he was blackmailing Lena.

The old man had a lot on his plate.

Lena rubbed her eyes, trying to clear her vision. The room was stuffy and hot, but that wasn't the problem. She was pretty sure she had a fever. Her hand was already sweating through the fresh Band-Aids she'd found in the first aid kit. The flesh underneath was raw and hot. She had heard from Delia Stephens that they were going to wake Brad in the morning. Lena would go over first thing and find a nurse to take a look at her injury. She'd probably need a shot and have to answer a lot of questions.

There would be worse questions tonight. She would have to tell Jared what was going on. At least part of what was going on. Lena didn't want to burden him with the whole truth. And she hadn't laid herself in front of an oncoming train for nothing. Losing Jared on top of giving up her badge was the kind of sacrifice she was not willing to make.

Lena turned back to work. The videotapes she'd been watching for the last two hours ranged from tedious to boring. She should've just gone home but Lena felt a weird sense of duty toward Will Trent. He'd made her into a reluctant Cinderella. Lena figured it would take until midnight to watch all these tapes, around the same time her badge turned into a pumpkin.

She had found the good stuff early on. According to the

time code, last night at eleven-sixteen and twenty-two seconds, the fire door at the back of Jason's building was opened. Lena was familiar with the layout from her own days with campus security. The dorm, the cafeteria, and the back of the library formed an open U with loading docks in the middle. The school didn't let students use the area as a shortcut because a kid had fallen off one of the docks several years ago and broken his leg in three places. The resulting lawsuit had been a hard blow, and they'd blown even more money putting in xenon lights that lit up the place like a Broadway stage.

The camera over the exit door recorded in color. The light coming through the door when it was opened showed xenon blue. Then the camera jerked and showed the ceiling with a pie-shaped wedge of blue light cutting the darkness. The door was closed, and the ceiling went dark.

At eleven-sixteen and twenty-eight seconds, a figure came into the second-floor hallway. The camera wasn't night-vision equipped, but the light from the open dorm room picked out the form. Jason Howell's clothes were bulky, the same as Lena had seen when the kid was lying dead in his bunk. Jason looked around nervously. His movements were panicked. He had obviously heard a noise, but he dismissed it easily enough. At eleven-sixteen and thirty-seven seconds, he went back into his room. From the sliver of light in the hall, she could tell he'd left his door slightly ajar.

The killer took his time climbing the stairs. Maybe he wanted to make sure Jason was caught truly unaware. It wasn't until eleven-eighteen on the dot that the second-floor camera tilted up. The killer wasn't as adept this time.

Lena imagined he'd slipped on the stairs. The camera had only tilted slightly, at an angle rather than straight up, and she worked the pause until she caught sight of the tip of a wooden baseball bat. The rounded end was easily distinguishable, but the Rawlings logo gave it away. She recognized the lettering style from her softball days.

At eleven-twenty-six and two seconds, the xenon light once again flashed against the first-floor ceiling as the exit door opened. The killer had taken roughly eight minutes to end Jason's life.

Marla knocked on the door as she walked into the room. Lena paused the tape she was staring at – the digital film of the empty parking lot in front of the library. 'What is it?'

'You've got a visitor.' Marla turned on her heel and left.

Lena tossed down the remote, thinking Marla Simms was one person she would not miss when she left this place. Actually, now that she gave it some consideration, Lena could not name one person in town she couldn't live without. It seemed odd to feel so detached from a group of people who had comprised her world for the last several years. Lena had always thought of Grant County as her home, the police force as her family. Now, she could only think about how good it would feel to finally be rid of them.

She pushed open the metal fire door and walked into the squad room. Lena stopped when she saw the woman waiting in the lobby, instantly recognizing Sheila McGhee from the picture Frank had taken out of Allison's wallet. They had all been sitting on a bench in front of the student center. The boy Lena now knew was Jason Howell had his arm around Allison's waist. Sheila sat beside her niece, close but not too close. The sky was deep blue behind them. The leaves had started to fall.

In person, Sheila McGhee looked thinner, harder. Lena had thought from the photo that she was local town trash, and now she guessed Sheila was the Elba, Alabama, version of the same. She was the sort of stick thin you got from eating too little and smoking too much. Her skin hung limply from the bones of her face. Her eyes were sunken. The woman in the photo had been smiling. Sheila McGhee looked like she would never smile again.

She nervously clutched her purse in front of her stomach as Lena approached. 'Is it true?'

Marla was at her desk. Lena reached across and pressed the buzzer to open the gate. 'Why don't you come back?'

'Just tell me.' She grabbed Lena's arm. She was strong. The veins along the back of her hand looked like braided pieces of twine.

'Yes,' Lena confirmed. 'Allison is dead.'

Sheila wasn't convinced. 'She looked like a lot of girls.'

Lena covered the woman's hand with her own. 'She worked at the diner down the street, Mrs. McGhee. Most of the cops who work here knew her. She was known to be a very sweet girl.'

Sheila blinked several times, but her eyes were dry.

'Come back with me,' Lena offered. Instead of leading her to the interrogation room, she went into Jeffrey's office. Oddly, Lena felt a sudden pang of loss. She understood that somewhere in the back of her mind, she'd thought that in ten, maybe fifteen years, she'd rightfully have this office. Lena hadn't realized the dream was even there until she'd lost it.

Now wasn't the time to dwell on her own broken dreams. She indicated the two chairs on the other side of the desk. 'I'm so sorry for your loss.'

Sheila sat on the edge of the seat, her purse in her lap. 'Was she raped? Just tell me right out. She was raped, wasn't she?'

'No, she wasn't raped.'

The woman seemed confused. 'Did that boyfriend of hers kill her?'

'No, ma'am.'

'Are you sure?'

'Yes, ma'am.' Lena sat down beside her. She kept her hand in her lap. The skin was hotter than before. Every heartbeat shot a throb through her fingers.

Sheila said, 'His name's Jason Howell. She's been seeing him a couple of years. They weren't getting along lately. I don't know what was going on. Some kind of disagreement or something. Allison was torn up about it but I told her to just let him go. Ain't no man worth that kind of misery.'

Lena flexed her hand. 'I've just come from the college, Mrs. McGhee. Jason Howell is dead. He was murdered last night.'

She looked as shocked as Lena had felt when she'd heard the news from Marty. 'Murdered? How?'

'We think he was killed by the same man who murdered your niece.'

'Well...' She shook her head, confused. 'Who would kill two college students? They didn't have a dime between them.'

'That's what we're trying to figure out.' Lena paused, giving the woman time to recover. 'If you could think of anybody in Allison's life, a person she mentioned, maybe something she'd gotten mixed up in that she couldn't—'

'That don't even make sense. What could Allison do to anybody? She never hurt nobody.'

'Did she ever tell you about her friends? Talk about anybody in her life?'

'There was that Tommy. He's retarded, got a thing for her.' Realization dawned. 'Have you talked to him?'

'Yes, ma'am. We cleared him of the crime.'

She kept clutching the purse in her lap. 'What about that landlord? Seemed like he had a jealous girlfriend.'

'They were both in Florida when the crime was committed.'

Tears moistened her eyes but didn't fall. She was obviously trying to think of someone else who could have done this. Finally, she gave up, taking a short breath and letting it out between her lips. Her shoulders slumped. 'None of this makes sense. None of it.'

Lena kept her own counsel. She had been a cop for fifteen years and she had yet to work a murder case that made much sense. People always killed for the stupidest reasons. It was depressing to think that life held such little value.

Sheila opened her purse. 'Can I smoke in here?'

'No, ma'am. Would you like to go outside?'

'Too damn cold.' She chewed at her thumbnail as she stared at the wall. The rest of her nails were chewed to the quick. Lena wondered if Allison had picked up the habit from her aunt. The girl's nails had been painfully short.

Sheila said, 'Allison had a professor she was mad at because he gave her a bad grade.'

'Do you remember his name?'

'Williams. She's never made a C on a paper in her life. She was pretty upset about it.'

'We'll look into that,' Lena told her, but she'd already talked to Rex Williams. He'd been in New York with his family since Saturday afternoon. A call to Delta confirmed his alibi. 'Did Allison have a car?'

Her eyes shifted to the floor. 'It was her mama's. She kept it in Judy's name because the insurance was cheaper that way.'

'Do you remember the make and model?'

'I don't know. It was old, held together by spit and rust. I can look it up when I get home.' She clutched her purse as if she was ready to leave. 'Do you need me to do that now?'

'No,' Lena told her. She was fairly certain Allison drove a red Dodge Daytona. 'Did you talk to your niece much on the phone?'

'Once a month. We got closer after her mama passed.' A look crossed her face. 'I guess it really is just me now.' She swallowed hard. 'I got a son in Holman stamping out license plates. About the only thing he's ever done right in his life.'

She meant Holman State Prison in Alabama. 'What's he in for?'

'Being stupid.' Her anger was so palpable that Lena resisted the urge to lean back in her chair. 'He tried to rob a liquor store with a water pistol. That boy's been in prison more days than he's been out.'

'Is he affiliated with a gang?'

'Well, who the hell knows?' she demanded. 'Not me, that's for sure. I ain't talked to him since they sent him up. Washed my hands of it all.'

'Was he close to Allison?'

'Last time they were together was when she was thirteen, fourteen. They were out swimming and he held her head under the water until she threw up. Little shit ain't no better than his daddy.' She started rummaging around in her purse, but then seemed to remember she couldn't smoke. She pulled out a pack of gum and shoved two pieces into her mouth.

'What about Allison's father?'

'He's living in California somewhere. He wouldn't know her if she passed him on the street.'

'Was she seeing a counselor here at school?'

Sheila gave her a sharp look. 'How did you know about that? Was it the counselor did it?'

'We don't know who did it,' Lena reminded her. 'We're looking into all angles. Do you know her counselor's name?'

'Some Jew. A woman.'

'Jill Rosenburg?' Lena knew the psychiatrist from another case.

'That sounds like it. Do you think she could'a done it?'

'It's not likely, but we'll talk to her. Why was Allison seeing Dr. Rosenburg?'

'She said the school made her.'

Lena knew freshmen were required to see a counselor once a semester, but after that, attendance was left to them. Most students found better ways to spend their time. 'Was Allison depressed? Was she ever suicidal?'

Sheila looked down at her torn fingernails. Lena recognized the shame in her face.

'Mrs. McGhee, it's all right to talk about it in here. All of

367

us want to find out who did this to Allison. Even the smallest bit of information might help.'

She took a deep breath before confirming, 'She cut her wrists eight years ago when her mama died.'

'Was she hospitalized?'

'They kept her for a few days, gave her some outpatient therapy. We were supposed to keep it up, but there ain't no money for doctors when you can barely put food on the table.'

'Did Allison seem better?'

'She was good off and on. Like me. Probably like you. There are good days and bad days, and as long as there aren't too many of either, you get along with your life fine.'

Lena thought that was one of the most depressing ways to live your life that she had ever heard. 'Was she taking medication?'

'She said the doctor gave her something new to try. Far as I could see, it wasn't helping much.'

'Did she complain about school? Work?'

'Never. Like I said, she put on a good face. Life is hard, but you can't get down about every shitty thing that happens to you.'

'I found a picture of you in Allison's wallet. She was with you and Jason. It looked like you were all sitting on a bench in front of the student center.'

'She kept that in her wallet?' For the first time, Sheila's features relaxed into something close to a smile. She searched her purse again and found a photograph that was a match for the one in her niece's wallet. She stared at the image a long while before showing it to Lena. 'I didn't know she kept a copy for herself.'

'When was it taken?'

'Two months ago.'

'September?'

She nodded, smacking her gum. 'The twenty-third. I had a couple of days off and thought I'd drive over and surprise her.'

'What was Jason like?'

'Quiet. Arrogant. Too touchy. He kept holding her hand. Stroking her hair. Would've drove me up the wall having some boy pawing me like that, but Allison didn't care. She was in *love*.' She put enough sarcasm in her voice to make the word sound obscene.

Lena asked, 'How much time did you spend around Jason?'

'Ten, fifteen minutes? He said he had a class, but I think he was nervous around me.'

Lena could understand why. Sheila didn't seem to have a high opinion of men. 'What made you think Jason was arrogant?'

'He just had this look on his face like his shit don't stink. You know what I'm saying?'

Lena had a hard time reconciling the chubby grad student she had seen on Jason's student ID with the arrogant prick Sheila was painting. 'Did he say anything specifically?'

'He'd just bought her this ring. It was cheaper than dirt, and not good for her color, but he was all puffed out like a peacock about it. Said it was a promise ring to buy her a nicer one by Thanksgiving.'

'Not by Christmas?'

She shook her head.

Lena sat back in the chair, thinking about what the

woman had said. You didn't give people Thanksgiving Day gifts. 'Did either of them say anything about expecting some money to come in?'

'Ain't no money coming in for either one of 'em. They were poor as church mice.' Sheila snapped her fingers. 'What about that old colored man at the diner?'

Lena had thought Frank Wallace was the only person who still used that word. 'We've talked to Mr. Harris. He's not involved in this.'

'He was hard on her, but I told her it was good she was learning how to work with the colored. You look around big corporations now and they're filled with black people.'

'That's true,' Lena said, wondering if the woman thought her brown skin was the product of a bad home-tanning experiment. 'Did Allison have other friends that she talked about?'

'No. There was just Jason all the time. Her whole world was wrapped up in him, even though I kept telling her not to put all her eggs in one basket.'

'Did Allison date anyone in high school?'

'Nobody. She was always about her grades. All she cared about was getting into college. She thought it would save her from . . .' She shook her head.

'Save her from what?'

A tear finally fell from her eye. 'From ending up exactly the way she did.' Her lip started to tremble. 'I knew I shouldn't let myself hope for her. I knew something bad would happen.'

Lena reached over and took the woman's bony hand. 'I'm so sorry about this.'

Sheila straightened her spine, making it clear she didn't need comforting. 'Can I see her?'

'It'd be better if you waited until tomorrow. The people who are with her now are taking care of her for you.'

She nodded, her chin dipping down once, then jerking back up again. Her eyes were focused somewhere on the wall. Her chest rose and fell, a slight wheeze to her breath from years of smoking.

Lena looked around the room, giving the woman some time to pull herself together. Until yesterday, she hadn't been in Jeffrey's office since his death. All his stuff had been sent to the Linton house after he died, but Lena could still remember what the room had looked like – the shooting trophies and photographs on the walls, the neatly stacked papers on the desk. Jeffrey had always kept a small framed picture of Sara by the phone. It wasn't the sort of glamour shot you'd expect a husband to have of his wife. Sara was sitting on the bleachers at the high school. Her hands were tucked into a bulky sweatshirt. Her hair was blowing in the wind. Lena supposed the scene had a deeper meaning, just like her picture of Jared at the football stadium. Jeffrey tended to stare at the picture a lot when he was in the middle of a difficult case. You could almost feel his desire to be home with Sara.

The door cracked open. Frank looked in. He was visibly angry, fists clenched, jaw so tight with fury it looked like his teeth might break. 'I need to see you.'

Lena felt a chill from his tone, like the temperature in the room had dropped twenty degrees. 'I'll be there in a minute.'

'Now.'

Sheila scrambled to stand, taking her purse with her. 'I'll be going.'

'You don't have to rush.'

'No.' She glanced nervously at Frank. There was fear in her voice, and Lena suddenly understood that Sheila McGhee was a woman who had been on the receiving end of a lot of anger from the men in her life. 'I've taken up your time when I know you've got better things to do.' She took out a piece of paper and handed it to Lena as she rushed toward the door. 'This is my cell phone number. I'm staying in the hotel over in Cooperstown.' She turned away from Frank as she left the room.

Lena asked, 'Why did you do that? She was obviously scared.'

'Sit down.'

'I don't—'

'I said sit!' Frank slammed her into the chair. Lena nearly fell back onto the floor. 'What the hell is wrong with you?'

He kicked the door closed. 'What the fuck are you doing?'

Lena glanced out the window into the empty squad room. Her heart was in her throat, the pounding making it hard for her to talk. 'I don't know what you're talking about.'

'You told Gordon Braham that Tommy didn't mean to stab Brad.'

She rubbed her elbow. It was bleeding. 'So?'

'Goddamn it!' He pounded his fist on the desk. 'We had a deal.'

'He's dead, Frank. I was trying to give his father some peace.'

'What about *my* peace?' He raised his fists in the air. 'We had a fucking deal!'

Lena held up her hands, afraid he would hit her again.

She'd known Frank would be mad, but she had never seen him this furious in her life.

'Stupid.' He paced in front of her, fists still clenched. 'You're so fucking stupid.'

She told him, 'Lookit, calm down. I took the blame for everything. I told Trent that it was all my fault.'

He stared, slack-jawed. 'You did what?'

'It's done, Frank. It's over. Trent's on to the homicides. That's where you want him. We both know Tommy didn't kill that girl.'

'No.' He shook his head. 'That's not true.'

'Have you been to the college? Jason Howell was murdered last night. There's no way—'

He gripped his fist in his hand like he had to stop himself from punching her. 'You said Tommy's confession was solid.'

Lena's voice took on a pleading tone. 'Listen to what I'm saying.' She could barely catch her breath to speak. 'I'll take the fall for everything. Dereliction of duty. Negligence. Obstruction. Whatever they come up with, I'll take it. I already told Trent you didn't have anything to do with it.' He started shaking his head again, but Lena didn't stop talking. 'It's just me and you, Frank. We're the only witnesses and our stories will be exactly the same, because I'll say whatever you want me to say. Brad didn't see what happened in the garage. For better or worse, Tommy's not going to come back from the grave and tell anybody different. It's all gonna be whatever we tell them.'

'Tommy—' He put his hand to his chest. 'Tommy killed—'

'Allison was killed by someone else.' Lena didn't know

why he couldn't accept this. 'Trent doesn't care about Tommy anymore. He's all excited about a serial killer.'

Frank's hand dropped. All the color left his face. 'He thinks—'

'You don't get it, do you? Listen to what I'm saying. This case just went into the stratosphere. Trent's got his lab guys down here processing Jason Howell's dorm top to bottom. He's going to have them in Allison's room, the garage, out at the lake. Do you think he's going to care about some stupid spic cop who let a kid kill himself in her custody?'

Frank sat heavy in Jeffrey's chair. The springs squeaked. How many times had she sat in this office with Jeffrey and heard that chair groan as he sat back? Frank didn't deserve to be here. Then again, neither did Lena.

She said, 'It's over, Frank. This is the end of the line.'

'There's more to it, Lee. You don't understand.'

Lena knelt down in front of him. 'Trent knows the 911 transcript was changed. He knows Tommy had a phone that's missing. He probably knows you took that picture from Allison's wallet. He sure as hell knows Tommy went back into those cells with my pen and used it to cut his wrists.' She put her hand on his knee. 'I already told him he can tape my confession. You were at the hospital. No one will blame you.'

His eyes worked back and forth as he tried to read her face.

'I'm not working a scam here. I'm telling you the truth.'

'The truth doesn't matter.'

Lena stood up, frustrated. She was handing him everything on a platter and he was shoving it back in her face. 'Tell me why not. Tell me where this blows back on anybody but me.'

'Why couldn't you just follow my orders for once in your miserable fucking life?'

'I'm taking the fall!' she yelled. 'Why can't you get that through your head? It's me, all right? It's my fault. I didn't stop Tommy from running out into the street. I didn't stop him from stabbing Brad. I screwed up the interrogation. I badgered him into writing a false confession. I let him go back into the cells. I knew he was upset. I didn't frisk him. I didn't put him on suicide watch. You can fire me or I can resign or whatever you want. Take me in front of the state board. I'll swear on a stack of Bibles that it was all my fault.'

He stared at her as if she was the stupidest human being walking the face of the earth. 'That easy, huh? You do all that and then you just walk away.'

'Tell me where I'm wrong.'

'I told you to stick to the story!' He banged his hand so hard against the wall that the glass rattled in the window. 'Goddamn it, Lena.' He stood up. 'Where's that boyfriend of yours, huh? You think you're gonna squirm out of this so easy? Where's Jared?'

'No.' She pointed her finger in his chest. 'You don't talk to him. You don't ever say anything to him ever. You hear me? That's the deal. That's the only thing that keeps my mouth shut.'

He slapped away her hand. 'I'll tell him whatever I damn well please.' He started to leave. Lena grabbed him by his arm, too late remembering his injury from the garage.

'Shit!' he screamed, his knees buckling. He swung his

fist around, slamming it into her ear. The inside of Lena's head clanged like a bell. She saw stars. Her stomach clenched. She tightened her grip on his arm.

Frank was on all fours, panting. His fingers dug into the skin on the back of her hand. Lena tightened her grip so hard that the muscles screamed in her arm. She leaned down to look at his gnarled old face. 'You know what I figured out this morning?' He was breathing too hard to answer. 'You have something on me, but I've got even more on you.'

His mouth opened. Saliva sprayed the floor.

'You know what I've got?' He still didn't answer. His face was so red that she could feel the heat. 'I've got proof about what happened in that garage.'

His head jerked around.

'I got the bullet you shot me with, Frank. I found it in the mud behind the garage. It's going to match your gun.'

He cursed again. Sweat poured down his face.

'Those classes I've been taking? The ones you've been making fun of?' She took pleasure in telling him, 'There's enough of your blood at the scene for them to get an alcohol level. What do you think they're going to find? How many swigs did you take from that flask yesterday?'

'That don't mean anything.'

'It means your pension, Frank. Your health insurance. Your good fucking name. You stuck around all these extra years, and it won't mean a damn thing when they fire you for drinking on the job. You won't even be able to get hired on at the college.'

He shook his head. 'It's not gonna work.'

Lena took some liberties with the truth. 'Greta Barnes

saw you give Tommy that beat-down. I bet that nurse of hers can tell some stories, too.'

He gave a strained laugh. 'Call them in. Go ahead.'

'If I were you, I'd be careful.'

'You don't see it.'

Lena stood up and wiped the grit off her pants. 'All I see is a tired old drunk.'

He struggled to sit up. His breathing was labored. 'You were always so sure you were right that you couldn't see the truth if it was standing there in front of you.'

She took the badge off her belt and threw it on the floor beside him. The Glock she carried was her own, but the bullets belonged to the county. Lena ejected the magazine and thumbed out each round. The bullets gave off satisfying pings as they hit the tile floor.

He said, 'It's not over.'

She pulled back the slide and ejected the last round in the chamber. 'It is for me.'

The door was stuck. She had to yank it open. Carl Phillips stood at the back of the squad room. He tipped his hat at Lena as she walked out of the office.

Marla swiveled in the chair, her arms crossed over her large chest as she tracked Lena's progress through the room. She leaned down and pressed the buzzer for the gate. 'Good riddance.'

There should have been some kind of pull, some kind of loyalty, that made Lena look back, but she walked out into the parking lot, inhaling the wet November air, feeling like she had finally freed herself from the worst kind of prison.

She took a deep breath. Her lungs shook. The weather had cleared up a little, but a strong, cold wind dried the sweat on her face. Her vision was sharp. There was a buzzing in her ears. She could feel her heart rattling in her chest, but she forced herself to keep moving.

Her Celica was parked at the far end of the lot. She looked up Main Street. The waning sun was making a brief appearance, giving everything a surreal blue cast. Lena wondered how many days of her life had been spent going up and down this same miserable strip. The college. The hardware store. The dry cleaners. The dress shop. It all seemed so small, so meaningless. This town had taken so much from her – her sister, her mentor, and now her badge. There was nothing else that she could give. Nothing left to do but start over.

Across the street, she saw the Heartsdale Children's Clinic. Hareton Earnshaw's billion-dollar Beemer was parked in the lot, taking up two spaces.

Lena passed her Celica and kept walking across the street. Old man Burgess waved at her from the front window of the dry cleaners. Lena waved back as she climbed the hill to the clinic. Her hand was killing her. She didn't think she could wait to go to the hospital tomorrow morning.

During Sara's tenure, the clinic had always been well maintained. Now, the place was starting to go downhill. The driveway hadn't been pressure-washed in years. The paint on the trim was chipped and faded. Leaves and debris clogged the gutters so bad that water flowed down the side of the building.

Lena followed the signs to the rear entrance. There were cheap stepping-stones laid in the dead grass. At one time, there had been wildflowers back here. Now there was just a mud track leading to the creek that ran through the back of the property. The torrential rains had turned it into a fast-flowing river that looked ready to flood the clinic. Erosion had taken hold. The channel was wider now, at least fifteen feet across and half as deep.

She pressed the buzzer by the back door and waited. Hare had been renting space in the building since Sara left town. Lena had to think that Sara would've never let her cousin work alongside her when she owned the clinic. They were close, but everybody knew Hare was a different kind of doctor from Sara. He saw it as a job, whereas Sara saw it as a calling. Lena was hoping this was still the case, that a doctor like Hare would view her as a billable office visit instead of a blood enemy.

Lena pressed the buzzer again. She could hear the bell ringing inside along with the quiet murmur of a radio. She tried to flex her hand. There was less movement now. Her fingers were fat and swollen. She pulled back her sleeve and groaned. Red streaks traced up her forearm.

'Shit,' Lena groaned. She put her hand to her cheek. She was burning up. Her stomach was sour. She hadn't felt right for the last two hours, but it all seemed to be catching up with her at once.

Her phone started to ring. Lena saw Jared's number. She gave the buzzer by the door one last push before answering. 'Hey.'

'Is this a bad time?'

She paced in front of the door. 'I just quit my job.'

He laughed like she had told an unbelievable joke. 'Really?'

She leaned her back against the wall. 'I wouldn't lie to you about that.'

'Does that mean you'd lie about other things?'

He was kidding, but Lena felt her heart drop when she

thought about how all of this could've blown up in her face. 'I want to get out of town as soon as possible.'

'All right. We'll start packing tonight. You can move in with me and we'll figure out later what you're going to do.'

Lena stared at the river. She could hear the rush of the current. The sound was like boiling water in her ears. Even though the rain had stopped, the river was still rising. She conjured the image of a huge wave crashing down the hill, flooding out the street and taking away the police station.

'Lee?' Jared asked.

'I'm all right—' Her voice caught. She couldn't start crying now or she'd never stop. 'I should be home in an hour or two.' Her throat started to tighten. 'I love you.'

She ended the call before he could answer. Lena looked at her watch. There was a doc-in-the-box in the drugstore over in Cooperstown. Maybe she could find a physician's assistant who needed some cash and wouldn't ask questions. She pushed away from the wall just as the back door opened.

Lena said, 'Oh.'

'I didn't see your car out front.'

'I'm parked across the street.' Lena held up her hand, showing the dangling Band-Aids. 'I . . . uh . . . kind of have a problem I can't take to the hospital.'

There was none of the expected reluctance. 'Come on in.'

The smell of bleach hit Lena as she walked into the building. The cleaning staff had been thorough, but the stench made her stomach turn.

'Go into exam one. I'll be right there.'

'All right,' Lena agreed.

Being in the doctor's office seemed to give her body permission to hurt. Her hand was throbbing with every heartbeat. She couldn't pull her fingers into a fist. There was a high-pitched noise in her ears. Then another one. She realized she was hearing sirens.

Lena bypassed the exam room and went to the front of the building to see what was going on. The pocket door to the front office took some coaxing to open. The blinds were drawn, the room dark. She turned on the lights and saw the source of the odor.

Two gallon jugs of bleach were on the desk. Leather gloves soaked in a stainless steel bowl. Cotton swabs and paper towels littered the floor. A wooden baseball bat was laid out on a sheet of brown craft paper. Blood was embedded in the letters around the Rawlings logo.

Lena put her hand to her gun, but she was too late. She felt a drop of blood trickle down her neck before her body registered the pain of the cold steel of a knife pressing into her skin.

FOURTEEN

Charlie Reed bounded down the dorm stairs with a smile showing under his mustache. He was in a white clean suit, covered head to toe in Tyvek. 'Glad you're here. We were just about to start the magic.'

Will tried to return his smile, but the effort failed. Charlie was a forensics expert. He had the luxury of looking at cases through the lens of a microscope. He saw bone and blood that needed to be photographed, analyzed, and catalogued, where Will saw a human being whose life had been ended by a cold-blooded killer who seemed to be doing a very good job of evading justice.

Despite Will's earlier hopes, none of the evidence they'd found so far had been useful. Jason Howell's Saturn station wagon was remarkably tidy. Aside from some breath mints and a couple of CDs, there was nothing personal in the car. The blanket Will had found in the bathroom stall held more promise, but that had to be analyzed in the lab. This process could take a week or more. The hope was that the killer had injured himself or leaned against the blanket, leaving trace evidence that might link him to the crime. Even if Charlie found DNA in the material that did not belong to Jason, they could only run it through the database and hope that their killer was in the system. More often than not, DNA was a tool used to rule out suspects, not track them down.

'This next bit should go a little faster.' Charlie leaned down and rummaged through one of the open duffel bags at the bottom of the stairs. He found what he was looking for and told Will, 'Suit up. We should be ready in five minutes.' He bounded back up the steps two at a time.

Will grabbed one of the folded clean suits from the pile at the bottom of the stairs. He tore the package open with his teeth. The suit was meant to limit skin and hair transfer to the crime scene. It had the added bonus of making Will look like a giant, elongated marshmallow. He was tired and hungry. He was pretty sure he smelled, and though his socks were dry now, they had dried in such a way as to feel like sandpaper rubbing across the blister on his heel.

None of this mattered. Every second that ticked by gave Jason and Allison's killer the freedom to move about freely, planning his escape or, worse, planning his next murder.

Will glanced at Marty Harris. The man was still guarding the front door with his usual degree of thoroughness. Marty's head was back against the wall, glasses askew. His soft snores followed Will up the stairs.

Charlie knelt in the middle of the hallway, adjusting a fixture on top of a tripod. There were three more tripods spaced evenly across the hall, going all the way to the bathroom. Similarly Tyvek-suited men all adjusted gauges as Charlie told them to go up or down. They had been here for hours. Photographing the scene, graphing the measurements of the hall, the bathroom, Jason's room, his desk and his bed. They had documented every item from the inside out. Finally, they had given Dan Brock permission to remove the body. Once Jason was gone, they had taken more photos, diagrammed more graphs,

383

and finally started bagging any evidence that seemed pertinent to the case.

Jason's laptop was toast, soaked to the core. There was a Sony Cyber-shot with some provocative photos of Allison Spooner in her underwear. All of Jason's school-work and notebooks seemed to be what you'd expect. His Dopp kit contained the normal toiletries and no pre-scription bottles. The strongest drug he had in the room was an expired bottle of Excedrin PM.

Jason's cell phone was more interesting, if not more helpful. The contacts list contained three numbers. One belonged to Jason's mother. She wasn't pleased to be talking to the police twice in one day about a son she apparently didn't care that much about. The second number dialed the main switchboard to the physical engineering building, which was closed for the holiday. The third belonged to a cell phone that rang once, then announced that the voice mailbox was full. The cell phone company had no record of who the number belonged to – it was a pay-as-you-go deal – an expected revelation considering none of these kids seemed to have good enough credit to get a phone in their own names.

Will assumed the cell phone with the full mailbox belonged to Allison Spooner. She had called Jason fifty-three times over the weekend. Nothing came in after Sunday afternoon. Jason's only outgoing call had been made to his mother three days before he died. Of all the details that Will had discovered about the victims in this case, Jason Howell's sad, lonely life was the most depressing.

'Almost ready,' Charlie said, the excitement building in his voice.

Will stared into the hallway, wishing he never had to see this place again. The dingy tan linoleum on the floors. The scuffed and dirtied white walls. Making it worse was the lingering smell of Jason's body, even though the kid had been removed several hours ago. Or maybe it was all in Will's mind. There were crime scenes he had visited years ago that felt like they'd left their mark on his nasal passages. Just thinking about them could evoke a certain odor or bring a sour taste into the back of his throat. Jason Howell would forever be trapped in the pantheon of Will's bad memories.

'Doug, move that a little to the left,' Charlie said. He'd divided the crime scene into three areas: the hall, Jason's room, and the bathroom. They had all agreed that their best bet was finding something in the hallway. The group of assembled men hadn't needed to articulate the problems associated with looking for DNA in a communal boys' bathroom, but Will could tell none of them were looking forward to crawling around on that particular floor.

Charlie tinkered with the light on the tripod. 'This is the ME-RED I told you about.'

'Nice.' Will had already gotten an earful about the extremely fascinating qualities of the Mobile Electro-magnetic Radiation Emitting Diode, which as far as Will could tell was fancy jargon for a gigantic black light that had a longer range than the Wood's lamps that had to be carried around by hand. The lights would pick up visible traces of blood, urine, and semen, or anything else that contained fluorescent molecules.

For the traces that were less visible, Charlie and his team had sprayed the hallway with Luminol, a chemical that reacts to the presence of iron in blood. Crime shows had made the general public well aware of the blue glow emitted by Luminol when the lights were turned off. What they hadn't shared was that the glow usually lasted around thirty seconds. Long-exposure cameras had to be used to record the process. Charlie had set these up on tripods in all four corners of the hallway and staggered more around the entrance to Jason's dorm room. For good measure, he had tilted the security camera back down to capture it all in real time.

Will stood at the mouth of the stairs, watching the team make last-minute adjustments. He wondered if the murderer had paused here on the stairs to psych himself up for the kill. It was all so premeditated, so well thought out. Enter through the back door. Push up the cameras. Go up the stairs. Weapons in hand. Gloves on. Plan ready: Incapacitate Jason with the bat. Drag him to the bed. Cover him with the blanket. Stab him repeatedly. Hide the blanket in case it contained any trace evidence. Go back down the stairs. Leave by the back door.

Was it really as calculated as that? What went through a person's mind before they went to someone's dorm room, their home, and fractured their skull with a baseball bat? Would the killer's pulse quicken? Would his stomach tighten the way Will's did when he thought about the gruesome crime scene? There had been so much blood, so much brain and tissue, spattered around the room that Charlie and his team had been forced to make a grid so that they could clear a path to fully document the carnage.

What kind of person could stand over that bed and methodically stab another human being?

And what about poor Jason Howell? Lena was probably right that the killer had known Jason well enough to hate him. Despise him. What kind of trouble had the kid gotten himself into that he would become the object of such fury?

'I think we've got it.' Charlie grabbed a handheld video camera and pulled Will toward Jason's room. He told Doug, 'Go get the lights.' Doug took off down the stairs and Charlie explained the plan to Will. 'First we'll see what the Luminol brings out, then we'll go to the black light.'

'Ready?' Doug called.

'Ready,' Charlie yelled back.

The hall went dark. The Luminol responded quickly. Dozens of small, elongated circles glowed blue just outside Jason's open doorway. They were smeared where the killer had tried to wipe them up, but the pattern was easy to follow. The drops revealed his movements. After stabbing Jason to death, the killer had walked out of the room, heading toward the stairs, then changed his mind and doubled back toward the bathroom.

'The original plan was probably to take the blanket with him,' Charlie said. He held the video camera low, documenting the drips. Will could hear the steady, slow click of the long-exposure cameras capturing the evidence.

He asked, 'What about this?' A larger stain, more like a puddle, was on the floor just beside the bathroom entrance. Three feet above it was a patterned mark on the wall.

Charlie twisted up the LCD screen of the camera. Will saw the images in double as he recorded the luminescent blobs. 'Our killer comes out of the room, heads toward the stairs, then he realizes the blanket is dripping. He goes toward the bathroom, but first—' Charlie pointed the camera toward the glowing stain on the floor. 'He leans something against here. I'd guess a bat or a club. That's the mark on the wall.' Charlie zoomed in close to the wall where the top of the weapon had rested. 'Uh-oh, fingerprint.'

Charlie got down on his knees and pointed his camera at an almost perfect circle. 'Gloved, it looks like.' He zoomed in closer. The glowing dot started to fade. 'We're losing it.'

The Luminol's reaction time varied depending on the content of iron in the blood. The dot slowly disappeared, then the puddle on the floor was gone. Charlie muttered a curse as the hall was plunged back into darkness.

Charlie rewound the camera to look at the print again. 'He was definitely wearing gloves.'

'Latex?'

'Leather, I think. There's a grain.' He showed Will the LCD, but the light was too intense for him to see anything but a blob. 'Let's see if it still shows up under the diodes.' He called, 'Black light, please.'

There were a couple of popping noises, then a steady hum. The hallway lit up like a Christmas tree, illuminating every protein-based fluid ever left here.

'Impressive, right?' Charlie's lips glowed a bright blue, probably from the Vaseline in his lip balm. He knelt down on the floor. The blood trail that had glowed so brightly minutes before was barely visible. 'Our killer did a good job cleaning up after himself.' He took a few more photographs. 'Good thing he didn't use bleach or we wouldn't be able to see any of this.'

'I don't think he planned to leave a mess,' Will said. 'Our guy is careful, but the only things he probably brought with him were the weapons – the knife and a bat or club. He used the blanket on the bed to catch the spatter. He tried to leave with it, then like you said, he changed his mind because it was dripping.' Will felt himself smile as he remembered, 'There's a supply closet beside the stall where I found the blanket.'

'You're a genius, my friend.' They both went into the bathroom. Charlie flipped on the lights. Will clamped his hands over his face, feeling like his eyeballs were being stabbed.

'Sorry about that,' Charlie apologized. 'I should've warned you to close your eyes and open them slowly.'

'Thanks.' Spots exploded in front of his eyes with every blink. Will put his hand on the wall so he wouldn't trip over his own feet.

Charlie stood in front of the supply closet with his video camera. 'We can check the photographs, but I'm sure this door was closed when we got here.' His hands were still gloved. He carefully turned the knob.

The closet was shallow, a metal shelving unit taking up most of the space. There was nothing unusual about the contents of the shelves: gallon jugs of cleaning products, a box of rags, sponges, two toilet plungers, a mop tucked into a rolling yellow bucket. Two spray bottles hung from a bungee cord on the back of the door. Yellow liquid for spot-cleaning stains. Blue liquid for windows and glass.

Charlie documented the contents of the shelves with the camera. 'These cleaners are industrial grade. They're probably thirty percent bleach.'

Will recognized the Windex label on one of the spray bottles. He had the same cleaner at home. It contained vinegar to help cut the grease. 'You can't mix vinegar and bleach, right?'

'Right. It forms a chlorine gas.' Charlie followed Will's gaze to the spray bottle. He laughed as he made the connection. 'I'll be right back.'

Will let out a deep breath that he felt like he'd been holding for the last two days. Bleach glowed just as brightly as blood when sprayed with Luminol, obscuring any evidence. Vinegar, by contrast, formed a natural bond with iron, making it more visible when it was sprayed. That explained why the spots in the hall glowed with such intensity. The killer had used the Windex to clean up the floor. He might as well have drawn an arrow to the bloodstains.

Charlie was back with Doug and another assistant. They worked in tandem, taking photographs and handing Charlie the brush and powder to check the Windex bottle for fingerprints. Charlie was methodical, starting from the top down, going from one side of the bottle to the other. Will had expected him to find fingerprints immediately. The bottle was half full. The janitorial staff must have used it. The closet wasn't locked. The students would have access.

'It was wiped down,' Will guessed. The trigger and the area around the grip were clean.

'Don't give up on me yet,' Charlie mumbled. The brush swept back and forth across the label. All of them knelt down as Charlie dusted the bottom surface.

'Bingo,' Will whispered. He could see a partial finger-print on the bottom of the bottle. The black practically glowed against the dark blue liquid.

'What do you see?' Charlie asked. He took a flashlight

out of his pocket and shone it on the clear plastic. 'Holy Christ. Good catch, eagle eye.' He traded the flashlight for a piece of clear tape. 'It's a partial, probably the pinky finger.' He sat back on his heels so he could transfer the tape to a white card.

Will said, 'His gloves would've been bloody. He had to take them off to clean the floor.'

Charlie stood up with Doug's help. 'We'll drive this to the lab right now. I can wake some people up. It'll take time, but it's a good print, Will. This is a solid lead.' He told his assistant, 'The other evidence is in the van. There's a pill bottle in my tackle kit. Grab that, too.'

Will had forgotten about the bottle in Tommy Braham's cabinet. 'Did you field-test the capsules?'

'I did.' Charlie started down the hall toward the stairs. The black lights bounced off their white Tyvek suits. 'It's not coke, meth, speed, or any of the usual suspects. Was the kid into sports?'

'I don't think so.'

'It could be a steroid or a performance enhancer. A lot of younger guys are using those to bulk up now. The Internet makes them easy to get. I sent some photos back to Central to see if they recognize the label or capsules. A lot of these dealers are into branding. They keep their labels consistent so their product gets advertised.'

Tommy didn't strike Will as interested in weight lifting, but he'd been a skinny kid. Maybe he wasn't happy with that. 'Did you find any fingerprints on the bottle?'

Charlie stopped at his tackle box. He pulled out the pill bottle, which had been sealed in a proper evidence bag instead of the Ziploc Will had found in the kitchen. 'I lifted two sets. The first was adult, probably male. The second was a partial webbing.' He indicated the skin between his thumb and index finger. 'I don't know if it's male or female, but I'd guess whoever wrote those words on the label held it in her hands while she did. I'm saying "her" because it looks like a woman's handwriting.'

'Can I keep the bottle? I want to show it around and see if anybody recognizes it.'

'I already have some of the capsules in the van.' Charlie gave him the bag as they walked down the stairs. 'You still want a lift to the Braham house? I think I can spare one of my guys to process the garage now.'

'That'd be great.' Will had forgotten his Porsche was still at the Taylor Drive house. He checked the time on his phone. Knowing it was already past ten o'clock made Will feel even more exhausted than he had before. He thought about Cathy Linton's dinner invitation and his stomach rumbled.

Downstairs, Marty was awake by the door. He was talking to a large man who was his exact opposite except in skin color.

'You Agent Trent?' The man slowly made his way over. He was built like a linebacker who'd gone to seed. 'Demetrius Alder.'

Will was too busy unzipping his clean suit to shake the man's hand. 'Thank you for cooperating with us today, Mr. Alder. I'm sorry we've kept you out so late.'

'I gave Lena all the tapes. I hope she comes up with something.'

Will assumed he would have heard from her hours ago if Lena had found anything of note in the security footage. Still, he told Demetrius, 'I'm sure they'll prove useful.'

'The dean wanted me to give you his number.' He

handed Will a card. 'He had me check all the buildings. We didn't find anything else. All the dorms are empty. Somebody's coming to fix the cameras first thing after the holiday.'

Will sat down so he could pull off the rest of the suit. He remembered something Marty had said earlier. 'What about the car that was hit by the security camera?'

'It was parked in the loading dock. Good thing it was empty. Camera busted straight through the hatchback window.'

'Hatchback?' Will stopped worrying about the suit. 'What kind of car was it?'

'I think it was one'a them old Dodge Daytonas.'

The rain had turned into a light sleet by the time Charlie's van reached the tow yard. Gusts of wind shook the vehicle. Water pooled in the parking lot. There was no way to get to the front door without getting soaked. Will felt his socks getting wet again. The blister on his heel was so raw that he was starting to limp.

'Earnshaw's,' Charlie said, and Will guessed he meant the sign glowing over the building. There was a whippet-thin older man standing in the doorway dressed in bib overalls and a baseball cap. He held the door open for them as they ran into the building.

'Al Earnshaw.' The man offered his hand to both of them. He told Will, 'You're Sara's friend, right? My sister's told me a lot about you.'

Will guessed that explained the man's uncanny resemblance to Cathy Linton. 'She's been very kind to me.'

'Sure she has.' Al bellowed a good-natured laugh, but he

slapped Will on the arm hard enough to throw off his balance. 'Car's in the back.' He motioned them toward the door behind the counter.

The shop was large, with the usual array of girlie calendars and posters of sexy, bikini-clad ladies washing cars. There were six lifts, three on each side. The tool chests were neatly lined up, their covers locked down tight. Al had turned on the propane heaters, but the cold was still biting. The roll-up doors in the back rattled from the wind. Allison's Dodge Daytona was on the ground by the last lift. The back windshield was buckled in the center, just as Demetrius had said.

Will asked, 'Did you call Allison to let her know you had her car?'

'We don't call people when we tow them. Signs are up all over the school with our number. I figured the owner got a ride home for the holiday and we'd get a call when they got back and saw the vehicle wasn't there.' Al offered, 'Tommy's Malibu is on the lot if you want to see it.'

Will had forgotten about the young man's car. 'Did you figure out what was wrong with it?'

'Starter was stuck again. He was crawling under there and hitting it with a hammer to get it unstuck.' Al shrugged. 'I went ahead and fixed it. Gordon's truck doesn't have much more life left in it. He'll need something to drive.' He took a rag out of his pocket and wiped his hands. The gesture had the hallmark of a nervous tic. His hands were as clean as Will's.

Will asked, 'Did you know Tommy well?'

'Yep.' He tucked the rag into his pocket. 'I'll leave you guys to it. Just holler if you need me.'

'Thank you.'

Charlie walked over to the car. He put his tackle box on the floor and opened the lid. 'Sara?' he asked.

'She's a doctor in town.' He corrected, 'I mean, Atlanta. She works at Grady Hospital. She grew up here.'

Charlie handed him a pair of latex gloves. 'How long have you known her?'

'Little while.' Will took a longer time putting on the gloves than the task warranted.

Charlie got the message. He opened the car door. The hinges squealed loudly. Lionel Harris had been right about the condition of the Daytona. It was more rust than paint. The tires were bald. The engine hadn't been started in days but the smell of burning oil and exhaust filled the air.

'I guess the rain got to it,' Charlie said. The dash was a sturdy molded plastic, but the cloth seats were wet and moldy. A stream of water had poured in from the busted hatchback, soaking the carpets, flooding the footwells. Charlie pulled up the front seat and water sloshed onto his pants. School papers floated in the murky liquid. The ink had washed away. 'This is going to be fun,' Charlie muttered. He was probably wishing he was back at the campus with his fancy lights. 'I suppose we should do this right.' He took his video camera out of the tackle box. Will walked around the car while he got everything ready.

The trunk was held down with a frayed bungee cord. The glass was safety-coated with a transparent sheet that held the shattered pieces of the window together. Will had a spiderweb view inside the messy trunk. Allison was as sloppy as Jason was neat. Papers were scattered around, their ink smudged from the rain. Will saw a flash of pink.

'That's her book bag.' He reached down to loosen the bungee cord.

'Hold on, now.' Charlie backed him off. He checked the rubber gasket around the window to make sure it was doing its job. 'Looks like it held,' Charlie told him. 'Still, be careful. You don't want a sheet of glass coming down on your head.'

Will figured there were worse things that could happen. He waited patiently as Charlie focused the camera on Will, narrating in an official-sounding voice for the benefit of the tape. 'This is Agent Will Trent with the Georgia Bureau of Investigation. I'm Charles Reed, also with the bureau. We are at Earnshaw's Garage on Highway 9 in the city of Heartsdale, which is in Grant County, Georgia. It's Tuesday, November twenty-sixth, at approximately ten thirty-two in the evening. We are about to open the trunk of a Dodge Daytona reportedly belonging to murder victim Allison Spooner.' He nodded, indicating Will could finally proceed.

The bungee cord was stretched to its limit. Will had to put some muscle into unhooking it from the bumper. The hatchback was heavy, and he remembered Lionel saying the pistons were blown. Allison had used a broken-off broom handle to prop it open. Will did the same. Tiny pieces of glass rained down as he opened the hatch all the way.

'Hold for just a second,' Charlie said, zooming in on the book bag, the papers, and fast-food trash.

Finally, he gave the okay to remove the bag.

Will grabbed the strap. The bag had some heft to it. Despite the pink, the fabric looked waterproof. Under the camera's watchful eye, he pulled back the thick zipper.

There were two heavy books on top, perfectly dry. From the drawings of molecules on the outside, Will assumed these were Allison's chemistry texts. There were four spiral-bound notebooks, each with different-colored covers. Will flipped through these for the camera, the pages blurring. He guessed these were Allison's class notes.

'What's that?' Charlie asked. A slip of paper was sticking out of the blue notebook.

Will unfolded the page. It was half a sheet of college-ruled paper. The side edge showed where it had been ripped away from the spiral. There were two lines of text on the page. All caps. Ballpoint pen. Will stared at the first word, trying to make out the shapes of the letters. His reading was always worse when he was tired. His eyes refused to focus. He held up the paper to the camera, asking, 'You want to do the honors?'

Thankfully, Charlie didn't find the request odd. He narrated in his camera voice, 'This is a note found in the pink book bag reportedly belonging to the victim. It reads, "I need to talk to you. We'll meet at the usual place."'

Will looked back at the words. Now that he knew what they said, he could better make out the letters. He told Charlie, 'The "I" looks familiar. It's similar to the one written on the fake suicide note.' He pointed to the torn bottom half of the page for the benefit of the video camera. 'The note found at the lake was written on the bottom half of a torn sheet of paper.' Will recalled Charlie's words, ' "I need to talk to you. We'll meet at the usual place." And then you add the last part from the fake suicide note, which is "I want it over."'

'Makes sense.' Charlie's voice changed again as he announced that he was stopping the tape. Wisely, he didn't want to record their speculation for a future defense attorney to show in court.

Will studied the letters on the page. 'You think a man or a woman wrote this?'

'I have no idea, but it doesn't match Allison's handwriting.' Will guessed he was using the girl's class notes as a comparison. Charlie continued, 'I saw some of Jason's homework in his room. He wrote in all caps like that.'

'Why would Allison have a note like this from Jason?'

Charlie guessed, 'He could've been an accomplice to her murder.'

'Could be.'

'And then the killer decided he didn't want to leave any witness.'

Will's brain was starting to hurt. The theory didn't add up.

Charlie offered, 'I'm not a professional, but I'd say the writing in Allison's journal matches the writing on the pill bottle.'

'Her journal?'

'The blue notebook. It's obviously some kind of journal.'

Will thumbed through the pages. Slightly less than half the notebook was filled. The remaining pages were blank. He checked the printing on the front of the plastic cover. The number 250 was in bold type with a circle around it. He assumed that was the number of total pages. 'Doesn't this seem like a weird choice for a diary?'

'She was twenty-one. Were you expecting one of those girlie leather-bound lock-and-key deals?'

'I guess not.' Will flipped through the pages. Allison's handwriting was awful, but her numbers were legible.

There were dates at the top of each entry. Some entries were as long as two paragraphs. Sometimes, there was just a stray line or two. He flipped to the last entry. 'November thirteenth. That was two weeks ago.' He checked the other dates. 'She was pretty consistent up until that point.' He flipped to the front page. 'The first entry was on August first. That's a pretty short diary.'

'Maybe she starts a new one every year on her birthday.'

Will remembered Sara's notation on the whiteboard at the funeral home. Allison Spooner's birthday was two days before Angie's. 'She was born in April.'

'Can't blame me for trying.' Charlie picked up his camera. 'I guess we should get some of this on tape. Anything pop out at you?'

Will stared at the open journal. Allison's handwriting looked like a series of loops and squiggles. He patted his pocket. 'I think I left my glasses in my glove compartment.'

'Bummer.' Charlie turned off the camera. 'I'll run you by your car so you can get started. Between this and the Braham place, I'm going to be pulling an all-nighter, too.'

FIFTEEN

Lena felt another ripple of tremors working its way through her body. It was like an earthquake, a slow rumble and then the world turned upside down. Her teeth started to chatter around the gag in her mouth. Her muscles quivered, working their way into full spasm. Her feet kicked. She saw flashes of light. There was no use fighting it. She could only lie there and wait for the sensation to pass.

With agonizing slowness, the spasms subsided. Her body began to relax. Her jaw loosened. Her heartbeat slowed, flopping in her chest like a fish caught in a net.

How had she let herself get into this situation? How had she been so easily fooled?

She was hog-tied, an entire length of rope wrapped around her body, her hands, her feet. Even without the bindings, she doubted she could do anything but lie there and sweat. Her clothes were saturated. The concrete beneath her had wicked the moisture so that she was surrounded by a pool of her own making.

And it was cold. It was so damn cold that even without the shaking, her teeth wanted to chatter. She could barely feel her hands and feet. Dread filled her body when she thought about another attack coming on. She wasn't going to be able to hold on much longer.

Was it the infection in her hand? Was that the reason she

couldn't stop shaking? The throbbing had turned into a stabbing pain that ebbed and flowed with no discernible pattern. Her life wasn't flashing in front of her eyes, but she couldn't stop thinking about what had brought her here. If she managed to get out of this place, if she managed somehow to get free, then everything had to change. The fear flooding through her body had brought with it a clarity that Lena had never known. For so long, she had tricked herself into thinking that she held back the truth to protect other people – her family, her friends. Now she could see that she was only protecting herself.

If Brad managed to pull through, she would apologize to him every day for the rest of her life. She would tell Frank that she was wrong about him. He was a good man. He'd stuck by Lena all these years when a smarter man would've dropped her for the worthless friend she was. Her uncle had gone through hell with Lena. She had pushed him away so many times that it was a miracle he was still standing.

And she had to find a way to get Sara Linton alone. Lena would bare her soul, confessing her complicity in Jeffrey's death. She hadn't killed him with her own hands, but she had put him in harm's way. Lena had been Jeffrey's partner. She was supposed to have his back, but she had stood silently by while she watched him walk into the fire. She had practically pushed him in that direction because she was too much of a coward to face it on her own.

Maybe that was what was causing the seizures. The truth was like a shadow creeping through her soul.

Lena twisted around her good hand to reach her watch. The rope bit into her wrist. The pain barely registered as she pressed the button for the light.

Eleven fifty-four.

It was almost midnight.

Lena knew she had left the station around six. Jared would be wondering where she was. Or maybe Frank had gotten to him. Maybe Jared was on his way home to Macon right now.

Jared. The truth would lose him to her forever.

The punishment fit the crime.

Her jaw clenched. She closed her eyes, feeling another wave coming on. The tremble moved down her shoulders, through her arms and into her hands. Her feet kicked. She felt her eyes roll back. There were noises. Grunting. Screaming.

Slowly, Lena opened her eyes. She saw darkness. Her mind suddenly came back to her. She was tied up. She was gagged. Sweat covered her body. The stench of sweat and urine filled the air. She pressed the button on her watch. In the soft glow she could see the skin of her wrist. Red lines streaked up toward her shoulder, toward her heart. She looked at the display.

Eleven fifty-eight.

It was almost midnight.

WEDNESDAY

SIXTEEN

Sara listened to the kitchen clock tick as the hands moved past midnight. She had been sitting at the table staring at the pile of dirty dishes stacked in and around the sink for longer than she cared to remember. It wasn't just lethargy that kept her rooted to the chair. Her mother's kitchen makeover included two dishwashers that were so modern it was impossible to tell whether or not they were running, yet she still insisted on hand washing her china and all the pots and pans. Or, insisted that Sara do the chore, which made Cathy's anachronistic ways even more outrageous.

The mindless task should have been a welcome end to Sara's day. Working at Grady Hospital was like trying to stand still on a spinning merry-go-round. The flow of patients never ebbed, and Sara generally was juggling twenty cases at any given time. Between consultations and her usual workload, she saw an average of fifty to sixty patients during any twelve-hour shift. Slowing all this down, focusing on just one patient at a time, should have been an easier task, but Sara found that her mind worked differently now.

She realized that the constant pressure of the ER was a gift in many ways. When Sara had lived in Grant County, her life had taken on a far more leisurely pace. She usually ate breakfast with Jeffrey in the morning. Two or three times a week, they had supper with her family. Sara was the team doctor for the local high school football team. She helped coach volleyball in the summer. Her free time was infinite if she managed her schedule right. Going to the grocery store could take several hours if she ran into a friend. She clipped articles from magazines to share with her sister. She'd even joined her mother's book club, until they started reading too many serious books to make it fun anymore.

By contrast, the fast pace of her work in Atlanta kept Sara from thinking about her life too much. Usually by the time she finished dictating her charts, all she could do was drag herself home and take a bath before falling asleep on the couch. Her days off were equally wasted with what she now saw was busywork. Her chores were something to get out of the way quickly. She scheduled lunches and dinners so that she didn't have too much time alone with herself. Alone with her thoughts.

All of her usual crutches had disappeared in the basement of Brock's funeral home. An autopsy certainly required a great deal of attention, but after a point, the motions were rote. Measure, weigh, biopsy, record. Neither Allison Spooner nor Jason Howell had left any remarkable clues in their deaths. The only thing that bound them together was the knife that had been used to kill them. The stab wounds were nearly identical – each made by a small, sharp blade that had been twisted before it was removed to ensure maximum damage.

As for Tommy Braham, Sara had found only one item that stood out: the boy had a small metal spring in the front pocket of his jeans, the type that you usually found in a ballpoint pen.

The hall light snapped on. Cathy yelled, 'Those dishes aren't going to wash themselves.'

'Yes, Mama.' Sara glared at the kitchen sink. Hare had come for dinner, but she guessed the spread put on was really intended for Will. Cathy loved cooking for an appreciative audience and Will certainly fit that bill. Her mother had used every piece of china in the house, serving coffee in teacups with saucers, which Sara thought was very sweet until her mother informed the table that Sara was going to wash every last piece. Hare had brayed like a donkey at the expression on her face.

'Try twitching your nose while you stare at them,' Tessa offered as she came into the kitchen. She was dressed in a billowing yellow nightgown that formed a tent over her belly.

'You could always offer to help.'

'I read in *People* magazine that dishwater is bad for the baby.' She opened the refrigerator and stared at the mountains of food inside. 'You should've watched the movie with us. It was funny.'

Sara sat back in her chair. She wasn't up for a romantic comedy right now. 'Who called a while ago?'

Tess pushed around the Tupperware containers lining the shelves. 'Frank's ex. You remember Maxine?' Sara nodded. 'He's still refusing to go to the hospital.'

Frank had suffered a mild heart attack at the police station this afternoon. Fortunately, Hare was down the street at the diner or things might have been a lot worse. Five years ago, Sara would have rushed to Frank's side. Today, when she had heard the news at the funeral home, all she could muster was sadness. 'What did Maxine want?'

'Same as usual. To complain about Frank. He's a

stubborn old coot.' Tessa put a tub of Cool Whip on the table and went back to the fridge. 'You all right?'

'I'm just tired.'

'Me too. Being pregnant's hard work.' She sat down across from Sara with a leg of fried chicken in her hand. She scooped it into the Cool Whip.

'Please tell me you're not going to eat that.'

Tessa offered her the leg.

Despite her better judgment, Sara tried the ungodly mix. 'Wow. It's sort of salty and sweet at the same time.' She passed the leg back to her sister.

'I know, right?' Tessa dipped it into the tub again and took a bite. She chewed thoughtfully. 'You know, I pray for you every night.'

Sara laughed before she could catch herself. She apologized as quickly as she could. 'I'm sorry. I just . . .'

'Just what?'

She thought now was as good a time as any for the truth. 'I didn't think you really believed in all that.'

'I'm a missionary, you dumbass. What do you think I've been doing with my life for the last three years?'

Sara struggled to dig herself out of an ever-deepening hole. 'I thought you wanted to go to Africa and help children.' She didn't know what else to say. Her sister had always enjoyed life. Sometimes it felt like Tessa was enjoying it for both of them. Sara had always had her mind on school and then work. Meanwhile, Tessa dated whom she pleased, slept with whoever struck her fancy, and never made apologies for any of it. 'You have to admit that you're not a typical missionary.'

'Maybe not,' she allowed, 'but you've got to believe in something.'

'It's hard to believe in a God who would let my husband die in my arms.'

'You can't fall off the floor, Sissy. If somebody throws you a rope, then you better start climbing.'

Cathy had told Sara as much when she'd first lost Jeffrey. 'I'm glad you've found something that gives you peace.'

'I think you've found something, too.' Tessa had finished the chicken leg, but she used the bone to spoon up more Cool Whip. 'You're different from when you first got here. You're doing the work that you want to do.'

'I don't know about that.'

'Where's Will?'

Sara groaned. 'Please don't start that again.'

'The next time you see him, take that band out of your hair. You look prettier with it down.'

'Please, please stop.'

Tessa reached out and took her hand. 'Can I tell you something?'

'As long as it's not advice on chasing after a married man.'

She squeezed Sara's hand. 'I'm really in love with my husband.'

Sara gave a careful 'Okay.'

'I know you think Lem is boring and too earnest and too self-righteous, and believe me, he can be all those things, but a thousand times a day, I hear a song, or I think of something funny, or Daddy says one of his stupid puns, and the first thing that comes into my head is "I want to tell Lem about this." And I know that halfway around the world, he's thinking the same thing.' She paused. 'That's what love is, Sara, when there are so many things about

409

you that you only want one person in the world to know.'

Sara remembered how that felt. It was like being wrapped in a warm blanket.

Tessa laughed. 'Good Lord, I'm gonna start crying. When Lem gets home, he's gonna think I'm some kind of basket case.'

Sara put her hand over Tessa's. 'I'm glad you've found someone.' Her words were genuine. She could see that her sister was happy. 'You deserve to be loved.'

Tessa smiled knowingly. 'So do you.'

Sara chuckled. 'I walked right into that.'

'I'd better get to bed.' She groaned as she stood. 'Wash your hands. You smell like chicken and Cool Whip.'

Sara smelled her hands. Her sister was right. She stared again at the full sink, thinking she might as well start on the dishes so she could go to bed. She groaned as loudly as Tessa had when she got up from the table. Her back was hurting her from leaning over all day. Her eyes were tired. She rummaged under the cabinet for the dish liquid, hoping that her mother was out so she would have a legitimate excuse to leave the dishes until morning.

'Crap,' Sara mumbled, finding the Dawn behind a full box of dishwashing powder that her mother had never opened. She heard footsteps in the hall. 'Did you come back for the Cool Whip?' she asked. Tessa didn't answer, but Sara was sure that she was there. 'Don't tell me you're here to help.' She went into the hall and saw not Tessa, but Will Trent.

'Hey.'

He stood in the center of the hall. His leather briefcase was at his side. There was something different about him that Sara couldn't quite put her finger on. He looked the same. He was even wearing the same clothes she'd seen him in for the last two days. There was definitely something wrong, though. He had a sadness about him that cut straight through.

She waved him into the kitchen. 'Come on in.' Sara put the dish liquid on the counter. Will hovered in the kitchen doorway.

'I'm sorry,' he said. 'Your sister let me in. I was staring through the window in the door trying to figure out if y'all were still awake. I know it's late.' He stopped, his throat working as he swallowed. 'It's really late.'

'Is everything okay?'

He nervously moved his briefcase from one hand to the other, then back again. 'Please tell your mother I'm sorry I couldn't make it to dinner. We had a lot to do, and I—'

'It's all right. She understands.'

'Did the autopsies—' He stopped again, wiping his forehead with his sleeve. His hair was wet from the rain. 'I was thinking while I was driving over here that maybe Jason's murder was a copycat.'

'No,' she told him. 'The wounds were identical.' Sara paused. Obviously, something awful had happened. 'Let's sit down, okay?'

'That's all right, I—'

She sat down at the table. 'Come on. What's wrong?'

He glanced back toward the front door. She could tell he didn't want to be here, but he seemed incapable of leaving.

Sara finally took his hand and pulled him to the chair. He sat, the briefcase in his lap. 'I'm sorry about this.'

She leaned forward, resisting the urge to hold his hand. 'Sorry for what?'

411

He swallowed again. She let him speak in his own time. His voice was low in the large room: 'Faith had her baby.'

Sara put her hand to her mouth. 'Is she all right?'

'Yeah, she's fine. Both of them are fine.' He took his cell phone out of his pocket and showed her a picture of a red-faced newborn in a pink knit hat. 'I guess it's a girl.'

Faith had given the baby's weight as well as her name in the message. Sara told him, ' "Emma Lee." '

'Eight pounds, six ounces.'

'Will—'

'I found this.' He put the briefcase on the table and opened the locks. She saw a stack of papers, an evidence bag with a red seal. He pulled a college notebook with a blue plastic cover from one of the pockets. Black finger-print powder spotted the cover. 'I tried to clean it up,' he said, wiping the grime on the front of his sweater. 'I'm sorry. It was in Allison's car and I . . .' He flipped through the pages, showing her the scrawled handwriting. 'I can't,' he said. 'I just can't.'

She realized that Will hadn't looked at her once since walking into the room. He had such an air of defeat about him, as if every word that came from his mouth caused him pain.

Sara's purse was on the counter. She got up and found her reading glasses. She told Will, 'Mama fixed a plate for you. Why don't you eat something and I'll start on this?'

He stared at the notebook in front of him. 'I'm not really hungry.'

'You've already missed supper. If you don't eat that food, my mother will never forgive you.'

'I really can't—'

Sara opened the warming drawer. Her mother had

cooked for an army again, this time roast beef, potatoes, collards, green beans, and snap peas. The cornbread was wrapped in aluminum foil. Sara put the plate in front of Will, then went back to get silverware and a napkin. She poured a glass of iced tea and found some lemon in the refrigerator. While she was up, she turned on the oven so that she could warm the cherry cobbler sitting on the counter.

She sat down across from Will and opened the notebook. She looked at him over her glasses. He hadn't moved. 'Eat,' she said.

'I really—'

'That's the deal,' she told him. 'You eat. I read.' She stared at him, making it clear that she wasn't going to back down.

Reluctantly, Will picked up the fork. She waited until he had taken a bite of potatoes to open the spiral-bound notebook.

'Her name's on the inside of the cover with the date, August first.' Sara went to the first page. '"August first. Day one."' She thumbed through the pages. 'Each entry has the same format. Day two, day three . . .' She flipped to the back. 'All the way to day one hundred four.'

Will didn't comment. He was eating, but she could tell he was having difficulty swallowing. Sara could not imagine his frustration over having to have the journal read to him. He clearly took it as a personal failure. She wanted to tell him it wasn't his fault, but obviously, asking for Sara's help had taken so much out of him that she couldn't risk pushing him any further.

She returned to the first page. '"Day one,"' she repeated. '"Prof. C was sarcastic today. Cried later for

413

about twenty minutes. Just couldn't stop. Was really annoyed in Dr. K's class because D behind me kept passing notes to V and I couldn't concentrate because they kept laughing." '

She turned the page. ' "Day two. Cut myself shaving my leg pretty bad. Hurt all day. Was two minutes late for work but L didn't say anything. Felt paranoid all day that he was going to yell at me. Can't take him being mad." '

Sara kept reading, page after page of Allison's thoughts on L at the diner and J who had forgotten that they were supposed to meet for lunch. Every notation described Allison's feelings about the situation, but never in florid detail. She was either happy or sad or depressed. She cried, usually for a period of time that seemed unusually long given the circumstances. Despite the emotional revelations, there was something clinical about the telling, as if the girl was an observer watching her life go by.

Getting through the entire journal took over an hour. Will finished his supper, then ate most of the cobbler. He folded his hands on the table and stared straight ahead at the wall. He paced until he realized the distraction slowed down her reading. When Sara's voice started to falter, he got her a glass of ice water. Eventually, he noticed the dishes in the sink, and she read over her shame as he turned on the faucet and started cleaning. Her legs started to cramp from sitting so long. Sara ended up standing by him at the sink, so at least there was the appearance of her helping. Will had made it through all the pots and pans and was starting on the china when Sara finally reached the last entry.

' "Day one hundred four. Work was all right. Concentration bad all day. Slept nine hours last night.

Took a two-hour nap during lunch. Should have studied. Felt guilty and depressed all day. No word from J. I guess he hates me now. Can't blame him."' She looked up at Will. 'That's it.'

He glanced up from the bread plate in his hands. 'I counted all the pages. There are two hundred fifty.'

She checked the front cover, noting the page count. The girl hadn't torn out any pages. Sara told him, 'She stopped writing two weeks before she died.'

'Something happened two weeks ago that she didn't want to write down.'

Sara put the notebook on the table and grabbed a towel. Will was doing a much more thorough job than Sara ever had. He changed out the water often and dried everything as he went along. There wasn't much space left on the counters, so he'd made educated guesses about where things went. Sara would have to go back through and put the pots and pans in their proper place, but she didn't want to do that in front of Will now.

He saw the towel in her hands. 'I've got this.'

'Let me help.'

'I think you've helped enough.' She thought he was going to leave it at that, but Will told her, 'It's been worse today than usual.'

'Stress is a contributing factor – when you get tired or if something emotional happens.'

He scrubbed hard at the plate in his hands. Sara saw that he hadn't bothered to roll up his sleeves. The cuffs of his sweater were soaked. He said, 'I've been trying to dig a new sewer line to my house. That's why my laundry is behind.'

Sara had been expecting a non sequitur, but she'd hoped

he could hold off for a few moments longer. 'My father built this house with money from people who try to do their own plumbing.'

'Maybe he can give me some pointers. I'm pretty sure the trench I started is filled in by now.'

'You didn't use a trench box?' Sara stopped drying the plate. 'That's dangerous. You shouldn't go past four feet without shoring up the sides.'

He gave her a sideways glance.

'I'm my father's daughter. Call me when you're back in Atlanta. I know my way around a backhoe.'

He picked up a bread plate. 'I think you've done me enough favors to last a good long while.'

Sara watched his reflection in the window over the sink. His head was down as he concentrated on the task at hand. She reached back and loosened her ponytail. Her hair fell to her shoulders.

She said, 'Go sit down. I can finish the washing.'

Will glanced up at her, then did a double take. She thought he was going to say something, but he picked up another plate and dunked it into the soapy water instead. Sara opened the drawer to put away the silverware. Her hair hung down in her face. She was glad for the cover.

He said, 'I hate leaving dishes lying around.'

She tried for levity. 'Don't let my mother hear that. She'll never let you leave.'

'I had this foster mother named Lou once.' Will waited for her to look up in the window. 'She worked all day at the supermarket, but she came home at noon to fix me lunch no matter what.' He rinsed the plate and handed it to Sara. 'She always got home after I'd gone to bed, but one night I heard her come in. I went into the kitchen and

416

there she was in her uniform – it was brown, too tight for her – and she was standing in front of the sink. It was piled with all the plates and dishes and leftover food from lunch. I hadn't done anything while she was gone. I just watched TV all day.' He glanced up again at Sara's reflection. 'Lou was standing there looking at the mess in the sink and just bawling. Like, the kind of crying you do with your whole body.' He took the next dish off the pile. 'I went into that kitchen and cleaned every single dish I could find, and for the rest of the time I was there, I never made her have to clean up after me again.'

'Did she try to adopt you?'

He laughed. 'Are you kidding? She left me alone all day except for lunch. I was eight years old. They took me away when the school counselor noticed I hadn't been to class in two months.' He pulled the drain on the sink. 'She was a nice lady, though. I think they let her have an older kid.'

Sara asked the question before she could stop herself. 'Why weren't you ever adopted? You were an infant when you entered the system.'

Will kept his hand under the stream of water as he adjusted the temperature. She thought he was going to ignore her question, but he finally said, 'My father had custody of me at first. The state took me away after a few months. They had good reasons.' He plugged the drain so the sink could fill. 'I was in the system for a while, then an uncle showed up and tried to make a go of it. He meant well. I hope he meant well. But he wasn't really equipped to take care of a child at that point in his life. I was in and out of his house, in and out of foster homes and the children's home. Eventually, he gave up. By that time I was six years old and it was too late.'

417

Sara looked up. Will was staring at her reflection again.

He said, 'You've heard about the six-year rule, right? You and your husband were trying to adopt. You must've heard it.'

'Yes.' Sara felt a lump in her throat. She couldn't look at him. She dried the saucer again, though not a drop of water was left on the surface. The six-year rule. She'd heard the phrase in her pediatric practice, long before Jeffrey had ever suggested they adopt. A child who had been in the system more than six years was considered tainted. Too many bad things had happened to him by then. His memories were too fixed, his behaviors too ingrained.

Years ago, someone in Atlanta had heard this warning, too. Probably from a friend or maybe even a trusted family doctor. They had gone to the children's home, seen six-year-old Will Trent, and decided he was too broken.

He asked, 'Does that journal sound like a twenty-one-year-old girl's journal to you?'

Sara had to clear her throat so she could speak. 'I'm not sure. I didn't know Allison.' She forced herself to think about his question. 'It seems off to me.'

'It doesn't sound like a "Dear Diary" sort of thing.' He started on the last stack of dishes. 'It's more like a long list of complaints about people, professors, her job, lack of money, her boyfriend.'

Sara admitted, 'She sounds kind of whiny.'

'The point of whining is so other people hear you and feel sorry for you.' He asked, 'Does she sound depressed?'

'There's no doubt about that. The journal makes it clear that she was having a very rough time of it. She tried to kill herself once before, which points to at least one depressive episode in her past.'

'Maybe she was in a suicide pact with Jason and a third person.'

'That's a pretty awful way to die if you want to kill yourself. Pills would be much easier. Hanging. Jumping off a building. Also, I think if there was a pact, they'd do it together.'

'Did you find any signs of drug use on Tommy, Allison, or Jason?'

'No outward signs. They were all healthy, of average or above average weight. The blood samples and tissues are on their way to Central. We'll get something back in a week to ten days.'

'Charlie and I were kicking around this theory that Jason could have been involved in Allison's murder. We're pretty sure the killer used him to lure Allison to the lake. Or at least his handwriting.' He turned off the water and wiped his hands on his jeans as he walked to his briefcase. 'This was tucked inside the journal.'

Sara took the plastic evidence bag he gave her. There was a note inside. 'That paper looks familiar.' She read the words. ' "I need to talk to you. We'll meet at the usual place." '

Will added the phrase from the suicide note. ' "I want it over." '

Sara sat down at the table. 'Jason wrote Allison's fake suicide note.'

'Or, he wrote the entire note to somebody else, and that somebody tore off the bottom half and left it in Allison's shoe as a warning to him.' He saw the flaw. 'But then why did Allison have it in her notebook?'

'No wonder your brain is tired.' Sara's head was starting to ache just thinking about it.

Will took another plastic bag out of his briefcase. 'I found this in Tommy's medicine cabinet. Charlie field-tested it, but he's not sure what's inside.'

Sara rolled the pill bottle around to read the label through the plastic. 'That's strange.'

'I was hoping you'd know what it is.'

' "Tommy, do not take these," ' she read. 'I'm not a handwriting expert, but it seems to me that Allison wrote this. Why would she tell Tommy not to take them? Why not just throw them away?'

Will didn't offer her a quick answer. He sat back in his chair, staring at her. 'They could be poison, but if you had poison, why would you stab somebody in the neck?'

'What are these letters on the bottom of the label?' Sara unclipped her reading glasses from her shirt so she could see. 'H-C-C. What does that mean?'

'Faith tried to run the initials through the computer, but I'm not sure how effective the search was. The picture I took wasn't very good and . . .' He indicated his head as if there was something wrong with it. 'Well, you know I wasn't much help.'

'Have you ever had your vision checked?'

He gave her a puzzled look, as if she should know better. 'Needing glasses isn't my problem. I've had this all my life.'

'Do you get headaches when you read? Feel nauseated?'

He gave a half-shrug and a nod. She could tell she wasn't going to get much more time on the subject.

'You should see an ophthalmologist.'

'It's not like I can read the chart.'

'Oh, sweetheart, I can shine a light into your eyes and tell if your lens is focused.'

420

Her endearment hung awkwardly between them. Will stared at her. His hands were on the table. He was nervously twisting his wedding ring.

Sara scrambled to hide her embarrassment. She grabbed the pill bottle and held it up for him. 'Look at the small print for me.' Will held her gaze a moment longer before looking at the bottle in her hand. 'Now, stay still.' She carefully slid her glasses onto his head, then held up the pill bottle again. 'Is that better?'

Will obviously didn't want to, but he looked at the bottle anyway. He glanced back at Sara, surprised, before he looked at the bottle again. 'It's sharper. It's still not right, but it's better.'

'Because you need reading glasses.' She put the bottle back on the table. 'Come to the ER when you get back to Atlanta. Or we can go to my old place tomorrow. You've probably seen the children's clinic across from the police station. I used to have special eye charts for—' Sara felt her mouth drop open.

'What is it?'

She took back her glasses and read the fine print on the label again. 'H-C-C. Heartsdale Children's Clinic.' Sara had been considering all the illegal reasons behind the bottle of pills and none of the legal ones. 'This is part of a drug trial. Elliot must be running it out of the clinic.'

'A drug what?'

She explained, 'Pharmaceutical companies have to do drug trials on medicines they want to bring to market. They pay for volunteers to participate in the studies. Tommy must have volunteered, but I can't see him meeting the protocols. If there's one rule that governs these studies, it's that the participants have to give

421

informed consent. There's no way Tommy could do that.'

Will sounded skeptical. 'Are you sure that's what this is?'

'The number at the top of the label.' She pointed to the bottle. 'It's a double-blind study. Each enrollee gets assigned a random number by the computer that says whether they get the real drug or the placebo.'

'Have you done a trial before?'

'I've done a few at Grady, but they were surgical or trauma related. We used IVs and injections. We didn't have placebos. We didn't give out pills.'

'Did it work the same way as a regular drug trial?'

'I suppose the procedures and reporting would be the same, but we were working in trauma situations. The intake protocols were different.'

'How does it work if it's not in a hospital?'

Sara put the bottle back down on the table. 'The pharmaceutical companies pay doctors to run studies so that we can have yet another cholesterol-lowering drug that works about as well as the twenty other cholesterol-lowering drugs that are already on the market.' She realized her voice was raised. 'I'm sorry I'm so angry. Elliot knows Tommy. He knows he's disabled.'

'Who's Elliot?'

'He's the man I sold my practice to.' Sara kept shaking her head, disbelieving. She had sold her practice to Elliot so that the children in town would be helped, not experimented on like rats. 'This doesn't make sense. Most studies don't even involve children. It's too dangerous. Their hormones aren't fully developed. They process medications differently than adults. And it's almost impossible to get parents to consent to their children being tested with experimental drugs unless they're deathly ill and it's a last-ditch effort to save them.'

Will asked, 'What about your cousin?'

'Hare? What does he have to do with this?'

'He's an adult doctor, right? I mean, his patients are adults?'

'Yes, but—'

'Lena told me he rents space at the clinic.'

Sara felt sucker-punched. Her first instinct was to defend Hare, but then she remembered that stupid car he'd forced her to look at in the pouring rain. She had seen a BMW 750 in an Atlanta showroom that retailed for over a hundred thousand dollars.

'Sara?'

She pressed her lips tightly together to keep herself from talking. Hare at her clinic pushing pills on her kids. The betrayal cut like glass.

Will asked, 'How much money can a doctor make from running a drug trial?'

Sara had trouble forming words. 'Hundreds of thousands? Millions if you go around and speak at conferences.'

'What do the patients get?'

'Participants. I don't know. It depends on what stage the trial is in and how long you have to participate.'

'There are different phases?'

'It's based on risk. The lower the phase, the higher the safety risk.' She explained, 'Phase one is limited to around ten or fifteen people. Participants could make ten to fifteen thousand dollars depending on the trial, whether it's in-patient or not. Phase two expands to around two or three hundred people who get four or five grand each. Phase three is less dangerous, so the money is lower. They enroll thousands of people for hundreds of dollars.' She shrugged. 'The amount of money they make depends on how long the trial lasts, whether they need you for a few days or a few months.'

'How long do the big trials last?'

Sara put her hand on Allison's notebook. No wonder the girl had been obsessed with recording her moods. 'Three to six months. And you have to submit journals on your progress. It's part of the supporting documentation to track side effects. They want to know your moods, your stress level, whether you're sleeping and how much. You know all those warnings you hear at the end of the drug commercials? That's straight out of the journals. If one person reports headaches or irritability, it has to be included.'

'So, if Allison and Tommy were both involved in a drug trial, their records would be at the clinic?'

She nodded.

Will took a moment to think it through. He picked up the bottle again. 'I don't think this is going to be enough to get a search warrant.'

'You don't need one.'

SEVENTEEN

Lena heard the steady sound of dripping water. She opened her mouth around the gag as if she could catch the drops. Her tongue was so swollen that she was afraid she'd choke on it. Dehydration kept her body from sweating. The only thing she had to fight the cold were her shivers, and her muscles were so weak they were refusing to comply. When she pressed the button for the light on her watch, the blue glow captured the red streaks in her wrist like a burning brand in her flesh.

She shifted, trying to take some of the weight off her shoulder. Sitting up was not an option. The room spun too much. Either her arms ached or her legs shot through with pain every time she tried. Because her hands and feet were tied together, every movement required a co-ordination that she no longer possessed. She stared into the darkness, thinking about the last time she had gone for a run outside. It had been unseasonably warm. The sun had been high on the horizon, and when she jogged around the track at the college, she could feel the heat beating down on her face, then her back. Sweat dripped off her. Her skin was hot. Her muscles were primed. If she thought about it long enough, she could almost hear her shoes on the track.

Not shoes on a rubber track. Shoes on wooden steps.

Lena strained to hear the footsteps making their way

down into the basement. There was a sliver of light underneath the door in front of her. Scraping sounds indicated something heavy was being moved – metal across concrete. Probably storage shelves. The sliver of light glowed brighter under the door. Lena closed her eyes as she listened to a key scraping in the deadbolt lock. The door opened, and Lena slowly opened her eyes, letting them adjust to the blinding fluorescents.

At first, there was a halo behind the woman's head, but then Darla Jackson's features came into view. Lena saw the streaked hair, the fake fingernails. Oddly, Lena's first thought was to wonder how the woman had managed to viciously murder two people without breaking her nails. She must redo them every night.

Darla walked down the stacked cinder blocks that served as stairs to the lower part of the basement. She knelt on the floor in front of Lena, checking to make sure the rope was still tightly tied. Incongruously, she put her hand to Lena's forehead. 'Still with us?'

Lena could only stare. Even if her mouth wasn't gagged, she doubted she could say anything to the nurse. Her throat was too dry. Her brain was having difficulty holding on to one thought at a time. She couldn't form the words to articulate her questions. Why had Darla done this? Why had she killed Jason? Why had she killed Allison? It didn't make any sense.

'You're in the basement of the clinic.' Darla pressed her fingers to Lena's wrist, for all intents and purposes acting like a caring nurse instead of a savage murderer. Hours ago, Lena had interrupted Darla cleaning blood off the bat that had slammed into the back of Jason Howell's head. She was bleaching the gloves she had used, trying to hide

426

evidence. And now she was checking Lena's pulse and trying to see if she had a fever.

Darla told her, 'This is some kind of bomb shelter or tornado shelter or something.' She looked at her watch a few seconds longer. 'I doubt Sara remembers it's even down here. I found it a while ago when I was looking for a place to stash some files.'

Lena glanced around the room. With the light on, she could see the concrete walls, the small metal door. Darla was right. They were in a bunker.

'I never liked Tolliver much,' the nurse said. 'I know a lot of people blamed you for what happened, but he could be a prick, let me tell you.'

Lena kept staring, wondering why the woman was picking now to open her soul.

'And Sara's no better. Thinks she walks on water because she got that medical degree. I used to babysit her when she was little. Nothing but a little know-it-all.'

Lena didn't bother to try to disagree.

'I never wanted to kill you,' Darla said. Lena felt a laughing sound in her throat that came out more like a groan. 'I just gotta get out of town, and I know you won't let me do that if I let you go.'

She had that right.

'Daddy had a heart attack.' She sat back on her heels. 'You know Frank's my daddy, right?'

Lena felt her eyebrows go up. A flood of adrenaline let her brain think for the first time in hours. Frank had mentioned his daughter when they were driving away from Allison Spooner's homicide scene. Did he know then that Darla had committed the crime? He sure as hell was covering up for her. Lena couldn't even remember all the things he had hidden from Will. The photograph. Tommy's phone. The 911 call. Was this what Frank meant when he said that Lena couldn't see what was right in front of her? Christ, he was right. She didn't know the truth when it was staring her in the face. How many other clues had she missed? How many other people were going to be hurt because Lena was so blind?

'Do you carry a purse?'

The question was so strange Lena thought she was hearing things.

'A pocketbook?' Darla asked. 'Where do you keep your keys?'

Lena didn't answer.

'I can't take that piece-of-shit Accord out of town. The engine light's been on for weeks. I thought I'd get a new one once the checks cleared, but . . .' She checked Lena's pockets and found her key ring. Her house key was on there, in addition to the keys for Frank's Town Car and Lena's Celica. 'You got any money on you?'

Lena nodded because there was no use lying.

Darla checked Lena's back pocket and pulled out two twenties. 'Well, I guess that'll pay for gas.' She tucked the cash into the front pocket of her uniform. 'I'm gonna have to ask Daddy for some money. I really hate that.' She smoothed down the pink material of her uniform. 'I guess I should feel some remorse about what's happened, but the truth is that I just don't want to get caught. I can't go to prison. I can't be trapped like that.'

Lena kept staring at her.

'If they'd'a just left me alone and kept quiet, none of this would've happened.'

Lena tried to swallow. She could hear her heart doing

that weird, flopping beat in her chest. She must be more dehydrated than she thought. Her hands and feet were numb. Her legs tingled. Her body was shutting down blood flow to the extremities in order to keep the core functioning.

'Daddy and me don't get along too good.' Darla tucked her hand into the front pocket of her smock. 'I get the feeling most days he'd prefer you was his daughter, but we don't get to choose our family, do we?' She pulled out a syringe. 'This is Versed. It'll take some of the anxiety off and put you to sleep. I'm sorry I don't have enough to put you to sleep for good, but this should make it easier. You're not gonna live much longer – maybe five or six hours. That infection in your hand's spreading pretty quick. You're probably already feeling your heart slowing down.'

Lena felt her throat try to swallow.

'What happens is, your body starts to shut down. Your nerves go crazy. Usually there's a lot of pain. Sometimes you're awake for it, sometimes you're not. Do you want the shot?'

Lena looked at the capped syringe. What kind of choice was that?

'Nobody's gonna come save you. The clinic's not gonna open again until next Monday, and by then the smell's the only thing that's gonna let them know you're here.' She glanced over her shoulder. 'I guess I should leave the door exposed so they don't have to look much. Some of the people here ain't been too bad.'

Lena tried to speak, to form the only word that mattered in all of this: *why?*

'What's that?'

Lena groaned the word again. Her lips couldn't meet because of the gag, but the question was clear enough to her ears. 'Why?'

Darla smiled. She understood what Lena was asking, but she wasn't about to give an answer. Instead, she repeated her offer, waving the syringe in the air. 'You want it or not?'

Lena shook her head, vehement. She couldn't black out. She couldn't let go. Her consciousness was the only thing she had any power over.

Darla took the cap off the syringe and jabbed the needle into Lena's arm anyway.

EIGHTEEN

Sara waited in her car for Will to come down from the apartment over the garage. He had asked for a few minutes to change into clothes that were less dirty than the ones he'd worn all day. Sara had welcomed the time to regain her composure. Her anger had settled to a low simmer, but she would've thrown the car in gear and driven to Hare's house right now if not for Will. Why was she surprised that her cousin was mixed up in something so seedy? Hare had never hidden the fact that he liked having money. Sara liked it, too, but she wasn't willing to sell her soul in the process.

The car door opened. Will climbed behind the wheel. He was wearing a white button-down shirt and a fresh pair of jeans. He gave her an odd look. 'Did you wash my clothes?'

Sara laughed at the suggestion. 'No.'

'All my clothes are washed. And ironed.' He picked at the crease on his jeans. 'And starched.'

She knew only one person who ironed jeans. 'I'm sorry. My mother enjoys doing laundry. I can't explain it.'

'It's fine,' he said, but she could tell by his strained tone that he was slightly put out.

'Did she mess anything up?'

'No.' He adjusted the seat so his head wasn't pressed into the ceiling. 'I've just never had anybody wash my clothes for me before.' The gearshift had a learning curve, but he figured it out quickly, putting the engine into drive. He turned off the windshield wipers as he pulled into the street. The rain had slacked off. Sara could actually see the moon peeking out between the clouds.

He said, 'I was thinking about the suicide note.'

'What about it?'

'How about if Jason wrote it, and Allison was supposed to deliver it to a drop?'

'You think they were blackmailing somebody?'

'It's possible,' Will said. 'Allison may have changed her mind about the blackmail without telling Jason.'

'So, she tears off the bottom part of the note, the bit that says, "I want it over," to leave at the drop for the killer?'

'But the killer has already made up his mind to kill her. He's followed her into the woods. We know he's opportunistic. He used the blanket when he killed Jason. Maybe he saw the note as another opportunity.' Will glanced at Sara. 'The fake suicide note was in Jason's handwriting at the scene of Allison's death. Except for Tommy getting mixed up in all of this, the first person who would've been interviewed is the boyfriend.'

She finally put it together. 'The killer wanted to frame Jason for Allison's murder. If they were trying to blackmail him, that certainly would've gotten Jason off his back.'

'Tell me about these drug trials. How do they work?'

'They're complicated, and they're not all bad.' She felt the need to tell him, 'We need drug trials. We need new medicine and new breakthroughs, but pharmaceutical companies are corporations with shareholders and CEOs who like to get paid. There's more money in finding the next Viagra than curing cancer.' She added ruefully, 'And

432

it's a hell of a lot more profitable to treat diseases like breast cancer rather than prevent them from happening in the first place.'

Will slowed the car. Even without the rain, the street was still flooded. 'Don't they need Viagra to fund the cancer stuff?'

'Last year, the top ten pharmaceutical companies spent seventy-three billion dollars on advertising and less than twenty-nine billion on research. Tell me where their focus is.'

'Sounds like you know a lot about this.'

'It's a pet peeve of mine,' she admitted. 'I never wanted free pens and notepads with drug logos on them. I wanted medication that worked and that my patients could afford.'

Will stopped the car. 'You know, I think I'm going the wrong way.'

'It's a circle.'

He put the car in reverse, then made a wide U-turn. Sara knew exactly where they were. If they had gone a few yards farther down the street, they would've passed her old address.

'So,' Will said. 'How does it work? The drug company gets a new drug it wants to test, and then what?'

She couldn't think how to acknowledge his kindness, so she answered his question instead. 'There are two types: drugs of affluence, or lifestyle, and drugs of need.' He gave her a look. 'I'm not making that up. It's Big Pharma's designation. The need drugs are what we tested at Grady. They're for serious or life-threatening illnesses, chronic diseases. Usually, universities and research hospitals handle need drugs.'

He slowed the car again to navigate the deep water. 'And affluence?'

'Generally, that's handled by your average everyday doctor or lab. There are all kinds of announcements in medical journals. What you'd do is petition to run a study. If you're approved, the drug company sets you up and pays for everything. TV, radio, and print ads. File clerks and office furniture. Pens and paper. And then, when it's over, they pay the doctor to fly around the world talking about how fabulous their new drug is, all the while insisting that he's incorruptible because he doesn't own stock in the company.' She thought about Elliot and his Thanksgiving vacation. 'That's where the real money is. Not the stock, but the expertise. If you're involved in an early phase of a study, you can make hundreds of thousands of dollars just by opening your mouth.'

'So, why wouldn't a doctor want to do this if it's so much money?'

'Because if you do it right, there's not a lot of money in it. I mean, yes, you make money, but you're doing paperwork, not medicine. We all know it's a necessary evil, but it can be a really bad side of the business. Some doctors set up research mills. The drug reps call them "high-end rollers," just like in Vegas. Their clinics can have fifty different studies going on at the same time. There are a handful in downtown Atlanta, conveniently near the homeless shelter.'

'I bet there are a lot of students at the college who are looking to make some fast money.'

'Some of my indigent patients enroll in study after study. It's the only thing that keeps them from starving. But it's big business if you work it right. There are websites for professional guinea pigs. They fly around the country raking in sixty, eighty grand a year.'

'The doctors don't track the patients to make sure they're not gaming the system?'

'All you have to show is your license, sometimes not even that. They stick your name in a file. From then on, you're a number. Everything they collect on you is self-reported. You can tell them you're a stockbroker with insomnia and acid reflux when you're really a homeless wino looking for pocket money. They're not running background checks. There's no central database of names.'

'So, Tommy answers an ad and tries to enroll in one of these trials. Then what?'

'They would screen him both medically and psychologically. There's different criteria for each study, and each participant has to meet the guidelines, or protocols. If you're really smart, you can fudge your way onto a study.'

'Tommy wasn't really smart.'

'No, and he wouldn't have passed the psych evaluation if it was properly administered.'

'Wouldn't the doctor be in charge of that?'

'Maybe, maybe not. There are good doctors out there who do it right, but the bad doctors never see the trial participants. They're just paperwork that has to be signed off on. They usually go in on a Sunday and "review" all three hundred cases before the enforcement rep gets there Monday morning.'

'Who takes care of everything then, nurses?'

'Sometimes, but it's not required that they have any medical training. There are CROs, Clinical Research Organizations, that offer temp staffing for doctors

435

running studies. At least they have some training. There was a doctor in Texas who had his wife doing everything. She accidentally switched the trial drug with medication for her dog. One doctor had his mistress in charge. She told the participants to double up on missed doses and half of them ended up with permanent liver damage.'

'Okay, so Tommy makes it through the psych evaluation. Then what?'

'He goes through the medical workup. He was healthy; I'm sure he passed that. Next, he gets the pills. He has to keep his journal. He goes in to give blood and urine or just to check in, probably once a week. The person who talks to him takes his journal and her report, what's called source notes, then enters them into the case report. The doctor only sees the case report.'

'Where would the system break down?'

'Exactly where you said. Tommy obviously had a reaction to the medication. He was getting into arguments with people, which we know from the police incident reports. His altered mood would have shown up in his journal. Whoever interviewed him during his office visits would immediately know something was wrong.'

'And if this person wanted to hide the fact that Tommy was in trouble?'

'They could lie on the case report form. It's entered into the computer and transmitted directly to the drug company. No one would know anything was wrong unless they compared it to the source material, which gets boxed and put into storage as soon as the study ends.'

'Would it ruin the study if Tommy was wigging out?'

'Not necessarily. The doctor could classify him as a protocol violation. That means he doesn't meet the guidelines for being enrolled in the study. Which, with his disability, he didn't belong in anyway.'

'What about Allison?'

'Her suicide attempt should've exempted her, but if she didn't self-report, they wouldn't know.'

'Who gets in trouble for Tommy being enrolled in the study?'

'No one, really. You can always plead ignorance to the ethics committee. By law, every study has to have an internal review board that's in charge of maintaining ethical standards. They're comprised of people from the community. Doctors, lawyers, local businessmen. And always a priest or a minister, for some reason.'

'The ethics committee gets paid by the drug company, too?'

'Everybody gets paid by the drug company.'

'What about Tommy? When does he get his money?'

'At the end of the study. If they paid them ahead of time, most of them wouldn't come back.'

'So, if the trial was nearing the end, then Tommy had a payday coming. And Allison, too. Maybe Jason Howell.'

Sara didn't want to think about who had the biggest money motivation in this sordid mess. 'For a three-month trial, it wouldn't be out of the question that they would each be looking at around two to five thousand dollars for their participation.'

Will pulled into the parking lot of the clinic. He put the gear in park. 'So, where's the problem? We've got doctors making lots of money. Participants getting paid. Tommy shouldn't have been in the study but it's not like he was going to bring the whole thing down. Why would anyone kill two people over this?'

'The key is going to be finding out how many more participants were experiencing mood alterations like Tommy. Allison was depressed. You can read that in her journal. Tommy was acting out lately, getting into arguments when he never had before. He killed himself in jail. I don't want to let Lena off the hook, but he could've been suicidal from the medication. In a study, if you get clusters of adverse events, it's immediately shut down.'

'So, it would be in the doctor's best interest not to have one of these adverse clusters. Not if he stood to make a lot of money on the trial.'

Sara pursed her lips, thinking of Hare. 'Right.'

She stared out the window at the clinic. The front door was illuminated by the headlights. She could see the familiar layout of the lobby.

Will got out of the car and walked around to get the door for her. 'I probably shouldn't go inside with you. I know you're the rightful owner and I've got your permission and all that, but the law is very strict about me looking through medical records. You're going to have to play the concerned citizen and tell me what you find.'

'It's a deal,' she agreed, though it occurred to her that he wouldn't be much help reading the records anyway.

Sara walked to the front door with her keys in her hand. She couldn't remember the last time she had been inside the building, but she didn't have time to reflect. Just as she slid the key into the lock, she turned toward the police station. The movement was natural, something she had done every morning because Jeffrey usually waited across the street to make sure she got safely inside.

The streetlights were bright, the night air crisp, finally clear of rain. She saw a shadow standing by the window to

Jeffrey's office. The man turned. Sara gasped. Her knees started to give.

Will got out of the car. 'Sara?'

She ran without thinking, pushing past Will, going down the hill toward the station. 'Jeffrey!' she screamed, knowing it was him. His broad shoulders. His dark hair. The way he walked like a lion ready to pounce. 'Jeffrey!' She stumbled as she reached the parking lot. The asphalt ripped her jeans. Her palms were scraped.

'Aunt Sara?' Jared jogged toward her with his father's easy gait. He knelt in front of her, hands on her shoulders. 'Are you okay?'

'I thought you were—' She put her hand to Jared's face. 'You look—' She threw her arms around his shoulders and pulled him as close as she could. Sara couldn't help herself. She wept like a child. All the memories she had kept at bay for so long came flooding back. It was almost too much to bear.

Jared rubbed her back, soothing her. 'It's all right,' he whispered. 'It's just me.'

His father's voice. Sara wanted to close her eyes and pretend. To lose herself completely. How many times had she stood in this parking lot with Jeffrey? How many mornings had they driven to work together, kissed each other goodbye in this very parking lot? And then he would stand at the door to the station, watching her make her way up the hill, checking to see that she got inside safely. Sometimes, she could feel his eyes following her, and it took everything Sara had not to run back across the street for another kiss.

Jared asked, 'Are you all right?' There was a tremor in his tone. She was scaring him. 'Aunt Sara?'

'I'm sorry.' She dropped her hands into her lap. She didn't know why she was apologizing, but she kept repeating the words. 'I'm so sorry.'

'It's all right.'

'I thought you were—' She couldn't finish the sentence. Couldn't say his father's name.

Jared helped her stand up. 'Mama says I look just like him.'

Sara couldn't stop the tears streaming down her face. 'When did you find out?'

'It's kind of hard to hide.'

She laughed, the sound high-pitched and desperate in her ears. 'What are you doing here?'

He glanced at Will. Sara hadn't noticed him walk up. He stood a few feet away, obviously trying not to intrude. She told him, 'This is . . .' She forced herself to say the name. 'This is Jeffrey's son, Jared Long. Jared, this is Will.'

Will's hands were shoved deep in his pockets. He nodded at the boy. 'Jared.'

'Why are you here?' Sara asked. 'Is it because of Frank?'

Jared scratched his eyebrow with his thumb and forefinger. Sara had seen Jeffrey make the same gesture countless times. It meant he was upset, but didn't quite know how to talk about it. Jared looked at Will again. There was something going on between them that Sara couldn't follow.

She repeated her question. 'Why are you here?'

Jared's voice cracked. 'Her car is here. I don't know where she is.'

'Who?' Sara asked, but she already knew the answer. Lena's Celica was still in the lot.

'She was supposed to be home six hours ago.' He

directed his words to Will. 'I've been to the hospital. I tried to get in touch with Frank. I can't find anybody who knows where she is.'

'No,' Sara breathed.

'Aunt Sara—' Jared reached for her but she put her hand flat to his chest, holding him back.

'You can't be seeing her.'

'It's not what you think.'

'I don't care. It's wrong.'

He reached for her again. 'Aunt Sara—'

She stepped back, stumbling into Will. 'You can't do this.'

'It's not what you think.'

'Not what I think?' she demanded, her voice rising in anger. 'What am I thinking, Jared? That you're sleeping with the woman who murdered your father?'

'It's not like—'

Will grabbed Sara by her waist as she lunged at Jared. 'She killed him!' Sara screamed, pushing Will away. 'She killed your father!'

'He killed himself!'

She raised her hand to slap his face. Jared stood absolutely still, facing her, waiting for the blow. For her part, Sara felt frozen. She couldn't strike him, but she couldn't drop her hand, either. It divided the air between them like a knife waiting to fall.

'He was a cop,' Jared said. 'He knew what the dangers were.'

She dropped her hand, because now she really wanted to hurt him. 'Is that what she told you?'

'It's what I know, Aunt Sara. My father loved being a cop. He was doing his job, and it got him killed.'

'You don't know who she really is. You're too young to understand what she's capable of.'

'I'm not too young to know I love her.'

His words were like a punch to her chest. 'She killed him,' Sara whispered. 'You don't know what she took from me. From you.'

'I know more than you think.'

'No, you don't.'

Jared's voice turned sharp. 'He was doing his job, and he pissed off the wrong people, and nobody could've stopped him. Not you, not Lena, not me, not anybody. He made his own decisions. He was his own man. And he was stubborn as hell. Once he made up his mind, there was no talking him out of doing exactly what he wanted to do.'

Sara didn't realize she was backing up until she felt Will behind her. She gripped his arm, forcing herself not to falter. 'She's twisted the story to fool you into feeling sorry for her.'

'That's not how it is.'

'She's a master at manipulating people. You can't see that now, but it's true.'

'Stop saying that.' Jared tried to take her hand. 'I love her. And Jeffrey loved her, too.'

Sara couldn't speak to him anymore. She couldn't be here. She turned into Will, burying her head in his chest. 'Get me out of here. Please, just take me home.'

Jared said, 'You can't leave. I need your help.'

Will kept his arm around Sara as he guided her across the street.

Jared jogged to keep up. 'You've gotta help me find her. I don't know where she is.'

Will's voice was hard. 'You need to move on, son.'

'Somebody sliced her tires. She's not answering her cell phone.'

Will kept his arm around Sara, helping her up the hill. She looked down at the grass on the front lawn. The roots had been washed out. Clumps of mud slipped beneath her shoes.

Jared said, 'She called me on her cell at six o'clock. She said she'd be home in an hour.' He tried to block their path, but Will swept him away with one hand. 'She quit her job!' he screamed. 'She told me she quit!'

They had reached the clinic parking lot. Will opened the car door and helped Sara inside.

Jared slammed his hand on the hood. 'Come on! She's missing! Something's wrong!' He rushed around the car and got on his knees in front of the open door. His hands pressed together as if in prayer. 'Please, Aunt Sara. Please. You've got to help me find her. Something's wrong. I know something's wrong.'

There was so much anguish in his face that Sara felt herself falter. She looked at Will, saw the concern in his expression.

His voice was low, steady, when he told her, 'She hasn't checked in with me.'

Jared was crying. 'Please, just check the clinic for me. I know her hand was hurting her this morning. Maybe she went for help. Maybe she fell down or she's sick or—'

Sara closed her eyes for a moment, trying to separate her emotions. She wanted so badly to leave, to never hear the name Lena Adams again as long as she lived.

Will said, 'Sara.' Not a question, more like an admission of guilt.

'Go,' she told him. There was no use fighting it.

Will cupped his hand to her face so she would look at him. 'I'll be right back, okay? I'm just going to check the clinic for him.'

Sara didn't respond. He closed the car door and she leaned back in the seat. The engine was off now, but the moon was so bright in the sky that she didn't need the headlights to see the two men at the front door of the clinic. Lena didn't even have to be present to control the men in her life. She was like a succubus, her siren song clouding their logic.

Will glanced at Sara as he turned the key in the lock. She studied Jared with some detachment. He was thinner than his father. His shoulders hadn't filled out. His hair was longer than Jeffrey had kept it, more the length he'd worn in high school. An image flashed in her head: Lena's hand gripping Jared's hair. She had taken everything now. Her path of destruction had ripped through every part of Jeffrey's legacy.

Sara turned her head as the two men went inside the clinic. She couldn't look at Jared anymore. It hurt too much. It hurt too much to even be here. She slid over the console and got behind the steering wheel. She pressed the button to start the engine. Nothing happened. Will had taken the key with him.

Sara got out of the car, leaving the door open. She looked up at the full moon. The glow was remarkably bright, illuminating the ground in front of her. She remembered a Civil War letter Jeffrey had read to her a long time ago. It was written by a lonely wife to her soldier husband. She was wondering whether or not the same moon was shining down on her lover.

444

Sara walked to the back of the clinic. There was a sign with Hare's name on it, but her anger about the drug study had long dissipated. She couldn't dredge up any sympathy for Allison Spooner or Jason Howell or even poor Tommy Braham, who had somehow gotten caught in the middle of it. All of her emotions had dwindled to a dull ache. Even her hatred for Lena was gone. Trying to stop her was tilting at windmills. There was nothing Sara could do to stop her. If the world fell down, Lena would still be standing. She would outlive them all.

The yard behind the clinic was a mud pit. Elliot hadn't bothered to keep up anything. The picnic tables were gone, the swing set dismantled. The wildflowers Sara had planted with her mother were long dead. She stood on the bank of the stream. It was a river now, the shush of churning waters drowning out all sound. The big maple that had given so much shade over the years had fallen into the current. Its canopy barely touched the opposite side of the shore. As Sara watched, chunks of earth fell into the water and were quickly whisked away. Her father had taken her fishing on these shores. There was a field of large rocks a half mile down where catfish swam in and out of the eddies. Tessa had loved climbing on top of the granite to lie in the sun. Some of the boulders were as high as ten feet tall. Sara guessed they were underwater now. Everything in this town, no matter how strong, eventually got washed away.

Sara heard a branch snap behind her. She turned around. A woman in a pink nurse's uniform stood a few feet away. She was out of breath. Her makeup was smeared, mascara ringing dark circles under her eyes. The plastic red nails on her fingers were chipped and broken.

'Darla,' Sara realized. She hadn't seen Frank's oldest daughter in years. 'Are you all right?'

Darla seemed reticent. She glanced over her shoulder. 'You heard about Daddy, I guess.'

'Is he still refusing to go to the hospital?'

She nodded, again looking behind her. 'Maybe you could help me work on him, get him to let them run some tests.'

'I'm probably not the best person for that job right now.'

'He piss you off?'

'No, I just—' Sara felt logic start to intrude. It was almost three in the morning. There was no conceivable reason for Darla to be here. 'What's going on?'

'My car broke down.' Darla glanced over her shoulder for a third time. She wasn't looking at the clinic. She was looking at the police station. 'Can you give me a lift to Daddy's?'

Sara felt her body reacting to a danger she couldn't quite put her finger on. Her heart was pounding. Her mouth was spitless. This wasn't right. None of this was right.

Darla indicated Sara should walk ahead of her to the parking lot. Her tone turned hard. 'Let's go.'

Sara put her hand to the back of her neck, thinking about Allison Spooner at the lake, the way her head had been held down while the knife sliced into her throat. 'What have you done?'

'I just need to get out of here, all right?'

'Why?'

Darla's tone turned even harsher. 'Just give me the key to your car, Sara. I don't have time for this.'

'What did you do to those kids?'

'The same thing I'm going to do to you if you don't give me that fucking key.' There was a glint of light at Darla's waist, then a knife was in her hand. The blade was about three and a half inches long. The tip was sharpened to a menacing point. 'I don't want to hurt you. Just give me the key.'

Sara took another step back. Her foot sank into the sandy shore. Panic gripped her throat like a hand. She had seen what Darla could do with the knife. She knew the woman had no qualms about killing.

'Give me the key.'

Sara heard the roar of the river swelling behind her. Where was Will? What was taking so long? She looked left and right, trying to decide whether to run.

'Don't,' the woman said, guessing her thoughts. 'I'm not going to hurt you. I just want the key.'

Sara could barely speak. 'I don't have it.'

'Don't lie to me.' Darla checked the station again. She hadn't once looked at the clinic. Either she had already taken care of Will and Jared or she didn't know they were still inside. 'Don't be stupid, honey. You've seen what I can do.'

Sara's voice shook as she asked, 'What happens if I give it to you?'

Darla stepped forward, closing the space between them. The blade was steady in her hand. She was less than three feet away now. Within striking distance. 'Then you can walk home to your mama and daddy and I'll be gone.'

Sara felt a momentary sense of relief before the truth hit her. It couldn't work that way. They both knew Sara wouldn't go home. She'd cross the street to the police station and tell them everything that had happened. Darla wouldn't make it to the city limits before every squad car in the county surrounded her.

The woman repeated, 'Give me the key.' Without warning, she slashed the blade through the air. The metal made a whistling sound as it passed in front of Sara's face. 'Now, dammit.'

'Okay! Okay!' Sara put her trembling hand in her pocket, but her eyes were on the knife. 'I'll give you the key if you tell me why you killed them.'

Darla stared at her in cold appraisal. 'They were blackmailing me.'

Sara took a small step back. 'The study?'

Her arm relaxed, but the blade was still close. 'Students kept dropping out, not showing up when they were supposed to. I got Jason to double up his blood work and do an extra journal. He pulled Allison into it, then they got Tommy involved. We were gonna split the money fifty-fifty. Then they got greedy and decided they wanted all of it.'

Sara could not take her eyes off the knife. 'You were trying to frame Jason for killing Allison.'

'You always were smart.'

'Did Hare know?'

'Why do you think I'm leaving town? He found Tommy's paperwork. Said he was going to report it to the ethics panel.' For the first time, she showed remorse. 'I didn't mean for Tommy to get hurt. He didn't know anything about it. I couldn't have them looking too hard at the case reports.'

'Tommy doubled up on his pills,' Sara guessed. 'He was enrolled twice, so he took twice the dose. That's why his moods were altered. That's why he killed himself, isn't it?'

'I'm done fucking around with you.' She straightened her arm. The knife was a few inches from Sara's throat. 'Give me the key.'

Sara allowed herself a glance back at the clinic. The door was still closed. 'I don't have it.'

'Don't lie to me, bitch. I saw you in the car.'

'I don't—'

Darla lunged. Sara stepped back, holding up her arm in defense. She felt the blade slice open her skin, but no pain followed. All she could feel was heart-stopping panic as the ground under her feet suddenly gave way, sending them both tumbling backward.

Sara's back slammed into the ground. Darla reared up, the knife raised above her head. Sara tried to scramble, instinctively rolling onto her stomach before she realized this was exactly the position Allison Spooner had been in when the blade plunged into her neck. Sara tried to roll back over, but Darla's weight was too much. She gripped the back of Sara's neck. Sara pushed with her hands, kicked with her feet, did whatever she could to get out from under the woman.

Instead of feeling the blade sink into her flesh, Sara felt the earth tremble, the ground again give way beneath her. There was another feeling of free fall. The roar of the river got louder as she fell face-first into the icy water. Sara gasped as the cold enveloped her. Water poured into her mouth and lungs. She couldn't tell which direction was up. Her feet and hands found no purchase. She flailed, trying to find air, but something was holding her down.

Darla. She could feel the woman's hands gripping her waist, fingers digging into her skin. Sara struggled, pounding her hands into the woman's back. Her lungs were screaming in her chest. She brought up her knee as hard as she could. Darla's hold loosened. Sara pushed herself up to the surface, gulping air.

'Help!' she yelled. 'Help!' Sara screamed the word so loud that her throat was raw from the effort.

Darla shot into the air beside her, mouth gaping open, eyes wide with panic. Her hand clamped around Sara's arm. The riverbank was a blur as the current shot them downstream. Sara dug her nails into the back of Darla's hand. Debris slapped against her head. Leaves. Twigs. Limbs. Darla held tight. She had never been a good swimmer. She wasn't trying to pull Sara down. She was holding on for her life.

The water changed from a low roar to a deafening scream. The rock field. The jutting granite stones Tessa and Sara had climbed as children. She saw them up ahead, scattered like teeth waiting to rip them in two. Water split around sharp edges. The current turned violent as it hurtled them forward. Thirty feet. Twenty feet. Sara grabbed Darla under her arm and pulled as hard as she could, thrusting her forward. The crack of the woman's skull against the granite reverberated like a ringing bell. Sara slammed into her. Her shoulder crunched. Her head exploded.

Sara fought the dizziness that wanted to take over. She tasted blood in her mouth. She wasn't moving downstream anymore. Her back was pinned to a large crevice in the rock. White water pounded against her chest, making it impossible for her to move. Darla's hand was trapped between Sara's back and the granite. Her lifeless body waved like a tattered flag. Her skull was open, river water flooding into the gash. Sara could feel the woman's hand slipping. There was a violent jerk, then the current whisked her downstream.

Sara coughed. Water poured into her open mouth, flooded up her nose. She reached above her head, feeling flat stone. She had to turn around. She had to find a way to climb on top of the rock. Sara bent her knees and braced the soles of her feet against the granite. She tried to push up. Nothing happened. She screamed, trying again and again with the same result. The water was peeling her off the rock. She was sliding, losing her grip. Her head dipped beneath the surface. She struggled to stay up. Every muscle in her body shook from the effort. It was too much. Her shoulder screamed with pain. Her thighs were aching. Her fingers were losing their grip. There was no fighting it. The water was too strong. Her body continued sliding down the rock. Sara took a deep breath, gulping in air just before her head dipped below the surface. The constant sound of the rushing water turned to complete and total silence.

Sara pressed her lips tightly together. Her hair floated out in front of her. She could see the moon above her, the bright light somehow managing to pierce the water's edge. The rays were like fingers reaching toward her. She heard something underneath the quiet in her ears. The river had a voice, a gurgling, soothing voice that held a promise that things would be better on the other side. The current was speaking to her, telling her it was okay to let go. Sara realized with some shock that she wanted to. She wanted to just give in, to go to that place where Jeffrey was waiting for her. Not heaven. Not some earthly ideal, but a place of quiet and comfort where the thought of him, the memory of him, did not open like a fresh wound every time she breathed. Every time she walked in the places they walked. Every time she thought of his beautiful eyes, his mouth, his hands.

Sara reached through the water, touching the fingers of moonlight shining down. The cold had turned into a shroud of warmth. She opened her mouth. Air bubbles traced up her face. Her heartbeat was slow, lethargic. She let her emotions wash over her. She let herself feel the luxury of surrender just one more second before she forced herself back to the surface, twisting her body around so that she could find hold on the rock.

'No!' she screamed, raging at the river. Her arms shook as she clawed her way up the rough surface of the stone. The water gripped her like a million hands trying to drag her back in, but Sara fought with every fiber of her being to drag her way to the top of the granite.

She rolled over onto her back, staring up at the sky. The moon was still gloriously shining down, the light reflecting off the trees, the rocks, the river. Sara laughed, because she was sick of the alternative. She laughed so hard that she started coughing. She pushed herself up to sitting, and coughed until there was nothing left inside.

She breathed deeply, drawing life back into her body. Her heart pounded wildly in her chest. The cuts and bruises riddling her skin started to make themselves known. Pain woke every nerve ending, telling her she was still alive. Sara took another deep breath. The air was so crisp she could feel it touching every part of her lungs. She put her hand to her neck. The necklace was gone. Her fingers did not find the familiar shape of Jeffrey's ring.

'Oh, Jeffrey,' she whispered. 'Thank you.'

Thank you for letting me go.

But go where? Sara looked around. The moon was so bright it might as well have been daytime. She was in the middle of the river, at least ten feet from either bank. Water churned white around the smaller rocks that surrounded her. She knew some of them went at least eight feet down. She tested her shoulder. The tendon clicked, but she could still move it.

Sara stood up. There was a weeping willow on the bank, its waving tendrils beckoning her to the clearing underneath its branches. If she could get to one of the smaller rocks without being swept away, she could stand on top and jump to shore.

She heard a branch snap. Leaves rustled. Will came into the clearing. His chest heaved up and down from running. He had a rope coiled in his hands. She could read every emotion on his face. Fear. Confusion. Relief.

Sara raised her voice to be heard over the rushing water. 'What took you so long?'

His mouth opened in surprise. 'Errands,' he managed, still breathless. 'There was a line at the bank.'

She laughed so hard she started coughing again.

'Are you all right?'

She nodded, struggling against another coughing fit. 'What about Lena?'

'She was in the basement. Jared called an ambulance, but . . .' His voice trailed off. 'She's in bad shape.'

Sara leaned her hands on her knees. Yet again, Lena needed help. Yet again, it fell to Sara to pick up the pieces. Oddly, she didn't feel the usual reluctance or even the anger that had been her constant companion since that awful day she had watched her husband die. Sara felt at peace for the first time in four years. Tessa was right – you couldn't fall off the floor. Eventually, you had to get up, dust yourself off, and get back to the business of living.

'Sara?'

She held out her hand toward Will. 'Throw me some rope.'

NINETEEN

Will slowed the Porsche to turn onto Caplan Road, trying to follow the directions Sara had given him. She had drawn arrows by the street names, and as long as Will held the sheet of paper in the right direction, he should be able to make it to Frank Wallace's house without losing his way. Sara had even given him her reading glasses, which were so small on his face that he looked like Poindexter's idiot cousin. Still, she was right. The glasses worked. The words on the page in front of him still did their tricks, but at least they were sharper.

His phone rang, and Will fished around in his pocket, steering with his knees for fear of dropping the directions. He saw Faith's number in the caller ID.

'Where have you been?' she demanded. 'I've left two messages on your cell. I even called Amanda.'

'Aren't you supposed to be on maternity leave?'

'Emma's asleep and I'm sick of being in this stupid hospital.' She began a litany of complaints that started with the bad Jell-O and quickly segued into breast tenderness.

Will stopped her there. 'I got my bad guy.'

'What?' Faith's voice went up in surprise, and he realized that she'd had no great hope that he would solve the case so quickly.

'Thanks for the vote of confidence.'

'Oh, shut up. You know I'm just annoyed because you did it without me.'

Faith wasn't given to sudden fits of emotional honesty. Will knew better than to pursue the point. Instead, he told her about the drug trial and the lengths that Darla Jackson had gone to in order to take out her blackmailers and get rid of Lena Adams.

Faith asked, 'How much money are we talking about?'

'We don't know how many records she was falsifying. Maybe tens of thousands of dollars.'

'Holy crap. Where do I sign up?'

'No kidding,' Will agreed. The money would've come in handy. He wasn't looking forward to going back to Atlanta and digging up his front yard again. 'Lena's still at the hospital. I think they're going to keep her for a while.'

'I'm surprised Sara helped her.'

Will had been surprised as well, but he guessed being a doctor meant you couldn't pick and choose who you saved. Still, there hadn't been much talking while Sara hooked up the IV and ordered Jared to get Lena water, then more blankets, then more water. Will wasn't sure how much of this was meant to help Lena and how much of it was designed to keep Jared from having a nervous breakdown. Either way, it had worked to bring a much-needed level of calm to the situation.

Jared had been frantic from the moment they entered the children's clinic to search for Lena. His erratic behavior had cost them several valuable minutes. He'd kicked down doors that weren't locked. He'd overturned desks and toppled filing cabinets. By the time Will had found the locked basement door, the young man was so spent that he'd barely had the strength to help Will break it down.

And then Jared's second wind had kicked in. He'd rushed downstairs, heedless of anyone hiding in the shadows. They had found another locked door at the back of the basement. Deep ruts were cut in the concrete where metal shelving had once covered the entrance to what had to be a bomb shelter. An old but sturdy deadbolt held the door firmly in place. Jared had pounded away, popping off the steel like a pinball, nearly dislocating his shoulder, before Will came back with a crowbar from the workbench.

Will had to admit that he didn't think of Sara until after the door was pried open. Lena was barely awake, shaking with fever. Her body was drenched in sweat. Jared cried as he untied the rope from her hands and feet, begging Will to get help. That was when Will had gone upstairs to find Sara. He was staring at her empty BMW when he heard her screams from the river. It was sheer luck that she'd managed to call for help before Darla pulled her back down into the water. It was even better luck that the rope that was used to tie up Lena was long enough to help Sara get back to safer ground.

Not that she had needed it. Will was pretty sure she was capable of taking care of herself. He wouldn't have been surprised to see her walk on water after the hell she had survived.

On the phone, Will heard a baby gurgle and another woman talking.

Faith's voice was muffled as she said something to the nurse. She told Will, 'I need to go. They brought Emma for her feeding. Didn't they, baby?'

Will waited through several seconds of baby talk before her voice returned to normal. 'I'm glad you're okay. I was worried about you down there on your own.' There was a strain to her voice, as if she was about to cry. Faith had been pretty emotional these last few months. Will had hoped the baby's birth would send the crazy train back to the station, but maybe it would take a while for her hormones to get back to normal.

'I should probably go,' he told her. 'I'm almost at Frank's.'

She gave a loud sniff. 'Let me know what happens.'

'I will.'

He heard the phone rattle around in the cradle and assumed that was Faith's way of ending the call. Will tucked his cell phone back into his pocket. He checked a street sign against the directions and took a turn. There was an arrow pointing over to the other side of the paper. His lips tugged up into a smile. Sara had drawn a smiley face for him.

He slowed the Porsche again, looking for street numbers. Will checked each mailbox, comparing the addresses to the directions. Halfway down the street, he found what he was looking for. Frank's house was a one-story cottage, but there was nothing quaint or cottagey about it. An air of sadness hung over the place like a dark cloud. The gutters sagged. The windows were dirty. The garden gnome was surprising, but the empty bottles of Dewar's by the trashcan were not.

The screen door opened as Will got out of his car. Lionel Harris laughed at him, obviously enjoying the surprise.

'Good morning,' he said. 'I heard y'all went for a swim last night.'

458

Will smiled, though he felt the cold sweat come back like a sudden rain. He couldn't get the image out of his mind of Sara standing on top of that rock. 'I'm a little surprised to see you here, Mr. Harris.'

'Just dropping off a casserole.'

Will's confusion must have been obvious. The old man patted him on the back. 'Never underestimate the power of a shared history.'

Will nodded, though he still didn't understand.

'I'll leave you to it.' Lionel gripped his cane as he walked down the porch steps. Will watched him walk into the street. A neighbor waved him over and he stopped for a chat.

'Frank's waiting for you.'

Will turned around. There was a woman standing at the door. She was older, with stooped shoulders and unnaturally red hair. Her makeup was caked on in the same style that her daughter preferred. Will saw the finger of a bruise under the woman's eye. The bridge of her nose was swollen. Someone had punched her recently, and very hard.

'I'm Maxine.' She pushed open the screen door for him. 'He's waiting for you.'

As depressing as Frank's house was on the outside, the inside was far worse. The walls and ceiling had yellowed from years of cigarette smoke. The wall-to-wall carpet was clean but worn. The furniture looked like it had come from a 1950s model home.

'Back here.' Maxine gestured for him to follow her down the hall. Opposite the kitchen was a small bedroom that had been turned into a cluttered office. At the back of the house was a dingy bath with avocado green tile. Frank

459

was lying in a hospital bed in the last room. The shades were all drawn but the sunlight glowed behind them. The room was dank and sweaty. Oxygen tubes were clipped to Frank's nose but his breathing was still labored. His skin was yellow. His eyes were clouded.

There was a chair by the bed. Will sat down without having to be told.

'I'll be in the kitchen,' Maxine told them. 'You'uns let me know if you need anything.'

Will turned in surprise, but she'd already left the room. He turned his attention back to Frank. 'Julie Smith?'

The older man's deep baritone had been reduced to a low tremble. 'I had her call Sara.'

Will had assumed something like this had happened. 'You already knew Tommy had killed himself before Sara got there.'

'I thought . . .' Frank closed his eyes. His chest slowly rose and fell. 'I thought it would be better if Sara found him. That there would be fewer questions.'

It could have easily worked out that way. Sara knew Nick Shelton. She could have unwittingly smoothed things over. 'Why did you have Maxine say that Allison had a boyfriend?'

One shoulder went up. 'It's always the boyfriend.'

Will guessed that was true enough, but Frank had lied so many times over the last few days that Will didn't know whether the man was capable of being honest. Lionel Harris had a point about change. Not many people could pull it off. There had to be something awfully bad or awfully good to compel a person to turn their lives around. It was obvious to Will that Frank was past any life-changing revelations. Even without the oxygen tank, he smelled sick, like his body was already rotting. Will knew that there came a point in every person's life when it was too late to change anything. All you could do was wait for death to make you inconsequential.

Frank winced as he tried to get more comfortable in the bed.

'Can I get you anything?'

He shook his head, though he was obviously in pain. 'How's Lena?'

'The infection's bad, but they think she'll pull through.'

'Tell her I'm sorry,' Frank said. 'Tell her I'm sorry about everything.'

'All right,' Will promised, though if he had his way he would never talk to the woman again. He didn't think Lena Adams was all bad, but there was just enough of her that was tainted that left a bad taste in Will's mouth. 'Why don't you tell me what happened?'

Frank stared openly at Will. His eyes watered. 'You got kids?'

Will shook his head.

'Darla was always rebellious, pushing me, pushing Maxine.' He stopped to catch his breath. 'She disappeared on us when she was seventeen. I didn't even know she was back in town until I saw her outside the clinic.' He coughed. Fine specks of blood dotted the bedsheet. 'She was taking a cigarette break.'

'Why did she call the police on Tommy?' The act seemed risky considering her criminal enterprises.

'I don't know if she was trying to scare Tommy or punish me.' Frank reached for the glass of water on his bedside table. Will helped him, holding the straw so he could drink. Frank swallowed, the noise painfully loud in the tiny room. He sat back with a slow groan.

Will asked, 'What did you do when you read the incident report about Tommy's dog?'

'I went to the clinic and asked her what the hell she was doing.'

'Darla's name wasn't in the report.'

Frank didn't answer.

Will was sick of pulling teeth. 'You've done thousands of interviews, Chief Wallace. You know what questions I'm going to ask. You've probably already got a list in your head.' He paused, waiting for Frank to make this easy. After a full minute, Will realized nothing was ever going to be easy with this man. He asked, 'What did Darla say when you confronted her?'

'She told me she was being blackmailed.'

'About the drug trial?'

'It wasn't just the two kids she was lying about. It was a lot of them. She had a system going – getting them to double up on the rolls so it looked like more kids were in the study, then they'd split the checks when they came in.'

'Were they all blackmailing her?'

'Just Jason and Allison.'

'She told you their names?'

'No.'

Will studied him, trying again to figure out if he was lying. It was an exercise in futility. 'What did Darla tell you about the blackmailers?'

'She thought she could pay them off, get them off her back. One of them was graduating soon. She thought if she gave them enough money they'd go away.'

'How much did she ask you for?'

'Ten thousand dollars. I didn't have it. Even if I did, I wouldn't'a given it to her. I spent so much money bailing her out so many times. I couldn't throw away more.'

Will noticed the man had not considered a second option, which was arresting his daughter and sending her to prison for her crimes.

Frank continued, 'She worked so hard to get her nursing degree. I never thought she'd . . .' His voice trailed off. 'I didn't know.'

'She's been in trouble before.'

Frank would only nod.

'Bad checks,' Will supplied. Darla's fingerprints were on file. They matched the print on the Windex bottle Will and Charlie had found in the dorm bathroom closet. Will made an educated guess. 'She was in trouble before that.'

Frank gave a tight nod. 'I'd get calls every now and then. Professional courtesy, one cop to another. Austin. Little Rock. West Memphis. She was taking care of old people, skimming their money. She was good. She never got caught, but they knew it was her.'

Will had found many times that there was a fine line between knowing someone was guilty and proving it. Being a cop's daughter had probably given Darla an extra layer of protection.

'I was sure Tommy killed that girl. I just didn't want anything to come back on Darla.'

'You did everything you could do to make sure Lena's case was solid.'

He stared at Will with rheumy eyes, obviously trying to guess what he knew.

The truth was that Will didn't know anything for certain. He guessed that Frank had hidden evidence. He guessed that Frank had delayed the call center in Eaton sending the audio of Maxine's voice on the 911 call. He guessed that the man had impeded an investigation, acted with reckless endangerment, and blindly if not willfully contributed to the deaths of three people.

As Frank had said, there was knowing and then there was proving.

'I never wanted to get Lena involved in any of this,' Frank said. 'She didn't know nothing about any of it. It was all down to me.'

Will imagined Lena would say the same thing about Frank. As long as he lived, he would never understand the bond that held them together. 'When did you figure out that Darla was involved?'

'When Lena—' He started coughing again. This time, there was so much blood that he had to spit into a tissue. 'Jesus,' Frank groaned, wiping his mouth. 'I'm sorry.'

Will fought to keep his stomach under control. 'When did you figure it out?'

'When Lena told me there was another kid got killed the same way . . .' His voice trailed off again. 'I couldn't see Darla doing this. You'll understand when you have kids. She was my baby. I used to walk the floor with her at night. I watched her grow from a little girl into . . .' Frank didn't finish his words, though it was obvious what Darla had grown into.

'When's the last time you saw her?'

'Last night,' he admitted. Then, instead of making Will ask the right questions, he volunteered, 'We got into a fight. She said she had to leave town. She wanted more money.'

'Did you give it to her?'

He shook his head. 'Maxine had a couple hundred bucks in her purse. They got into a fight. Pretty bad.' He indicated the oxygen tank, the rails on his bed. 'By the time I got up, she had Maxie on the ground, beating her.' Frank pressed his thin lips together. 'I never thought I'd live to see anything like that – a child wailing off on her own mother. My child. That wasn't who I raised her to be. That wasn't my kid.'

'What happened?'

'She stole the money. Took some out of my wallet, too. Maybe fifty bucks.'

'We found almost three hundred dollars on the body.'

He nodded, as if that's what he expected. 'I got a call from Brock this morning. Said she was pulled out downriver from the granite field.' He looked at Will as if he didn't quite believe the information.

'That's right. She was near the college.'

'He said I didn't need to see her right now. Give him time to clean her up.' Frank's breath caught. 'How many times have you said that to a parent who wants to see their kid, only you know the kid's been beaten, cut, fucked up six ways to Sunday?'

'A lot of times,' Will admitted. 'But Brock's right. You don't want to remember her like this.'

Frank stared at the ceiling. 'I don't know if I want to remember her at all.'

Will let his words hang between them for a few seconds. 'Is there anything else you want to tell me?'

Frank shook his head, and again, Will wasn't sure whether or not to trust him. The man had been a detective for over thirty years. There was no way he hadn't at least suspected his daughter was involved in these crimes. Even if Frank didn't want to say it out loud, surely he knew deep down that his inaction had at the very least cost Tommy Braham and Jason Howell their lives.

Or maybe he didn't know. Maybe Frank was so good at deceiving himself that he was certain he had done everything right.

'I should let you get some rest,' Will offered.

Frank's eyes were closed, but he wasn't asleep. 'I used to take her hunting.' His voice was a raspy whisper. 'It was the only time we got along.' He opened his eyes and stared at the ceiling. The only sound in the room was the quiet hiss of the oxygen tank beside his bed. 'I taught her to never aim for the heart. There's ribs and bone all around it. Bullet ricochets. You end up chasing the deer for miles waiting for him to die.' He put his hand to the side of his neck. 'You go for the neck. Cut off the stuff that supplies the heart.' He rubbed the sagging skin. 'That's the clean kill. The most humane.'

Will had seen the crime scenes. There was nothing humane about the murders of Allison Spooner and Jason Howell. They had been terrified. They had been butchered.

'I'm dying,' Frank said. His words were no surprise. 'I was diagnosed with cancer a few months ago.' He licked his chapped lips. 'Maxine said she'd take care of me as long as I gave her my pension.' His breath caught in his chest. He gave a strained laugh. 'I always thought I'd die alone.'

Will felt an overwhelming sadness at the man's words. Frank Wallace *was* going to die alone. There might be people in the same room with him – his bitter ex-wife, a few blindly loyal colleagues – but men like Frank were destined to die the same way they had lived, with everyone at arm's length.

Will knew this because he often viewed his own life and death through a similar lens. He didn't have any childhood friends he'd kept in touch with. There were no relatives he could reach out to. Faith had the baby now. Eventually, she would find a man whose company she could tolerate. There might be another baby. She would probably find a desk job to take some of the stress out of her life. Will would recede from her life like a tide rolling back from the shore.

That left Angie, and Will had no great hope that she would be a comfort to him in his old age. She lived fast and hard, showing the same reckless disregard that had landed her mother in the coma ward at the state hospital for the last twenty-seven years. Marriage, if anything, had pushed them further apart. Will had always assumed that he would outlive Angie, that he would find himself alone at her graveside one day. This image always brought him great sadness tinged with a modicum of relief. Part of Will loved Angie more than life itself. Another part of him thought of her as a Pandora's box that held his darkest secrets. If she were to die, she would take some of that darkness with her.

But she would also take part of his life.

Will asked Frank, 'Do you need me to get you anything?'

He coughed again, a dry, hacking sound. 'No,' he answered. 'I'm fine on my own.'

'Take care of yourself.' Will made himself reach out and touch Frank's shoulder before he left the room.

Sara was in the front yard with her greyhounds when Will pulled into the Linton driveway. The side of her face was bruised. The cut on her arm had needed stitches. Her hair was down, brushing across her shoulders.

She looked beautiful.

The dogs ran to greet him as he got out of the car. Sara had dressed them both in black fleece jackets to fight the cold. Will petted the excited animals as much as he could without falling over backward.

Sara clicked her tongue and they stopped accosting him. She asked, 'I take it Frank wasn't much help?'

Will shook his head, feeling a lump come into his throat. He used to be good at hiding his thoughts, but somehow Sara had cracked the code. 'I don't think he has long.'

'I heard.' She was obviously conflicted about the impending death of her longtime family friend. 'I'm sorry that he's sick, but I don't know how I feel about him as a person after all of this.'

'Maybe he could've stopped it – for Jason, at least.' Will added, 'Then again, people don't see what they don't want to see.'

'Denial doesn't hold up as a good excuse. Darla could've killed me. She *would've* killed me if the bank hadn't given out.'

Will didn't look up because he didn't want Sara to know what he was thinking. Instead, he leaned down to scratch Bob's ear. 'Frank's ex-wife is with him. At least he's not going to die alone.'

'Small comfort.'

'I think it is,' he countered. 'Some people don't get that. Some people just—' Will stopped himself before he started to sound like a blubbering child. 'Anyway, I don't think I'm ever going to find out what really happened this week.'

'Do you need to?'

'I don't guess so. Nothing will bring Tommy back, but at least his name is clear. Darla's not going to hurt anyone else. Frank's in his own prison.'

'And Lena gets away clean yet again.'

She didn't sound as bitter as she had before. 'We'll see.'

Sara laughed. 'You want to make a bet?'

Will tried to think of a clever wager, something that involved him taking her to dinner when they got back to Atlanta, but he was too slow.

She said, 'Brock called this morning. He found Lena's Toyota key in Darla's front pocket. I guess she was planning on taking Lena's car and leaving town.'

He remembered the Celica's sliced tires. Someone at the station had given Lena a parting gift. 'Darla must've seen you get out of your car and decided to upgrade her ride.' Will had always known that the killer was good at improvising. 'Did Hare say what made him check the files for Tommy's name?'

'He'd seen Tommy in the clinic a couple of times. It's not unusual for kids that age to still go to their pediatrician, but Tommy was there a lot, at least once a week. Hare got curious after the suicide and checked the paperwork for Tommy's name.' Sara pulled the leash as Billy tried to pee on the side of Will's car. 'He confirmed what Darla said. He was going to the ethics committee to report the protocol breach.'

'That's good, right? He was doing the right thing.'

'I suppose, but he's not going to stop running trials.' She gave a rueful laugh. 'Let me correct that: he's going to stop running trials out of my building, but he's still going to keep running them.'

'Did you find out what he was testing?'

'An antidepressant. They're going to try again next spring with a different dosage.'

'You're kidding me.'

'It's a billion-dollar business. One in every ten Americans is on antidepressants, even though placebo studies show a lot of them get absolutely no benefits whatsoever.' She nodded back at the house. 'Hare's inside, which is why I took the dogs for a two-hour walk in the freezing cold.'

'Your folks aren't mad at him?'

She sighed heavily. 'Oh, my mother will forgive him anything.'

'I guess that's what families do.'

She seemed to think about what he said. 'Yeah, they do.'

'I talked to Faith this morning.' She'd sent so many baby pictures to Will's phone that the memory was almost full. 'I've never heard her happy before. It's weird.'

'Having a baby changes you,' Sara told him. 'Obviously, that's not something I've learned from personal experience, but I can see it with my sister.'

Bob leaned against his leg. Will reached down and scratched him. 'I guess I—'

'I was raped.'

Will kept his mouth closed because he didn't know what to say.

'In college,' she continued. 'That's why I can't have children.' He'd never noticed how green her eyes were, almost emerald. 'It took years for me to tell my husband. I was ashamed. I wanted to think it was behind me. That I was strong enough to get past it.'

470

'I don't think anyone could ever say you're not strong.'

'Well. I've had my bad days.' She let out Billy's leash as he sniffed around the mailbox. They both stared at the dog as if he was far more fascinating than reality dictated.

Will cleared his throat. The moment was too awkward. It was also cold outside, and he guessed Sara didn't want to stand in front of her parents' house all day watching him struggle to come up with something meaningful to say. 'I should start packing my stuff.'

'Why?'

'Well . . .' Will was tongue-tied, and painfully stupid. 'The holiday. Your family. I'm sure you want to be with them.'

'My mother's cooked enough for fifty. She'd be crushed if you didn't stay.'

He couldn't tell if the offer was genuine or if she was just being polite. 'My front yard's kind of a mess.'

'I'll help you when we get back to Atlanta.' She smiled mischievously. 'I'll even show you how to use a backhoe.'

'I don't want to impose.'

'Will, it's not imposing.' She took his hand. He looked down, tracing his thumb along her fingers. Her skin was soft. He caught the scent of her soap. Just being close to her like this made him feel warm, like that empty place in his soul might have the chance of being filled one day. He opened his mouth to tell her that he wanted to stay, that he wanted nothing more than to get two thousand more questions from her mother and watch her sister's sly smile as she glanced back and forth between them.

And then his cell phone chirped in his pocket.

She wrinkled her nose. 'What's that?'

'Probably another baby picture from Faith.'

She gave him that same flirty smile. 'Let me see.'

Will felt incapable of denying Sara any request. He used his free hand to find his phone. He'd seen Emma Lee Mitchell from every conceivable angle, and he was sure she was a sweet baby, but at the moment she looked like an angry red raisin in a pink knit hat.

Sara flipped open the phone. Her smile quickly faded. 'It's a text.' She showed him the phone, then seemed to realize herself. She turned it back and read aloud, ' "Diedre finally died. Come home." '

Will felt a sudden pang of grief. 'Angie's mother.' He looked down at her hand. She was still holding his hand.

'I'm sorry.'

Will hadn't cried since he was sixteen, but he felt tears threatening to come. He struggled to speak. 'She's been on life support since I was a kid. I guess she finally . . .' His throat was so tight he could barely swallow. Angie claimed to hate her mother, but she had visited her at least once a month for the last twenty years. Will had gone with her many times. The experience was awful, heart wrenching. He had held Angie so many times while she sobbed. It was the only time she let her guard down. The only time she surrendered herself to Will.

He suddenly understood Lionel Harris's words about the power of a shared history.

'Sara—'

She squeezed his hand. 'You should go home.'

Will struggled to find the right words. He was torn between wanting to be with Sara and needing to be with Angie.

Sara leaned in close, pressing her lips to his cheek. The wind draped her hair across his face. She put her mouth to his ear and told him, 'Go home to your wife.'

So he did.

THREE WEEKS LATER

EPILOGUE

Lena stood in the cemetery looking down at Jeffrey Tolliver's headstone. It seemed stupid to put flowers on an empty grave, but the things inside that coffin were more tangible than a jar of ashes. Brad had contributed a paper target from his first qualifying round at the police academy. Frank had put in his citation book because Jeffrey was always yelling at him for being late with the reports. Lena had donated her gold shield. The one she carried up until three weeks ago was a duplicate. Dan Brock had slipped it in with the other items because they both knew there was no way she could do it herself.

All the businesses on Main Street were closed the day Jeffrey's coffin was lowered into the ground. Jared hadn't attended the funeral either. His resemblance to his father had been brought to his attention years before. He didn't want to distract the mourners. He didn't want to bring Sara that sort of pain.

He wanted to be in town, though. He wanted to feel close to his father, to see the place where Jeffrey had lived and loved. He'd met Lena outside the diner. She was sitting on the curb, thinking about all the things she had lost. At first, she'd thought Jared was Jeffrey. Of course she'd thought he was Jeffrey. He was more than a spitting image. He was a walking ghost.

Maybe part of Lena was drawn to him because of the

resemblance. She had worshipped Jeffrey too much to ever consider anything romantic. He was her mentor. He was her hero. She had wanted to be the same kind of cop he was. The same kind of person. She hadn't realized until he was gone that he was just a man.

'Why aren't you at the funeral?' Jared had asked her.

And Lena had told him, 'Because I'm the person who killed your father.'

Jared had spent two hours listening to Lena pour her heart out, then another two hours arguing about how it wasn't really her fault. His youth made him passionate, a staunch defender of his quickly formed opinions. He had just signed up for the police academy. He hadn't yet seen the horrors of the world. Hadn't yet figured out that there was such a thing as a truly irredeemable person.

Was she irredeemable? Lena didn't want to think so. She had a fresh start ahead of her. A clean slate on which to write the rest of her life. The police review board had returned a verdict of no fault in Tommy Braham's suicide. Will Trent's report was long on supposition and short on evidence, especially since Lena had never gotten around to taping that confession. Gordon Braham was moving to Florida to be closer to his wife's people. He had filed a class-action lawsuit along with Jason Howell's mother against Hareton Earnshaw and the drug company that had sponsored the trials. He'd signed a paper indemnifying the Grant County force in exchange for an undisclosed sum.

Lena had gone through two operations and a week in the hospital, but the damage to her hand was surprisingly limited considering the hell she'd gone through fighting off a nasty staph infection. Therapy was bringing movement back to her fingers. She was right-handed anyway.

All her left hand needed to do was hold up her badge when she was making an arrest. And she would be making a lot of them soon. Gavin Wayne had called two days ago to let her know the job on the Macon force was still available. Lena had told him yes without a second thought.

She was a cop. It was in her blood. Her nerve had been tested. Her resolve had faltered. But she knew without any doubt that there was nothing else in the world that she wanted to do.

She leaned down and placed the flowers on Jeffrey's grave. He was a cop, too. Not the same kind of cop as Lena, but different paths could still lead to the same destination. Jeffrey would understand that. He had always given her the benefit of the doubt.

Lena looked across the row of headstones lining the cemetery. She'd already put flowers on her sister's headstone. Frank Wallace didn't have a marker yet, but she had brought him some daisies because she knew he liked them. He'd left her some money in his will. Not a lot, but enough for Lena to sell her house at a loss and still pay off her mortgage. She had donated the rest to a nonprofit legal fund established to help cops who got on the wrong side of the law. Something told her Frank would've approved.

Not that she needed his approval anymore. Lena was sick of worrying what other people thought about her. Part of looking ahead to her new life required her never to look back. The only things she was taking with her from Grant County were her clothes and her fiancé, neither of which she thought she could live without.

'Ready?' Jared was sitting in his truck. He leaned over and pushed open the door.

Lena slid across the seat so he could put his arm around

her. 'Are things going to be okay with you and Sara?' He'd had coffee with her this morning. Lena gathered things hadn't gone well.

'Don't worry about it.' Jared's jaw tightened as he put the car in gear and pulled out onto the road. He didn't like giving bad news. 'Aunt Sara will come around.'

'I wouldn't hold my breath.'

He kissed the top of her head. 'She just doesn't know who you are.'

'No, she doesn't.'

He reached down and turned on the radio. Joan Jett started singing about her bad reputation. Lena stared into the rearview mirror. She could see the road disappearing behind her, Grant County getting smaller with every mile. She wanted to feel something for the place – a sense of loss, a sense of nostalgia. All she felt was relief to have it finally behind her.

Did Sara Linton know Lena? Probably better than anybody else alive. But Jared didn't need to know that. He didn't need to know about the mistakes Lena had made, or the people whose lives she had ruined. Things were going to be different in Macon. This was her clean slate. Her new beginning.

Besides, Lena had never told a man the truth in her life. She wasn't about to start now.

ACKNOWLEDGMENTS

My appreciation to the usual suspects: Victoria Sanders, Kate Elton, and Kate Miciak. I'd also like to add Gail Rebuck, Susan Sandon, Richard Cable, Margie Seale, Robbert Ammerlaan, Pieter Swinkels, Silvie Kuttny-Walster, Berit Boehm, Per Nasholm, Alysha Farry, Chandler Crawford, and Markus Dohle. And I guess Angela Cheng-Caplan, if she can handle the love.

Isabel Glusman, thank you for your letters, and Emily Bestler, thank you for raising such a great kid. Dr. David Harper helped me figure out how to kill people. Dr. David Worth helped me figure out eyeballs. Any mistakes are my own. Trish Hawkins was instrumental in giving me insight into the complexities of dyslexia. Debbie Teague, you are such a trouper for sharing your experiences; every time I write about Will, I think of your amazing strength of spirit. Mo Hayder: thanks for all the free research on scuba diving, suckah! To Andrew Johnston I offer my apologies for you know what, and no, there's no compensation. Same goes for you, Miss Kitty.

Thanks to Beth Tindall of Cincinnati Media for all the usual web crap. Jamey Locastro can arrest me anytime. Fiona Farrelly and Ollie Malcolm were very gracious helping me figure my way around the thing that involves the plot of this story, which I won't mention here in case people read this before they read the actual book, which they shouldn't be doing anyway. Thanks also to the folks who helped by discussing this subject matter but didn't want to be named for obvious reasons. To Speaker David Ralston: I thank you very much for introducing me to some great people. GBI Director Vernon Keenan and John Bankhead, thanks for your time. I will never fire a shotgun again without thinking of our lovely day outside the women's prison. I hope I've honored the work y'all and all the agents and support staff at the GBI do for the great state of Georgia.

My daddy made me soup and cornbread during critical times, which I may have conflated because of the cornbread and soup, which – did I mention? – I will probably need more of. D.A. showed amazing perseverance through this whole process. As always, you are my heart.

To my readers: y'all are the best. For further reading, try the *GPZ* anthology, check out issue 15.05 of *Wired* magazine, or, if you really want to get upset, investigoogle Jessie Gelsinger. For those of you with a wild hair, GPGP.net is an interesting site as well. Hey, folks, while you're online, check me out on Facebook or my website, karinslaughter.com. I love getting letters, but please remember this is a work of fiction.